HIGHEST PRAISE FOR JOVE HOMESPUN ROMANCES

"In all of the Homespuns I've read and reviewed I've been very taken with the loving rendering of colorful small-town people doing small-town things and bringing 5 STAR and GOLD STAR rankings to readers. This series should be selling off the bookshelves within hours! Never have I given a series an overall review, but I feel this one, thus far, deserves it! Continue the excellent choices in authors and editors! It's working for this reviewer!"

—***Heartland Critiques***

We at Jove Books are thrilled by the enthusiastic critical acclaim that the Homespun Romances are receiving. We would like to thank you, the readers and fans of this wonderful series, for making it the success that it is. It is our pleasure to bring you the highest quality of romance writing in these breathtaking tales of love and family in the heartland of America.

And now, sit back and enjoy this delightful new Homespun Romance . . .

HEAVEN MADE

by Teresa Warfield

HEAVEN MADE

TERESA WARFIELD

J

JOVE BOOKS, NEW YORK

HEAVEN MADE

A Jove Book / published by arrangement with
the author

PRINTING HISTORY
Jove edition / December 1995

ISBN: 0-515-11748-X

A JOVE BOOK®
Jove Books are published by The Berkley Publishing Group,
200 Madison Avenue, New York, New York 10016.
JOVE and the "J" design are trademarks
belonging to Jove Publications, Inc.

PRINTED IN THE UNITED STATES OF AMERICA

10 9 8 7 6 5 4 3 2 1

For Michael Patrick, my best St. Louis friend who never fails to make me smile and laugh. I love you, Mike.

ACKNOWLEDGMENTS

THIS BOOK WAS written during a tough time, during absolute chaos in my life. Without the support and encouragement of a number of people, I doubt seriously whether I could have finished *Heaven Made*. Special thanks must be given to my champions:

Judith Stern . . . For always believing in me, even when I doubt.

Evan Fogelman . . . For having a hand in this one even though he didn't get a percentage. (laugh) Evan, you helped push me to the finish line with your undying encouragement and zany enthusiasm.

Debbie Krauss and Ron and Michelle Brocious . . . For always having a bed ready when I call, and for making my trips back to Cleveland tolerable. Words of thanks are inadequate. I know what being on the run feels like.

Beth Sprosty . . . For not judging me.

❖ ❖ ❖

PROLOGUE

Philadelphia, 1841

IN THE END—or the beginning—Olivia acted impulsively, driven by fear, determination and desperation, by the fact that she knew eight-year-old Janey was only days away from being either murdered or sent to a sanitarium. *He won't . . . he'd have to kill me or send me away first,* Olivia swore to herself as she raced down the dim upstairs hallway, a lamp dangling from one hand, a bag from the other. He . . . her Uncle Edward . . . a monster . . . the Devil himself . . . Satan, Lucifer, Evil incarnate. She would not stand for any more.

She had never stood idly by, not really. Which was why she had gone nearly mad the many times he locked her in her room. She had listened to his curses, to his rages, and she had seen Janey afterward. Janey, a child, innocent, troubled, haunted . . . It was only a matter of time before he disposed of her somehow.

But that would never happen. Olivia would see to that.

He was gone tonight, really gone. Soused with his favorite whore in a Market Street tavern, or so Harry, the footman, had reported an hour or so ago. After that, Olivia had started gathering a few belongings, putting things together. Oh, he had been gone and soused many times before. But during those times Olivia had not had the courage or the resources to do what she had decided to do tonight, what her mind screamed at her to do. Now she would not think about not having the courage—she would act. Now she would not think about the fact that she had scraped and stolen and sold—she would grab Janey and flee. Go far away. To the other side of the earth if need be.

Soused with his favorite whore . . . That meant he would be gone virtually all night. It meant he would stumble home early in the morning, some time around dawn. It meant that Olivia had hours in which to get started, hours in which to travel miles. *Miles*. If anything were amiss in the house when he returned he would fly into a rage and take off after Janey. But he would not find her this time. This time he would search and search, and once he sobered a little he might realize that Olivia was gone, too. And then he might realize that something was really amiss. But none of that would happen until morning.

Janey jerked awake when Olivia threw a cloak over her and lifted her. She stared at Olivia with glazed eyes. Olivia smiled and smoothed her hair. "We're going for a ride, Janey. You can snuggle against me in the carriage and sleep."

Any other eight-year-old child might have raised objections and questions. *Is it morning? Is something the matter? Why are you rousing me in the middle of the night for a carriage ride?* But Janey simply wrapped her arms around Olivia's neck and laid her head on Olivia's shoulder. *She knows what I'm doing,* Olivia thought, *and she wants me to—she won't object. She hates him so much for the cruel monster that he is, her own father, that she wants me to take her away.*

So it had come to this. A sad state of affairs, Olivia's father would have said.

Edna Ferguson, the housekeeper, was there suddenly, helping Olivia, saying, "Wait, I'll pack some things," and Olivia became tense and unsure. She had never quite trusted the sharp-eyed Mrs. Ferguson. But then she had never quite trusted Harry, the driver, either. Until that morning when he had put the notion of running away into her head. She had gone to the carriage house, thinking to tell the groom she wished to make a few calls that afternoon, and Harry was there, cursing over the welts on one of the horse's legs, welts the master had put there. "He flies into tempers, doesn't he?" Harry had asked, shaking his head. "Why, no thing deserved such a beating, not an animal . . . and surely not a child." Olivia had caught his eye, held his meaningful gaze. And then in the softest voice she'd ever heard Harry use, he had said that if she ever took up the notion to take little Miss Janey somewhere safe, he'd be glad to help her. He had two young girls of his own and Miss Janey had an awful lot of falls and misfortune, and he'd bet his own life that they weren't falls and misfortune at all but bruises and cuts brought down by the evil hand of Edward Morgan. Now that he'd put it all together he planned to look for other employment. But not for several weeks, he said, letting her know that she had at least that much time in which to decide if she wanted to do something and if she wanted him to help her. "After that," he said, "I'll leave word where I can be reached." Of course, after he was gone, arranging matters might be more complicated.

A savior, a godsend . . . an angel sent from heaven. And now, here was Mrs. Ferguson helping, too, stuffing some of Janey's clothes into a bag, and Olivia felt ashamed when she wondered briefly what the woman stood to gain. A terrible thought, for surely Edna Ferguson would be fired if her employer ever learned that she had packed for them, and a fired housekeeper would have a difficult time finding other employment. She took a great risk; there were other servants in the house who might report her misdoings if they ever learned of them. *I must trust her,* Olivia decided. She had no choice really.

Mrs. Ferguson stuffed the bag full, then grabbed it along with Olivia's and turned toward the door. Olivia held Janey and the lantern. She turned at the same time she heard the housekeeper gasp, and she caught her own breath at the sight of Uncle Edward, swaying slightly, his eyes narrowed, his neckcloth loose and rumpled. He stood barring the doorway, but Olivia suspected him to be drunk enough that she might very well shove him aside if need be. He was still strong when drunk, but he was also clumsy. And she was so determined right then, she wondered if she might be stronger.

"Where the devil do you think you're headed, Missy? With a collection of my money, too, no doubt, and my daughter. Did you think I wouldn't notice? That I'm an imbecile?" he demanded, his speech slurred as he attempted to strut forth. "That I wouldn't discover that you had something planned?" He wobbled, and Olivia said a silent prayer that he would fall. Then she could rush by him and downstairs. Instead he bumbled toward her, glaring, reeking of drink. Janey was awake now, breathing fast and gripping Olivia's shoulders, her little fingers biting into Olivia's flesh.

"Mr. Morgan, leave them be," Edna Ferguson said, stepping forth, her shoulders squared. "No one is going to allow you to hurt that child anymore, ever again. We shall all—"

"Out of my way, woman!" he roared, shoving her aside, unbalancing both her and himself in the process. She crashed into the chest of drawers, upsetting a lamp that was not lit (thank God), books, and several brass bookends.

Olivia's gaze fastened on one of the bookends. She shouldn't . . . but she had to if Janey were to stand a chance. She was not a murderer . . . but perhaps she wouldn't kill him. Mrs. Ferguson stood up, looking dazed but otherwise unharmed. Uncle Edward was trying to get to his feet, but he was so drunk he slipped, then slipped again.

Olivia put Janey and the lamp down, quickly, before Uncle Edward could gain his footing. Then, without allowing herself to think, having already made up her mind, she grabbed one of the bookends, lifted it over her uncle's head, closed her eyes, and brought it down. She heard him puff air, felt him collapse at her feet. *Sweet Jesus, forgive me . . .*

When she opened her eyes, she saw Uncle Edward lying facedown, the back of his head wet with blood. Mrs. Ferguson stood, wide-eyed, her hands clasped over her mouth. Janey yanked on Olivia's hand, trying to pull her toward the door. The housekeeper suddenly flew into motion, grabbing their bags and the lantern and urging Olivia and Janey from the room. The trio rushed downstairs, past the library, the drawing room, and the kitchen.

"We knew you would flee one day soon," Mrs. Ferguson said at the back entrance, breathless now. "Things have gotten too bad, and then that doctor was here the other morning, looking at Miss Jane, and he said . . . he said . . ." She flushed. Her eyes glittered. "Doesn't matter. What matters is that you take her away. Get on a train or a coach going west. Decent cities have sprung up in places out there, I hear. Find one and hide. Go on now. Harry has a carriage."

Olivia and Edna were thinking alike.

"What will you do, Mrs. Ferguson?" Olivia had to ask. "What will you do?" If, by chance, Uncle Edward lived, he would make certain that Mrs. Ferguson paid for her part in this. Olivia knew him . . . knew how evil he could be.

"Never mind me," the woman said. "Take that child away from here. You are her only hope. Go—now!"

It was true . . . she was Janey's only hope.

Though Janey was heavy, Olivia took the bags from the housekeeper and raced down the steps and halfway up the stone walk. Then she stopped, turned, and raced back, her heart pounding.

Mrs. Ferguson gave her an astonished look. "What in the name of the Father . . . ? Go, now, if you want a better life for that child, if you want her to have a life at all, and she deserves one. She deserves—"

Olivia wrapped one arm around Edna Ferguson's neck and squeezed, overwhelmed suddenly with gratefulness and with more fear than she had ever known. *What if I've killed him? What if . . . ?*

She and Janey were leaving, and she planned to do exactly what Mrs. Ferguson suggested, get on a train or a coach and keep traveling west until she found a decent city in which she and Janey could start over, be free and happy. But oh, to know that she had the understanding and support of at least two of the staff here meant everything to her. Everything. Her mother was long dead. Her father had died last year. Every other family member she had told things to did not believe her. Her aunt had offered that if she was so unhappy with Edward she could come and live with her. But Olivia had refused to leave Janey, and Uncle Edward had refused to let Janey go.

"I know you're scared nearly out of your mind," Mrs. Ferguson said, stroking her back, being mother, father and every absent caring relative at the moment. "But the truth is, that child won't live to see her ninth birthday if you don't take her away. Now go, and may the loving hand of God watch over you."

Olivia had never known Edna Ferguson like this. Oh, she had sensed her affection in an occasional fond look, a tender smile, but for the most part the housekeeper had always been solemn and distant. Olivia felt a pain in her breast for a friendship lost before it had a chance to grow and blossom, a lovely spring flower crushed just as it pushed its way up through the winter snow.

She and Janey went, fleeing along the path again. Olivia whispered a silent prayer . . . reached the carriage . . . watched Harry lift Janey and put her inside where it was dark but safe. Olivia then lifted her skirts and let Harry hand her up, and finally, she settled on the seat opposite Janey as Harry shut and latched the door.

Seconds later, the carriage jolted forth, its wheels turning, creaking, moving it along, taking her and Janey away.

Olivia gripped the strap above her head and squeezed her eyes shut. She would never look back. She and Janey would go forward from there. They would settle somewhere and make a new life for themselves, free of nightmares, of horrible memories and wretched pain. And someday perhaps Janey would laugh and be carefree again . . . find her voice again.

CHAPTER ONE

A SHRILL BLAST roused Olivia from heavy sleep, making her blink and wrinkle her brow in confusion. A small room . . . dark woodwork . . . a gleaming brass doorknob . . . light spilling in from a small window . . . Janey's hair in her face as the girl snuggled close . . . the hard bunk beneath them . . .

The room seemed to shift suddenly, swaying to and fro, and Olivia oriented to her surroundings. They were on a steamer that was either just now leaving Cincinnati, Ohio, or arriving in another port. She couldn't be sure which. Normally a blast like that would have made her sit straight up, and it would have jolted Janey awake. But both of them were exhausted.

At the Cincinnati dock Olivia had made the quick decision, after she and Janey had been bumped and prodded and overcome by people on the ship from Pittsburgh, to rent a cabin this time around. That awful trip had taken place after they'd already spent days in a cramped coach going from Philadelphia to Pittsburgh.

She had thought about stopping in both Pittsburgh and Cincinnati and renting a room at a hotel for at least one night. But the urgency of getting as far away as possible as quickly as possible made her trudge on, and so she and Janey had boarded one ship after another. If Uncle Edward was alive, their disappearance was doubtless an embarrassment for him, something he was having to explain to relatives and friends—but of course, he would think of something . . . he would say that she, Olivia, had gone mad, had stolen from him and then kidnapped his only child. Truthful accusations, no less, except for the part about her being mad—and he was surely enraged and searching in every crack and crevice of Philadelphia, and perhaps beyond, by now. But of course, he was most likely dead . . . Dead. There was also the matter of money. While Olivia had plenty for now, she couldn't be certain of what might lie ahead, and the cost of a hotel room now had seemed a frivolity. She knew she would have to find work wherever she and Janey ended up, and she wasn't sure what kind of work might be found by a woman newly arrived in a western settlement. So for now she was frugal. Except for this expense—the cost of the cabin they occupied right now.

She had a great sense of traveling to an entirely different world—after all she'd hardly journeyed outside of Philadelphia in her entire life, as she realized when she and Janey stepped out of that stage in Pittsburgh and she glanced around at a city that had the potential to be as fine as Philadelphia one day but that was crude and harsh for now. Oh, Philadelphia had its harsh areas, parts she would never dream of passing through alone. But most of the streets were paved, and there didn't seem to be as many shanties as in Pittsburgh. Certainly no one pitched tents around the outskirts of the city. People were rude and brazen in Pittsburgh, too, bumping up against a person and not bothering to apologize. Men made lewd comments. Women and children stared.

The crowd on the ship departing from that city had been much the same, and Olivia and Janey had not been able to escape the noise and confusion because Olivia had made the mistake of buying deck passage. "Take a place," the man who took their tickets had told her as she switched her and Janey's heavy bags from one hand to the other. And as instructed, they'd taken a place on the main deck, the only open space there seemed to be by that time, between crates of chickens and two filthy men who reeked of alcohol. Olivia had felt their eyes on her, raking her, and she'd lifted her chin and stared straight at them, silently promising to rip their eyes out if they even thought about coming closer. She and Janey had had more than their share of drunkards.

A stagecoach, a ship, and now another ship . . . and possibly another one after this one. Who knew?

Olivia shifted on the small bunk, groaning at the pain that shot through her neck. She should go see if the ship was just leaving Cincinnati or arriving in another city. But she was so tired. So very, very tired. Tired and dirty and hungry. She had bought fruit and sandwiches from a vendor at the wharf, had paid handsomely for them in fact, and she thought that if she moved at all it would be to wash some of the dirt and perspiration from her body, and then eat. After that she would sleep more. She would not leave the cabin just yet and go up to the deck to see where they were. If they were arriving somewhere and the cabin was rented to someone else, a knock on the door would alert her.

She forced herself to move from the bunk. Luckily, in Pittsburgh she had bought a canteen which she filled with water and corked, as she had resolved to do earlier, during the stagecoach ride. She and Janey had had no water then except for the few sips a gentleman had given them from his canteen. Smart man, Olivia had thought, and before boarding the ship, she had found a shop that sold canteens.

All along the way, during the journey to wherever she and Janey would make their new home, Olivia meant to observe and learn and follow examples. Until now she had led an easy life for the most part, something of which she had always been vaguely aware, something of which she was now even more aware. She had never in her life gone so many days without bathing or at least washing. (How many days now? She wasn't sure . . . she didn't even know what day it was, if the truth be known.) She had never gone so many days without a moment of privacy, without a bed on which to rest, without servants to prepare her meals. She had been sheltered, at least by her father, and told what areas of Philadelphia she should never venture into, either alone or with her maid, and so she had never seen many of the things to which she had recently been exposed in Pittsburgh and Cincinnati. Drunkards with lewd remarks—sober men with lewd remarks, too—women in skimpy gowns with painted faces and suggestive words—The poor and starving, the orphaned. The expectant yet dirty faces of people who said things like, "We're headed west . . . Missouri, Iowa, Kansas . . . There's land to be had everywhere. Everywhere!"

She ripped material from the hem of her chemise, held the piece of cloth over the mouth of the now opened canteen, and tipped the container until it wet the material. The water was cold on her hands, face, and neck. But oh, it felt good! Marvelous. Soothing. The cloth came away dirty, and she thought she must look a sight—a fright, that was.

She glanced at Janey, who now lay curled in a ball on the bunk, and she wandered over and covered the girl with the one blanket they had been provided. Not the best cabin Olivia had ever been in in the course of her limited travels, but it was one of the last available, or so the man she had spoken to had said at the time. No matter. It provided privacy and relative quiet, though she heard people banging around above, people shouting, babies crying, chickens squawking, pigs snorting, voices out in the hall as people passed the cabin. Well, more quiet than they had had in days, in what seemed like months.

Olivia thought about rousing Janey, washing her from head to toe, helping her dress in clean clothes, and urging her to put food in her belly. But Janey was snoring lightly, resting comfortably for the first time in days and days, and Olivia did not have the heart to wake her. At the moment she obviously needed sleep more than she needed food, water, a bath, and clean clothing. Sweet little Janey with her dark hair and lashes, with her big blue eyes that hid so much hurt. *Will she ever again be the happy, carefree girl I remember from two years ago, a time that seems amazingly remote?* Olivia wondered.

Had it really been such a short time ago that she and Janey had run along the garden paths barefoot and plucked tiny fish from the small pond in the clearing there? They had watched the fish wriggle in their open palms, then they had put the fish back. Later they had snatched beef and bread from under the cook's nose and raced out to the garden and had a little feast, a little picnic, complete with ants and flies and sunshine and whispering trees. Janey had told her how Edward drank so much of late, how she didn't like it, how he was so very mean when he drank.

He had us all fooled, Olivia thought now, shuddering at the sight of her stringy, dirty hair as she glanced into the small beveled looking glass she had produced from her bag. People always commented about her beautiful golden hair. She grimaced, hating the way it looked and felt right now so grimy and dirty, hating the way she looked and felt—apprehensive, uncertain, quivering inside, her eyes dull and frightened. She hated not knowing what lay ahead for her and Janey.

I killed him . . . murdered him . . . he couldn't have survived that blow.

The self-accusation always crept forth to haunt her—almost every time she closed her eyes, almost every time she sat still for too long. She glanced at Janey and shook the thought from her head. She had had no choice. No choice at all.

He had us all fooled, she thought again as she began removing the pins that were still left in her hair. On the outside, he had always managed to appear composed to friends, family, and business acquaintances, continuing to represent his clients and attend suppers and balls and other social events without flaw. At home, behind closed doors, he had been far different, fooling even Olivia's father—so much so that her father, when he knew he was dying, had left her in the care of this brother of his. *He hangs by a thread,* Olivia had thought to herself many times afterward as she watched Uncle Edward at the social events and then at the house on Pine Street. And she didn't know how he did it, how he fooled so many people. Except that he was clever. He knew he teetered on the edge of ruin. Sometimes she thought it even scared him, the thought that the drink might just be taking control of his life, that there were things he later couldn't remember having done. At some point, she had even begun to pity him, at times when he looked at

Janey, who was bruised and wounded from his latest episode, and shock crossed his face, fleeting but there nonetheless. He had started locking her and Janey in their rooms occasionally because he thought they had the power to ruin him, that they might tell people he beat Janey at times. And then he had figured out that no one would believe them.

His sister had come to him, betraying Olivia, informing him that their niece had approached her and told her horrible things about him, and that she'd told Olivia, "Edward would never do that." Olivia had tried to tell other family members, but all refused to believe her. Or else they were scared of him themselves. Olivia had never been sure of which it was, or the reason for their reticence, and soon she had stopped going to anyone at all, knowing that she and Janey were alone in this. Truly alone. Until the day she had spoken to Harry in the stable. Then she knew they had an ally, someone who would help them escape.

Dear Harry. He had given her money the night she had taken Janey and run. She had opened her mouth to refuse it, of course, snapping her lips together when she saw the look in his eyes. He would be taking them to the stagecoach station and leaving them there to board the next conveyance heading west. He wanted to do more, but what more could he do besides go along with them? And he couldn't leave his wife and daughters. He could at least do this much . . . give her money. Know that Mistresses Olivia and Jane wouldn't starve, though starvation would be much better than the fate that might await them if they stayed in Philadelphia. Olivia had smiled and kissed Harry on the cheek—yes, kissed him!—to his great surprise. She had told him that she had some money, though she wouldn't dare tell him how she had come by it because she feared that Harry would then look at her in a different way, with less respect. She wasn't a common thief, really, and when she had access to the trust her father had left her, she meant to pay it all back. But Harry had looked so worried, so pale, so distraught with concern, and when he pressed the bag of coins in her hand, she had squeezed her eyes shut and choked back the refusal. Once she and Janey were settled and she found employment—perhaps as a seamstress (she was qualified to teach, but people might want to know more about her . . . her background, her family, where she was from, and she could not risk that, not for a long time anyway)—she would repay him, too. Harry first, she had decided, watching him climb up onto the driver's seat of the carriage, flick the reins, and head off down the street. Harry first.

Olivia had spent the past days worrying about Edna Ferguson, too, wondering what had happened to the housekeeper after the two girls escaped. If Uncle Edward had survived the blow, he would have made certain that Edna Ferguson was punished for her part in the scheme. And what about Harry? Had his role been discovered? And if so, what had become of him?

The entire situation—the traveling, the worry, the not knowing how things had turned out with her uncle and with Edna and Harry—was overwhelming. Olivia was more weary than she had ever been in her life.

She brushed her hair, then changed her clothes, discarding the torn and dirty for the clean and intact. The crisp chemise and gray poplin she donned made her feel better, almost fresh. She ate. Beef that was too dry and chewy. Bread that was stale. Only the apple she devoured tasted delicious. But at least she had nourishment in her stomach, food that stayed down despite her worry that it might not, and despite the painful objections of her stomach that she was eating too much too fast after being famished.

She crawled back onto the bunk, snuggled up to Janey, and seconds later, fell asleep.

Janey woke her by stroking her face and kissing her chin. Olivia smiled and stretched, then tickled Janey in the ribs. The girl opened her mouth as if to laugh, but no sound emerged, something that always saddened Olivia. Janey squirmed herself right off the bunk.

Olivia washed her. She dressed her in clean clothes, too, and gave her food. Not once during the journey so far had

Janey looked frightened. Not once had she looked or acted reluctant, questioning with her eyes or tugging with her hands.

"Now that we're rested, fed, and somewhat clean, we should go out and breathe some air," Olivia suggested. Janey nodded an agreement. "But only a little," Olivia amended, "if the people and conditions on the deck of this ship are anything like they were on the last one."

Janey grimaced, then nodded to that, too.

So they ventured out, feeling somewhat refreshed by rest and nourishment.

It was evening, Olivia's favorite time of day—the same time of day it had been when they boarded this ship in Cincinnati, which made Olivia wonder again what day it was and how long they had slept. It was the time of day when she and her father had always finished reconciling the books in his Walnut Street shop, then strolled home. Except in the wintertime. Then, his driver always came for them. But during the summer and fall, and often during the spring, they always walked the two miles home, arm in arm, talking about their days and other subjects. Evenings with her father had always been a quiet, peaceful time, and Olivia cherished her memories of them and him.

The glowing sun melted over the riverbank, strewn with trees and undergrowth, and over distant hills. The water was different from what it was like in Cincinnati. Wider, murkier. The land seemed to roll on forever, green, lush, wild . . .

"You're some two hundred miles down into the Ohio River from Cincy, ma'am," a riverman in a steamer cap told her when she asked where they were. "Another two hundred b'fore we slide into the Mississippi, an' another hundred an' fifty or so b'fore we settle into St. Louie."

So far from home. From Philadelphia, where she had been born and raised, where her mother and father were buried.

Olivia nodded, thanked the man, and walked on, Janey holding fast to her hand as they followed the sound of music, a lively tune on a violin. The main deck was crowded with people, animals, and belongings (from bags to small pieces of furniture), and it was lit with lanterns that dangled from railing posts. An area had been cleared, and couples were dancing, kicking up their heels, clapping their hands, dipping, smiling, laughing. The men had rolled up their shirtsleeves. The women lifted their skirts nearly to their knees. As indecent as the sight was, Olivia stood and watched the gaiety, breaking into a smile when Janey squeezed her hand; glancing down Olivia saw the girl's eyes sparkling. It was about time they had fun. They deserved to have fun.

"'Tis Timber John's birthday," a little balding, red-faced Irishman told Olivia, pressing a mug into her hand. "Drink up, now. An' the lassie there, too!" He tweaked Janey's cheek, gave her a grin, then he was off.

Olivia laughed at the sight of him in his shirtsleeves, kicking up his heels in the dance area. He ran up to a man, tapped his arm, and when he got the man's attention, pointed off to something and spoke earnestly. While the man looked away, the little Irishman made off with the man's dance partner, a slender, bright-eyed, blond woman who laughed and missed a few steps. They were off a few seconds later, the two of them, twirling and dipping, tapping and skipping. Realizing he'd been tricked, her original partner rushed after them. The impish troublemaker scampered away giggling, darting between couples and dance partners. He grabbed one man's hat and smacked the blond woman's man on the rear with it. Then he raced off again, and her partner darted after him this time. People doubled over with laughter. Janey jumped up and down a little, giggling . . . a sweet sound. One Olivia had not heard in a long time.

"Janey, you—"

"Quite the mischievous leprechaun, isn't he?" a man said behind Olivia.

She turned and found herself staring into the prettiest set of brown eyes. Eyes a man should not be allowed to possess. Deep and rich and gazing at her from the depth of the man's soul. He wore dark trousers and a white shirt, the sleeves flapping slightly in the evening breeze. A beard shades darker than his blond hair peppered his jaw, and his face was strong, consisting of planes and angles, all seeming to change intensity and shape every few seconds in the glowing sunset and flickering lamplight. He dipped his head toward the mug Olivia held, asking, "Have you tried his brew?"

Smiling, Olivia glanced down at the mug, which she hadn't yet raised to her lips. "Brew? Pray tell, what are the ingredients?"

"Ah . . . ingredients. Let me see," he said, rubbing his chin as Olivia dared another look at him from beneath her lashes. He noticed; he paused longer than he might have otherwise, considering her more than the contents of her mug. "A snake or two from the Mississippi, a barrel of frogs—hence the jumping about"—he waved a hand at the merrymakers in the dance area—"a pinch of this and that from the forest . . . all combined to make certain that the person or persons who consume it have a jolly time."

It smelled harmless, like a sweet berry punch, and so Olivia lifted the mug to her lips. "In that case . . ." She tipped the mug and drank a good amount of the brew, watching him over the rim as he broke into a grin. She handed the rest to Janey and watched as the girl finished it.

"Dr. Alan Schuster, on my way to attend business in St. Louis," he said, bowing slightly, presenting himself to Olivia.

Manners had been ingrained in Olivia, and she offered him her hand and her name. "Olivia . . . Monroe," she said, her heart quickening at the fact that she'd almost forgotten the new last name she had concocted. *For our protection,* she had told Janey. *And we might have to tell a few other stories, too. Lying is not right, but our lies are not meant to hurt anyone, and we have no choice.* "And this is Jane, my sister."

Olivia half expected Janey's head to whip up at that, with a question in her eyes: *Your sister?* Olivia watched her to see how she would react. Janey did look up, but only to give her a wide smile. Olivia smiled back, feeling relieved. The two of them . . . they would love to have been born sisters, and this was at least a chance to pretend.

"Ah. Your sister," Dr. Schuster said, bending over her hand, brushing a kiss on the back of it. His gaze never left her face, and Olivia had the disturbing notion that he didn't believe that she and Janey were sisters. "Where are you from? East, surely. You have a refined manner that's in scarce supply in this part of the country."

She nodded. "East . . . Boston." From the outer corner of her eye she again watched to see if Janey would react, this time to the fact that they weren't from Boston at all, but from Philadelphia. But Janey had fastened her gaze on a group of children who were playing with a handful of dice, rolling them, shouting points, then rolling the die again.

"Boston . . . Now that you've a bit of Timber John's brew in you, would you like to have a try at a jig?" he queried, affecting a brogue.

It was silly and insane, the idea of dancing such a dance. Besides, something about the doctor made her uncomfortable. Perhaps it was the way he repeated her words: *your sister . . . Boston . . .* An odd sensation crept under Olivia's skin and warned again, with a little more bite this time, that he didn't believe her. But really, it made no difference whether he did or not. After this evening and after they disembarked in St. Louis, she might not ever see him again. And just as well.

"You're far removed from Boston, m'lady," he said leaning close and flashing his eyes at her.

He was far too charming. Olivia laughed a little, then felt Janey's hand slip beneath hers. In a flash, Olivia's hand was back in Dr. Schuster's, and Janey was pointing toward the dance area.

"Well, you're a sprite after my heart," the doctor told Janey. Olivia laughed more and let him lead her out into the dancing. Janey would not wander, at least not far. She never did.

He showed her the skips and kicks, the dips and turns. After two rounds of the song, Olivia finally felt she was catching on, and she became as uninhibited as the other women dancers, lifting her skirts and dancing as she had never danced, wild and free. She clapped and laughed, felt her hair fall free and didn't care. She looked for Janey a few times, watched her clap, too, and the third time she glanced over, she spotted Janey playing dice with the other children. Another corruption. Olivia laughed at that thought, drank another mug of the leprechaun's brew, then danced more.

A few more dances, and she and the doctor, both feeling tired and breathless but exhilarated, found bench seats near the deck railing, where Olivia had a good view of Janey.

"I'm trying to remember when I last had so much fun," she said.

Chuckling, he dabbed perspiration from his forehead with a linen handkerchief, then smiled over at her. "And . . . ?"

"Perhaps it was when my mother was still alive. She loved to dance. I remember her twirling around the ballroom in our home in Phila—" She caught herself. She would never make a good liar. Never. "I lived for a time in Philadelphia when I was younger and—"

"Before your sister was born?" he queried, studying her, her face, her hair. Olivia suddenly wished for her hairpins, though they were long gone, doubtless scattered about the deck by now. She wished for a fan to cool herself, too, and for a glass of water to wet her dry mouth. She didn't intend for her and Janey to be found—certainly not without a struggle—by Uncle Edward, if he was still alive, or by authorities hunting her as his murderess, and the doctor's questions made her uncomfortable.

"Yes, I was younger than she is now at the time, much younger, and I remember so little about the city."

He studied her more, making her more uncomfortable. Olivia wanted to squirm on her seat, twist a portion of her skirt . . .

"You're here with a relative?" he asked. "Your father, since your mother is deceased?" Obviously he was trying to make conversation and find out more about her at the same time.

"No," Olivia responded, standing, deciding that enough was enough. He stood, too, and she looked up into his eyes, determined to put him off. He was far too inquisitive for her peace of mind. She and Janey were running, trying to get far from Philadelphia and the ugliness they had left there. She had no idea who this man was, not really—she knew only that he was traveling to St. Louis to oversee some business. If that was even true. If he had not been hired by Uncle Edward or the authorities. She hated to be so paranoid, but she had to think that way. She had to. Even if he had not been hired by her uncle or the authorities, the last thing she needed was to attract the attention of a man, of an ardent suitor. She shouldn't have allowed herself to get caught up in the merriment.

"I'm here with my husband," she lied. Then she gathered her skirts, turned, and walked off.

CHAPTER TWO

"IF I DIDN'T have bad luck, I wouldn't have *any* luck," Alan said, stuffing his hands into his trouser pockets and shuffling up to where an elderly woman, his companion during this journey, perched on a trunk, her crooked cane resting beside her. Ida Bogue tapped her boots against one side of the trunk and clapped her hands now and then, keeping time with the lively tune being played out a short distance away. Her silver curls shimmered in the lamplight, and her rosy cheeks and bright eyes revealed that she herself had had a bit of the brew being passed around in celebration of Timber John's birthday.

A couple of tussling young men crashed into the trunk, unbalancing Ida. Her cane went flying. She righted herself, then got riled up and scowled, ready to set off after the youngsters.

"Trifling boys. Infernal nuisances!" she growled. "Git on outta here b'fore I lodge a complaint with the Captain 'n' have the two of ya tossed offa this boat."

"Sorry, ma'am," one boy mumbled, wincing. The other fetched her cane.

Ida growled more, yanked her stick out of the boy's hand, and brandished the cane at the pups. "G'on. Git!"

"Wasn't meanin' to disturb ya. Wasn't meanin' to at all," the first boy insisted; then he and his companion turned heel and raced off.

Alan couldn't help a chuckle. Small as she was—weighing no more than one hundred ten pounds at the most and standing no taller than five foot three inches—Ida always held her own. Alan wouldn't have thought to intervene on the boys' behalf, saying, for instance, that it was an accident that they'd slammed into the trunk. Ida would have had a few words for him, too.

"Now what was it ya were sayin' there, Doc?" she croaked.

"I said, 'if I didn't have bad luck I'd have no luck at all.' " Alan sat on one edge of the trunk and watched people jig, all the while feeling Ida's sharp green gaze. Apprehension prickled the hair on the back of his neck.

She whacked him on the thigh with her cane.

Smarting, Alan jerked away. "What the—"

"Don't that just beat the nation!" she exploded. "Yer feelin' a mite sorry fer yerself there, Doc. That don't go, no how, no way. Ya hunkered all the way to Cinc'natti an' ya didn't do well there, not like ya thought ya'd do anyhow. Mebbe yer not meant to be in the steamboatin' bus'ness, 'at's all. No sense hangin' yer jaw over it. An' that gal that just put ya off . . . Well, mebbe she's got her own troubles."

"Ida, you—"

"Don't gimme that look, mister, like a cock that just got his tail feathers burned an' don't want nobody knowin'. Durn right I saw it—I saw the whole thing. Ain't much gets past me. Truth is, tail feathers or no tail feathers, if ya like the gal ya go after 'er, an' if ye're really wantin' to be in the steamboatin' bus'ness ya go after it, too. When this thing docks in St. Louie, ya get on a boat goin' right back to Cinc'natti an' finish that bus'ness ya started."

Alan shook his head. "It's not that simple."

Ida jerked back, hissing in her throat. "Whadya mean? It's simple enough! Ya wanna build a boat an' ya want that feller in Cinc'natti to build it 'cause ya think he's the best there is. So ya hire him to build it, an' he builds it."

"He wants twice what he originally asked."

She squinted one eye. "Then ya give 'im a little buckshot an' tell 'im he's gonna build the boat, an' he's gonna build it fer the cost he told ya in the first place. Seems to me he knows ya want *him* to build the dadburned thing. Now how d'ya suppose he figured that one out? Weren't too cool dandyin' in there, was ya, Doc? He saw right through ya, just like I'm seein' right through ya now. Lord A'mighty!"

"Buckshot would not make him build my ship, Ida. It would land me in jail. Obviously he did guess that I want him, and no one else, to build the ship and—"

She whacked him again, her eyes sparking. "Tarnation! Haven't I told ya to git rid of those city ways? If ya don't gravel me sometimes . . . Where'd that gal go? Had a youngun with her, didn't she? There she goes!" she snapped, pointing her cane. "Go git 'er an' dance with her some more."

"I'm going to take that cane and snap it in two if you—"

She whacked him again. Thoroughly irritated, Alan snatched the stick from her. She set her jaw and glared at him.

"She's married, Ida."

"Well, she ain't wearin' a ring."

"Not all married couples wear rings. Her husband is aboard this ship."

"Didn't see him out there dancin' with 'er."

"He could turn up at any moment!"

"Then tell 'im he shouldn't oughtta be leavin' such a pretty gal alone 'round all these roosters!"

"My . . . *God*, but you're irritating, Ida Bogue, the most irritating, irrational woman I've ever come across!"

"Ya've got gumption after all. I'll give ya that, Doc," she said, scooting off the edge of the trunk. She snatched her cane back and pointed the straight end of it at him. "Ain't nobody ever dared grab this thing from me. Now I'm gonna go dance with a furriner."

And with that, the stubborn Iowa woman stumped off, leaving Alan scratching his jaw. He thought briefly about shouting at her that she shouldn't be dancing, that such foolery might just be the end of her, but he bit back the notion. Ida wouldn't listen to him. Ida rarely did.

She was definitely the most irritating woman he'd ever run across, his most independent, stubborn, *bull-headed* patient. When he had learned, some two months ago, that Ida was planning a spring visit to her sister's home in

Cincinnati, where she also meant to do a little mercantile business, Alan had determined to accompany her and conduct his business at the same time. Even as sick as she was with both lung and heart ailments, Ida refused to let anyone do for her what she felt she could do for herself. He'd known that before, but since this journey had begun she'd drilled the fact into his head. She walked by herself. Despite his objections, she toted her own luggage. She blasted anyone who got in her way. She was a hard lady, a product of the harsh Iowa plains, as long lasting and sturdy as the sod houses that nearly blended with that land. The boys who had dislodged her from that trunk had had no idea how lucky they were that she hadn't taken after *them* with her cane.

She had become his patient only this past fall, after years of watching him tend patients, years of observing, scrutinizing and criticizing. A makeshift doctor in her own right, she had her remedies—a leaf for this, a leaf for that, prepared in various ways—most of which she'd learned from the Indians before white settlers had invaded parts of what was now Iowa, claiming native lands, and before war had driven the Indians further and further west. She ran a dry goods store in Davenport, and one entire shelf in her little store was cluttered with bottles of her remedies. But none of them had worked when she cut the big toe on her right foot last fall and infection had set in.

Ida and her pride and stubbornness . . . By the time she came and asked Alan if he wouldn't mind having a look at her foot, gangrene had set in in the toe and she figured it had to go. She trusted him with a scalpel, it seemed, more than she trusted herself with a makeshift knife. She'd brought her own tin of whiskey, and she swigged it down before he began working, one of the few times Alan had seen even the smallest sign of weakness in Ida. He'd lifted a brow at the tin, and she'd grumbled at him, "Well, ya don't think I'm gonna let ya saw on me b'fore I have somethin' to deaden' things, do ya? Brewed it m'self, I did, an' it's the meanest stuff west of the Mississippi, too!"

Alan had noticed that she breathed funny at times,

wheezed and turned a little ashen, but he said nothing about that, concentrating on her toe instead. Afterward she had surprised him by telling him to listen to her ticker and her lungs and tell her why he thought they didn't work so good sometimes, more and more of late. She had a murmur and bronchitis, he said, and when he started to make a suggestion for treatment of the latter, she scampered away, wincing because of pain in the area where her toe had been, though she surely hadn't known that he'd seen her wince. Ida was a proud woman.

After that, he began visiting her store every few days, not at all surprised to see her there when he'd told her to go home and stay completely off of her feet for a few weeks. He left her medicine, saying carefully, "if you want to try it," and every so often he asked about the remedies she used. He really was interested, and he asked in a respectful manner so as not to irritate her. Of course, it didn't take much to irritate Ida. During the ensuing winter they went on a few calls together, and people lifted their brows and began talking about Ida and Dr. Schuster being seen around together—there'd never been any love lost between the two, after all. Ida had always had a lot of vinegar in her, as another of Alan's patients told him, and everyone was wondering how he'd tamed her. Alan laughed in disbelief; obviously no one ever witnessed the spats between himself and Ida, between a common-sense doctor and a grumpy old woman.

. . . if ya like the gal, go after 'er . . . give 'im a little buckshot an' tell 'im he's gonna build the boat . . .

Lord, he wished it were that easy. To Ida, everything was black and white. She charged through life with her pointed chin in the air and her cane in hand, and damn anyone who stood in her way. While that worked for Ida, Alan didn't conduct his affairs that way. The young woman was married, so that was that, and Nathaniel Cotton had been so unreasonable about the cost of building the ship that Alan refused, absolutely refused, to negotiate with the man further. In fact, he didn't even want to think about the ship and the negotiation with Cotton right now or anytime in the near future; he planned to stop in St. Louis and visit a friend for a bit, go home to Davenport, check on each and every one of his patients, *then* think about approaching another shipbuilder.

A flash of gold caught his eye, and he caught himself staring at Olivia Monroe, the woman who had snared his attention earlier. She had been laughing at Kevin McBride's mischievous leprechaun ways as he passed out brew and played pranks, her curls shimmering in the lamplight as they danced along her back. Her pallor and thinness had concerned Alan, but when he spoke to her and she glanced around at him, he saw that there was nothing sickly in the brightness of her blue eyes. Presently she was trying to coax her sister from a group of children. She spoke to the girl several times, and finally the child glanced up at her, scowled, then nodded.

What had he said to make her turn tail and run? He had given her a few appreciative looks, but nothing lewd. Perhaps she had acted as she thought any proper married woman should when any man besides her husband looked at her that way. She and the girl obviously had come up onto the deck alone—given the fashionable cut of her and the girl's dresses they surely were not deck passengers—and while the dance with him was acceptable, sitting with him and enjoying his attention apparently were not. Perhaps her husband was the jealous type and . . .

Why waste time trying to guess at why she had skittered away?

She cast another apprehensive glance at him, then she took the girl by the shoulders and led her away. Alan wondered at the fear in her eyes. He wasn't so frightening—at least he didn't think so. But then, if her husband was the jealous type and saw her talking to him, perhaps even looking at him, there might be retribution. Alan hated to think such thoughts, but over the years he'd seen examples of that sort of thing. He'd tended more than one woman who tried to attribute bruises and broken bones to falls.

He fetched himself another mug of birthday brew and sipped it while propping an elbow on the deck railing and leaning that way. Ida kicked her heels up, flirted with men twenty years younger than she by flipping her skirt at them, and in general gave everyone hell in the dance area, forcing men and women alike to try to keep up with her. She'd left her cane somewhere—though she could walk without it, it relieved her aching foot most of the time—but wherever she'd left it, Alan was certain it was in good care: her favorite beau, Curtis Campbell, had fashioned the cane for her last fall after hearing that she'd lost her toe, and Ida would not lose sight of that cane for the world. Any second now, Alan expected her to collapse and perish on the dance floor. But then, passing on in such a fashion would no doubt suit Ida's fancy, he thought, giving a chuckle.

During the second day of travel from Cincinnati, the *Star of Ohio* steamed into the wide Mississippi River some one hundred and sixty miles below St. Louis. Olivia and Janey took their meals in the ship's dining room and though they strolled the vessel for exercise during the afternoons and evenings, they steered clear of the main deck. Olivia knew they could run into the doctor just about anywhere on board, but staying away from the main deck, where she had met him, might decrease their chances of running into him at all.

Janey had again become her solemn self, rarely smiling, and Olivia regretted having pulled her away from the group of children the evening of the birthday party. *Will I always have to be as distrustful as I was with the doctor?* she wondered. She didn't want to be a paranoid individual but felt that she must be right now for the sake of her and Janey's survival. Soon they would settle somewhere, a place where Janey could form friendships if she wanted to, a place where they could feel safe and secure.

Olivia would never forget the moment she decided to make that place Iowa Territory, or rather, the moment she at least decided to investigate the land that was the topic of conversation between two women in the ladies' saloon the third afternoon of travel from Ohio.

"There's so *much* land opening up west of the Mississippi River that Albert couldn't decide where he wanted us to settle at first," one woman said to the other. She looked to be in her mid twenties, and she wore a fashionable black feathered hat that nestled securely on her dark curls, even when she tipped her head and looked down at the book that lay in her lap. "Then we read from this—Lieutenant Albert M. Lea's *Notes on the Wisconsin Territory; Particularly with Reference to the Iowa District*—and we decided to come have a look at the land. Lieutenant Lea says the soil is black and rich, that the land is beautiful, one grand rolling prairie, and that along one side flows the mightiest river in the world—the Mississippi. The climate is pleasant, too, from what I've read; the winters are much less harsh than those of northern Pennsylvania. We never had a home of our own in Pennsylvania, Albert and I. We married five years ago and have lived with my parents since. Western land is inexpensive, and it's good land. This is a chance for Albert and me to finally start our own life together and to become independent of my parents."

"I'd say—after already being married for five years!" the other, older woman remarked. She wore a prim evergreen traveling dress, and she was twice the size of her companion. For the last twenty minutes or so she clearly had been tolerating the younger woman's excited chatter, frequently glancing off at nothing in general, then fussing with her bodice, sleeves, and the folds in her skirts, then glancing off again . . . The woman with the black hat began rattling more descriptions of Iowa—"wooded bluffs and seas of wildflowers"—and the older woman stood abruptly. "Well, my husband has been up that way a time or two—he's in the banking business—and he agrees that the land is rich. But he doesn't agree with the way the government wrestled it from the Indians. A pity, he says."

"But there's more land farther west, an entire wilderness in which the Indians can hunt and fish and set up their villages. Besides, the government bought the land, Mrs. Sullivan," the other woman argued earnestly. "All Albert and I want to do is buy a piece of what's being offered and farm it. Towns are springing up all over, so it won't be like we're in total wilderness."

"Yes, well, the best of luck to you, Mrs. Sumner," Mrs. Sullivan said, giving a patronizing smile. She snapped open a fan and began flickering it beneath her chin. "My husband and son are surely waiting upstairs for me by now. Good afternoon."

"Good afternoon," the girl mumbled, staring after the departing woman as if wondering what she had said to offend her. Climbing the staircase from the saloon, Mrs. Sullivan soon disappeared beyond a door that opened onto the deck.

Only ten or twelve women currently sat in the ladies' saloon, relaxing on settees and around tables. Not wanting to mingle with the crowd upstairs but also not wanting to be cramped inside their small cabin, Olivia and Janey had wandered into the saloon nearly half an hour ago and now sat on a velvet-cushioned settee near the one Mrs. Sumner now occupied alone. Janey had leaned against Olivia's side and was now dozing. Mrs. Sumner pulled her surprised gaze from the staircase, opened her book, and began reading.

"Do you plan to settle near a town?" Olivia could not help but ask.

Mrs. Sumner glanced up, her eyes bright again at the fact that someone was interested in her topic after all. "Yes, but we're not sure which one yet. There's Burlington, Davenport, Dubuque, Iowa City . . . . We're just not certain yet. I think Albert wants to get there and have a look around. I imagine we'll spend a few days in Davenport and Dubuque anyway since they're river towns. Iowa City is almost fifty miles over from Davenport, not so far that traveling there is a hardship. Any farther and . . ." She blushed. "Albert worries. You see . . . I realized only a week ago that I'm expecting. He says that if we had known before we left Pennsylvania, we wouldn't be here now. But I'm glad I didn't realize before. My mother would have raised the roof about me traveling. Mothers, you know. Very protective. I hope I'm not so diligent even when my children are grown. Why, I'm twenty-four, a grown woman. But I'm probably offending you, you with your little girl and all, being a mother yourself. My mother—"

"How thrilled you must be!" Olivia managed to interject.

Mrs. Sumner's blush deepened. "I am—oh, I am! It's our first, and I was beginning to think it would never happen. But I think it was just meant to be this late, that's all. I mean, here we are, setting out on our own for the first time, and now a baby decides to come along at just the right time. Why, by the time my confinement approaches, Albert will surely have built us a home."

After introducing herself and learning that her new acquaintance was named Maddie, Olivia gestured toward the book. "Does it have a map?" she asked. "Where is Iowa Territory?"

"It is just upriver from Missouri," Mrs. Sumner said, coming over from her settee, intent on sharing her book, her eyes gleaming with excitement again. She sat to Olivia's left since Janey already occupied the space on Olivia's right. "If you go much farther west of Iowa Territory and Missouri, Albert says you'll be in complete wilderness—and Indian country, and the Indian skirmishes aren't so far in the past that you would want to do that. He's read this book and he's talked to a lot of people." She sat and began thumbing through pages. "Here we are . . . a map," she said, moving half of the book onto Olivia's map.

Olivia scanned the drawing. According to the map, the territory of Iowa was some two to three hundred miles up from St. Louis, a city that was a lot like Cincinnati in population and development, or so other passengers had told her when she'd asked about St. Louis. She wanted to settle somewhere small and relatively quiet, and that seemed to exclude St. Louis. But Iowa Territory might be an option. In fact, Iowa sounded like *the* option.

"Where are you from?" Maddie asked.

Olivia glanced up.

Maddie blinked. "I didn't mean to startle you. Please . . . read. We can talk later."

"Oh, I wasn't reading," Olivia said, forcing a smile. Heavens, but she nearly jumped out of her skin whenever anyone asked her a simple question! Yesterday afternoon another woman she had met here in this saloon had asked

Janey's age, and Olivia had hesitated before telling the woman that Janey was eight years old. "That's nice," the woman had responded just before casting Olivia a queer look, then moving on.

"I'm . . . We're from Boston," Olivia told Maddie. "I was thinking. Does this ship travel up into Iowa Territory?"

"No. Albert says we'll be changing ships in St. Louis."

"Do you know the name of the ship you'll be taking from there?"

"Not right off," Maddie said. "But I'll ask Albert later. He's sure to know."

Olivia gave Maddie her and Janey's cabin number so she would know where to locate them aboard ship. They agreed that if Olivia wasn't in at the time Maddie called, then Maddie would slip a note containing the name of the ship under the cabin door.

"I see it's getting near suppertime," Maddie said an hour or so later, after she had gone through a host of topics—her and Albert's life with her parents in Pennsylvania; the variety of people she'd met on the ship from Pittsburgh to Cincinnati and then during this journey, too; how she was so excited about the move that she'd hardly slept a night since the journey began . . . Olivia found her sweet but exhausting, undoubtedly the same way Mrs. Sullivan had viewed her, only Olivia had much more patience.

"I hope to see you again," Maddie said. "Perhaps in Iowa Territory somewhere soon, depending on where you and your husband and Albert and I settle."

Olivia thanked her for sharing her book and information about the new territory. Then, as she had done with the doctor on the main deck the other evening, she let Maddie Sumner go off thinking that she was married and that her husband was on board somewhere. She might not see either of them ever again, and letting them believe she was married was the safest course. In the doctor's case, it stopped him from pursuing her, and in Maddie's case, it safeguarded against questions. An unmarried woman traveling alone with a child was likely not a common occurrence, perhaps not a safe one either, and people were bound to lift brows.

Olivia looked down at Janey and found the child gazing up at her, her eyes wide. Olivia brought her head down close to Janey's and said softly, "Perhaps we've found a place to settle. Somewhere in the Iowa Territory. We shall at least go have a look at the land and the people."

Nodding, Janey slipped her arms around her cousin just under Olivia's breasts and squeezed. Olivia hugged the girl back. "Oh, Janey," she said, "look at us, wandering off to a new land. We're so brave. So very, very brave."

Janey sniffed, and Olivia realized that the girl was crying. She'd not seen Janey be so emotional in months, and it was actually a good sight, a comforting sight. At least Janey had not gone so cold inside, so distant, for the sake of self-preservation, that she was beyond healing.

CHAPTER THREE

THE STEAMER *BRAZIL* took them from St. Louis up into the wilds of northern Missouri and Iowa Territory, and though tension mounted when the ship braved rapids, driftwood, and numerous snags in the waterway, this section of Olivia and Janey's journey into what would be their new life was not as tedious as the other parts had been. Only a handful of passengers traveled on this ship, perhaps ten, as compared to the hundreds that had crowded the other two ships on which Olivia and Janey had traveled. The *Brazil*'s captain and crew were friendly and hospitable, making certain their passengers were comfortable, and yet they still managed to keep a close eye on the river, sending a yawl—a small riverboat—on ahead of them to check for depth and mood.

Olivia was thankful that Albert and Maddie Sumner were not aboard the *Brazil* during this particular journey, a surprise since this was the ship Maddie had indicated in the note she had slipped under Olivia's cabin door several hours after the two had talked in the saloon. Escaping Maddie would have been a nearly impossible feat on board a ship with only ten passengers, and though Olivia had a large store of patience, she doubted that she would have had enough to be completely civil if she had found herself spending days with the chattery Maddie by her side. And that was exactly where the woman would have been given the fact that Olivia and Janey were the only two females aboard the *Brazil* at the moment.

Though she in no way begrudged Maddie her excitement, Olivia was approaching her and Janey's new life in a serious, protective manner, and she wanted no interference, no questions, no odd looks, no prying. Maddie was inquisitive enough—and also compassionate enough, Olivia sensed—that she would eventually have asked a dozen questions, no doubt wondering where Olivia's husband was and soon learning from the crew that Olivia's husband was deceased. (Another concoction on Olivia's part because she couldn't have registered a husband, too, or she would have had to pay passage for three people instead of two, and . . . an unmarried woman traveling alone surely would raise far more brows than a widow traveling alone.) Then Maddie would have wondered why Olivia had lied to her and . . .

Olivia shuddered. She was telling lie upon lie upon lie. Conniving and scheming, weaving a web of untruths, and losing at least an hour of sleep over each and every one. The fact that she had stolen from her uncle, possibly murdered him, and kidnapped her cousin, all added to her sins. Once—back in St. Louis—she had started to pray for forgiveness, then she had clamped her mouth shut. Why pray for forgiveness now, when she knew she would tell another lie in five or ten or fifteen minutes . . . however much time passed before someone else asked where she was from and with whom she was traveling, and whatever else a curious stranger might choose to ask.

The farther upriver the steamer traveled, the more the forested banks of the Mississippi River gnarled and tangled and looked inhospitable. Now and then bluffs broke through the dark entanglements, their shelves extending over the gray water, and just about the time Olivia was ready to shake her head and tell Janey they had made a terrible mistake and would be going back downriver soon, probably on this very ship, she spotted not only a settlement but friendly people waving from a wharf.

"Burlington," a scruffy riverman leaned over to tell her, "an' I wouldn't recommend it if it was the last place in the territory—which it ain't. They look like they'd welcome ya all right. But ferrymen here charge strangers twice as much as they charge citizens, an' the damn boarding house and hotel people do the same—pardonin' my English, Mrs. Monroe."

Though his name was William Clift, the other crew members called him Turtle, supposedly because he worked as slow as one. But he had been pleasant to Olivia during the journey, and not in an unseemly manner either. In a fatherly sort of way, a way she had found refreshing and comforting. Without saying so, he seemed to have guessed early on that she was in a predicament and in a foreign place and needed gentle guidance. All along, whenever the *Brazil* hit a glitch in the Mississippi, which, he said, could be a downright hazardous river at times—shallow in places, running fast in others—he had taken the time to explain to her what the crew was doing to remedy the situation. In this way William Clift had made more than one stretch of this journey a little easier for her and Janey, and for that, and him, Olivia was grateful. She trusted him, too, which was something she could not say about anyone else she had met since leaving Philadelphia.

"So if you were a newcomer looking to settle and make a new home, you wouldn't settle in Burlington, Mr. Clift?"

"No, ma'am, I wouldn't," he said, looking her straight in the eye, reiterating what he'd said against it. If he wouldn't settle there himself, then Olivia had no wish to settle there.

"Where would you settle in Iowa?" she asked directly, though she knew he made his home in St. Louis. From their past conversations she at least knew that he liked parts of Iowa.

"Davenport or Dubuque," he responded without pause. "We'll be sittin' in Davenport in three to four hours, dependin' on how long we take here. You could stop there for a spell, an' if you find you don't like it, why, the *Brazil* makes runs up and down the river every two days—you could catch her when she comes back through. You could go on up to Dubuque then, an' see what you think of it."

Olivia smiled. "I'll do exactly that, Mr. Clifton. Thank you."

He nodded, then scampered off to help bring the ship into dock.

* * *

Her first glimpse of Davenport was a quaint but pretty one. Earlier, the day had been overcast, painting everything gray, making the river look dark and murky. But the sun had come out nice and bright right after the *Brazil* departed Burlington, and now the setting sun cast a red orange hue on the wharf, the frame houses and buildings, a steepled church, several cemeteries, the dirt streets and the people walking up and down them. A woman and a group of children waved and shouted from the dock, obviously happy to see the steamer, and when the ship pulled closer and Olivia heard the children's shouts of "Pa, Pa!" she understood why. The crew moored the ship, and then she watched a stout, burly male passenger run down the gangplank and scoop into his arms the entire group of children—two boys and two girls of assorted sizes. Next he hugged the woman, and Olivia stood watching the family scene, feeling a familiar, sad tug. Though she had been young—all of nine years old—when her mother died, she remembered enough about the warmness of her own family to miss the smiles, the laughter, the times she cherished in her heart. Her father's death had crushed her because not only did she miss him, but also the last shred of their family unit had gone with him into the grave. And now, if she ever married and had children, he would never see them, never know them.

Fighting back tears, Olivia turned away from the wharf and prepared to gather her and Janey's trunks.

"No, ma'am, Mrs. Monroe," William Clift said, stepping between her and the trunks. "You ain't totin' these. Why, we'll be docked here for a couple hours anyway. I'll help find you a room in town, then I'll come back for yer things."

Olivia thanked him, saying she greatly appreciated his help. Then she took Janey by the hand and followed him from the steamer.

They found a room quickly enough in one of Davenport's two boardinghouses. The proprietor's name was Charlotte Lind, a sweet-faced woman twice Olivia's age with graying black hair pinned in a chignon at the nape of her neck. Wearing a bright blue-and-white-checked gingham dress and a white smock, she answered the door with flour covering her hands and smudging her chin. "Well, Will Clift, I always have a room to let to any friend of yours," she said, beaming at Janey, then at Olivia. Laughing a little, she made an attempt to brush the flour from her chin with her forearm. "Lordy, but aren't I a sight! I was just digging in, making bread for the week. Come in here now."

The colors of sunset beamed into the common room through a western window. Colorful braided rugs covered the planked floor in places, and red curtains were tied back at the windows. The huge fireplace was empty, though a little pile of ashes had been swept to one side of the hearth. Three rough oak tables shot through with dark veins, a settle, and several small stools furnished the main room. Knitted coverlets of blue and green and other colors lay folded over the arms of the settles, and a collection of cracked and weathered books sat on a small shelf on the southern wall. Nearby, a narrow staircase led up to the second floor. The room was by no means plain, unless it was compared to Uncle Edward's home and the home Olivia had grown up in. But a home was not the furnishings, she quickly decided as she stood glancing around the cozy room, her hands on Janey's shoulders from behind. Olivia looked at Charlotte Lind's bright face, warm smile, and tender eyes, and the apprehension and fear that had knotted Olivia's stomach for more than a week now broke up a little. Though she had not decided whether or not Davenport was where she and Janey would make their home, being in a warm, welcoming place like Charlotte Lind's boarding-house while she took a few days to look around and make up her mind would certainly be a comfort.

"Well, let's go up and have a look at the rooms and then if you decide you want to stay, we'll talk about cost and meals," Charlotte said. "I realize I have competition up the street, albeit friendly competition—Malva Dodge and I are the best of friends—and you could just as well go up there."

Relief rushed through Olivia, and with it exhaustion, more emotional than physical. She walked numbly over to one of the little stools that sat beneath a window, and there she sat and closed her eyes. The unshakable fear of possibly having killed Uncle Edward . . . the fear of being pursued, caught and hung for robbery and murder . . . the fear, if he was still alive and if she were caught, of Janey having to go back, having to endure more abuse and possibly the horror of being sent to a madhouse because people whispered about her and about the fact that she had been withdrawn and hadn't spoken a word since her mother's death . . . The long days—more than a week—traveling, first in that bumpy, rattling stagecoach, then going from ship to ship to ship, running, not really knowing where they were going exactly, just west; not knowing what kind of people they would meet along the way; not knowing—still not knowing—who could or couldn't be trusted: just having solid walls around her and a floor that didn't move beneath her feet and being in such a sweet room with such caring people . . . mingled together, relief and joy and fear—overwhelmed her. And to her horror she sat on the stool and cried for the first time since leaving Philadelphia.

Janey was there suddenly, slipping her little arms around Olivia's neck, such sweet, solid comfort. Another set of arms slipped around Olivia, encompassing Janey, too. They were soft and motherly, and suddenly Olivia didn't feel strong inside anymore at all; she felt drained and vulnerable. Her weakness shamed her, and she wanted to run and hide. But Charlotte Lind whispered that it was all right to cry sometimes, when a person needed to, that tears shouldn't be held inside and that she had a feeling Olivia's *had* been held inside and that now the dam had burst. Hearing her, Olivia was comforted. She melted against Charlotte and cried more.

Charlotte led her and Janey to the back of the house, into the kitchen, as a mother might lead small children. She gave Olivia a warm drink, something that tasted like cider but that had more spice to it. Olivia drank it as Charlotte moved about the kitchen, heating water in a fireplace kettle, then drawing aside a curtain across the room and dumping the water into a large round tub that sat in an alcove there. Charlotte sprinkled dried flower petals in the water, then she removed Olivia's clothes and helped her into the tub. Olivia sank down into the water, thinking she had surely died and gone to heaven.

She had forgotten that people existed like William Clift, who had been so kind to her on the *Brazil* (where had he gone? he had been in the common room when her dam had burst, and she hadn't seen him since), and Charlotte, who was being so kind and motherly to her now, during a time when she so desperately needed motherly attention.

Charlotte produced a white shift for Olivia, then served her and Janey a delicious stew. Later, she tucked them in for the night, in a room that was just as warm as the common room, and in a bed that was just as soft as Olivia had imagined it would be.

Olivia was grateful for Charlotte's kindness, but the next day they argued over what Charlotte wanted to charge Olivia for boarding her and Janey—which was nothing.

"I won't accept charity," Olivia said as they sat together in the common room. "I have money."

"Charity?" Charlotte exploded. "Listen, Miss Boston, you're not out east anymore. People here help each other. I might need the favor returned sometime and—"

"What are you charging your other boarders?" Olivia had seen the man upstairs this morning, tall and gangly, dressed in a black suit. He had been coming out of his room at the same time she and Janey had been coming out of theirs.

Charlotte set her jaw. "That's none of your concern. Besides, he's not a woman who just lost her husband and decided to strike out west on her own with her sister—a mere child—because there's opportunity here. I don't know what kind of opportunity you think there is for a woman, except maybe teaching or the boardinghouse business. And you have to have a house for that. To have a house you have to have land to build it on first. Sure, there's land to be had, but it takes a strong back and strong arms to break sod."

"Charlotte, we were talking about the cost of boarding me and Janey," Olivia said gently, not wanting to quarrel.

"Spend your money on a piece of land," the other woman insisted. "Then spend it on materials to build a house."

"I would like to pay you."

"And I'm telling you I don't want your money."

"Then Janey and I will have to find another place to live as soon as possible."

Charlotte sat back in her chair and considered Olivia, finally shaking her head. "Stubborn girl. You ought to turn and go back to Boston. What are you going to do? I see a lot of people come through here, all ready to make new lives, and they all give different reasons why. Not that I ever ask questions. Not that I usually want to. But you . . . you make me want to ask questions. There you and your husband were in a home in Boston, and instead of staying, instead of keeping a roof over your head and good food in your belly, you sold everything and headed out here. Well, it's a rough land. It's not kind. You ought to go back to where you at least have relatives. And I'll tell you something—"

"You have no idea what our life was like, what it would be like if we went back," Olivia said.

"You had a roof and you had food."

"We had . . . pain!"

Charlotte stared at her, no doubt a hundred questions racing through her head. Olivia stood up and took Janey by the hand, leading her away from the rag dolls Charlotte had given her this morning and hurrying from the room. Yesterday Charlotte had been comforting; today she was being judgmental, making her feel like a fool for traveling west. Well, she hadn't had a choice, not really, at least not a good choice.

She went walking with Janey. They needed to have a look at Davenport anyway. Blast Charlotte! Olivia wasn't interested in "breaking sod," but if that was what she had to do in order to survive, to have a home and to make a good life for herself and Jenny in the West, then that was exactly what she would do. Of course, she had to find out what "breaking sod" meant before she could decide if she had to do it.

She also meant to find out if Davenport had any dry

goods stores, and if so, how many. She had helped her father at his mercantile many times over the years, and in the back of her mind was the thought that she could open one of her own, that teaching or running a boardinghouse were *not* the only professions a woman could enter into out here. Why, even a small town needed a place where its citizens could replenish their basic supplies and now and then purchase a little something extra, too. If she thought the possibility of opening a mercantile in Davenport was promising, then she just might do exactly that.

CHAPTER FOUR

NEARLY A WEEK after stopping in St. Louis, Alan and Ida arrived in Davenport on the steamer *Iowa,* one of the few ships that made regular runs up and down this section of the Mississippi. Ida had grumbled and groaned from the time they had docked in St. Louis until the time they left, and even some after they boarded the *Iowa,* saying that she wanted to get home and that she bet her store had gone nearly to ruin by now under Homer Whitworth's direction—although Alan knew she trusted Homer's business sense. She had planned to stay in Cincinnati longer, but she was glad that Alan had wanted to leave when he did because she also wanted to get back to Davenport and make sure her cat hadn't clawed anything else up lately because if the critter had, she was going to whap her a good one. And that Louise Gordon, the only person in the world she had ever called friend, better not be tipping the bottle again or else Ida was going to have at her, too. All in all, Ida was homesick, and Alan doubted whether she would have been able to stay away from Davenport for the entire two or three months he had originally planned for them to be in Cincinnati and St. Louis.

The *Iowa* arrived at the Davenport dock later than expected, having been delayed in Burlington when the pilot left the ship and did not return. Another pilot had had to be located, negotiated with, and boarded. The air was unseasonably cool for June, the temperature having dipped earlier in the evening. The time was nearing ten P.M., and lanterns still glowed here and there around town. John Brimmer, Davenport's sole attorney, was waiting near the wharf.

"Didn't expect ya back so early, Doc Schuster . . . Ida," he said. "Was ridin' by an' thought I'd stop. Here, lemme help with those trunks. I'll get Ida's and take her on home. You, Doc, you're gonna wanna go converse with Homer 'bout some things. He's gonna be su'prised to see ya, that's for durn sure." He chuckled a little as he stooped his six-foot five-inch frame and scooped Ida's trunk up over his shoulder as if it was as light as a small bag of flour. Since Alan had carried the trunk onto the ship, he knew that wasn't true. He knew that Ida's trunk weighed as much as a man. She had bought and bought items in both Cincinnati and St. Louis, and he wasn't sure how she had managed to stuff everything in the one trunk, but she had. "Yep, I'd say you're back a mite earlier than Homer knew," John said, and chuckled again. His blue eyes twinkled with mischief as he started down the gangplank. "Got anythin' in here for me, Ida?"

"Have I got anything for ya! Pshaw! Got a switch or two, jus' like when ya was a boy," Ida grumbled, tapping her way along behind him. "What's this 'bout Homer? Why's he have such a bug in his britches to talk to Doc? Why, las' time I saw Homer excited was when that mad bull took after 'im."

"Is he ill, John?" Alan asked, concerned himself.

"He might be in a bit," John responded and laughed again. "He jus' might be."

"Well, thank the Lord he waited till we got back," Ida said. "Least he could do, seein' how I left 'im in charge of the store an' Doc here left him in charge of his property, an' seein's how we're both payin' him a good lick. I don't partic'larly know what for since 'bout all Homer does is sit 'round smokin' that corncob pipe of his an' tellin' yarns."

John had a wagon waiting, but he didn't even seem to think twice about offering Alan a ride home. He loaded Ida's trunk, helped Ida up onto the buckboard, then hoisted himself up and folded his lean frame onto the seat. Rudeness was unlike John, and so Alan stared at him, dumbfounded for a few long moments.

"'He might be in a bit?'" Alan repeated John's words. "What exactly does that mean? Is Homer ill or isn't he?"

"Go see for yerself, Doc Schuster," John said jovially, then he jerked the reins, clicked his tongue at the horses, and the wagon creaked off.

Alan glanced around, finally approaching a boy who was stacking crates near the dock building. "Tommy Brewster, I trust that wound on your leg is healed by now?"

Tommy turned and straightened, hiking his baggy trousers up around his thin waist. The boy was twelve years old, but a stranger would never guess that. He was small for his age—the disease in his lungs was responsible for his stunted growth. Alan had first met Tommy more than a year ago, when his family had disembarked—having arrived, like Olivia, on the *Iowa*—and brought the boy to him. He had known almost immediately what was wrong with the frail, pallid child who couldn't seem to catch his breath and who was coughing up blood, and he regretfully told the family—tuberculosis. He also told them that he thought Tommy would succumb in a brief time, perhaps in a matter of months. But Tommy had surprised him. Not only was the boy still alive a year later, he seemed to have improved. He had even taken a job at the wharf to help his impoverished family. While a patient improving from tuberculosis was not unheard of, the disease never completely disappeared from his lungs, and sooner or later, the consumptive patient always expired. Right before Alan had left for Cincinnati, Tommy had cut his leg here at the wharf and had needed the wound stitched. The cut was a clean one; it had stitched easily and there was no reason why it shouldn't have healed well, except that wounds often took longer to heal on a diseased patient than on a patient who was healthy.

"Doc Schuster!" Tommy said, lifting both brows, looking startled out of his mind. "You're back early! You're not s'posed to be back yet. Why, you're not s'posed to be back for at least another month! Mr. Whitworth's gonna be su'prised."

Alan stopped in his tracks and shook his head. "John Brimmer didn't bother saying 'hello' either. He said nearly the same thing you just said, only he hinted that Homer needed to talk to me. And he implied that Mr. Whitworth might be ill."

Tommy hiked the trousers up again, then shifted from one foot to the other. "Well . . ." He grimaced, twisting his face. "He might *be*." He dipped his head, and his dark eyes flashed from beneath the strawlike, honey-colored hair that slipped over his brows and eyes. "I don't know, y'know," he said almost hesitantly.

Alan gave a slow nod. "I see that. And I can't for the world understand why Mr. Brimmer, and now you, are acting so odd about Homer."

"Reckon you'd better talk to Mr. Whitworth."

"I reckon I'd better," Alan said, aware that he sounded caustic. He dug bills from his pocket. "About that business proposition . . . fetching me a wagon and horse from the livery stable in exchange for a few dollars."

That straightened and brightened Tommy up. "Well, sure, Dr. Schuster. Sure!" He started off, ready to shoot up Main Street to the livery stable, eager to make a few dollars he would undoubtedly take home to his mother to help feed the family.

"There is one condition," Alan said, stopping him.

Tommy turned back, both brows raised again.

"You're not to run." Running might irritate his illness, and Alan would have none of that.

The boy broke into a smile. "Sure, Doc. Sure," he responded, then headed off again.

Even walking, Tommy didn't take long to fetch the wagon. Alan paid him out of the money left from renting the horse and conveyance from the livery, then he carried his trunk from the ship and placed it in the wagon bed. Tommy went back to stacking crates.

As always, Alan had his medical bag with him. He was eager to call on Homer at the little house the man occupied near the foot of Ripley Street and see for himself if Homer was sick, or getting sick. Or if something else was happening. He hated to jump to conclusions, but *something* was happening with Homer. John had thought Alan returning early from Cincinnati was amusing where Homer was concerned, and the look on Tommy Brewster's face when he had seen Alan was one of unpleasant surprise. Not to mention that both John and Tommy had brought up the subject of Homer, the very man Alan had hired to keep up his house and tend his animals while he was gone to Cincinnati.

His house. Was something wrong with his house, then? Had it caught fire and burned to the ground? Had his hens and his horses perished? Was everything gone?

Well, that was the worst scenario. The condition of his house and animals couldn't be *that* bad. And maybe it was simply a case of Homer being a little ill with something.

Homer wasn't home, Alan soon found out. He knocked and knocked on Homer's door, but there was no answer. He knocked on Homer's bedroom windowpanes, thinking the man might have "gone to bed with the chickens," as Ida might say. But he received no answer there either.

Damn. Why had John and Tommy left him wondering if Homer was ill? The concern creeping around under his skin was not going to let him go home until he went inside Homer's house somehow and made certain the man wasn't lying unconscious or dead.

Which is just what he did. He entered the dark house through a small, half-opened kitchen window, squeezing his way in and finally landing in a heap on the planked floor. He got to his feet and dusted himself off.

"Homer?"

No answer. Alan glanced around the room at the dark furnishings—tables and chairs, a settee, and a few trunks. A lantern sat on top of one of the trunks. Alan eased that way.

"Homer, are you here?"

Still no answer. He lit the lantern, then glanced around the room again, which now had orange glow. Once satisfied that Homer wasn't anywhere in the main room, Alan headed for the bedroom door, calling Homer's name again, listening for any kind of response, even a groan.

Homer wasn't in the bedroom either.

Alan sat on the edge of the bed there and ran a weary hand through his hair. He was tired—and relieved that Homer wasn't lying ill in his house somewhere, unable to say a word—and whatever Homer needed to talk to him about would have to wait until tomorrow. If he hadn't returned from Cincinnati and St. Louis so early the man wouldn't be able to talk to him about anything anyway. Homer occasionally went out "tipping the bottle" with Walt Lincoln and a few other old-timers and he very well might have done just that this evening. Alan didn't intend to wait for him. He meant to go home and make certain his house was still standing and his animals were still alive—those were his next concerns.

The bed boards creaked when he rose, and the next sound, the low growl of a dog, made him cringe. Breaking into Homer's house to check on the man, Alan had forgotten one important thing: that Minnow, Homer's dog, was not much of a guard because he slept so heavily. But once awakened, Minnow could be vicious. The first time Alan had made a medical call to Homer's house, when the man's late wife began having chest pains, Minnow had taken after him and torn the seat of his pants clean off. The mutt had done the same three times after that, until, at Alan's insistence, Homer had started locking him in a back room whenever the doctor called.

Minnow was awake. And Minnow would be after him.

Alan put the lantern down carefully, not wanting to tip it and catch the house on fire. Without the lantern in hand he could doubtless run faster, and he might reach the front door long before Minnow did.

He bolted from the tick and shot out of the bedroom and into the main room. Halfway across the floor he heard Minnow growl again and his heart thudded because he knew what was coming next.

He felt the back of his trousers rip. Minnow snarled and twisted his head back and forth, wrestling the material he had gotten into his jaws, trying to tear it off. Alan cursed and pulled, trying to get free. But Minnow had him—at least he had the seat of his trousers—and the beast didn't mean to let go.

Finally the material ripped free. Alan ran again, and when he glanced over his shoulder, Minnow was just dropping his prize. Alan knew what came next—the brute would be after more, only this time he might get a jawful of flesh, too. Alan didn't intend to stand still and wait for that to happen.

How, he didn't know, but he managed to unbolt the front door, open it, dart outside, and slam the portal shut a second before Minnow would have stuck his nose in the doorway. The dog began yelping as if he had been wounded. But Alan knew better.

He laughed at the doorway—at the dog on the other side. "You . . . rotten scoundrel! You're just sorry you didn't get a piece of me."

He stood just so for a long minute to give his heart a chance to slow down. Then he breathed a sigh of relief, cursed Homer Whitworth and Minnow, and started off for his wagon. After being gone for months, after making the long trip home, after dealing with Ida—listening to her and trying to reason with her about various matters, something that became more and more difficult to do the older she grew—after wondering if something was wrong with Homer and then being attacked by Minnow . . . he was going home to make certain his house was still standing and his animals were still alive. He was going home to have a bite to eat and to relax in his favorite chair and to look around at his favorite things. Home would be quiet, and after a while, boring, which was exactly what he needed. No belligerence from Ida, no mischievous chuckles from John, no apprehensive looks from Tommy, no snarling dog at his backside. No anything. Just home.

It didn't take him long to realize that things were amiss at home, too. He kept a lantern on a small table beside the front door, but when he reached for it, the lantern had disappeared, and so had the table. Now why had Homer moved the table? Alan always kept the curtains tied back at the three windows in the main room, allowing sunshine in during the day and moonlight in at night. But Homer must have pulled the curtains shut, too, because hardly a sliver of moonlight peeked into the room right now.

Alan started toward one of the windows, intent on opening the curtains—Homer couldn't have moved the window—and he rammed into the corner of something, upsetting it. The table. Alan grimaced, expecting to hear the lantern glass shatter. Instead only the table toppled over, crashing to the floor.

Like a blind man, he put his hands out in front of him, although his eyes had now adjusted somewhat to the darkness inside the house. He made out the shapes of furnishings, and if he wasn't just seeing things, Homer had rearranged everything, not just the table.

Feeling baffled, Alan shook his head. This wasn't like Homer. Normally the man didn't give a thought to the arrangement of furniture. In fact, Homer's own household furniture had not been moved since before his wife's illness and death. What had gotten into the man that he would go into someone else's home and rearrange everything? He shouldn't have, Alan thought irritably. No matter that Alan had left his house in Homer's care, in the care of a very competent individual. He just shouldn't have.

He rammed into something else, something that just touched the middle of his shins. It scooted a bit, grating across the floor. "Damn you, Homer!" Alan cursed, then moved on toward the window, now watching for items closer to the floor, too.

He reached the window and was just pushing open the curtains when he heard a floorboard creak. At first he wondered if someone else was in the house with him, then he checked the boards beneath his own feet, remembering that a floorboard had become worn somewhere beneath this particular window. He had stepped on it before, making it creak, and it creaked again now as he put his weight on it. He decided then that the sound had come from the floor beneath his own feet; no one was in the house with him.

He started toward the second window, forgetting to watch the floor. Halfway there, he stumbled over something else, and this time he went sprawling into a nearby chair, crashing over with it and hitting his shoulder on the corner of the fireplace. He heard a high-pitched screech, then the sound of hooves clattering, then a frantic bawling such as a calf or a goat or perhaps a lamb might make. Some young animal. He didn't keep animals inside his house. But then, Homer had been "minding the store" for a good month now. He had rearranged all the furnishings, and somewhere along the way, he apparently had decided that the addition of a calf, goat, or lamb might compliment the new arrangement.

Another animal joined in the bawling, emerging from somewhere in the darkness. Alan heard the muffled sound of a duck quacking, and he shook his head, wondering if he had hit it *and* his shoulder on the fireplace stones. Good God, his house seemed to have become a barnyard. No wonder John and Tommy had acted so queerly when they spotted him. No wonder both had implied that Homer might be ill. Homer just might be—after Alan got his hands on him.

Alan was just regaining his footing when something crashed down over his head, covering him to his shoulders. A bucket, and something was in the bucket, a thick, sticky, overpoweringly sweet-smelling liquid that was now oozing down his face. Molasses.

Someone was in the house, after all. No animal could have slammed the bucket down on his head.

He grabbed the bucket with both hands and pushed up. The molasses was so thick that the bucket stuck fast for a few seconds, then it went flying across the room, hitting someone in the process—Alan heard a gasp as he scrambled to his feet, ready to defend his home and himself.

He wiped molasses from his eyes, nose, and mouth, and he glanced around, trying to spot the intruder. But with more molasses dripping into his eyes, the room was darker than ever. He spotted movement to one side of the room, but for all he knew the shadow might be one of the animals. They were still bawling and quacking, and now racing around the room.

Alan wiped more molasses from his eyes just as a pistol

cocked. The clicking of the trigger being drawn back was unmistakable, even with the pandemonium caused by the animals.

"Get out," a woman said. "Get out right now." Her voice was firm but soft, and Alan immediately had a sense of having heard the voice before. Where, he wasn't sure, and right now, with a pistol aimed at him and with himself and his home being assaulted by animals and some unknown person, he didn't have time to think about why the voice sounded familiar.

"I'm not go—" A shot cut him off. Alan dropped to the floor, expecting to feel a bullet slam into him. Instead, it whizzed by him and shattered something on his right. He had no idea what had been damaged since he had no idea where everything was located in his house anymore, or even if all his belongings were still here.

"*You* get out!" he shouted, growing more outraged by the second. "I have no idea who—"

Another shot. Panicking, the animals bawled and quacked more than ever. A hoof stepped on his ankle, and he yelped. When the animal decided to go over him rather than around him, Alan scrambled away, his temper flaming now. Enough was enough. He had wanted to come home to his nice quiet house and his nice quiet life. Instead he had come home to bedlam.

He got to his feet again, and this time he spotted the woman, looking harmless and oblivious in a flowing white shift, one arm extended in front of her. But she wasn't harmless: She held a gun and she was trying to shoot him and he had to do something now before one of her crazy bullets hit him.

He stooped and charged at her, hoping he would reach her before she fired again. He came at her from the side, realizing she could see about as well in the darkness as he could. He grabbed her around the waist and they tumbled to the floor just as she screamed and the pistol fired again. The bullet went whizzing by, and she screamed again as she struggled, beating and kicking at him.

Someone else hit him repeatedly with a pillow—on the

head and on the back, arms and shoulders. The pillow burst and feathers flew everywhere as Alan tried to catch a glimpse of the second assaulter. The animals ran wild, making twice as much noise now, and the woman screamed again just as the front door slammed open.

"What'n the blazes is goin' on?" John Brimmer demanded, holding up a lantern. "Doc . . . ? Is that you?"

Holding up another lantern, Ida stumped in behind John, casting a squint around the room, assessing. Behind her came Walt Lincoln, chewing a wad as usual and screwing up one side of his face the way he did whenever something was amiss. He stuffed his hands into his trouser pockets and threw a glance at the front door. "You get in here now, Homer, an' face all the trouble you've caused. Lord Almighty. Come on an' have a look."

"Get off of Mrs. Monroe, Doc!" John ordered. Two lengthy strides put him in front of where Alan and the woman had been struggling on the floor, and with several lithe movements, he grabbed Alan by the upper arms and put him on his feet a good distance away from the woman. John stood between the two of them. "See here now," he said, anger reddening his face as he glared at Alan. "I know it's yer house, Doc, but she's as harmless as a castrated bull. Lord . . . she's a woman!"

"She just shot at me twice!" Alan shouted, above the din of animal noise. He blew a feather out of his mouth. "Look at me. Molasses, feathers . . . bullets! She's not harmless!"

Ida cackled.

"*What* is so funny?" Alan demanded.

Ida sobered. "Lower yer voice, Doc, afore I get a gun an' start shootin' at ya myself. The way yer feathered, I've a mind ta do that anyways, you lookin' like a bird an' all."

"Homer, I'm gonna come after you if you don't get in here," Walt warned.

Alan glared at Ida. John turned to help the woman who had shot at Alan up off of the floor.

"Where is Homer?" Alan suddenly demanded. "What in the hell did he do to my home? And who in the hell is—"

He had turned to point a finger at the woman, but the sight of her, her loose hair now tossed back to reveal her face, stopped him in his tracks.

He might not have been able to recall the voice right away (given time, he would have), but he damn sure knew the face. She was the woman he had danced with that evening on the steamer between Cincinnati and St. Louis, the woman whose golden hair and pretty blue eyes had caught his eye. The woman who had shied away from him the moment he asked a few questions. She stood looking at him now with her hair, disheveled from their tussle on the floor, cascading around her shoulders and down her back. In ordinary circumstances she might have appeared harmless. But she was still holding a pistol, and although his imagination might be playing tricks on him, Alan swore the weapon was still smoking.

"What are you doing here?" he demanded. His tone and the question were all wrong. He was gruff because he had arrived home to find all the furnishings rearranged in his house, animals wandering the place, and her attacking him and shooting at him. He had meant the question to mean *why are you in my home?* because he truly did not understand what she was doing here. But he was short-tempered and the question had run out of his mouth in an insulting way. Hell, there wasn't a good way to ask what she was doing here, why she had been sleeping in his home when he had left the house in what he had thought was Homer's capable care.

He suddenly had no patience. He wanted to sleep. He would deal with this tomorrow, sort it out then. Right now, he wanted them all out—her, the animals, John, Ida, Walt, Hom—"

"Where is Homer?" he demanded again.

Homer appeared in the doorway, looking sheepish and even smaller than usual—which was already pretty small, since he was only five feet two inches tall—and Alan tore off after him. But John reeled Alan in with one hand at the end of his long arm and told him to stay put.

"Now, see here, Doc . . . I know it's yer home an' all . . . ," John began again.

"His home?" the strange woman blurted. "You're the doctor? What are *you* doing here?"

"It's my home," Alan announced indignantly.

She tilted her head and regarded him in a haughty way. "Not at the moment."

Alan's jaw fell open. He snapped it shut. "It's my home until I decide it's not my home anymore. Until I decide to sell . . ." A thought dawned on him, a startling suspicion, and he jerked his head around to look at Homer. "Did you sell my house?"

Homer dipped his head, looking as though he wanted to shrivel up and blow away. "No, Doc Schuster, I didn't sell it."

Relief. But only a little.

"Then what is the meaning of this?" Alan demanded just as one of the two goats decided to lower his head and plow into his leg. "Damn—Ah!" He shoved at the goat, trying to push it away and nurse his thigh at the same time.

"Leave him alone!" the woman objected, and Alan quickly realized that she was defending the animal, not him.

She marched over, put her arm around the goat's neck, urged its head toward her, and began rubbing the animal's neck and talking to him. "There now, Edwin. It's all right now. Annie's safe and you're safe . . . everyone is safe. This horrible man is not going to touch you again. Ever again," she said, and her eyes seemed to spark as she looked up at Alan, daring him to touch the goat again.

"He's your goat?" Outrage, anger, and now disbelief sparked Alan's own temper. First she had assaulted him, and then her goat had rammed him with a horn. "Who's Annie?" he demanded, growing more impatient with this madness. "And just what the devil are you doing in my house? What are these animals doing in here? Who moved my furniture? Homer, I want answers!"

If anything, Homer shrank back more.

"Don't even think about disappearing!"

"Simmer down!" John said.

"Homer, I reckon we shoulda bought an extry bottle or two, tha way this night's goin'," Walt drawled, leaning against the door frame. He had produced a small knife and was using the tip to clean dirt from beneath his fingernails.

"It's like this, Doc," John said. "Ya left Homer in charge of things here an'—"

"Ya oughtta be boiled an' plucked, attackin' that girl that way," Ida decided aloud, glaring at Alan.

Alan seethed. "For once, Ida Bogue, keep your thoughts to yourself!"

"I mostly do," Ida retorted. "But not when I see the likes of what I just seen, you thrashin' all around on the floor with that gal. I cain't help but—"

"Ida, that's enough!" John bellowed. "Like I was explain', Doc . . ."

"I don't want an explanation tonight! I want everyone out of my house."

Alan marched over and batted another goat away from munching on one corner of his settle. "I want sleep. I want quiet. And I want all animals, human or otherwise, gone from my house!"

Another shot whizzed by Alan's head. He cursed and ducked just as the shot lodged in a nearby wall. John ducked, too, and a few seconds passed before either of them decided to peek around the chairs behind which they had sought shelter. Homer had disappeared from the doorway, and the animals were running wild again, making noise, their eyes crazy with fear. Ida shook her head while Walt went on cleaning from beneath his nails.

The woman Alan had met on the ship lowered her pistol. But she glared at Alan with a look that could have shot bullets. "Do *not* touch my goats!"

"Damn crazy woman," Alan muttered, and he rushed across the room after her again and grabbed the pistol from her hand. "You're in *my* home and you're shooting at me!"

"It happens to be my home right now!"

"It's *my* home! I hold the deed to the land. I hold the—"

"Both of ya, stop!" John commanded.

That quieted them. Alan and the woman stood glaring at

each other. She stood a good four inches shorter than he, but she didn't seem the least bit intimidated.

"I am sick to death of brutes," she said under her breath, and Alan was almost certain that no one but him heard her remark.

"Now . . . I know ye're upset, Doc," John said, his voice lower than before. "I under—"

"No matter what anyone says, I'm not going anywhere for a time and neither is my sister." The woman made the announcement in a soft voice, but the thrust of her chin and the glitter of her eyes made Alan realize how serious she was. He stared at her as she put her arm around the shoulders of the girl who had been with her on the ship and held the child close. "I signed a rental agreement with your agent for the duration of the summer," she told Alan. "Of course, you might physically force me out of this house and off of this property, Doctor. You might . . . with a fight. And then I will sue you and Mr. Whitworth for breach of contract."

Even the animals quieted at that.

"Doc, I . . . She was lookin' for a place, see, wanderin' all around town, just lookin'," Homer said quietly from the doorway, having decided to reappear. "You said you'd be gone a good three months, maybe longer. I figured that was the whole summer and what harm could come from rentin' her your house for a piece while she arranged to have one of her own built. She's lookin' to open a mercantile in Davenport, and—"

"At the very least," the woman said.

"I said I would be gone for perhaps two months, Homer," Alan responded irritably. "You had no right to rent my house out. And you—"—he turned back to the woman—"you had no right to destroy it in such a manner."

She lifted a fine brow. "*'Destroy it?'* Begging your pardon, Doctor, but rearrangement of furnishings hardly constitutes destruction. As for the animals, I bring them in at night for their protection."

"And I suppose you'll bring the horses in next?"

"Perhaps."

Ida chuckled. "She's got a backbone, Doc. Would ya look at that? A fine backbone."

"Everyone . . . out," Alan announced again.

"You might wanna rethink that decision," John advised.

"Why? She signed a rental agreement, but what kind of 'rental agreement' could it possibly be? Homer drew it up." Ordinarily, Alan wouldn't think of insulting Homer by insinuating that the man couldn't draw up a valid legal agreement. But Homer had rented out his home, for God's sake.

"Oh, it's a good one, all right," John said.

"It can't be," Alan insisted.

"Get yer head outta yer rear an' listen to John Brimmer, Doc, a fine law man around these parts," Ida said, and Alan almost could hear her thinking *before I whap ya with my cane.*

"And just why should I do that?" he asked smartly.

"Most likely 'cause I drew up the agreement," John responded a little quietly. "And I'm legal. I didn't especially wanna be the one to tell ya."

The duck began quacking, disrupting the silence that followed John's admission. In the doorway, Homer shifted from one boot to the other. Walt cleaned another fingernail and considered Alan through a squinted eye, probably wondering what he would do now. But what could he do? John was an attorney, and if he had drawn up the agreement himself and he said it was valid, it probably was.

Ida leaned over on her cane more than she usually did, as if her leg and foot were tiring, and she gave Alan a grim look. "Charlotte'll put ya up," she reassured, and a little tender compassion from Ida was a rare thing indeed.

Alan straightened his shoulders and raked a hand through his hair. "Good . . . *God!* All right, then . . . John, since you seem to be my self-appointed legal representative in this matter—not that I have much of a choice—there are a few points I would like to negotiate in the rental agreement."

John shook his head. "Signatures are already affixed, Doc. Caint' do it."

"And for how long a period is she my tenant?" Alan asked, staring straight at the woman, the intruder.

"Until the end of August."

"I uh . . . I have the first month's rent for ya, Doc," Homer volunteered.

Alan glared. He felt drained. He needed a drink. He needed to sleep. He needed to find a place to live until the end of August.

"Might buy ya a new pair of trousers with part of it," Ida said, cackling a little. "Minnow must've been at ya. I see ya still like red drawers."

"Where is your husband, Mrs. Monroe?" Alan asked suddenly. Even as tired as he felt, his mind was busy working, remembering their meeting on the ship and wondering how she had ended up here, in Davenport, in his home.

She flinched.

"She's a widow woman," Homer said.

"Oh? Did her husband perish between here and the Ohio River?"

"I'm your renter, Doctor," she answered coldly. "That's all. I'm not obligated to answer your questions."

"Come on now, Doc," John said. "Give it up for the night. Let's go an' let the lady get some rest."

Sighing, Alan held her furious gaze for a long moment, and behind the fury he glimpsed fear. Fear that he might ask more questions? Fear that he might try to cause her more trouble? Fear overall? Well, he suddenly couldn't blame her. She obviously had been sleeping when he stumbled in. She had assumed he was an intruder, just as anyone in the same situation might have. If her husband *had* died somewhere between here and the Ohio River, then she must feel alone and frightened, on guard for anything and everything. And his throwing a temper tantrum, being a "brute," because Homer had rented out his home only made the situation worse.

"I'll need to pick up some of my things tomorrow," he told her.

She nodded, and Alan made his way to the front door.

CHAPTER FIVE

After the doctor, Homer Whitworth, Walt Lincoln, and John Brimmer filed out, the elderly woman who had burst into the house with Mr. Brimmer stayed behind for a moment to introduce herself to Olivia. Ida Bogue seemed gruff and brash, but she told Olivia that she thought she was right in standing her ground and that that pistol had been a good idea, too. She was a woman living alone herself, and she'd do what she had to do to protect herself if an intruder broke into her home.

"Ya've done a right fine job of rearrangin' things 'round here," Mrs. Bogue said, glancing around the room. "Better than when Doc Schuster lived here, I guarantee ya. Don't know 'bout them an'mals stayin' in here at night, but I know 'bout an'mals comin' to be like yer own younguns. So ya wanna open a merc'tile?"

"Yes," Olivia said, now sitting and holding Janey on her lap. The sight of the doctor's struggle with her cousin had scared Janey nearly to death, and the girl was still trembling. "I don't necessarily want to compete with you, Mrs. Bogue. It's just that my father ran a mercantile, though he had many other business interests, and I spent hours helping him every day because we liked being together."

"I don't reckon you'll be competin' with me. It's Harvey Tirado an' the other men 'bout town you'll be competin' with. See, there's other stores, an' Harvey's had plans now for a good six months to open up another dry goods in Davenport. Harvey gets on the bandwag'n 'bout ever'thing. Why, when that border skirmish started, Harvey was the first one down yonder all set up to fire on those Missour'ans. I've given 'im a good whap a time or two, tryin' to put some sense in 'im. But I reckon ya cain't put sense in a body that thinks he's got more'n his share of it. Ain't it funny ya ended up here, right here in Davenport? There we all was on that ship, Doc dancin' with ya, then ya runnin' off. An' now here ya are. Yep, things have a mighty funny way of comin' together."

Olivia caught her breath. She hadn't been able to see Dr. Schuster's face well during the confrontation moments ago because his entire upper body had been covered with molasses and feathers. She had forgotten the name of the inquisitive doctor with whom she had danced that evening aboard the ship she and Janey had boarded in Cincinnati. She was shocked to realize that the raving man she had just encountered was that man, that doctor.

"Ye're lookin' a mite ill. All the excitement, I reckon," Mrs. Bogue said. "G'on back to bed now. I 'magine those boys're waitin' for me outside. You an' yer gal there come by my store t'morrow. Got some hard candy for the youngun an' a sliver or two of advice for yerself—'bout openin' up yerself a place."

Olivia agreed to go by the store tomorrow. Mrs. Bogue was right about the excitement, though. All Olivia wanted right now was to calm Janey and the animals, who still looked skittish and frightened. She watched Ida Bogue use her cane to tap her way over to the door. Then the old woman turned back and cackled at her. "Hee-hee! If Doc Schuster don't look tar-'n-feathered! I ain't never seen anythin' so funny, an' I been 'round these parts goin' on fifty years, back long afore too many settlers came along. Ya sure ain't one ta hide behin' a door an' not defend yer home an' yer relations. Ya have a backbone," she said, cackling more. Then she walked through the doorway into the night, the sound of her tapping cane fading along with her laughter.

Olivia hurried over to shut the door, and then she returned to Janey, who looked up at her with wide, frightened eyes. She pulled Janey back onto her lap, held her close, and stroked her hair. She called to Edwin and Annie, the goats she had saved from abuse by buying them three days ago from their owner, who had been hitting them with a whip to force them into his barn. Though she wasn't certain either responded to the names she had given them, they did respond to her soothing voice, crying as they hurried over to her.

Nothing much—except gunshots—fazed Martha, the duck Olivia had rescued from Charlotte's kettle two days after arriving in Davenport; despite the pandemonium that had taken place in this very room less than ten minutes ago, Martha was settled on the hearth with her beak tucked under her wing. Why, she hadn't even quacked an objection when Charlotte had been about to chop off her head! Olivia had shouted "Stop!" and Charlotte's small ax had frozen in midair, thank goodness. The duck was their supper, Charlotte had said, and Olivia had snatched Martha from her hands, saying they wouldn't have live duck as long as she was a boarder. "Give her back and she won't be a live duck much longer," Charlotte responded, and Olivia thought that was the most awful, most cruel thing she had ever heard anyone say.

Charlotte shrugged. "Well, you've gotta kill 'em to eat 'em. I bought that duck for our supper. Now give her back."

But Olivia wouldn't. Instead, she paid Charlotte for the duck and then she took Martha upstairs.

Charlotte had walked around muttering the entire next day: "Never heard of such crazy goings-on. Saving a duck from the kettle, paying somebody to not kill it. Giving it a name! That's strange behavior. Why, people've been called mad for less than that. I never, ever agreed to board a duck!"

Olivia had stood her ground, keeping Martha in the room upstairs and intensifying her search for a house to rent. Now that she had Martha, too, she surely couldn't go to another boarding house—who would take in her, a child, and a duck? And if she left Martha to wander outside, particularly at night, someone might snatch her, thinking, as Charlotte had, that she would make a good meal. No, Olivia needed a house complete with a small barnyard. Besides, there was more than Martha to consider. Olivia might need a horse eventually, and a place to put it, too.

She had gone all over town, up and down Main Street, up and down Ripley Street and what was known as Brimstone Corner, the area around which nearly the whole settlement was centered. Homer Whitworth, who was minding Ida Bogue's store for a time while she was away visiting her sister in Cincinnati, had told Olivia that he wasn't sure who had given the corner that name, but that most likely the name came because of the hot style of preaching that went on in the churches there. Some services were held in tents, and if a person stood around the corner on a Sunday morning, he might hear the gospel being shouted from one establishment to the next; he might hear praises being sung and people repenting for last week's sins, and he might hear prayers being cried out. The corner was fairly quiet every other day of the week, but come Sunday . . . Well, Homer had said, if she was looking for religion for herself and her girl, Brimstone Corner was the place to find it.

Their first few days in Davenport, Olivia and Janey had wandered the town, and Olivia introduced them to various people and inquired if anyone knew of any rental property. They met Frank Coates, a carpenter; Elijah Stephenson, a blacksmith; John Brimmer, a lawyer by profession; and Walt Lincoln, a farmer who, according to John, strode along most of the time not letting much bother him. They met numerous other people, too, and found most everyone friendly and welcoming. They attended a church service their first Sunday in Davenport, and Olivia had been invited to join several sewing circles and to participate in the upcoming pie-baking contest that would help raise funds for the erection of a new church building. Though she kept asking about rental property, she received the same answer each time: although land could be bought in and around Davenport, no one knew of a house for rent.

John Brimmer had called on her at the boardinghouse the evening of her and Janey's second day in town. He came offering her a nice smile and a box of confections and asked if she would consider a walk around town with him the following afternoon. She would indeed, she had answered without hesitation, liking him well enough. Homer Whitworth had called right afterward, nearly bumping into Mr. Brimmer as he walked out of the boardinghouse, and he had asked if she would consider having dinner with him the following afternoon. Certainly, but she had to be back in time to go walking with Mr. Brimmer, she explained, since she had already promised him she would. Homer had looked disappointed for a moment, then he had agreed to have her back in time. And later that day, he had returned, saying that he might know of a rental property that would be available until the end of summer.

Olivia was excited by what Homer told her, and after discussing the matter with him the following day over supper in Davenport's one hotel, she had then told John all about it. John had expressed concern that she enter into a written legal agreement—otherwise, what if Homer and the doctor changed their minds at some point? He knew all about the law, he said, being a graduated student of the profession, and he wanted to make certain her rights were protected. She didn't have to pay him a penny either; he'd just go to Homer and offer his services. Homer hadn't liked the idea of John being involved, but Olivia had agreed that they should have a signed and witnessed legal agreement, which was exactly what the two men had come up with in the end.

Charlotte had shaken her head at the entire proceeding, on one hand saying in a serious tone that Olivia needn't bother—she and Janey could stay at the boardinghouse as long as they needed to—and on the other hand laughing and saying that Homer and John were both scampering along, each trying to do everything right because they were vying for Olivia's attention. "Like strutting roosters, trying to get the hen's notice," she said, and laughed again. "Homer represents the property and John's got the legal know-how. Sure is funny, watching this all go on."

In the end, the signed agreement put Olivia in the modest but comfortable doctor's home until the end of August, when he was expected to return from his business in

Cincinnati. She hadn't considered at the time that the Davenport doctor might be the same doctor she had met on the ship she and Janey had taken from Cincinnati—that inquisitive man whose questions she had finally evaded by claiming that she was traveling with her husband. She had had no reason even to suspect that he was. Besides, she couldn't even remember that doctor's name. And . . . Davenport and the surrounding area had three doctors, excluding Ida Bogue, who, Olivia understood from John, had numerous remedies of her own for ailments.

Overall, from her first day here, Olivia had found Davenport interesting and most of its people warm and friendly, and so when William Clift from the *Brazil* came calling on her shortly after John and Homer both saw her and Janey out to the rental house, she told him she had decided to stay. He was delighted for her, that she had found a comfortable place to live and that she and her sister were faring well. The *Brazil* had been scheduled to depart shortly after he had left her at Charlotte's boardinghouse, and so he had gone on. But he had thought of her often in the days since, wondering how she and Janey were getting along and if she'd found Davenport to her liking. If not, he'd been prepared to tell her that the *Brazil* would take her on upriver. Mr. Clift had visited with her and Janey a while longer, and then he'd gone off to report back to his ship. Olivia had stood outside the two-bedroom house that she and Janey would call home for the next few months and she had tipped her face up to heaven and said a prayer of thanks that she and Janey *were* faring well, that they had found good people to settle near, a growing community that would be good for business once she opened her store, and a nice home. She had seen families sleeping in tents on the outskirts of Davenport, and she knew how fortunate she and Janey and their animals were to have shelter.

After leaving Olivia in possession of the house, John offered Alan a ride in his wagon to Charlotte's boardinghouse. But Alan, feeling irritated with John, Homer, and even Ida, didn't acknowledge the offer. Instead, he walked off to the wagon he had rented from the livery stable and went directly to the boardinghouse by himself. Tomorrow he would look at the rental agreement John had drawn up—just to be familiar with it. There still might be some way to make Mrs. Monroe vacate his house. She could surely find another residence—he would even help her find another one. His was taken—by him.

As late as the hour was, Charlotte was not too shocked to see him, although his appearance made her jaw drop open. Like everyone else, she was surprised that he and Ida had returned from Cincinnati so soon, but she seemed to know exactly why he appeared on her doorstep asking if she had a room available. She promptly set up a bath for him, and when he finished bathing, she led him up to the same room that Mrs. Monroe and her daughter had occupied for a few days right after they'd shown up in Davenport, or so Charlotte informed him.

"She's an independent woman, that's for sure," Charlotte said, talking about Mrs. Monroe, shaking her head as she turned the coverlet down on the bed. "I won't charge a woman on her own even a penny, and Olivia Monroe didn't like that, not at all. She called it charity and she let me know right then and there that she intended to look for another place for her and her girl to live if I didn't intend to charge her the same as I would charge anyone. She said she had money to pay me. Maybe she did, maybe she has plenty of money. But a woman on her own in these parts can't be too careful. I told her to use her money to buy herself a piece of land and have herself a house built. She wouldn't hear any more, and then when she left, I found ten dollars on the table in here. Ten dollars! I didn't want to charge her anything, and even if I had charged her, the bill wouldn't have come to ten dollars total. That's robbery. But I reckon she's used to how things are done in Boston. Well, she'll find out real quick that things aren't done the same out here."

"Yes, she will," Alan agreed.

"I reckon you'll be staying here for a while," she remarked, her eyes filled with questions.

He removed soap and a razor from his trunk and placed

them beside a wash basin on a small table. "Not if I can find a way to dislodge her."

Charlotte stared at him, worry wrinkling her brow. "Dislodge her? Why, Dr. Schuster, I know it's your home. But you can't imagine the trouble Mrs. Monroe went to to find herself and her girl a place to stay for a few months until she can buy a piece of land and have a home built. Why, she was fresh off the *Brazil* when she came here and—"

"Homer told me how much trouble she went to," he grumbled. "Why couldn't she have stayed here in the interim? This is a comfortable room—and she would have had you to cook and clean for her."

"I told you she was stubborn about wanting to pay me. And she wanted nothing to do with my cleaning. She was learning to do for herself, she told me one morning after I got on her for making her bed. Why, she was here just yesterday, wanting to know if I would teach her how to make butter if she bought a cow." Charlotte sighed. "She'll only be there until the end of August, Doc. That's not such a long time."

Alan tossed her an impatient look. "Charlotte, I'm tired. I went home earlier this evening thinking I would go right to bed. Instead, I encountered chaos and a stranger in my home. I was hit, shot at, then informed that my house was rented out for the next two months. Understandably, I'm going to sleep."

Nodding slowly, she told him what time breakfast and supper were served at the boardinghouse. Then she bade him good night and left the room, closing the door behind her.

Alan stripped off his clothes, lay on his back on the bed, and went to sleep.

I can't believe I shot at him.

Olivia woke the next morning with that thought running circles in her head. In her entire life, she had never even held a pistol in her hands, though she had seen her father load one several times. She had found the one she had used last evening in a desk drawer in one of the bedrooms, and she had loaded it and put in under her bed, thinking that she should keep a loaded gun handy—she was a woman living alone with a child and a few animals, after all. She didn't have a man around in the event that something happened. She had met many nice, friendly people in Davenport, but she had also seen the saloons and gaming houses, and the men loitering outside of them leered at her every time she walked down the opposite side of the street. If people asked around about her, heard that she was a widow, and realized that she lived without the benefit of male protection, they might decide to come calling. She had held and aimed the pistol a few times, wanting to get used to the feel of it in her hands, because if any of those men did decide to call, she meant to be ready for him.

That was what she had been thinking when she had heard the table crash over last evening—that one of the saloon men had decided to call. She had eased from her bed and quietly pulled out the pistol, breathing deeply in an attempt to calm herself. Her hand had been shaking so badly that even if she normally could have fired accurately and hit her target, she wouldn't have been able to at that moment. Her plan had been to blind the intruder by disabling him a bit with a bucket of molasses, then shoot him while he couldn't see to grab her.

She had frozen with the pistol in her hand, horrified by what she was contemplating doing—actually killing a fellow human being—which had given him time to yank the bucket off of his head. Then she had known that he was probably angry enough that if she didn't shoot him, he might do more than sexually assault her; he might kill her. So she had shot at him, scared that she'd hit him, scared that she hadn't. Then she'd shot at him again, and then again when he was claiming that the house was his and he was trying to force her and Janey and the animals to leave.

This morning, with soft sunlight penetrating the curtains and Edwin and Annie sleeping on the floor beside her bed, Olivia couldn't believe she had fired the last shot just to see

Dr. Schuster scramble. It had been a childish thing to do, the result of a flaring temper, and she was ashamed.

She should apologize.

That was exactly what she would do—apologize.

As she rose, dressed, and brushed her hair, she thought about how terrible he must feel, returning to his home at night only to find out that his "agent" had rented it out to someone for the next two and a half months. Last night her only thought had been that she was not going to stand still and silent while she and Janey were booted out of the home they had found and for which she was paying good money. They had spent some exhausting and uncomfortable days and weeks traveling, they had finally established a home, and no one was going to take it from them. The fact that Dr. Schuster had not authorized Homer to rent out his property had shocked her. Not that she had ever thought to ask Homer Whitworth if he was authorized to rent the property. After all, an agent was a legal representative. John Brimmer should have asked the question since he had drawn up the paperwork. But still . . . the fault came back to Homer in the end. John, like her, might have assumed that Dr. Schuster had authorized the rental.

Sleep—and thought—had shed new light on the entire matter. This morning, Olivia found that she was furious with Homer and irritated with John but felt sorry for Dr. Schuster. As she fried eggs in a skillet over a small fire in the fireplace while waiting for Janey to wake up, she decided to go talk to all three of them today.

Janey soon awoke. She and Olivia ate a breakfast of eggs, biscuits and milk, and then Olivia helped Janey dress. The girl was calm this morning. Still, Olivia worried.

"What happened last night was terrible, Janey," Olivia said as they walked up Ripley Street a little later. "The man you thought was hurting me . . . Dr. Schuster . . . I don't know that he would really hurt us. You see, we're living in his house right now because he went to another city for a while and asked Mr. Whitworth to care for the house while he was gone. Mr. Whitworth thought Dr. Schuster wouldn't mind if he let us live in the house. But Dr. Schuster doesn't want anyone living in his house. I imagine he wanted to come home to his house last night and go to sleep, like us. I thought he was someone who was breaking in to try to hurt us. But he was really just coming into his own house to go to bed for the night. Do you understand?"

Janey twisted her lips and scowled for a minute, considering what Olivia had said. Then her expression cleared, and she nodded.

"We need to go see them—Dr. Schuster, Mr. Whitworth, and Mr. Brimmer—and talk to them about the house. I'm not sure what will happen. Dr. Schuster may still want us to leave the house. I shot at him last evening because I thought he was a bad man breaking in to hurt us and . . . I plan to ask if he will honor the agreement made between Mr. Whitworth, Mr. Brimmer, and myself. But if he won't, I think we should look for another house." That was a terrible prospect, going around town looking for another house, asking high and low if anyone knew of any rental property. But Olivia didn't know another way to remedy the situation peacefully. She had found a nice town for herself and Janey to settle in and she didn't want to endure a bitter, two-month disagreement with one of Davenport's citizens. Particularly when he hadn't known anything about his house being rented out.

Janey looked a little dejected, shuffling along with her chin tilted down now. Olivia couldn't stand Janey looking disappointed.

"The lady who was with the men last evening . . . her name is Mrs. Bogue, and she owns the store Mr. Whitworth has been taking care of," Olivia said. "She said for you and me to come by there today. She wants to talk to me about us opening a store, and she has some hard candy for you."

That brightened the girl up a bit; Janey glanced up at Olivia and smiled. She slipped her hand into her cousin's and squeezed, and she and Olivia continued on down the street, finally reaching Charlotte's boardinghouse.

CHAPTER SIX

CHARLOTTE HERSELF ANSWERED the door, even though it was usually answered by Sally, the hired girl who helped Charlotte clean and cook. The proprietor smiled in a knowing, amused sort of way. Wearing a white smock tied around her waist and a broom in one hand, Charlotte stepped off to the left side of the doorway, giving Olivia and Janey room to step into the house.

"Let's see now, is this about the butter-making or about the fact that the doctor isn't taking kindly to you renting his property?"

"Charlotte," Olivia admonished, clenching the side of her skirt. "I gather you're boarding Dr. Schuster? Janey and I thought we might check here before going to Mrs. Bogue's store and asking if she knew where he was staying."

"He's here. Along with the chip on his shoulder."

Olivia didn't like the sound of that. She clenched the skirt tighter, lifted it slightly, and walked into the boardinghouse with Janey. "I know he must have been in an awful temper when he came here last night after learning that Mr. Whitworth had rented his house to me and Janey."

"A bit." Charlotte shook her head and laughed a little. "I didn't dare ask about the feathers—or about him smelling like molasses."

"Oh. Good," Olivia said, glancing away, feeling her face warm. "Well . . . is Dr. Schuster available, Charlotte? I'm mean, is he awake yet, and if so, could you tell him that Janey and I would like to speak with him?"

Charlotte wasn't one to ask too many questions in an

uncomfortable situation; Olivia had realized that about the woman during her and Janey's first day at the boardinghouse, and she was thankful for it. Charlotte had probably formed the habit over years of taking in boarder after boarder, each with a different dilemma or situation.

"He came down for coffee and breakfast just a little while ago, then he went off back upstairs," Charlotte said. "I'll go knock on the door and see if he's still awake. He looked pretty tuckered out last evening when he turned up on my doorstep. Must have been the journey."

Olivia smiled uncomfortably at that, knowing full well why he had looked "tuckered out" when he had shown up on Charlotte's doorstep. Olivia and Janey sat at a table in the common room while Charlotte went upstairs.

Moments later, Charlotte stuck her head back into the common room, saying, "He'll be right down."

Olivia looked at Janey and they exchanged grim looks. Certainly Dr. Schuster had been in a temper upon arriving here last evening. After all, he had just learned that he couldn't simply go home where everything was familiar, take off his boots, and relax. Olivia hoped that sleep had cooled his temper somewhat, but Charlotte was gone from the doorway before Olivia could ask about his disposition this morning.

Would he insist that she and Janey move out of the house? Would he be as inquisitive about her as he had been aboard the *Star of Ohio?* Would he believe that the "husband" with whom she had told him she was traveling had died during the trip from St. Louis? Did he have a list of questions for her, questions that might eventually lead him to discover her lies and then to discover the truth? That Janey was not her sister, that she had kidnapped the girl and possibly killed Janey's uncle; that she had stolen a bundle of money from Uncle Edward's safe to ensure that she and Janey did not starve, and that they had the funds to begin a new life for themselves somewhere? Would he interrogate her until she broke down and finally told him the truth herself? Finding her installed in his house, he just might be angry enough to do exactly that, and then he might follow that up with making sure that she stood trial and either hung or went to jail.

Sweet Jesus . . . How in the world had she and Janey ended up in the same town in which he lived?

Olivia ran a forefinger up and down the basket handle and tapped the toe of her boot on the floor, fighting a tremble of apprehension and fear. She didn't want to face him this morning. No, she did not.

"Good morning," Dr. Schuster said from the doorway, and Olivia nearly leaped out of her skin.

"Good morning," she responded, smiling nervously as she stood. "Forgive me. I was deep in thought."

He nodded. "You'll forgive *me,* I trust, for staying here beside the doorway while we talk. Only last night you shot at me, and now I see you have a covered basket in hand."

Olivia glanced down at the basket, then back up at him, wrinkling her brow and then cringing when she realized what he was inferring. She took three steps forward, put the basket on the floor a short distance from his feet, then stepped back to stand beside Janey again.

She waved her hand at the basket. "Look for yourself, Dr. Schuster. I don't carry a pistol with me. Davenport has its share of men who think nothing of looking at women in a distasteful manner, and so I thought I should keep a loaded pistol nearby in the event one of them decided to call. That's who I thought you were, Dr. Schuster. I had no idea that you were the landlord—the owner of the property—returning so soon. But that's no excuse for the way I fired at you after I knew who you were. I thought you were about to toss me and Janey out into the night and I . . . I was in a temper, too, you see." She motioned to the basket again. "We made cinnamon buns this morning and thought you might like some."

She began twisting her hands in front of her stomach, twisting them so much that the tips of her fingers were turning red—a nervous habit she had had for years. She stood there watching Dr. Schuster, wondering what his reaction to her explanation and apology would be once he finished studying her.

Olivia felt a little hand cover hers, and she glanced down and saw Janey shaking her head no, meaning that Olivia shouldn't twist her hands so hard. Janey had always told her that, but now, because she couldn't speak, Janey had to take Olivia's hands and make her stop twisting them.

"I know," Olivia told the girl softly. "I shouldn't." She dropped her hands down to her side, then returned her gaze to Dr. Schuster, who now stood studying them both.

"You thought I was an intruder, and I might have done the same thing," he said finally.

Without the molasses and feathers, and in the morning light shining in through the room's two windows, Olivia found him handsome, but in a different way than she had on the ship that evening. That evening he had seemed friendly and playful, his hair lifting slightly in the evening breeze. Today, although his blond hair appeared soft and thick, it was also neatly combed, and his pretty brown eyes did not dance with merriment. Reserved and unsmiling, he walked toward the basket, stooped, and lifted the material covering the cinnamon buns.

A long second passed, then he glanced up and grinned a crooked grin at Janey. "Well, they didn't explode in my face. Tell me, is Annie of an age and maturity that she can be milked yet?" he asked the girl.

Janey hesitated, glancing up nervously at Olivia. Finally she looked back at the doctor and shook her head no.

"Well, when she is, I like goat's milk, and I'd be pleased if you brought me some one afternoon. What's your name?"

Janey stared at him, unable to tell him.

Olivia stepped in front of her cousin, wanting to shield her from unnecessary questions and embarrassment. She spoke in a rush, wanting to air her every thought on the matter of his home and the rental agreement and her intentions regarding them both: "Dr. Schuster . . . about the house . . . I thought we should talk. I had no idea that you were coming back so soon, I had no idea who you even were really, that we had met already and that you were from Davenport . . . that you owned the house and property . . . the "homestead," as Mr. Whitworth calls it. I signed the rental agreement with the best of intentions, and I would have had every piece of furniture back in its original position by the time Janey and I moved out at the end of August.

"I understand how you must have felt last evening, coming home and finding Janey and me there and your belongings arranged differently. I thought you were an intruder, but you must have thought *I* was an intruder, and for that, I apologize. I would have written to you myself in St. Louis had I known that you hadn't been informed of the rental agreement, and now that I know that you never were—and now that the shock of last evening is over, I'm ashamed of the way I behaved—I don't intend to hold you to it. Janey and I were traveling west with my husband, and when he died during the journey between here and St. Louis, I was suddenly in the position of deciding where to settle and of finding a decent home for myself and Janey. But I wouldn't dream of putting anyone out of his home, and if you decide that Janey and I must move today, I'm certain that Charlotte will rent us a room again while I search for another house. I ask only that our animals—Annie, Edwin, and Martha—be allowed to stay in your barn until such time. I had Martha here before, and Charlotte surely would not allow such a thing again." Olivia grimaced. "Martha's quacking nearly drove Charlotte mad, you see."

Dr. Schuster lifted both brows. "I see . . . Martha is the duck?"

Olivia nodded. "Dr. Schuster, Janey and I like Davenport and its people, and we've no wish to make an enemy of anyone here. We want peace, and if giving you your house back will ensure that we have it, then that is what we will do."

He bypassed the basket, approached her, and took her by the elbow. "Mrs. Monroe, why don't we sit—"

Janey had grabbed hold of his forearm, a wild, fearful look in her eyes, and was pulling on him, trying to make him let go of Olivia.

"Janey, no," Olivia said, understanding. "Remember what

I told you during the walk here? That he thought I was an intruder and that he won't hurt me?"

Janey quieted, although her brow was still wrinkled. She stared at Olivia, her lips clenched so tightly they were beginning to turn white.

"It's all right, Janey," Olivia soothed, placing her hand over the girl's and maintaining eye contact with her. She lowered her voice to a whisper: "Never again. It's all right."

"I won't hurt your sister—I promise," Dr. Schuster assured Janey, and Olivia was thankful for his words.

Janey finally released his arm.

"Please . . . sit," he told Olivia and Janey as he motioned to one of the tables in the room. "I'll go see if Charlotte has some milk to go along with those cinnamon buns. They smell delicious."

Olivia lifted the basket from the floor, placed it on the table, and she and Janey sat down. Olivia wanted to breathe a sigh of relief when Dr. Schuster smiled at her just before leaving the room. He appeared reserved, yes, but at least he wasn't hostile this morning. Hostility from him might have made her take Janey by the hand and leave the boardinghouse as quickly as possible.

He returned a short time later with two glasses of milk, and he sat them on the table in front of Olivia and Janey. Then he sat opposite Olivia at the table, smiling when she thanked him, studying her again in a way that made her want to squirm on her seat or twist her dress again. *He's trying to decide if I really mean what I said*, Olivia thought, *that I won't hold him to the rental agreement if he wants me and Janey to move.*

At the same time Alan sat thinking as he watched her, *How modestly pretty she is this morning.* She wore a gray bonnet, trimmed with blue ribbon, and her hair was caught back in a chignon at the nape of her neck, although a few curly strands wisped around her ivory face. She was clad in a modest dress, but one that most Iowa women might only dream of wearing, one of expensive gray and blue satin that buttoned up nearly to her chin and that swished whenever she moved. She somehow conveyed a virtuous air.

Although . . . last night, and that evening aboard the ship, she had been a raving beauty without even realizing it—or so it had seemed. Both times her hair had flown wild and free around her face—while she argued with him, brandishing that pistol, and earlier while she danced, reveling in the gaiety. For a time aboard the ship, her blue eyes had shimmered with joy. But he had also seen them glitter with fear—when he had asked her questions, and last night when they had argued about who had a right to be living in his house.

And the child . . . Janey . . . she was afraid of him, too, afraid that he meant to hurt her sister. She had latched onto his arm, and Alan had no doubt that she would have defended her sister to the death if need be.

Virtuous . . . and honorable. It was his house and it had been rented out without his knowledge. Now he had returned, and although she had fought him last evening, today she was willing to move out despite the rental agreement, simply because he hadn't known that Homer had rented out his property.

But Alan didn't know if he could let her do that, even though he'd told Charlotte last night that he meant to find a way to "dislodge" her. He didn't know if he could live with forcing Olivia Monroe and her wide-eyed, frightened-looking sister out of the house *they* had probably started calling home until he had shown up last evening. But if not, then he was stuck in the boardinghouse. And he would be without his shed in which he sometimes saw patients.

"We started wrong," he told Olivia. "Last night, I mean. I apologize. That evening aboard the ship . . . I enjoyed teaching you the dances, and I'm delighted to meet you again." *And to know that you no longer have a husband* he wanted to say. But that would be improper, her grief being so recent—and even if it weren't recent. "Last night never should have happened," he continued, "and I intend to make sure that nothing like that ever happens again if I have to leave my home in someone's care—and I may have to. The . . . You signed that agreement in good faith, and while I felt differently last evening, today I don't like the thought of you leaving the house when you and your sister are already comfortable there."

She looked relieved suddenly, unclasping her hands on the table and smiling over at her sister.

"But neither can I stay here."

She glanced back at him, anxiety making her eyes glow again.

"There's a room built onto one side of the barn, and I work there sometimes," he explained. "I ride out on calls most of the time, but occasionally patients come to me, and I can't run an office out of Charlotte's boardinghouse."

"I understand," Olivia said.

"Therefore, I have a proposition."

She waited, folding her hands again, her gaze lingering on him.

"We can all stay at the house."

Her eyes widened. "Dr. Schuster, I couldn't . . . What are you thinking . . . assuming? That we need a home so much that I . . ." She stood abruptly, her face flushing as she smoothed her hands down over her waist and skirt, soothing her ruffled feathers, ready to march out of the boardinghouse.

He stood, too. "Mrs. Monroe, I meant nothing indelicate. Please, listen to the rest of my proposition."

She regarded him for a long moment, then she sat again. But she watched him suspiciously from the corner of her eye.

"You and your sister should continue living in the house, having full use of all the furnishings and the surrounding yard outside. I'll live in the room off the side of the barn and share the barn with the two of you until the rental agreement expires at the end of August. In the interim, I'll help you locate a nice piece of land and arrange to have a home of your own built."

Her eyes widened in shock again, but in a good kind of shock this time. She liked the idea, he could tell; her entire face brightened, and she took a deep breath and puffed up her chest. He wondered if she had any idea of how beautiful and fashionable she looked in the gray and blue silk dress and bonnet, how well the colors suited her, how well the dress fit her; how delighted he was any time anyone brought a little culture to Davenport. Two summers ago, the actress Josephine Gavin and her theater troupe had come through Davenport, set up a tent, and performed plays beneath it, to the delight of many Davenport citizens, including himself. The church people all up and down Brimstone Corner had objected, of course, but then they objected to just about everything but preaching and prayer.

"That's . . . that's very generous, Dr. Schuster," she finally managed once the shock wore off a bit. "Thank you."

"If you'll agree to it, thank *you,* Mrs. Monroe. I realize that the legal agreement John Brimmer drew up is probably valid, but even if it weren't, as I said, I can't see making you and your sister move right now when you're already in the house, especially since the agreement is in effect only until the end of August."

"You . . . you promise to stay in the barn?" she asked, clearly uncertain. She had put the fingers of one hand to her throat in a protective gesture, and her face was flushed again, too.

"Yes," he responded without hesitation. "Although . . ."

She straightened her shoulders, preparing herself.

"I would like to come out now and then to call on patients and such."

"Oh—of course." She laughed a little—at herself mostly, he thought. Then she pretended to sober up and give him a severe look.

"Well," he said, sighing, "one must jest. It's not often that a bachelor comes home to find a woman and child ensconced in his home. It's not often that he returns home to find that he has no home at all." He pulled a face, trying to look as sad as possible.

She gave him an understanding smile. "Dr. Schuster, I am sorry. Here, have a cinnamon bun," she said, pulling one from the basket.

He smiled back, then reached out to take the bun from her. Their fingers touched for no more than a few seconds, but they were the longest seconds Alan thought he had ever experienced. Her skin was soft, and above the cinnamon smell there was her smell, the scent of roses, sweet and fresh, enhancing the summer morning. Her eyes were like a clear sky, an endless baby blue. A second later they flickered with shock and apprehension, and Alan took the bun and pulled his hand back, not wanting her to bolt from the room.

He wondered why she didn't seem distressed over her husband's recent death. Perhaps she simply hid her grief well. But a woman of her station usually wore widow's garb for at least six months, didn't she? He knew nothing about her marital relationship, whether or not she had even loved the man she had married or if he had loved her, but he certainly wouldn't think of asking her anything about her marriage.

He was relieved that she had come here in an amiable state of mind, not still angry over the events of last evening and not brandishing that pistol, and that they had reached an agreement about the house. In fact, as he sat across the table from her, bit into his cinnamon bun and watched her do the same, he found it hard to believe that this poised, well-mannered woman and the woman he had encountered last night in his home were one and the same. But they were, and he liked her today—very much.

"What do your patients do when you're away, Doctor?" Mrs. Monroe asked as her sister began eating a bun. Olivia Monroe leaned over the table and spoke to him more, in a lower tone this time, as if disclosing a secret. "The last thing I want to do is irritate anyone in the town in which Janey and I have decided to settle."

Not irritating anyone in Davenport was clearly of great importance to her given the fact that, twice now, she had mentioned not wanting to do it. "Two other physicians practice here," he explained, meaning in Davenport. "We often trade opinions, and we call on each other's patients whenever any one of us has to be away. I don't leave the area often, usually only a few times a year to call on friends in Chicago and St. Louis. I had business in Cincinnati, and Ida was visiting her sister," he said to explain his and Ida's presence there in case Mrs. Monroe wondered about that, too.

"I see."

He and Janey finished their cinnamon buns, and Janey drank her milk. Olivia offered Alan the glass of milk he'd brought her, and Alan took it since she didn't seem to want it. He drank it a little at a time, in between more bites of another cinnamon bun.

"These are delicious. You're to be commended, Mrs. Monroe."

She thanked him, but she also blushed—and cringed a little, too.

"So if you hear someone rummaging around in the barn this evening or tonight, you won't come out and shoot me?" he asked, grinning.

She shook her head adamantly, blushing more, looking suddenly as if she'd like to crawl under the table. "Besides, I didn't shoot you."

He laughed. "No, but you gave it a good try. The animals . . . ," he ventured, knowing he needed to broach the subject of her goats and duck staying in the house at night.

She knew exactly why he mentioned them. "I'll keep them locked in the barn at night, I promise. Although . . . Annie doesn't like the barn and may cry for a time. And Edwin stumbles into things in the dark. The adjustment may not be easy for them."

He nodded, understanding.

"Janey and I are supposed to meet Mr. Whitworth for dinner this afternoon, and then he plans to take us out to look at a cow I may purchase," she said, as if preparing him for the fact that she had to leave in a few minutes. "Charlotte has agreed to teach me how to make butter. Surely with the milk and butter and eggs . . ." She stopped herself, looking at him warily. "I forgot. They're your eggs since they're your hens, Dr. Schuster. Mr. Whitworth was selling them in Mrs. Bogue's store for you, but then when he rented the homestead out to me, he said he supposed he was renting the chickens, too."

Alan sighed and shook his head. Homer . . . What would he think of next? "Well then, I guess they're your chickens for the time being, and while you're 'renting' the chickens, I imagine the eggs are yours to do with as you please, too. But those hens lay fine eggs, and I'd be most appreciative if you would think about sparing one or two a day."

"Dr. Schuster, of course!" she said, clearly surprised that he thought she might not.

"Then everything is settled. You'll live in the house for the next few months, and I'll live in the room beside the barn. You won't shoot at me when you hear me rummaging around, and you'll spare one or two eggs a day. Do we need another written agreement?" he teased.

She shook her head in all seriousness until she realized he was jesting, and then she smiled and shook her head at him. "Janey and I promised Mrs. Bogue we would call on her, so we should be going soon," she said, glancing down at her lap, treating Alan to a fine view of her long dark lashes—and how pretty they were, splayed against her upper cheeks. She glanced up at him again, and he thought he might drown in the clear depths of those eyes.

"I'm certain Ida will be delighted to see the two of you."

Olivia Monroe nodded, then she tested the bonnet ribbons beneath her chin, tightening them. She and her sister rose, and Alan rose, too, to walk with them to the front door of the boardinghouse. There, Mrs. Monroe turned back to bid him good day. Alan dipped his head and returned the good wishes.

"Our arrangement should be interesting, Dr. Schuster," she said, smiling again.

He liked her sweet smile, perhaps too much, perhaps more than he should, given the fact that he was her landlord. He thought about reaching for her hand and kissing the back of it. But their agreement was a business arrangement, nothing more, and Alan meant to leave the relationship that way to avoid gossip. While they were living on the same homestead, he didn't want them to appear too friendly, otherwise people would talk and speculate, and Olivia

Monroe was a lady, the type of woman who minded having her reputation ruined.

"Yes, it should be," he agreed, hoping he didn't seem too cool. He felt her studying him as he opened the door for her.

She still looked a little baffled when she and her sister stepped out into the warm sunshine and started off up the street.

CHAPTER SEVEN

DAVENPORT WAS LAID out in no particular order, as was the case with many western settlements, as Charlotte told Olivia. There was most always a Main Street and a Front Street, and then if buildings, shanties, and tents were erected in any sort of fashion at all, there might be passages in between them that eventually were given names. Davenport had managed a collection of streets—Ripley, Le Claire, First, Second, Third, Fourth, Fifth, Sixth, and a few others—mostly between times when tents came down and buildings were erected.

A sense of pride and anxiousness to have the little community settled and prospering filled the air, with businesses springing up one beside the other, hardware stores, gun shops, tobacco shops, boot shops, meat markets, barbers, dry goods . . . Saloons and gaming houses were interspersed here and there, in tents and shabby-looking gray buildings that were concentrated mostly on Main and Front Streets. The tents that were occupied by businesses almost always gave way sooner or later to buildings, Charlotte had said, and because this had become quite common in Davenport during the past year or so, the settlement had started attracting smart minds and settlers with an eye toward making something both of themselves and of the community. The town had even vied for a time to become the territorial capitol. Most people traveled overland on the journey west—another piece of Charlotte information—since they brought their worldly possessions with them, which they packed and piled into the beds of huge wagons. Once they reached the

Mississippi River, they ferried over and either began looking for land right then and there or they traveled farther into territory that was, for the most part, untouched.

Bogue's Dry Goods was located near the middle of Front Street, its false front rising a good two stories above a barber shop on the right and a tobacco shop on the left. The building itself was only two stories tall. Ida lived in several rooms on the second floor; the others were used for storage. She purchased most of her goods from wholesale dealers in Cincinnati and had the goods shipped here, usually on the steamers. Most of the items she carried, displayed in cabinets and on open shelves, were practical and, in most cases, necessary: pots, cups, eating utensils, and tools such as axes, plows, sheep shears, scythes, cowbells, mule collars, wooden planes, mallets, and chisels. But aside from the necessary items a person might need to build and then run a homestead in Iowa, Ida also stocked items for pleasure and comfort—perfumes, parasols, purses, gold timepieces, darning tools, mittens, hair combs and brushes, jewelry, shoes, boots, bonnets, and an assortment of clothing for men, women, and children, from frocks to homespun dresses and trousers.

Ida made most of the clothing herself, or so Mr. Whitworth had told Olivia the first time she had browsed through Mrs. Bogue's store, and if she didn't have it and you wanted it made, Ida could most likely stitch it up for you in a day or two. She kept bolts and bolts of material and spindles of thread and other sewing items in a room off the back of the main room, and that was where she sat stitching much of the time, rocking in her old rocker, humming spry tunes and occasionally tapping her foot. Ida Bogue could be as aggressive as a grouchy old hen, Mr. Whitworth had warned, but then she'd survived a few things in her time—Indian attacks, fires, tornadoes, floods, the deaths of two children and three husbands—and although she frequently frustrated people who really knew her and shocked those who didn't, most people came to understand Ida after associating with her for a time.

"Ya came here with a plan, an' that's the way it's gotta

be," Ida said as Olivia and Janey settled on chairs placed around the bolts of material in the back room. The homespun Ida purchased from farmer's wives was drab—gray, brown, dark blue—as homespun was inclined to be. But the calicoes, ginghams, and silks—"have to have silk on hand in case some big somebody comes through here wantin' some," Ida had said as they walked into the room—were colorful, brightening the place. Currently, the proprietor was stitching together two blue-and-white gingham pieces of a dress.

The cowbell that hung above the front door of the shop always rang, calling Ida (or her substitute) up front, if anyone entered the store. Before Ida's return, Olivia and Janey had spent a few hours in the store with Homer Whitworth and John Brimmer on two separate afternoons, and Olivia had observed how the place was run.

"Folks who don't come with a plan most always end up bein' found somewhere, dead an' dried up in some corner or out 'n the prairie grass," Ida said. "That, or they jes' wander here 'n there, starvin' an' lookin' like they're gonna blow away any second. There's nothin' easy 'bout buildin' a life or startin' over—or gettin' along if ye're a woman an' ya suddenly find yerself without yer man. Ye're not all caught up in grief 'bout yer husband's death, an' that's good, too. That's real good. Janey, did ya help yerself to some candy when ya came in?"

Janey smiled a little, but said nothing, as usual. She shook her head no, meaning she hadn't helped herself to the candy. Janey was a polite enough child that she would never think of doing such a thing.

"Well, ya go on an' have some. It's right up front, by the . . . Shoo! I reckon ya know where it is since ya was in here a time or two when Homer was mindin' the place. Go on 'n help yerself."

Janey hesitated, looking at Olivia, silently asking with her eyes if Olivia would go with her. Since leaving Philadelphia, they hadn't spent more than moments apart, and then only when Olivia had danced with Dr. Schuster aboard the steamer between Cincinnati and St. Louis.

"I'll go with her," Olivia said, taking Janey's hand.

"Gotta let 'em fend for themselves sooner or later," Ida said. Then her voice lowered a notch. "But I reckon she's been through the mill. Don't run off now, though. Ya come right back, the two of ya. We've gotta bit more gabbin' to do."

Janey chose several pieces of red-and-white-striped candy, then she and Olivia returned to the back room where they spent the greater part of the afternoon with Ida Bogue. Olivia found pieces of another dress to stitch together, and Janey busied herself with a box of wooden toys in one corner of the room, while Ida spoke more about her wholesale merchants in Cincinnati, and how she and her second husband had opened up an early trading post in what was now Iowa Territory. But, of course, back then it had been part of Wisconsin Territory. With her third husband, she had opened this store, and up until a few years ago she had made trips about every third month up to Prairie du Chien, a trading post where she had made a sizable profit by trading goods and supplying the post with produce she bought from farmers in Scott County, where Davenport was located. Of course, that had been while her third husband, who often minded the store while she was away, was still alive.

"Of course, Herbert never did like me goin' up to that post alone," Ida said, "but he wasn't one to travel, havin' the gout an' all. B'sides, he knew once I made up my mind to do something he might as well git outta my way. He took a real bad spell come that fall, long about '41, I guess it was, an' I buried him down 'n the cem'tery. Least he got that. Rob and Jessup, they're both laying under four feet o' prairie, out where the Sauk Indi'ns roam right now. I say 'right now' 'cause there's no guarantee that's where they'll stay since they follow the buffalo. Or where the gov'ment'll leave 'em. There's already talk of pushin' 'em west more." She paused for a few seconds, looking off at nothing in particular, just seeming to gather her breath and her thoughts.

"I've seen a lot out here, that's fer damn sure. It ain't no place for a body to take any time at all feelin' sorry for herself, 'at's for sure, too. So ya lose yer man. Ya get another one if that's what ya wanna do an' ya go on. Wasn't I talkin' 'bout when I used to go up tradin' to Prairie du Chien an' how Herbert didn't like it?"

Smiling, Olivia nodded.

Ida cackled a little at herself. "Mind's old. It goes off here an' there . . . ever'where. I've done so much an' seen so much, sometimes I forget where I am an' what I'm doin' at the time. But that's what it's all about. Yessum. I came out here young with my first husband an' helped get the land ready fer more people. They've been comin' fer years now, an' I'm old, an' now . . ." She glanced down at the pieces of the dress. "Now, it's almost time to let the younguns, like yerself an' that girl over there"—she dipped her head at Janey—"take over."

"My toe, my toe . . ." she said suddenly, and she grimaced and glanced down at her foot at the same time.

"What is it, Mrs. Bogue?" Olivia asked, concerned.

"My toe . . . Herbert takin' so sick an' dyin' an' then Doc Schuster takin' my toe the next year, why, 'at's what put a stop to me goin' up tradin' at the post. Have to use that cane now, an' I can't get on as fast as I used to. But that's what I was gonna tell you—someone oughtta be tradin' up yonder at the post. You plow up space for a garden, get one in, then come this fall, bring in the crops, buy up the farmers' extra wheat, corn an' pork an' bacon—they always need winter money—an' take it all up to Prairie du Chien an' do yerself some tradin'. Doesn't look like the other merchants 'round Davenport are int'rested in doin' it. But I'm tellin' ya, there's business to be had doin' it."

"I've never plowed or planted a garden in my life," Olivia said quietly. She glanced up at Ida, who was now studying her. "But I'm willing to learn—anything I need to learn."

Ida twisted her brow and nose, forming more wrinkles on her face as she planted another five or six stitches. "I reckon ya've already got Homer an' John both wantin' to get ya to the alter, an' I imagine there's a line of other roosters—it ain't often bach'lor women turn up 'round these parts, an' men here, they like havin' a woman to cook for 'em an' clean an' breed."

Olivia looked away, knowing she would have choked had she been eating anything at the moment. *Breed?* Ida Bogue certainly said anything that came to mind.

The elderly woman cackled again. "Shocked ya with that one, didn't I? Well, that's what they're int'rested in, an' ya might as well know it up front. Might as well use it to do what ya've gotta do, too."

Now Olivia turned crimson; extreme heat crept up from between her breasts, covered her neck, and engulfed her face. She felt as if she were on fire, like she needed a very long drink of water. "Mrs. Bogue—"

"Call me Ida. That's how we do things out here. Don't go 'round callin' the people planted here 'Missus this' an' 'Missus that.' Maybe jes' folks passin' through."

"Ida, then." Olivia shifted. "Ida . . . while I've heard that some women must resort to . . . to selling themselves . . . during difficult times, I—"

"Tarnation!" Ida exploded. "I didn't mean *that.* I jes' mean ya've got Homer an' John sniffin' 'round ya already so ya might as well do something with 'em. Make 'em a good supper or dinner, bake 'em a pie—they both like pies—then make mention that yer in need of havin' a little plowin' an' seedin' done. Cain't tell me ya don't even know how to flirt. Ever' woman figures that out sometime in her life."

Olivia stared at her.

"Well?" Ida demanded.

"I know how to flirt," Olivia finally said, her voice cracking with shock. She couldn't possibly think of doing such a thing, of giving men sly smiles and looks and then suggesting she needed this or that done. She never manipulated anyone in any manner at any time.

"They're gonna come 'round whether or not ya flirt with 'em, 'cause that's jes' how men are when they get a whiff of a woman, 'specially a unattached woman."

"I don't know how to bake a pie," Olivia said suddenly. "I've never . . ."

Ida studied her again. "Lord, ya really don't," she said finally, narrowing one eye.

"Charlotte will teach me," Olivia remarked. "After she finishes teaching me how to make butter."

"No. *Before* she teaches ya how to make butter. We're already to the middle of June here, an' that ground's gotta be plowed an' seeded real soon if ye're gonna get any kind of harvest. Butter can wait. Doc never bothers with plowin' an' seedin'. He jes' plucks eggs out from under his hens 'cause he's gotta taste for eggs ev'ry day. But—"

"I know. He's agreed to let me and Janey continue to stay at the house through the end of August as long as he can stay in the barn and have a few eggs every day."

That lifted Ida's brows. "How'd that come about?"

"I talked to him before coming here. I called on him at Charlotte's boardinghouse. I told him that I knew it was his house and that since he'd known nothing about Mr. Whitworth renting it out to Janey and me, I would be willing to move out, provided my animals could still stay there. I was hoping he would be a gentleman and not hear of me and Janey moving out before the rental agreement expired. Heaven knows he was no gentleman last evening at the house. But Dr. Schuster restored some of my faith in him by insisting that Janey and I stay—and that took no flirting."

"Uh-huh," Ida said. "Don't think ya jes' bein' in the same room with him had any effect on 'im at all?"

"Mrs. Bogue," Olivia said sternly.

"Ida."

"Ida."

"I saw 'im lookin' at ya an' dancin' with ya on that ship—don't forget that, Missy . . . Ya've gotta get that rental agreement to go past the end of August," she said suddenly. "Ya won't harvest much till September, plantin' this late."

Olivia thought about that. She didn't know if Dr. Schuster would agree to extending the rental agreement, especially since she felt certain that he would much rather sleep inside his house than out in the room off the side of his barn. But she would do her best to get the ground plowed and seeded, just as Ida advised, then approach him about an extension.

As soon as possible, she had to get on her feet, get established in Davenport as a business woman, and what harm would come from flirting a little to do that? Homer Whitworth and John Brimmer *would* come calling whether or not she flirted with them because both men had their eyes on her. It wasn't as if she meant to make them promises of marriage. They would love the attention, Olivia told herself, trying to justify what she was contemplating doing. And only by telling herself that did she finally convince herself to go along with Ida's advice to flirt a little with Homer, John, and others, cook for them, then ask for their assistance if she needed it. It might not be a wise thing to do—trifling with men—but if done right, it would be a harmless sort of flirting.

Homer was glad to see her and Janey—as always. His hair was slicked back and neatly combed, and he wore a nice striped suit, probably the finest he owned, Olivia decided. His brown eyes were bright, as they always were whenever he approached her, and today, he had even splashed on some pleasant spicy-smelling cologne. All to take her and Janey to supper at the hotel and then out to look at a cow!

She tried flirting with him, she honestly did, sitting a little closer to him on the wagon seat, smiling a little more than usual and a little brighter, too. She thought about using her fan to flirt, flipping it open and smiling with her eyes over the top of it the way she had seen so many women do at balls and dinners in Philadelphia. Then she saw the glitter of adoration in Homer's eyes, heard his breath catch in his throat, and watched his chest move up and down rapidly. She couldn't do it to him—flirt with him just for the sake of having him plow and seed her a garden. Poor Homer was either going to fall off of the wagon seat at any second or have a heart attack.

"Shall we go?" she queried, glancing down, breaking their eye contact.

"Oh. Sure, Mrs. Monroe. Anything you say. They're

servin' a good dinner over at the hotel today. Should be just what we need," he said, flicking the reins. "Then we'll go on out to the Brewster place an' have a look at—"

"Look out!" Olivia grabbed Homer's hand, pulling back on the reins to stop the horses. He hadn't been looking in front of the wagon; he had still been looking at her when he flicked the reins, urging the horses to go, and so he hadn't seen the mother and child who started across the street in front of the horses. Olivia had glanced up just in time to spot them.

"You all right, ma'am?" Homer asked the mother, flushing, scrambling down off the wagon seat to check on her and her child. She held the boy's hand against her thigh as she stared, wide-eyed, at Mr. Whitworth.

"I believe you flustered the man," a male voice said to Olivia's right. Dr. Schuster stood there, half grinning, looking like he knew exactly why Homer had been so distracted.

Now was a fine time to click open that fan, Olivia decided, as heat crept up the back of her neck and then around, finally sweeping up over her face. In an instant, she had the fan open and was flickering it just below her chin as Homer went about dusting the boy off while apologizing profusely to the child's mother.

"We were discussing the animal I plan to look at and perhaps purchase today," Olivia told Dr. Schuster.

"I see . . . The cow?"

"Yes."

He raised his brows and nodded at the same time. "I've never known a man to become so worked up while discussing a cow. Homer is normally attentive, very careful of people crossing back and forth on the streets."

Olivia reddened more.

"Could he possibly be sweet on you, Mrs. Monroe?"

She gave a short laugh of disbelief and shock. "That's—that's hardly a suitable question to put to a woman who has been widowed for such a short time."

"And looks the part, too, I might add," he commented.

She studied him, realizing he was wondering why she

wasn't dressed like a woman in mourning. "I could wear widow's garb and mope about for six months or a year, Dr. Schuster, but I choose not to. I choose to go on, to do what I came west to do—make a life for myself and Janey."

That silenced him. The amusement in his eyes changed to respect. "I apologize," he said, dipping his head. "This must be a difficult time for you, finding yourself alone during such a transition."

"I have Janey," she said.

"I should've been payin' attention. I just should've been," Homer fussed as he climbed back up onto the wagon seat. "Doc Schuster!"—Homer visibly cringed—"didn't see you standin' there."

"Never fear, Homer. I don't plan to pull you down and pound on you for renting out my home. If I had been in the same position, having encountered a damsel in distress, I might have done the same thing."

"I was hardly a damsel in distress," Olivia objected.

"And now I hear that Mrs. Monroe plans to consult you about a cow she hopes to purchase?" Dr. Schuster asked Homer.

Homer's face turned beet red. "Well, yep, we're gonna go look at one."

"What a good Samaritan you are, Homer! First you find our Mrs. Monroe a house, then you help her find a cow . . . You have a heart of gold, Homer. A heart of gold."

"Now, Doc . . ."

"The two of you carry on," Dr. Schuster said, stepping away from the wagon. "Homer, be careful now. Watch the street, not Mrs. Monroe. I don't want to have to set any broken bones today or stitch up any lacerations made by horses' hooves."

Olivia wanted to crawl beneath the wagon. She was so embarrassed by Dr. Schuster's carrying on, by the implication that she had distracted Mr. Whitworth so much that he might not be competent to guide the horses and drive the wagon.

"Good day, Dr. Schuster," she said stiffly, feeling that she needed to be polite to him since she planned to ask for an extension on her rental agreement.

He tipped his head to her, grinned again, and then the wagon was off. Homer was uncomfortable with having rented out the doctor's house without Dr. Schuster knowing, Olivia was uncomfortable with the doctor's teasing about Homer's reaction to her, so both of them were glad to put distance between themselves and the Davenport physician.

"Sorry about the doc comin' back from his trip so soon," Homer said rather meekly as the wagon traveled along. "I woulda never offered for you to stay in the house if I'd known he was comin' back already, Mrs. Monroe. I was real scared you might not wanna see me today after all that carryin' on last night and after findin' out that I rented Doc's house without askin' him first. I shouldn't 'ave done that. I just shouldn't 'ave. But what's done is done, and there's no goin' back."

"No, you shouldn't have, Mr. Whitworth. But you're right—what's done is done," Olivia said, smiling. To reassure him, she patted his arm, not realizing her mistake until he turned to stare at her again instead of watching the road in front of them. She gently told him that he should watch the road, then she assured him that agreements between her and Dr. Schuster involving the house were fine, that they had worked out an agreement themselves. When she told him what that agreement was, he jerked, and Olivia wondered if he would fall off the seat.

"Why, Mrs. Monroe . . . Doc Schuster does his autopsies out 'n that barn room. You know, when somebody's murdered and it ain't clear who done it or how it was done exactly, and a doc cuts the body open and looks at the insides. Last summer he got appointed coroner for Scott County, and—"

"That's enough, Mr. Whitworth," Olivia said, horrified. Of course patients sometimes called on him at the homestead. *Dead* patients. Olivia glanced back at Janey to see how the girl was reacting. But Janey was fine, staring contentedly out at homes and buildings.

Homer looked meek again, drooping his head and shoulders and grimacing. "Sorry, Mrs. Monroe. I didn't mean to go into that. But he cain't *sleep* in that room."

"I'm afraid that's where he must sleep unless he wants to remain at Charlotte's boarding house," Olivia retorted irritably. "I had no idea that . . ." She put the back of her hand to her mouth, almost losing her breakfast when she thought of Dr. Schuster performing autopsies in the barn room. Well, not while she and Janey lived in the house, which was located not two hundred yards from the barn! And not while the animals stayed in the barn and she and Janey were in and out, taking care of them. Not on his life. She would talk to him about the matter as soon as possible, maybe even this evening when she returned to the homestead.

In the Davenport Hotel's dining room, she, Homer, and Janey were served potatoes and carrots, and strips of beef in broth. But with Olivia's stomach still turning, she ate perhaps three bites and then almost became ill. Autopsies in the barn! How many bodies a week did Dr. Schuster cut open and examine in that little room? And what did he do with the pieces when he finished? Olivia tried not to think about the matter, but her mind strayed back to it throughout the day.

After dinner, she, Homer, and Janey traveled to a small farm on the outskirts of town, where Olivia inspected a gentle-looking cow. Black circled her eyes, her tail was solid brown, her legs were white up to the knees, and the rest of her body was a mixture of white, brown, and black.

"How much milk does she give a day?" Homer asked the owner, Henry Brewster.

"A good two gallons, I'd venture," Mr. Brewster replied, stuffing his fingers beneath the waistband of his trousers. "She's in fine health. Could breed her again next year if yer of a mind."

"That's plenty of milk," Olivia said excitedly. "I'll take her. What are you charging for her?"

Mr. Brewster stated his price, and with Homer looking at her as if she were crazy, Olivia immediately began pulling bills from her reticule.

"I call her Eleanor," Mr. Brewster said as Olivia paid him. "After my wife. Didn't want to sell her, but I'm havin' hard times right now."

Olivia smiled and pressed the money into his hand. "I understand. Eleanor, she is. I've rented Dr. Schuster's homestead for the rest of the summer. You may visit Eleanor there anytime you wish."

He thanked her kindly while Homer tied Eleanor to the back of the wagon. Janey scooted to the end of the wagon bed where she reached out and stroked the cow's neck.

"Darn shame I've gotta sell her, but I ain't got a choice. See that hog over there?" he asked, motioning toward a pen where a black hog rooted around. "Gotta take him to Charlotte Lind in a bit. Already sold three of 'em his size to people in town."

Olivia froze. "Mr. Brewster . . . Charlotte will kill him."

He gave her a queer look. "Yes, ma'am, I reckon she will. An' then she'll have some fine pork on her table, too."

"But you mustn't let her do that," Olivia insisted, growing agitated.

"Mrs. Monroe, that's why people raise 'n' sell hogs," Homer said rather quietly. "For food."

"But look at him! He doesn't even suspect what will happen to him soon!"

"It'll be quick, Mrs. Monroe," Homer assured. "Charlotte uses a—"

Olivia covered her ears. "Enough about death for one day, Mr. Whitworth. Not another word. I'll not allow Charlotte Lind to kill that animal. What will Mrs. Lind be paying you, Mr. Brewster?"

"She already has. I'm just keepin' the hog here till it's time to—"

"Don't," Olivia said sternly. "Tell me what she paid you, and I'll double it. Then you can return Mrs. Lind's money."

"Now, Mrs. Monroe, what're you gonna do with a hog?" Homer asked, his voice rising. He was growing a little agitated himself, shifting from boot to boot over and over. "You already snatched that duck off of Charlotte's table, and she ain't—"

"Right out from under her ax, I did!" Olivia said, raising her chin. "And I would do it again. How much, Mr. Brewster? You said you're having hard times right now. Surely you don't mean to turn down my offer? Twice as much . . ."

He stated the price, quietly and uneasily. Then he inhaled deeply and a second later released a gust of air. "Lord, but Mrs. Lind's not gonna like this."

Olivia gave him a tight smile. "She'll understand."

She put more bills in his hand. Then she handed her reticule to Janey, who was still petting Eleanor. "I'll be right back," she told Homer Whitworth and Henry Brewster, and she set off for the hog pen, lifting her skirt to avoid patches of mud.

"Where're you goin', Mrs. Monroe?" Homer called.

"To fetch my hog!"

"Wait a minute. Wait a minute. That ain't the—"

"To fetch her . . . In her fine clothes an' fancy hat . . . It ain't like he's a dog you can just whistle or call fer." Mr. Brewster laughed loud and hard.

Olivia spun around and fixed a haughty gaze on him that silenced and sobered him almost immediately. She turned back and unlatched the barnyard gate.

"Don't do that, Mrs. Monroe. Don't go in there!" Homer warned. "I'll get him for you. Just wait a minute."

"Nonsense, Mr. Whitworth. I must learn to do for myself. I'm not exactly in Boston anymore, as Charlotte has reminded me a few times."

She stepped into the barnyard and sank up to her ankles in mud and other matter, a mixture of grass and vegetable waste—and animal waste if the wretched smell was any indication.

Olivia held her breath, released it, held it again, for longer this time as she stared down at the soiled hem of her dress. She released that breath along with a small cry—"Mr. Whitworth?"—and when she lifted her skirts, she saw only the tops of her boots.

She thought she might faint, the odor was so strong and awful. Why hadn't she noticed it before she marched into the pen? *Because you charged headfirst into the situation, as you are sometimes inclined to do, Olivia Morgan.*

She became aware of hoofbeats as she called for Mr. Whitworth again. He approached the gate, wincing, shaking his head, looking as though he didn't quite know what to do. She was about to snap at him to not just stand there shaking his head, to help her out of the mud and slop, out of this predicament. But then she caught a glimpse of a familiar figure on horseback drawing near the pen.

Dr. Alan Schuster. And my, how he was grinning now.

"Mrs. Monroe, if you're not shooting at me, you're trying to run people down in the street or you're frolicking in a hog pen," he teased.

Olivia dropped her skirts so he couldn't see that her boots were nearly completely sunk in the slop, and she mustered a smile—albeit a tight one—as she glanced at him.

"My . . . Dr. Schuster. You seem to be following me around today."

"Chance, dear lady. Chance," he said, sliding down off of his horse. "Homer, aren't you going to rescue her?"

That snapped Homer out of his state of shock. "Why, sure, Doc. I was just—"

"I hardly need to be rescued, Dr. Schuster," Olivia said, lifting her chin. For the life of her, she didn't like the way he teased Homer.

"She's fetchin' the hog she just bought from me," Mr. Brewster said smartly.

Olivia wanted to give the man another haughty gaze. Instead she continued smiling at Alan Schuster. "That's right. Now if you men would care to gawk at something else, I'll collect my hog and be on my way." Little did it matter that the wagon belonged to Homer Whitworth—for his part in the gawking, he could ride back into Davenport with the doctor, and she would return his wagon later, once she got the hog and Eleanor home.

"Mrs. Monroe, lemme help you," Homer offered, but now that Dr. Schuster had come along to have a laugh at her expense, Olivia was more determined than ever to collect the hog by herself.

The hog had come over to investigate her—thank goodness, since that meant she wouldn't need to walk farther into the pen. She found a coiled rope hanging on a post, and she looped and knotted one end and then slipped the loop up over the hog's head and neck. He smelled atrocious, and Olivia held her breath again and fought dizziness, hoping she wouldn't faint.

"Come along now," she urged softly and gently, tugging on the rope as she lifted her heavy boots from the mud and backed out of the pen.

"I see you were about to join him," Dr. Schuster teased, casting a glance down at her soiled hem and boots. He chuckled and shook his head. "Given your stubbornness and determination—"

Tearing the rope from Olivia's hands, the hog bolted from the gate suddenly, snorting, lowering his head and plowing the ground with his snout. He galloped out of the pen and charged right at Alan Schuster before the man could even think about moving. He barreled into the doctor's legs, knocking him on his backside and upsetting his horse. The gelding whinnied and skittered about, finally settling near the barn, and the hog raced off.

Homer ran after the animal while Mr. Brewster doubled over and began laughing so hard Olivia just knew he would split his side. Olivia herself laughed at the thought of how ridiculous this all was—the hog tearing into Dr. Schuster, and now . . . Oh! the sight of the Davenport physician seated on the ground looking stunned, furious, undignified, his legs sprawled out in front of him . . .

Janey laughed from the wagon bed, then she crawled toward the seat, jumped down from there, and raced off after Homer, looking as if she wanted to help chase the hog.

"At least I don't smell like animal waste, Mrs. Monroe," Alan Schuster chided, his brow dark with irritation.

Olivia laughed more. She gathered her skirts and started past him, tossing over her shoulder as she went: "At least I'm still on my feet, Dr. Schuster."

She heard him grumble more as she went off to help locate the hog. "I came to have a look at your arm, Henry," he snapped, "if you can stop laughing long enough to show it to me."

"Sure, Doc," Mr. Brewster said, still chuckling. "Sure. I've even got money to pay you this time around. She's somethin', ain't she? Mrs. Olivia Monroe. Didn't want me sellin' Charlotte that hog 'cause she said Charlotte would kill it—which she would, I reckon. She paid me twice what Charlotte did, then she went in there to get the hog herself, an' damn if she didn't do it. If something hadn't spooked it, she'd have it tied to her wagon already."

Olivia beamed. Well, at least she had shown them all—again—that she wasn't a weak, simpering female. Of course, after last night, Olivia didn't think Alan Schuster thought that anyway. But a reminder now and then was a good thing.

He might think twice about teasing her again, too, she thought, giggling to herself.

CHAPTER ✣✣✣ EIGHT

ALAN'S FIRST NIGHT in the barn room was anything but pleasant.

For hours he tossed and turned on the small cot he kept in the room, listening to the bleating goats, the snorting hog (Homer had finally caught him after a lengthy chase around and around the house, during which Henry Brewster had had another good laugh), and the quacking duck. Add to that the stirring of Eleanor the cow that Olivia Monroe had purchased that afternoon, and the clucking of the chickens and the stirring of the two horses Alan kept, and the barn was a noisy and annoying place.

The goats kept the entire animal gathering in an uproar, and several times Alan opened the door leading into the main barn and yelled at them to be quiet. The yelling was ridiculous, however, because it only made the goats bleat more. Alan thought about putting them out in the barnyard, but he had promised Olivia that they could stay in the barn at night. That was the agreement they had worked out. Besides, she had warned him that the goats might be scared the first night. Surely they would soon grow accustomed to staying in the barn and not cry anymore. But right now they were like babies trying to grow used to sleeping alone at night. Except they weren't sleeping alone. They had a host of animals to keep them company.

Alan was still irritated with that hog, and the more he went over in his mind the chaos that Olivia Monroe and that animal had caused out at the Brewster place, the more he swore to himself that the hog had rammed him and knocked him down on purpose. It seemed like a ridiculous thought—a hog doing anything but rooting and eating on purpose. Nevertheless, that was how it appeared. The animal had charged out of the pen and headed straight at him, knocking him clean off of his feet. It was rare that anyone or anything ever knocked him off of his feet—and he'd been involved in quite a few skirmishes over the years, particularly as a young hellion running around Chicago, where his family lived and where he had attended medical college.

Toward the middle of the night, he heard someone talking inside the barn, and he opened the door to see Mrs. Monroe sitting with the goats, stroking them and trying to soothe them. She had brought a lantern with her and placed it on the ground beside the stool where she sat. The hog was rooting around, and any second now, Alan expected—

He bounded from the room into the barn, catching the lantern just as it tipped. He straightened, raking a hand through his hair and cursing the hog, who squealed and tore off.

"*Dr.* Schuster," Mrs. Monroe scolded, standing as the hog tore through the hens, upsetting their nests. The squawking birds scattered, running under the goats, who cried louder. The cow objected, tossing her head and mooing. The horses turned in their stalls, whinnying at all the noise.

"*Mrs.* Monroe," Alan shot right back at her, thoroughly aggravated. "That hog nearly set this barn on fire. And he stinks. This . . . *chaos* must stop! I have seventeen patients to see tomorrow in various places around the county. I have two expectant female patients who are due any day, and this must stop!"

"Don't shout, Dr. Schuster," she said, tossing her unrestrained hair over her shoulder. He could barely hear her voice now over the noisy animals. "You're frightening them."

"They were this noisy before. I'm not frightening them."

"Yes, you are, and they were not this noisy before."

"Mrs. Monroe, if you heard them all the way into the house—which is undoubtedly the reason you're here—they were noisy."

"But not this noisy," she insisted.

He threw his hands up in exasperation. "Quiet them. Somehow, quiet them!"

"Don't shout, Dr. Schuster."

"And if I do, will you pull out another pistol and shoot at me again?"

She flinched. "Of course not. I apologized for doing that. I didn't know who you were. Besides, where would I hide a pistol? I have only my night rail . . ." She glanced down at herself, at her nightdress, and blushed profusely.

Alan groaned. In the middle of this pandemonium, she was embarrassed? "Never fear, Mrs. Monroe. I'm a doctor. I've seen many a woman in her night rail—and less. You're no different."

But she was. Indeed she was. Another lamp flickered on a stall rail not far behind her, making her golden hair shimmer. Her waist, hips, and thighs were shadowy but well-defined through the material of her shift. Her skin glowed, her eyes sparkled . . .

"I-I seem to be making a habit of greeting people in my night rail lately," she said uncomfortably.

Nevertheless she sat on the stool again and stroked the male goat, trying to quiet him. The hog had decided to plop down on a pile of hay in one corner, thank God, and the clucking hens were slowly but surely straightening their feathers, gathering their dignity, and returning to their nests. The duck decided to try and join them, and she was awarded with several quick pecks, which drove her back. She finally settled on the small haystack with the hog, gathering her own feathers around her and tucking her head under a wing. Only the goats kept up their noise and fussing, bleating despite Olivia Monroe's petting and gentle assurances.

"Give them milk," Alan suggested, desperately needing a few hours of sleep.

"And just where do I get milk?"

"You bought a cow."

"Oh. Yes . . . I bought a cow," she said, looking delighted by the reminder—and a little embarrassed at herself.

Alan shook his head in disbelief.

She left the goats and started to leave the barn altogether.

"Where are you going, Mrs. Monroe?" Alan demanded. "You have to quiet the goats. You've filled this barn with animals, and I refuse to take care of them."

She tipped her head and regarded him thoughtfully. "I don't recall asking you to take care of them."

"Just in case the thought occurred to you . . ."

"I'm going to get a bowl to put milk in for them."

"A pail would work fine. They're animals, not people."

"*People* are animals, Dr. Schuster, and every living, breathing thing deserves respect. When I met you onboard that ship, I would never have guessed that you could be so temperamental and—and . . . grumpy."

He straightened his shoulders. "Grumpy?"

"That is what I called you—grumpy."

He snorted with exasperation. "I think I'm returning home to my quiet house and my quiet existence as a country doctor, only I'm suddenly drowning in animals in my home and barn; my life has been disrupted by you and these . . . things, and you call me grumpy. Wouldn't anyone in the same situation be grumpy?"

She studied him for a long moment, looking incredibly pretty, incredibly furious. "I'm sorry your life has been 'disrupted,' " she said finally, grabbing the lantern and marching off to the left of him, suddenly not seeming to care that she wore nothing but her night rail, "and that is the last time I intend to apologize to you! Thank you for suggesting that milk might help quiet Annie and Edwin."

She snatched a wooden pail from a nail that protruded from a far wall, and she entered the cow's stall. Alan watched her pull up a little milking stool, sit on it, then hesitate as she stared at the cow's udders. Obviously, whatever her life in Boston had been like, it had not included milking a cow. She reached for a teat, too delicately, tugging on it in a way that would never draw out the milk.

She didn't know how to milk the cow, but she damn sure meant to try anyway.

Alan approached Olivia and the cow in the stall. He

stooped behind Olivia and reached around her, grabbing a teat in the groove of his thumb and hand and pulling down. Milk squirted into the pail.

"I don't recall asking for your help, Dr. Schuster," she said, her voice much lower than before.

Strands of her hair tickled his cheek, and he suddenly felt the urge to lean close and smell her hair. He turned his head and studied her profile, so perfect, so lovely—shimmery blue eyes, a small, rounded nose, a proud chin and jaw . . . full lips parted gently as she breathed in and out . . .

She swallowed. "Dr. Schuster, you—"

"If either of us is ever to get any sleep tonight, I suspect that you allow me to help you, Mrs. Monroe," he said softly.

She hesitated, drawing one side of her bottom lip in between her upper and lower teeth. Finally, she nodded, silently agreeing. How much pride she sacrificed in deciding to let him help her Alan couldn't be sure. But he guessed that it was quite a lot.

He showed her how to grip the udder, showed her how to tug down and how much force to use. He even showed her how to milk two teats at once. And all the while he was showing her he was painfully aware of her hair brushing his arm. Twice he made the mistake of glancing at her face, and she gave him a shy smile—a silent thank-you—one that made his heart beat faster and his groin warm. He suddenly felt like an adolescent boy again, afraid to touch but wanting to. Really wanting to.

"Is that enough, do you think?"

He thought it was—they had filled the pail halfway—but he wanted to say no because he wanted to stay this close to her, with his arms on either side of her and his chest touching her back. "I think it might be," he finally said.

"Well, is it or isn't it?" she asked softly, sounding a little breathless.

He suggested that they might need more.

She nodded, and they continued milking together. He stole more glances at her, and he thought she was aware of them even though she kept her gaze fastened on the cow.

Moments later, she said she thought they had enough milk, and she moved off the stool, taking the pail with her.

She poured half of the milk into another pail and offered a pail to each goat. They went after the milk hungrily, drinking and drinking while she petted them. She sat on a nearby pile of hay, and Alan stood at the stall door, watching her and the animals.

"They'll be quiet now," she told him, smiling again, and Alan thought crazily that he might be willing to put up with more nights of bleating for another of her sweet smiles.

Nodding, he returned to his little room and pulled the door shut. He lay down on the cot, but when he closed his eyes he saw her smile again, her sparkling eyes and her golden hair.

She's getting under my skin, he thought, disbelieving. But those damn animals . . . why in the world did she collect animals? He laughed, called himself grumpy, rolled over onto his side, and soon fell asleep.

"Tell me . . . give me one good reason, Mrs. Olivia Monroe, why I should teach you to make butter after you snatched two whole seasons of ham and bacon—not to mention duck—from my table," Charlotte said, standing in the doorway of her boardinghouse with her fists planted on her hips.

"Because I bought a cow, and I'll supply you with milk for a time?" Olivia offered, cringing. "Heaven knows Eleanor puts out more than Janey and I will ever drink. Besides, if I don't learn from someone how to make butter, the layers of cream on Eleanor's milk will have to be thrown out."

"That rich, huh?"

Olivia nodded.

"Come in here, then," Charlotte said, moving aside of the doorway. "I'll teach you, only because you offered to give me milk. But you didn't say for how long. 'For a time' could mean a few days or a week or—"

"A month?"

Charlotte planted a hand on her hip again. "Two animals

now, Olivia, and no telling how many meals. How much milk does she give?"

"Mr. Brewster said two pails a day, but I have a feeling it may be more than that. Dr. Schuster and I milked her last night and obtained nearly a pail, then I milked her this morning and obtained another pail and a half."

Charlotte's brows went up in surprise. "Your hands must be sore! I bet you never milked a cow before last night."

Olivia smiled indulgently.

"How about a pail a day for the summer?" Charlotte suggested. "Then we'll talk about a price at the end of the season."

They agreed on that.

Charlotte finally softened enough to greet Janey, and when Janey did nothing more than smile, offering no greeting in return, the boardinghouse proprietor remarked, "I'm beginning to think you don't talk at all, Miss Janey." If she had seen the look that Janey and Olivia exchanged afterward, she might have known that she hit on the truth. But she had already turned her back and started walking up the hall toward the kitchen.

"I've got some soured cream right here, ready to go into the churn," she said once they were in the kitchen.

Janey sat at Charlotte's big oak table and began playing with the bowls and spoons there, turning the bowls over and pretending they were drums.

"Have you figured out to let the milk sit for a bit so the cream rises to the top?" Charlotte asked Olivia.

Olivia nodded. "I already knew that."

"So you know how to skim it off?"

Again, Olivia nodded.

"You just never stuck around that Boston kitchen long enough to learn how to churn."

Olivia gave Charlotte a tolerant look. "I was probably with my dance or music instructor whenever butter was churned in our house. And of course when I was married, servants did all that."

"I might have known that," the older woman said.

Although Olivia was fond of Charlotte Lind, she was as

annoyed as always with her sarcasm. Still, she used her sweetest voice to say, "Charlotte?"

Charlotte narrowed one eye at her.

"Could you teach me how to make pies, too?"

The proprietor's brows shot up. "Shoo! Who are you looking to impress? So Doc Schuster taught you to milk that cow you bought. Are you planning on baking him a pie? Getting sweet on him? Lord knows most everyone in this town thinks Doc Schuster needs—"

"I just want to learn to bake pies," Olivia said, "particularly since I was invited to participate in the local pie-baking contest."

"Do you know how to cook *anything?*"

Olivia slid her finger around the edge of one of the bowls Janey had gathered. "A little."

"Nothing at all, I'd bet. How have you and this girl of yours been making it?"

Olivia sighed impatiently. "Charlotte, I need your help. Will you or will you not teach me to cook?"

"Oh, now we're not just churning butter and learning to bake pies. Now we're *cooking*."

"Charlotte—"

"All you had to do was ask," the older woman said, turning away to collect her jars of soured cream.

Relief went through Olivia. "Thank you."

Charlotte grumbled a response, then tossed Olivia an apron and a warning: "You're going to soil that pretty Boston dress. Might as well count on it. Then I suppose we'll have to teach you to do laundry."

It was never easy with Charlotte, but for all her groaning and complaining, Olivia suspected the woman loved her two new acquaintances. She even suspected that inside Charlotte was honored that Olivia had come to her and no one else and asked that Charlotte teach her to make butter, bake pies, and cook in general.

As Olivia tied the apron on, she smiled at Charlotte's back, thinking how she loved Charlotte despite her grumbling.

* * *

The following morning, when Olivia bought Janey several readers and herself a spade from Ida's store, Ida squinted her a skeptical look and said she figured this meant Olivia didn't intend to take her advice about getting Homer and John to do the plowing for her. Had she even learned to bake a pie yet? Ida wanted to know—and Olivia was proud to say that she had spent the entire last evening with Charlotte learning to do just that, and learning to cook other things, too, and that she was so excited about having learned so much the previous evening that she planned to go home and practice. In between cooking and baking today, she meant to dig up an area for a garden, too.

Ida cackled and shook her head, scoffing as Olivia went about gathering other items she needed—flour, sugar, cinnamon, coffee (in the event that Homer or John came calling), and dried herbs. Olivia paid Ida, then went on her way.

She bought vegetables from Homer, although he would have given them to her had she not insisted on paying for them. A grocer on Front Street had a supply of apples, and she bought a good number, enough to make at least two pies. When she and Janey set off for the homestead, she was also carrying the fresh chicken she had purchased from the butcher.

She had to put aside the thought that this had once been a living, breathing animal, she thought later as she unwrapped the pieces of chicken. Wasn't it ironic that she had saved two animals from Charlotte's butcher knife, and yet today she had gone to a butcher for the meat she needed to make a stew? But there was definitely a difference between seeing the meat already cleaned and having seen Martha and then the hog alive and moving, within minutes or days of appearing on someone's table as part of a meal.

Olivia lit a fire in the black cookstove and put the chicken on to boil. Janey scooted a chair up to the table where Olivia began chopping up onions and potatoes and carrots. Olivia hummed as she worked, singing to Janey, telling her that cooking was not nearly as difficult as she had thought it might be. She had watched Charlotte add this herb and that herb and although she couldn't remember exactly which ones Charlotte had added to the stew, she made a good guess, tossing in this and that, finally adding a good amount of salt and pepper.

She went on to the pie, having trouble rolling out the dough, which for some reason had turned out thick and too elastic. She rolled it more, and finally put it in the pie pan she had pulled from a cupboard, thinking that once it baked, it would be fine. She cut up the apples and let Janey place them in the pie. Then Olivia sprinkled the layers with cinnamon and sugar, and placed a top crust over the apple slices. Finally, feeling proud, she placed the pie in the oven and stirred the stew once more. Then she and Janey went outside to begin work on the garden.

Digging up the ground, breaking up the dirt, and removing the grass required much more work than Olivia had anticipated. But she was determined to have a garden, and so she continued working despite the fact that her hands were already sore from milking. Perspiration trickled down her face and under the high collar of her dress, which she finally unbuttoned to cool herself. Her back began aching, and her hands ached more, but she refused to quit. She would have the area she had chosen for a garden site dug up by this evening, and that was that.

Janey played with the goats, Edwin and Annie, running around with them. She carried Martha around for a while, although Olivia guessed that the duck was heavy for a girl Janey's size, and then she skipped over to the barnyard where she petted Eleanor, who had sauntered over to the fence. Janey seemed happy here in Davenport, almost carefree at times. Would she start talking again someday soon? Olivia wondered, as she frequently did. That was when she noticed the smoke wafting from the house.

The stew and the pie! She'd been so caught up in digging up the garden are that she'd forgotten about them!

Olivia dropped the spade and ran toward the house, throwing open the door and racing inside.

A thin layer of smoke was spreading throughout the

house, thicker smoke engulfed the kettle that contained the stew, and yet more smoke poured from the stove itself, probably from the pie inside. Olivia screeched, grabbed a thick cloth, and lifted the kettle, placing it on the table. She pulled open the oven door, coughing when smoke blew straight into her face.

Someone grabbed the cloth from her hand, pushed her out of the way, and pulled the pie from the oven. Or what was supposed to have been a pie. It looked more like one of the indelicate messes Eleanor made hours after she had made it and it had dried.

"Janey, you'll burn yourself!" Olivia warned. "Put the—"

"What are you doing?" Alan Schuster demanded.

"Where's Janey? Where's my pie?" Olivia asked frantically.

"Janey's outside. The pie's on the table. What the hell are you doing? Trying to burn the house down?"

"No! I was cooking and digging a garden. I forgot about the stew and the pie."

The smell of burnt food was almost overwhelming. Olivia began coughing.

"My . . . pie. I burned the . . . pie!"

She stumbled toward the table, wanting to see if there was some way she could salvage the pie. She was so tired from cooking this morning, then from working outside all afternoon, doing work her body was not accustomed to doing, and she was so disappointed that she had burned everything—*everything*—that she wanted to plop down and cry.

She coughed more, breathing smoke, and Dr. Schuster took her by the shoulders and forced her toward the front door. "Out," he ordered, urging her beyond the threshold. "Don't worry about the pie!"

"Don't worry about the . . ." Olivia twisted in his arms.

He held her tighter. "It's only a pie!"

"It's stew *and* a pie!"

"They don't matter—they're only food. It's more important that you breathe air right now, not smoke."

He reached down to take her hand in his, but Olivia yanked and snatched her smarting hand away. When she glanced down, several of the blisters that had formed while she was digging up the garden area had opened and drained. Dr. Schuster saw the open blisters, too, and stared at them in disbelief.

"Did you burn yourself?"

Now tears did well up in Olivia's eyes, despite her blinking and trying to fight them. Sniffing, she lifted her skirts between her thumbs and forefingers, trying not to open any more of the blisters, and without answering him, she ran to the barnyard where Janey now sat rocking on a rail, looking pale and scared nearly out of her mind.

"I'm all right," Olivia assured her. "I am . . . But I burned everything!"

Janey nodded, then grabbed her and hugged her.

"Mrs. Monroe, what were you doing? Didn't you notice smoke coming from the oven? Didn't you smell the pie burning?"

Olivia turned on the doctor. "*What was I doing?* Everything! Learning to cook and garden, only I burned all the food because I forgot about it, and now I have blisters on my hands, and the garden area is only half finished!"

"Were you tilling it yourself?" he asked, clearly shocked.

"I was *digging* it myself."

His jaw dropped open at that. He walked off, rounded the house, then returned moments later and studied her.

"What about asking someone to till the ground for you?" he suggested, his voice gentle.

"I have to learn to bake pies first," she said, sniffling more, still distraught.

He wrinkled his brow and studied her more, looking baffled. Then he pulled a handkerchief from his pocket and wiped her eyes and cheeks. "While there is probably some logic to learning to bake pies before asking someone to till the ground for you, it makes no sense to me. Here, blow your nose," he said in a quieter voice, trying to place the handkerchief in her hand. He shook his head, deciding against that, given the condition of her hands, and he held the handkerchief to her nose himself.

Olivia blew, and he wiped. Then he suggested that he

should take a look at her hands. Not knowing what else to do, and since he *was* a doctor, Olivia placed her hands in his care.

Alan had been riding up to the homestead, thinking to pick up some bottles of medicine before riding over to check on Malva Dodge, who had been suffering from a strong cough, and then continuing out a good ten miles to check on Elaine Merriam, a new mother and her one-month-old infant. He had seen smoke twisting from the house and Janey Monroe racing for the front door, looking frantic, terrified, her mouth wide open but no sound coming out. He had grabbed the girl and demanded to know where her sister was, but Janey hadn't answered him. She had been so terrified that all she could do was open her mouth as if trying to scream—no noise came out. Alan had picked her up and taken her to the safety of the barnyard, where he had put her on the top rail and told her to sit. He would go inside the house and get her sister. She shouldn't worry, he'd told her, and she should stay on the fence, not run after him. He didn't see flames coming from the house, but not knowing where the smoke originated, he wanted to take no chances. He didn't know if she would stay on the rail as he had told her to, but if her sister was inside the house and the house was on fire, he had to get Olivia Monroe out fast.

So he had barged into the house, into the thin smoke, and he had spotted Olivia right away, stooped beside the stove, a cloth in her hand as she prepared to reach inside through the smoke and pull something out. The smoke burned his eyes, and Alan knew that as close as she was to the stove, where the smoke originated, her eyes must be burning, too. She began coughing, and that was when he had grabbed the cloth from her and pulled the pie out of the oven himself.

Now, of course, he realized that the blisters on her hands were from the spade she had been using all afternoon. But blisters were blisters, however she had been injured, and they needed treatment.

He took her by the elbow and Janey by the hand and led them both through the barnyard and into the barn. There, he urged them toward his little room, where he intended to clean the blisters, put ointment on them, then wrap Olivia's hands.

She jerked away from him some two feet from the door. "I'm not going in there, and neither is Janey."

Alan shook his head. "Mrs. Monroe, my intent is only to treat your hands. Nothing out of the ordinary."

"In that room? Yes, there is," she insisted. Then she leaned toward him as if not wanting her sister to hear what she said next. "You do autopsies in that room. That's what you meant when you said that your patients sometimes come here."

He lifted his brows, wondering why the fact that he occasionally did autopsies in the back room should matter right now. He had felt no need to tell her that he did autopsies at his homestead. "I do perform autopsies here on occasion, when the need arises. Who told you that?"

"Mr. Whitworth did."

"Homer again!"

"I cannot believe you sleep in there."

He considered that. "Where am I supposed to sleep?"

She flinched.

"Are you expecting me to pull out an arm or a leg, or perhaps a dissected heart?"

"Dr. Schuster," she reprimanded hoarsely, her face going pale.

Laughing under his breath, Alan shook his head. "All right. Sit down over there," he said, motioning to a stool.

She went and sat where he indicated, and her sister sat on the ground beside her.

"See, Janey, your sister is safe," he assured the girl. "It was good of you to stay on the fence and not run after me."

Janey gave him a little smile. Alan remembered that when she had opened her mouth to scream, no sound had emerged, and suddenly he realized he had never heard the girl say a word. Perhaps she was still getting used to this new place, new land, and all the new people. Perhaps she was just very, very shy.

Alan brought a basin of water from the room into the barn, and told Olivia to put her hands into it. She did, grimacing, and he gently cleaned the open blisters, taking care not to upset those that were still formed. He went back to his room for the herbal salve Ida always mixed for him, and he applied that to the blisters, opened and intact. Then he again went back into the room and emerged with bandages, which he wrapped around Olivia's hands. She was quiet throughout his care. So was Janey, who sat watching him work.

"Now, why don't the two of you stay out here while I go check the house and see if the smoke has started clearing yet?" Alan said.

Olivia nodded, and he thought she looked defeated and vulnerable right then, with her shoulders slumped and her face tilted down. He put his hand beneath her chin and lifted, bringing her face up. It was smudged with dirt, and her eyes were larger and bluer than usual, though they possessed less sparkle. If not for Janey being in the barn with them and sitting so close, he might have kissed her and washed every smudge from her skin.

"Olivia Monroe, you finished the trip without your husband, you found a home, and you're doing a fine job of getting by on your own. You burned a pie, that's all, and I'd wager everything I own that you're not the first person to do that."

"I burned the stew, too."

"Yes, you did," he said, unable to suppress a grin—she looked like it was the end of the world. "But you have a good start on digging up the ground to plant a garden—and you didn't burn the house down."

Glancing down again, she tried to twist her chin away.

"Did you expect your first meal to be perfect, Mrs. Monroe?"

"Yes."

"Look at me."

She did.

"I caught my mother's finest curtains on fire once when I had a taste for fried fish and she was off working at the market in Chicago. The oil caught fire and blazed up and . . . well, I put the fire out, but I hid those curtains from my mother as long as possible, until she finally looked at me one day and asked me straight out, 'Alan, do you know where my curtains are?' My sister laughed because she knew what had happened to them; she had come home about the time I was stuffing them far back behind the porch steps. I couldn't sit for a while when my mother got finished with me that day, and I was never allowed to cook in her kitchen again either. Being the bachelor that I am, you can imagine how that was when I ventured out on my own. I can safely say I've scorched a few more curtains since then."

Olivia tipped her head and regarded him dubiously, a smile now playing on her lips. "You have not."

Alan put a hand to his chest. "Why, Mrs. Monroe, I swear to you on my pappy's grave that I have—and I don't often tell a lie. I am, for the most part, a man of impeccable character and dignity. Except when strange women shoot at me in my house and bleating animals keep me up half the night."

She scowled at him.

"Uh-uh," he said, shaking his head. "You were supposed to laugh."

She smiled again. But a second later, she sobered. "Do we still have a rental agreement?"

That caught him by surprise. "Certainly, since we still have a house."

"Dr. Schuster," she scolded, but this time she could not keep from laughing slightly.

"Mrs. Monroe. Of course we still have a rental agreement, provided that once you master the art of cooking, you fix me a meal. I've been enjoying Charlotte's fine meals, but now and then I'd like to eat a meal at home."

She happily agreed to do that, and Alan went off to see if the smoke had begun clearing from the house.

He opened all the windows and placed the pie and the pot that now contained a brown mixture and a few visible carrots that had not been cooked to oblivion outside on the porch. No doubt it would take a few days for the smell of burnt food to completely clear out of the house.

He returned to the barn and told Olivia that the house was

still smokey but that the smoke would surely clear at least by sundown and that the house should be fine for herself and Janey to sleep in tonight. She still looked meek and sorry and embarrassed, but at least tears weren't filling her eyes and streaming down her face anymore.

Alan gathered the medicines he needed from his room, and then he set off to call on Malva Dodge and Elaine Merriam—the new mother. He started to tell Olivia that he would be home by dark, but that sounded far too domestic, as if he were reporting to a wife, and she was hardly that. Instead he said, "I know you don't like suggestions, Mrs. Monroe, but a bonnet might be a good idea the next time you plan to spend a good deal of time in the sun. Your face and arms are sunburned."

Her mouth parted in surprise, and she touched her nose with the tip of two fingers. "I usually do. I completely forgot."

She looked cute—and pitiful—sitting on the stool, her face dirty (though he could see the sunburn under the dirt), her eyes wide, her hands (excluding her fingers and thumbs), covered with bandages. Alan almost felt that he shouldn't leave her, but Malva needed her medicine, and he needed to check on Mrs. Merriam, who was normally his patient but whose baby had been delivered by a fellow physician while Alan had been in St. Louis.

He left the barn without a glance back inside because if he had glanced back he would have been inclined to stay a little longer with Mrs. Monroe, or not leave at all. In fact, he mounted his horse and rode off still fighting the urge to look back and whistling as he went.

CHAPTER ❖ ❖ ❖ NINE

He didn't return home until late, when he found the goats causing another ruckus in the barn, tipping their heads up, bleating, running about and stirring up the chickens and the duck. Olivia was in the barn, trying to quiet them and milk the cow.

He couldn't see her when he first walked in, but he certainly heard her: "Ouch! Blast it all!"

Walking over to the cow's stall, from where her voice rose, Alan wondered what was wrong, but he also meant to tease her about the cursing. She seemed so proper at times, he would never have imagined her cursing. But he was hearing her, and he wasn't asleep, so he wasn't dreaming.

He stopped in his tracks at the stall door. "Mrs. Monroe, what are you doing? You'll break open more of those blisters, if you haven't already!"

"Why are you always asking what I'm doing, Dr. Schuster?" she said irritably. "What else would I be doing with my hands under a cow but trying to milk her? The milk calmed the goats last night, so I was thinking that it might help calm them tonight."

"Could I do the milking, Mrs. Monroe?" he asked, knowing that if he *told* her he would do it, she might object. One never knew with an independent woman; he had had enough experience with Ida to know that.

But Olivia surprised him by saying, "Please?", and Alan promptly put down his medical bag and went into the stall to milk the cow.

"Your face isn't quite as sunburned as I thought it was,"

he said over the bleating of the goats after he had taken Olivia's place on the milking stool. She wore a light blue wrap over her shift tonight, and the color enhanced her eyes. He stole glances of them as he milked the cow. Her hair was unpinned again, and he relished the sight of it waving down over her shoulders and back.

"It's sunburned enough," she said, glancing away, pulling her wrap closer around her.

It was on the tip of his tongue to tease her again, to remind her that he'd seen plenty of women in their nightclothes and in far less. But their growing awareness of each other stopped him. He knew that seeing her in her nightdress was far different from seeing any other woman.

"You're staring, Dr. Schuster," she chided, glancing at him quickly, then fastening her gaze on the straw-littered barn floor.

"You're something to stare at, Mrs. Monroe," he responded, "and I say that with the utmost respect."

Her lashes fluttered up again, and her lips formed a gentle smile. Then she turned away, moved out of the stall, and placed herself on the other side of the railing. A stream of milk missed the bucket. Alan laughed at himself and forced himself to watch what he was doing.

"Allow me to apologize for today's activity," she said presently. "I tried to do too many things at once."

"What did you have for dinner?"

"Slices of beef and bread from Charlotte. I thought she would never quit laughing when I told her what happened. Mr. Brimmer had dinner with us, as he and Mr. Whitworth sometimes do. Janey likes them and—"

"And you?" Alan asked, glancing at her.

"What?"

"Do you like them, too?"

She hesitated for a few seconds, fidgeting with her wrap again. "Of course, I like them. I like most everyone I've met in Davenport so far."

He nodded and went back to milking.

"Does it matter to you that I like Mr. Brimmer and Mr. Whitworth?" she queried after a time.

He stopped milking and lifted a brow at her.

"I mean . . . what I mean is . . . Mr. Brimmer and Mr. Whitworth both arranged to rent the house to me, and I thought . . . I don't want everyone to be at odds over the agreement."

"We're not at odds, I just haven't spoken to them since I returned," he said stiffly, and he went back to milking. He had thought she was asking because she wondered if he was jealous of John and Homer.

"You spoke to Homer briefly yesterday afternoon."

"I did—as briefly as possible."

"Don't you think you could consider forgiving him, please?" she said, huffing a little.

"In time I might."

"Dr. Schuster."

"Mrs. Monroe." He chuckled. "You have a way of scolding me."

He milked a little more as she wandered off to try to console the goats. Their bleating was beginning to give him a headache. He hoped the milk would shut them up. She had the patience of a saint, petting them, speaking softly to them; he himself would have put them out in the barnyard, and there they would have spent their days *and* nights.

She returned to the railing moments later. "That looks like the same amount of milk they had last night. It should be enough."

Agreeing, he stood, lifting the pail with him, and started from the stall. As he brushed the gate, his shirtsleeve caught on a nail.

Olivia reached over at the same time he did to try to free the material. Another fleeting touch of their hands, much like the one last evening, that made his blood pulse faster and made him want to touch her more. She glanced up at him during those seconds, quickly searching his eyes, and he barely resisted the urge to dip his head and kiss her. He wanted to . . . Oh, how he wanted to.

She freed the material, then produced another bucket. They divided the milk and sat together on a pile of hay while the goats drank. The animals soon settled on the barn floor, together on another cozy pile of hay, and Alan listened and smiled in pleasant disbelief, almost wishing he were one of those animals, as Olivia sang a ballad to them.

Once they had fallen asleep, she rose and wished Alan a good night.

"You are a different sort of woman, Olivia Monroe," he teased. "A very different sort of woman. Good night."

Smiling, she hurried from the barn, gripping her wrap again.

Alan woke with a start and listened, thinking the stirring of the animals had jolted him. But other than a few clucks from a hen, the animals were quiet. A lamp was glowing nearby—and he never left a lamp glowing at night.

He heard a sound from the far corner of the room, and when he glanced that way, Janey was there, holding the lamp in one hand and a slate against her chest with her other hand. She stood smiling at him, and Alan blinked, wondering if he was dreaming.

"What are you doing, Janey?" he asked, baffled. Why was the girl out here in the barn, in his room, watching him, smiling at him in the middle of the night? If it *was* the middle of the night. He really had no idea what time it was.

She drew close to the bed, a little angel in her white shift with her dark hair flowing around her shoulders. He sat up, and as she handed him the slate, he thought what an odd child she was, what a quiet child.

Alan took the slate, still staring at her, and she motioned to it, then she pushed it down flat onto his lap and tapped it. Alan looked down and read the words that were written on the tablet in a child's scrawl: *Thank you saving Livvy.*

He smiled up at her and inclined his head, acknowledging the words. But how odd that she had written him a message instead of just telling him thank you. He recalled thinking that he had never heard the girl speak, and he asked, "Would you read it to me? I'd like to hear you read."

She shook her head, declining.

"Can you read? If you can spell, you can surely read, Janey."

She shook her head again, and this time she put a finger to her parted lips, indicating her mouth.

"You . . . you can't talk?"

She shook her head again, then thought better and nodded. Alan wasn't sure what her answer was, though he suspected what it was, and he told her to nod if she couldn't speak. Janey nodded.

"But you can hear," he said, more to himself than her, puzzling over the matter. It might be the middle of the night, a time when most people's minds were cloudy, but he was accustomed to being awakened at all hours by relatives or friends of patients in need, and his medical mind was suddenly alert.

"I'm a doctor, Janey, do you know that?"

She nodded.

"Do you know what a doctor does?"

She scowled and nodded again.

"You don't normally like doctors?"

She shook her head no.

"Sometimes doctors have to hurt people to help them get well," he explained.

She nodded again, still scowling, not liking the fact that doctors sometimes had to hurt people to help make them well, but accepting it.

"Could I look at your ears and your throat, Janey? Could I shine a light into them?"

She twisted her mouth for a few seconds, then she nodded again.

Alan examined her ears and throat visually, then her throat manually, finding nothing out of the ordinary.

"Feels like everything is there," he teased. "Two ears and a neck and, my, what healthy tonsils you have, Miss Monroe!"

She grinned at that. Then she scooped up her slate and fled from his room.

Alan had a difficult time falling back to sleep. He thought about Janey, wondered why she could hear but not speak, wondered why her sister had not come to him and asked for his medical opinion. Of course, he and Olivia Monroe had had more than their share of differences these past few days, so maybe that was why she hadn't come to him. He wondered if Janey had ever been examined, and, if so, where. He intended to question Olivia tomorrow, and, in his troubled mind, tomorrow was not soon enough.

His life as a physician was unpredictable, however, and Curtis Campbell's son came calling the following morning while Alan was shaving, saying that his pa had taken a spill and needed medical attention. Olivia and Janey wandered into the barn right behind Charlie Campbell, carrying the baskets in which they always gathered eggs. If not for Curtis Campbell needing him, Alan would have questioned Olivia this morning.

Instead, Alan quickly finished shaving while Charlie saddled his horse. Then Alan grabbed his medical bag and rode off with Charlie.

Over supper the previous evening, John Brimmer had told Olivia that he would till and seed her a garden. Olivia hadn't even asked him to, and she hadn't batted a single lash or given him a single smile for the purpose of convincing him to till and seed her a garden. They had been eating their meal, Olivia having trouble with her utensils because of her wrapped and smarting hands, and John had asked what the devil had happened to her that her hands had to be bound with bandages. Reluctantly, Olivia told him that she had bought a spade, thinking to dig a garden, and that she had worked all afternoon, turning a good-sized area of ground. She left out the part about burning the stew and pie, of course, because it was embarrassing and because she wouldn't want John to think she was incompetent in the kitchen. After all, she had already sat through the humiliation of Charlotte's amusement over the afternoon's disasters.

John sat with his jaw hanging open for a good while after Olivia told him about her digging. "Why, Mrs. Monroe," he said finally, "a lady like yerself shouldn't oughtta be diggin' a garden in the blazin' afternoon sun. She shouldn't oughtta be diggin' a garden at all!"

"Sometimes a lady has no choice," Olivia said tightly. "I want a garden and I'm willing to turn the ground and plant a garden. In a few days my hands will be fine again, and then I'll finish the area."

"No, Mrs. Monroe, don't be doin' that. I'll borrow a friend's plow an' I'll be over tomorrow afternoon to turn that ground for ya. Don't concern yerself with it. Then we'll talk about what ya want planted an' we'll get it planted. Nope," he said when she opened her mouth to object. "I won't hear ya tellin' me no. I'll be there an' that's that."

He was, too. He arrived shortly after noon, while the sun burned down from straight overhead.

Dr. Schuster rode up almost right behind him, and he greeted John by inclining his head. Then he sniffed the air, glanced at Olivia, and lifted a brow. "Cooking again, Mrs. Monroe?"

She nodded uneasily, wondering if he meant to tell John how she had burned the stew and the pie yesterday. Mercifully Dr. Schuster flashed her a knowing grin, then walked off toward the barn. Earlier Olivia had put on another pot of stew, anticipating John's arrival and thinking he would be ravenous after tilling her garden area, and she beamed when he commented favorably on the smells wafting from the house.

"The way to a man's heart is indeed often through his stomach," Dr. Schuster called smartly to her from the barn doors. "But your smile alone might well have done the trick where John's concerned. You didn't have to cook again and risk—"

"Good afternoon, Dr. Schuster," Olivia said loudly and firmly.

Laughing under his breath, he dipped his head. "Afternoon, Mrs. Monroe." And with that, he disappeared into the barn.

John's two horses had just strained forward, pulling his plow over the ground while John guided it, when Homer approached in a wagon. And in the back of his wagon was another plow. Olivia stared at him, wondering how Homer had found out that she wanted a garden area turned, while John went on working, not noticing Homer.

But Homer appeared agitated. He stopped his horses and stood up, still grasping the reins, his brow wrinkled. "John Brimmer, I'm plannin' on plowin' that ground for Mrs. Monroe."

John twisted his head around, looking for Homer's voice. For a few seconds, he studied Homer, the wagon, and the tiller Homer had brought, then his face broke into a grin as his arms jerked up and down with the force of the plow turning chunks of earth. "'Pears I beat ya to it, Homer! Mrs. Monroe had me to supper last evenin', an' I told her I'd be over this afternoon to till her a garden. She put on a pot of stew fer when I'm done, too," John said proudly, and as soon as the words were out of his mouth, Homer's face screwed up, and Olivia knew she had a problem on her hands.

Whistling, John went on with his plowing. Homer jumped down from the wagon seat, his jaw jutting out with determination and anger as he began unloading his tiller. Once he had unloaded it, he unharnessed his horses from the wagon, lifted several yokes from the wagon bed, and tossed them over the horses' heads.

"Mr. Whitworth," Olivia said, hurrying down the porch steps, finally finding her voice. She hadn't known what to think when Homer had shown up, and she hadn't known what to do either when John had thrown in Homer's face the fact that she was cooking him a pot of stew. "You're certainly welcome to stay and have a bowl of stew," she told Homer. "However many bowls. But I—I don't believe I've marked a garden area so large that it requires two men to till it. I—"

"Mrs. Monroe, I'd already set my mind to come here today an' plow that garden for you. John Brimmer's a lawyer, not a farmer," Homer said, raising his voice and tossing that firm statement over his shoulder at John. "I bet he's never tilled a garden in his life. Year to year, he hires myself or Walt to do his tillin'. He might've been fine with that rental agreement, but he belongs in an office, not behind a plow. I know you want your garden—"

"What's that yer sayin' 'bout me, Homer Whitworth?" John demanded. He had stopped his horses with a single command, and now he marched toward Olivia and Homer, fixing a glare on Homer.

"I said . . . you've never been behind a plow."

"Well, I'm handlin' that one just fine, ain't I?"

"That's the crookedest piece of tillin' I've ever seen," Homer said, motioning to the ground John had already turned.

Olivia cleared her throat, thinking she should intervene before this confrontation developed into something more. Homer was angry because John was doing the plowing he thought *he* should be doing, and John was angry because Homer had insulted him. And neither man looked as if he intended to back down.

"Gentlemen, I—"

"Ya heard what the lady said, Homer. She needs just one man to plow her a garden, an' that man's me," John announced.

"Charlotte told you I was comin' over to do it, didn't she?" Homer accused. "You ate breakfast at her place this mornin', an' she told you. An' after she told you, you hurried around an' beat me over here, jus' to look good to Mrs. Monroe. Well, it ain't gonna work, John. You ain't never tilled a garden, an' I'm here now, so I'm gonna finish that mess you started."

"The hell ya are!" John exploded. "Beggin' yer pardon, Mrs. Monroe."

Olivia clapped her hands together and tried again: "Gentlemen, I—"

"Don't curse in front of a lady!" Homer shouted, balling his hands into fists. "An' don't curse at me!"

"Homer, we can work this out," John said, and Olivia released the breath she had sucked in at the sight of Homer's fists. Well, thank goodness John had decided to be rational. Now, if only Homer would too.

"Jus' load yer plow back in yer wagon an' go on home," John advised.

But Homer would not be deterred. He stomped over to his plow, gripped its handles, and barked a command at his horses. They jerked forward, and Homer held tight to his tiller as the blade began digging and turning the ground not ten feet in front of the house.

"What're ya doin'?" John yelled, clapping his hands to the top of his head. "That ain't what she's wantin' plowed. Homer Whitworth, yer crazy as a loon!"

Olivia had to object, too, but in a more diplomatic way. "Mr. Whitworth, as you are aware, I'm only renting this property, and I cannot have it destroyed. I—now, Mr. Brimmer, don't. Mr. Brimmer!"

John had snapped his arms down to his side and taken off after Homer, and the dark look on his face said he had had enough of this nonsense, quite enough, and that he meant to put a stop to it. Olivia stood with her arm outstretched, as if reaching to pull John back.

But now John would not be deterred. He grabbed Homer by the arm and yanked him around, and Olivia yelped when Homer swung his other arm and popped John clean across the jaw. Bellowing with rage, John snatched a handful of the front of Homer's shirt and lifted the smaller man off of his feet. John growled words while Homer blindly swung his arms and legs, finally unbalancing John. Both men tumbled into the freshly plowed dirt.

"*I'm* gonna . . . *plow* . . . her *gar*-den," Homer said, spitting every other syllable.

"Wrong, Whitworth, *I'm* gonna plow her garden," John said through what looked like a mouthful of dirt and grass.

"Stop it!" Olivia commanded. But neither man seemed to hear her; they were both so involved in fighting for the right to till her garden that nothing else mattered.

From the corner of her eye Olivia spotted movement near the barn. Dr. Schuster hurried out, glancing around in confusion at first. Then he spotted Homer and John tussling on the ground, and he ran toward them.

"John. Homer. Stop!" he ordered, reaching down to grab each of them by the scruff of the neck. Suddenly their anger was aimed at him—for interfering, Olivia supposed—and they both swung at him, knocking him off of his feet.

"John! Homer! Stop!" he shouted again. But even that did no good. Homer swung at John and caught Dr. Schuster in the shoulder. Dr. Schuster went after Homer, and John swung wildly, hitting both men.

John and Homer's confrontation over who was going to plow her garden area had gone even farther than she had been afraid that it might. Much farther. Now Dr. Schuster was involved in it, too, turning and swinging and cursing with Homer and John.

"Whadya reckon they're scufflin' about?" a voice asked over the commotion. Olivia twisted around and spotted Walt Lincoln propping his lanky form against the side of yet another wagon. Another wagon containing yet another plow—and Walt calmly standing there with a corncob pipe protruding from the side of his mouth and his arms folded across his chest while his friends fought.

"Mr. Lincoln, stop them!" Olivia shouted. "Stop them!"

He pulled the pipe from his mouth and studied it while twisting his lips. Then he glanced up at her. "Got a pol-i-cy, Mrs. Monroe, an' that is, I don't meddle in other folk's skirmishes."

Her eyes widened, and she stared at him in shock. He didn't meddle in other folk's skirmishes? *He didn't meddle . . . ?* John and Homer were beyond reason and perhaps seriously meant to hurt or kill each other, and he didn't meddle?

"Well, I do," Olivia said under her breath. She lifted her skirts and ran to the house.

She emerged moments later with her infamous pistol in hand. At a distance of two feet from the fighting men, she wrapped both hands around the weapon's handle, pointed the barrel at the sky, and fired.

The three men froze. Their heads jerked around, and they stared at her.

"Mr. Whitworth . . . Mr. Brimmer," she said sternly. "Get up, gather your plows, and leave."

"Yes, ma'am," Homer mumbled, his dirty face downcast. Olivia almost felt sorry for him. Almost.

"Whatever ya say, Mrs. Monroe," John said, glancing between her and the pistol as if wondering if she might decide to fire at the two of them. "Jus' . . . we're goin', Mrs. Monroe. We're goin' right now. Right this minute."

Homer and John walked off without looking at each other and began unhitching their horses from their plows.

"Of all the crazy things!" Dr. Schuster muttered, brushing dirt from his clothes and hair. "Mrs. Monroe, did it ever once occur to you that it might be dangerous to encourage them at the same time and in the same place?"

Olivia blinked. She wrinkled her brow in confusion, then she narrowed one eye at him. "What exactly do you mean, Dr. Schuster?"

"Homer and John. You've been trifling with them. Only today you decided to trifle with both of them at the same time and in the same place. You arranged for both Homer and John to plow your garden. Not a good idea."

Anger hit Olivia with such force that she almost couldn't breathe for a long moment. When her breath finally came, it burned her nose, throat, and chest.

"I have never trifled with any man," she said succinctly, staring straight at him. "Mr. Lincoln?"

"Yes, ma'am?"

"Have I trifled with you?"

"No, ma'am."

"Did you come to plow my garden area?"

"Yes, ma'am."

"Why?"

"Reckon I'm a neighborly sort of feller that way, Mrs. Monroe."

"Proceed then, Mr. Lincoln, and accept my gratefulness beforehand. If you're hungry afterward, I have a pot of stew in the house."

Olivia glared at Dr. Schuster for a few more seconds, then

she spun around and marched toward the house, intent on going inside. She hoped she would not have the misfortune of setting eyes on him again for the rest of the day, maybe for several days. It would take at least that long for her temper to cool.

CHAPTER TEN

Walt spent the afternoon plowing Olivia's garden area. Olivia spent the afternoon making butter with Janey, Dr. Schuster spent the afternoon in the barn room.

Actually, Olivia found herself wondering if he was even still in there, and if so, what was he doing that would require him to spend so much time in the room? He surely hadn't come out; she would have seen him since she and Janey were sitting on the porch taking turns at churning the butter. And then the ridiculous thought kept creeping into Olivia's head that maybe he had sneaked a body into the room in the middle of the night and was now—right now—performing an autopsy.

Olivia's stomach turned at that thought. Cutting up a body out in the barn? The thought almost made her nauseous, although it wasn't the thought of *where* he might be doing it exactly that made her stomach feel sour; it was the thought that he might be doing it at all, anywhere.

All through Walt's plowing and the butter churning, Olivia stole intermittent glances at the barn, wrinkling her brow more each time. She and Janey salted and molded the butter and wrapped it in brown paper. Charlotte had offered to let Olivia store her butter in a wooden box in the creek that ran behind the boardinghouse, and Olivia had gladly accepted the offer.

"We'll take it all over to Mrs. Lind's creek in a bit," she told Janey. Janey nodded, agreeing.

Smiling to herself, Olivia watched as Walt finished the last area of the garden. "Imagine how our garden will look in a month, Janey, with plants and vegetables growing all over!"

Janey's eyes brightened, and she rubbed her stomach and licked her lips.

Olivia bent to Janey's level and hugged the girl. "You're getting better. I can tell. Oh Janey, you're getting better. You're happy again," she said, smoothing hair from her cousin's face, "and I imagine it won't be long before you find your voice again. It's in there somewhere, I know it."

Janey leaned over and kissed Olivia's cheek. Olivia kissed her back, then suggested that they take the churn down to the well and clean it. While they were there, Walt came over and began cleaning himself, splashing water on his face, arms, and hands.

"I'll give it one more goin' through tomorrow an' then you can start your plantin'."

Olivia thanked him, then asked if he was hungry. The stew had finished cooking long ago and was sitting in the house waiting to be eaten.

"Hungry as a starvin' horse," Walt said, grinning. He cast a glance at the barn. "Doc Schuster sure is workin' hard on somethin' in there, ain't he?"

"Yes, he is," Olivia agreed, giving the barn another suspicious look. She gathered the churn and held out her hand to Janey. "Come along then, you two. I'm hungry, too."

Walt was enjoying his second bowl of stew when all the questions in Olivia's head about what Dr. Schuster had been doing in the barn all afternoon and was still doing finally got the better of her. She excused herself from the table, saying that she was going to see if Dr. Schuster might want to join them for supper.

"Reckon that's a good thing. He's got to have worked up an appetite by now," Walt remarked.

So Olivia went to the barn.

She thought about simply knocking on the door to Dr. Schuster's room and asking if he wanted to join them for supper. But if he *was* performing an autopsy in there despite knowing that she was uncomfortable with the thought of his doing that, he might conceal the evidence before answering her knock. She wouldn't have that. She wanted to know what he was doing; as queasy as the thought made her, she wanted to *see* what he was doing, because if he was performing an autopsy, she meant to confront him about it once and for all. No autopsies in the barn as long as she and Janey lived on the homestead. And that was final.

She at first thought there might be a crack between boards through which she might sneak a peak, but after examining every board on the wall shared by Dr. Schuster's room and the barn, Olivia realized there were no openings. Whoever had built the barn had made certain of that.

After only a minute of glancing around and thinking, she decided to climb up to the loft and look down on the room. She had never been up in the loft so she had no idea if his room and the barn shared the same ceiling. But if they did she could look down on his room from the loft and see what he was doing.

She climbed the loft ladder slowly, trying to prevent creaks that might alert him to the fact that someone was in the barn with him. The animals were still out in the barnyard, enjoying the bright day, so they surely couldn't be held accountable for any noises inside the barn. Olivia reached the top ladder step, then gathered her skirts higher and crawled up onto the loft and eased her way between loose hay and bales toward the area that overlooked Dr. Schuster's room.

The barn and his room did share the same roof, she soon discovered, and she was delighted with herself for having suspected this. The loft stopped where his room began, and that was more than Olivia had hoped for; she had thought the loft would extend over his room and she would have to find a space between floorboards through which to look down on him.

Hay had found its way beneath her skirt and into her hair, and as Olivia crept forward to peer down at his room she plucked strands and tossed them aside. The hay made her itch, and it tickled her nose. She fought down several sneezes, knowing that if she didn't Dr. Schuster would hear them and glance up and discover her.

The scene Olivia stared down upon made her heart leap up into her throat.

She couldn't see him, but she heard him. He was talking to himself, and Olivia heard the words *ligaments, tendons, amputations, stumps,* and *limbs*. He mumbled other words, things Olivia could not decipher. Nor did she want to decipher them. The sight of legs and arms piled on a large table near the far wall, their ends wrapped in paper, grabbed her attention.

Where had he gotten them? she had to wonder, but she took the question no further. Somehow her mind realized that the answer might very well drive her mad.

He mumbled more words, and finally he appeared within Olivia's line of vision. He stood with his back to her at yet another table, a smaller one on which rested another leg. He appeared to study the limb for a moment, then he moved away from the table, and Olivia saw that the leg had been sliced open at the knee. She clapped her hands over her eyes before she could see more.

She sneezed unexpectedly—she hadn't even felt a tickle this time. She sneezed again and again and again . . .

"Who's there?" she heard Dr. Schuster demand through the onslaught of sneezes.

Each sneeze jolted her, seized her, drove her closer to the edge of the loft. She managed to get her feet under her, her legs still bent at the knee, and turn away from the room below. Now that he knew someone was watching him, she meant to run to the loft ladder, not crawl. So far, he didn't realize who was watching him. And she couldn't risk his finding that out, not if he spent his nights digging up graves and robbing the bodies of arms and legs—and what else was she to assume? Since she had stumbled on to his gruesome secret he might decide to do away with her, and after killing her to silence her, he might decide to take *her* arms and legs.

It was all too horrible to ponder for long. And yet her mind wanted to imagine all sorts of things.

She had to escape the loft, grab Janey, and leave this place.

"Mrs. Monroe?" He called up to her in a tone of curiosity and disbelief, facing her now, looking up at her as he held a bloody scalpel with its point out.

Olivia sneezed again, her hardest sneeze yet, and the jolt sent her sprawling right out of the loft.

She landed on his tick, thank goodness, and began sneezing worse than ever. She had to get to the door and flee. But the sneezes gripped her and made movement difficult and slow.

"What the hell are you doing *now,* Mrs. Monroe?" he demanded, drawing close. His brow was wrinkled, his eyes flashed angrily, and he still held the scalpel, point out.

"Looking for . . ." She sneezed again and managed to ease toward the edge of the tick. "Martha isn't . . ."—another sneeze—". . . in the barnyard." Sneeze. "I heard quacking and thought she might have flown up into the loft," she said in a rush.

He narrowed his eyes. "Have you been romping around in the hay up there?" He reached out and plucked several strands from her hair.

Olivia yelped and jumped back, her eyes locked on the deadly point of his scalpel.

"I won't tell anyone!" she swore, feeling her heart pound in her throat. "I'll gather Janey and our things and . . ."—she sneezed again—". . . we'll leave right away, and I won't breathe a word to anyone."

His brows drew together in a crooked line. "A word about what?"

She stared at him. "About the . . . the . . . those," she finally managed, jerking her arm at the table on which the legs rested. "I won't tell anyone I saw them, and since I have no idea where you got them, even if someone questions me I can't tell them a thing because I really don't know where you got them. I was looking for Martha because I couldn't find her in the barnyard and I searched all over and thought she might be in the loft. So I went up there and I heard noises and looked down, and there you were with—with *those*. But I don't know where you obtained them. I have no idea, and now I think I'll just . . ."

"Mrs. Monroe," he said, hunching slightly and leaning forward. His eyes sparkled, and his tone and stance were menacing. At least that was how Olivia perceived them. "Where do you think I obtained them?" His voice had lowered and it was laced with insinuation.

She swallowed. "Wh—what?"

"The arms and legs . . . Where do you think I obtained them?"

She almost wished she would sneeze again. Sneeze right in his face and make him jump back. Then she would run for the door.

"I don't know. I really don't know," she said, hearing her voice tremble.

"Come now, Mrs. Monroe. Guess."

"No, I—"

"Guess."

His lips had twisted into a grin, a mad grin, and Olivia would have bolted for the door right then and there if he hadn't still been holding the scalpel.

"From—from . . . graves?"

His grin widened. "I *chop* them, then I *cut* them, then I—"

Someone knocked on the door and pushed it open without waiting for Dr. Schuster to answer. "Hey there, Doc. Just comin' to tell you—"

"Mr. Lincoln! Oh, Mr. Lincoln!" Olivia screeched, shooting off the tick and around Dr. Schuster, nearly knocking Walt Lincoln over when she grabbed him. "Thank God you're here. Thank God. He's been robbing graves . . . digging them up . . . cutting . . . taking the legs . . . Look at the pile of them on that table! Look at that one!" she said, pointing to the leg that rested alone on the smaller table, the limb that Dr. Schuster had sliced open at the knee.

Walt stared down at her in confusion and then in disbelief. "Mrs. Monroe, why—"

She grabbed the front of Walt's shirt and gave him a

fierce look. “Mr. Lincoln, we must do something. Do something right now! It’s our civic duty. We cannot allow this—this madness to continue! We must summon the sheriff, lock him up, make certain that all of Davenport knows he has been robbing graves, dismembering bodies, and bringing the pieces here to cut them up. Mr. Lincoln, we must—”

Behind her, Dr. Schuster began chuckling. His chuckles grew into outright laughter, laughter that was so strong it doubled him over and made his eyes water. Olivia watched him in growing amazement and horror.

“There, you see?” she said, turning back to Walt Lincoln. To her complete horror, he also was grinning now.

“You’re in on this with him, aren’t you?” she demanded softly. “Oh, my God. Oh, my . . .”

“Course I am,” Walt said, laughing a little. “I find the trees he needs an’ I chop ’em down—gotta have just the right kind of wood. Then I bring ’em here an’ help him chop ’em up into smaller pieces. Then he cuts ’em an’ whittles ’em an’ works ’em into just the right shape. Then he sells ’em to docs in St. Louis an’ Chicago, docs that have patients who’re in sore need of them arms an’ legs since they’ve lost their own for one reason or another. Doc Schuster makes ’em so good you’d think they was real. But honest, Mrs. Monroe, they’re wooden.”

Olivia stared at him.

Dr. Schuster continued laughing, and he was laughing so hard now that he plopped down in a nearby chair.

Olivia almost felt like a fool. Almost. Wooden legs and arms? Fashioned for people who had lost theirs? She didn’t—couldn’t—believe it.

She glared at Dr. Schuster. “What about that other one? The one on that table?” she demanded, pointing to the leg he had sliced open at the knee. “No wooden leg looks like that on the inside.”

“That one?” Walt asked.

“Yes, that one!”

“Well, I reckon if you look at it close you’ll see how rotten it is. You’ll see why Mrs. Simpson didn’t need it no more anyway, why it might even have kilt her, in fact, if Doc hadn't taken it off. It was hurtin' her so bad, like Ida's toe was hurtin' *her* so bad last fall, Mrs. Simpson just wanted it gone, wanted it outta her sight. She sure doesn't care what Doc does with it now that she ain't plagued with it no more. He didn't rob no grave to get that leg, Mrs. Monroe, an' you gotta understand, he learns from things like this. He learns how to make those wooden legs. He's studyin', tryin' to learn how to make legs an' arms that move for people. He didn't rob no graves," Walt said again, emphasizing the point.

An onslaught of emotions hit Olivia—anger that both Walt Lincoln and Dr. Schuster were laughing at her and that Dr. Schuster had had his most marvelous time yet teasing her; embarrassment that she hadn't realized that the arms and legs on the table were *wooden* arms and legs; humiliation at having sneezed so hard that she had fallen off the loft and landed right in the middle of what was apparently not just Dr. Schuster's living quarters at the moment but also his dissection laboratory; repulsion that, before she had interrupted him, he had been dissecting a leg he had recently amputated from some woman named Mrs. Simpson.

"You never got around to askin' him if he'd like to join us for supper, eh?" Walt asked her.

"No, Mr. Lincoln, I did not," she said succinctly.

"Is *that* why you were peering at me from the loft?" Dr. Schuster queried, still grinning. "Because you wanted to ask me to join you for supper?"

"From the loft?" Walt said, scratching one temple, clearly confused.

"From the loft," Dr. Schuster confirmed.

"What were you doin' up there, Mrs. Monroe?" Walt asked.

Olivia smoothed her skirt and squared her shoulders. "Never mind."

"Uh-oh. Watch out there, Walt. She may be about to pull out that pistol."

"Dr. Schuster!" she reprimanded.

"Yes, Mrs. Monroe?"

"I told you what I was doing in the loft."

"Yes, you did. Yes, you certainly did. Walt, did you happen to spot a duck out in the barnyard?"

"Why, I sure did, Doc. Waddlin' over to the hens, who don't seem to like it none."

Olivia's face burned. "I wouldn't invite you to supper if you were the last person on earth and I needed the company, Dr. Schuster! I believe you enjoy humiliating me."

"Now, Livvy . . ."

Olivia froze at the sound of the nickname Janey had always called her. Was it a coincidence that he had called her Livvy? Or had he and Janey been talking? But that was ridiculous—Janey couldn't talk.

"She cooked some fine stew, Doc," Walt said, rubbing his belly. "An' her an' her sister made some fine butter. She even baked bread. Why, word 'round town was she didn't know how to cook. Reckon I'm off to set people straight."

Word around town . . . ? People had been talking about her, speculating that she didn't know how to cook? Didn't they have better things to do than wonder if a newcomer knew how to cook? Blast them all! She would enter that pie contest and show them that she was no different from them, that she certainly did know how to cook.

She had had quite enough humiliation and embarrassment for one day.

Walt had started out the door. He turned back. "I'll be back to turn that garden one more time t'morrow, Doc. Thanks for the bottle of medicine. It shore helped clear up that jaw ache."

"There's no need to report to Dr. Schuster about my garden, Mr. Lincoln," Olivia said rather impertinently. The anger, embarrassment, humiliation, and repulsion were all too much. And now, on top of those feelings lay extreme curiosity and uneasiness about Dr. Schuster's use of the nickname Janey had always called her: was it merely a coincidence?

A thought suddenly hit her. She had told John that her garden area needed plowing, and Charlotte had apparently told Homer. But how had Walt known?

"Mr. Lincoln, how did you learn that I wanted an area tilled for a garden?"

"Why, Doc told me," Walt said as Dr. Schuster screwed up his face and shook his head at Mr. Lincoln. "If I'm havin' a problem an' he comes callin', I give him meat now an' then when I get around to butchering one of the stock. But this time, for payment, he said you was—"

"We'll see you tomorrow afternoon, then, Walt," Dr. Schuster interrupted, rushing forth to urge Walt to leave. But he was too late. Olivia already knew what Walt had been about to say.

"He said I needed someone to plow my garden?"

"Yep. Doc here, he cares about everybody. But he was pretty upset that you got out there an' tried to dig that ground by yourself. Real proud—said you had more determination an' spirit about you than any other woman in Iowa, exceptin' Ida—but real upset. Said you had blisters all over your hands."

"More determination and spirit . . . ?" Olivia had lifted both brows.

"That's what he said. Meant it, too."

"Did he?" Olivia had lowered her voice and fixed a wondering gaze on Dr. Schuster.

"He did," Alan said, dipping his head. "And I give you a fine example . . . Not many women, even Iowa women, would climb up to a loft to spy on someone below."

Olivia made a sound of exasperation in her throat. She grabbed one side of her skirt and spun around, heading for the door. She had started to soften a little where he was concerned, feeling touched that he would compliment her to Walt. Then he had decided to tease her again.

"I was not spying, Dr. Schuster," she said smartly, her cheeks burning with color.

She left the barn in a huff, cut between chickens in the barnyard, and marched straight for the house, slamming the door after she crossed the threshold. Janey was sitting on the floor before the hearth, playing with the rag dolls Ida had given her.

"I swear, Janey, I've never lost my temper more with

anyone than I lose it with Dr. Schuster," Olivia said, crossing her arms and plopping down into a chair. "Of course, I've never had anyone tease me the way he does."

Janey gave her a little smile and went back to playing with her dolls.

After Walt left, Alan washed his hands over the basin he kept in his room, dressed himself in fresh clothing, and headed for the house. Along the way he plucked a small white flower from the ground, wondering if he could talk Olivia into offering him a bowl of her stew despite her having said she wouldn't invite him to supper if he were the last person on earth and she needed company. He smiled, remembering her indignation, that way she had of huffing up her chest, lifting her chin, setting her jaw, and looking like a ruffled hen.

He had never seen anything as funny as the shock on her face when he had acted the part of the mad doctor—a grave robber, at that. At that point he had thought the overly curious Olivia Monroe had needed to be taught a lesson. So she had decided to climb up to the loft and spy on him, had she? She hadn't counted on something up there making her sneeze uncontrollably. She hadn't counted on falling over the side of the loft and onto his bed. And she certainly hadn't counted on coming face to face with the mad doctor, who just happened to have his scalpel in hand. When Alan realized that she thought the wooden arms and legs were real, cut from freshly dug-up victims, he hadn't been able to resist—he had played the role in which she had cast him to the hilt, fighting laughter, trying to affect an insane look. And she had fallen for it, fallen completely.

The skirmish this afternoon between John and Homer and then between John, Homer, and himself was even rather humorous now, hours removed. He had thought Homer showing up shortly after John to plow Olivia's garden area downright comical, and really, his own landing in the dirt rolling around with Homer and John after he tried to break up their fight was comical, too. What wasn't comical was the thinking he had done after returning to his room. It had made him grow serious about the entire subject of Olivia Monroe—herself, her sister, and all five of her animals.

John and Homer had been scampering around for days, unable to do Olivia's bidding fast enough. Certainly neither had been able to get his plow to the homestead fast enough upon learning that she needed a little tilling done. But then, he was scampering around himself where she was concerned, wasn't he? At least, in his own way he was. Instead of taking Walt up on his offer of meat this winter in exchange for medical services, he had asked if Walt would mind doing some plowing for Mrs. Monroe.

He was not going to act like John and Homer, groveling and fighting for that woman's attention, for any woman's attention, or so he had grumbled at himself during the hours immediately proceeding the skirmish. But inside . . . secretly he was pleased that she had chosen Walt to plow for her since Walt had been his choice, and that thought had surprised him since he had never made a conscious decision to vie with John and Homer for her attention.

But why couldn't he? And why shouldn't he? He didn't intend to make a fool of himself as he thought they were doing, but for a number of years now he had wanted to marry and start a family, although he wouldn't settle for just any woman. He wanted someone to love, cherish and trust—beyond anything, to trust—and after one lengthy courtship that had ended in disaster, he had resigned himself to waiting until that special woman came along.

Well, perhaps Olivia Monroe was that special woman. Stubborn, determined, and with a knack for finding trouble . . . but perhaps she was the woman he had been waiting for. He had spent these past hours wondering about that as he dissected the joint of the leg, searching for more secrets and clues about how it worked and how it could be reconstructed.

Knocking on his own door seemed odd, but the house was rented out to Olivia right now, and knocking was common courtesy. She opened the door a moment later and stood looking at him, appearing fresh as a spring flower in a dress of yellow-and-white gingham. She had braided her hair to one side, and the long golden plait hung nearly to her waist, ending in a curl just below a white ribbon. Her bright eyes sparkled in the evening light; to the west the colors of sunset melted low across the sky.

Alan held out the flower to her. "Could we call a truce if I apologize for playing such a dirty trick on the woman who fell down from heaven into my room earlier this evening?"

She studied him for a moment, finally unable to resist a slight smile. She plucked the flower from his hand, lifted it to her nose, and inhaled.

"I *was* spying on you," she admitted. "And I must say, now that I've considered it, it was funny that I mistook those wooden legs for real ones."

He nodded. "Yes, it was."

"I felt so silly. I still feel silly. I came here and kept asking myself, 'how could you have done that, Olivia? How?' It was so obvious once I really looked at them that they were made of wood. But that real one . . ." She put the fingers of one hand to her throat. "How can you do that, Dr. Schuster?" she almost whispered, glancing over her shoulder, probably to make sure Janey wasn't anywhere close, listening. "You cut up body parts? Body parts that have been amputated?"

"It's the nature of my profession, Mrs. Monroe. A friend in St. Louis teaches at a medical college there, where cadavers are in ready supply and body parts can be studied daily. Out here, I don't have that luxury. If someone is in unfortunate health and requires an amputation, why not take the opportunity to study the limb? The more I study the human body, the better. My knowledge of treating ailments and of performing surgery increases every time I study a cadaver or part of a body. A difficult thing for you to understand, Mrs. Monroe, but I could show you a list of surgeries I've done that I perfected on a cadaver before deciding to perform them on a living person."

"I suppose, Dr. Schuster," she said, having paled somewhat. "Still, I don't know how anyone has the stomach for such things."

"Speaking of stomachs, I was wondering if you had any more of that stew . . ."

She broke into a smile and stepped aside. "Of course I do. Come in and have a bowl."

Alan walked into the house and glanced around. He hadn't been inside the house since the afternoon she had burned the food, and he entered the house now in an entirely different state of mind than he had been in that day. Tonight he entered the house feeling curious, wondering what a woman's touch—specifically Olivia Monroe's touch—had done for it.

CHAPTER ✤ ✤ ✤ ELEVEN

OLIVIA MONROE HAD been busy brightening and cheering up his home. She had hung fresh new curtains, a light shade of blue, tied back with strips of blue-and-white-checked material. She had arranged his beige sofa and the settle that Homer had made for him on opposite sides of the hearth, tossed a braided rug on the floor between them, and placed his two small side tables on either side of the sofa. Several leather-bound books lay on one of the tables, and Janey's slate and a reader sat on the other. Alan's two chairs with their backs carved out like fiddles, gifts from Ida (who rarely gave gifts), now sat near the windows on either side of the fireplace. A knitted throw—red, orange, green, and brown—had been tossed over the arm of one chair, and on the floor to one side of the other chair a collection of what looked like dried apples and reddish brown sticks filled a large woven basket. Near that sat a basket filled with toys—rag dolls, wooden wagons and horses, strings of colorful beads . . .

The air inside the house smelled of cinnamon, and beneath that smell were others: freshly baked bread, pungent spices, Olivia's perfume—the light scent of roses. In the kitchen area, potatoes, carrots, and ears of dried corn filled other baskets, and another braided rug decorated the floor there, too.

Alan found himself wondering about the bedrooms and whether Olivia had worked her magic there, too, and made them as warm and inviting as she had made the rest of the house. Doubtless she had.

The thought struck him that this was no longer just a house, it was a *home.* A place where a family could gather around the hearth and visit or engage in some activity that might draw them closer together—read a book or simply sit and talk about hopes and dreams. Meals could be shared here. Children could be shared here.

"I know you're not used to seeing it look like this," Olivia said uncomfortably, hurrying over to tidy the knitted throw. "The house, that is. I plan to change it all back when Janey and I leave. I remember how it was, and I'll arrange all the furniture, everything, back the way it was when we came."

"I like it now," Alan said.

Olivia turned around and gazed at him as if he'd lost his mind. "What? That night . . ." She clasped her hands in front of her. "You hated it. You were angry that I moved your furniture."

"I was angry that someone was living in my house without my knowledge. I was angry that nothing was familiar. I'd just spent weeks traveling, spending days and nights among unfamiliar things," he explained. He waved a hand, encompassing the room. "But this is not unfamiliar. You've taken the same furnishings and just . . . dressed them and the room up. Yes, it was familiar before you changed everything. But it was also dull. Now it's not just a house. It's a home."

She looked surprised for a few seconds. Then she beamed, breaking into a wide smile, her eyes sparkling. "I'm relieved that you like it," she said, and her eyes made a circle around the room. "Ida gave us the dried apples and cinnamon. One of the church ladies brought us the throw. The curtains . . . I made the curtains—"

"You did?"

She nodded happily. "I do stitch a fine seam. I might not have learned to cook while I was growing up—although I definitely learned the art of snatching food from under the cook's nose—but I learned to sew and embroider."

"Ah. Speaking of cooking . . ."

"The stew," she said, and hurried toward the stove.

Janey emerged from the bedroom, and when she spotted

Alan, her face brightened, and she smiled. She hurried over to him, took him by the hand, and led him to the sofa, where she urged him to sit. There, she picked up the slate and began to write.

"Writing me another message?" he asked, teasing her a little.

Nodding, Janey caught her bottom lip between her teeth and drew letters.

"She's been writing you messages?" Olivia asked, freezing with a pot lid in hand.

The alarm edging her voice surprised Alan. Why would she be alarmed by Janey's writing him messages? Well, she actually had written him only one message, thanking him for saving Olivia from what she had thought was a fire. But Olivia's strange tone prompted Alan to make the quick decision not to tell her that. Deceptive of him, but he had questions to ask her about Janey anyway, and if she thought that Janey had already been telling him about herself, perhaps Olivia would explain Janey's inability to speak without his having to prompt her.

"Yes, she has," Alan said, catching and holding Olivia's gaze.

She opened her mouth, glanced down at the lid, inhaled, then pursed her lips, as if stopping whatever she had been about to say. "I see. I'll get your stew." And she busied herself doing that.

She turned cool after that, aloof and preoccupied.

She served him a bowl of stew, placing it on the table for him along with a plate containing several slices of bread. Nearby sat another plate on which rested a small mound of butter.

"Is this the bread and butter you made?" he asked, trying to be friendly. "The bread and butter Walt raved about?"

She nodded, and went off to one of the bedrooms while Janey settled in the chair opposite him. He was beginning to sense adoration or something akin to adoration from the girl, and he considered it cute and sweet.

Olivia returned from the bedroom moments later, went to

a tub that sat atop a small cabinet, and began washing pots. She had her back to Alan and Janey.

"This is good stew," he told Janey, and she nodded, agreeing.

She had brought the basket of toys with her to the table, and she pulled out numerous wooden blocks in which capital letters had been carved on each of their four faces. She began arranging the blocks, and he watched and continued eating as she did. From where he sat the letters were upside-down, but he made them out easily enough. When her little project—(which Alan suspected was huge for her)—was complete, she had spelled *LIVVY ANGRY.*

Alan raised his brow. He hadn't considered her angry. He had considered her uncomfortable. But then, Janey knew her much better than he did. He hardly knew Olivia Monroe at all. "Is she?" he queried in a low voice.

Janey nodded.

"Why?"

She shrugged. Then she twisted her mouth and shook her head as if she was not happy with her sister's anger. Not happy with it at all.

"Who made the blocks for you?" Alan asked as quietly as possible. Olivia seemed oblivious so far to his "conversation" with Janey, and he wanted to keep it that way, though he doubted that Olivia could hear them anyway above the clanging of pots.

Very slowly, concentrating by intermittently clasping her lips together, Janey spelled *HARRY.*

"Who is Harry?" He didn't know anyone locally by the name of Harry. Was Harry someone from Olivia and Janey's past in Boston? Perhaps Harry was Olivia's deceased husband.

DRIVER, Janey spelled.

"In Boston?"

NO.

"Where?"

She studied the blocks, wrinkling her brow and nose, twisting her lips, then finally trying a number of combinations: *FILLU, FELLA, FILADEL, FILADELFIA.*

Alan sounded out the last combination several times, finally coming up with, "Philadelphia?"

"Janey, what are you doing?" Olivia demanded in a hoarse whisper, now standing near the table. He and Janey had been so engrossed in their questions and answers that they hadn't heard Olivia approach.

Janey shrank back as if she had done some terrible thing. Alan glanced at Olivia, at her pale face and at her hands which gripped a dishrag so tight that her joints had gone white.

"Put the blocks away, Janey," Olivia said, her tone less harsh now—as if the acuteness of her shock had eased a little. "Go put the basket back where it belongs."

"What's wrong?" Alan asked, wanting to see how Olivia would react. "She was only spelling words for me."

"I think it's time we milked the cows and put the chickens and other animals to bed," Olivia told Janey. "After you put the basket away, change your dress, Janey, so you don't soil your nice one. I'll be along to do the same in a moment."

Rather unhappily—her entire face drooped—Janey piled the blocks back into the basket, then went off to put the basket back in its proper place. Once she had disappeared into the bedroom, Olivia rounded the table and settled her alarmed gaze on Alan.

"Why were you questioning her?"

"They weren't questions beyond the ordinary—who made the blocks for her, for example, and when she spelled Harry, I asked who Harry was. Natural curiosity, since no one by the name of Harry resides in Scott County. Why do innocent questions make you nervous?"

"They don't," she said, and her gaze skittered off for a second, then back.

"Mrs. Monroe . . . they make you extremely nervous. Anyone could see that," Alan remarked gently.

"I do not want you questioning her. I do not want anyone questioning her. Janey had a difficult life up until the time we came here. I want—"

"What does *Janey* want? A friend?"

Olivia cocked her head and lifted her chin, preparing for a fight. "I am Janey's friend."

"She befriended me because she thinks I saved her sister's life," Alan said. "I'm concerned about her, that's all. She hears yet she doesn't speak. There's nothing abnormal about her mouth or throat that I can see, no growths or abnormal presentation of the structure of the vocal cords. She's—"

"You examined her?" Olivia demanded, paling again. "You examined her without my consent?"

Alan studied her, watching her grip the material harder, watching her tense so much that every bone in her neck became prominent. "I examined her with *her* consent."

"You had no right to—"

"You are her guardian?"

"Yes!"

"You have legal documentation of that?"

She stared at him for a long moment, more alarm filling her eyes. "You have no right. Don't do this. Please, don't do this. I act in Janey's best interest. I—"

"No. You don't. For some reason Janey doesn't talk. Instead of wanting a physician to examine her to see if the problem can be corrected, you—"

"She's been examined by enough physicians!"

Olivia had become thoroughly agitated, her hands wildly twisting her skirt, her eyes bright and frightened.

Alan decided to proceed more gently.

"Janey didn't mind the examination. Olivia, if she had resisted, even by shaking her head no once, I wouldn't have proceeded. She didn't."

"I don't remember giving you permission to use my first name," Olivia said, and Alan shook his head in disbelief. Not even a gentle approach was effective with her where Janey was concerned.

"I'm not going to bite you or Janey," he tried to assure Olivia. "I didn't ask questions, nor will I ever ask questions, with harmful intent. I'm concerned."

"Don't be," she said, her voice hoarse again.

She hurried from the table, opened a door to one of the bedrooms, and fled inside.

Alan started to follow her, not liking the fact that she had run away. He stopped himself, however; given her hostility toward him and the fact that she seemed panicky and frightened right now, this was clearly a bad time to approach her.

Why? he wondered. Why would his concern with Janey's inability to speak frighten Olivia to the point of hostility? She had almost seemed like an animal backed into a corner by a predator. Only he wasn't a predator. He was a concerned physician. And Janey's inability to speak warranted his professional attention.

Janey didn't come to the barn with Olivia to help clean up after the animals and settle them in for the night. Alan came out and began milking Eleanor before Olivia could get to the chore, and although she gave him a sour look when he started, she thanked him afterward without looking at him.

"Has Janey ever spoken?" he asked, handing her the pail of milk.

She took it from him in silence, refusing to answer his question, refusing even to acknowledge the question. When she turned away and started to walk off, Alan wanted to grab her arm and turn her back around. But he resisted that urge, knowing that forcing her to face him might be the worst thing he could do at this point. He sensed that Olivia would have to make up her own mind to talk to him about Janey, and that an attempt to force her might make her all the more determined not to. Dealing with Olivia was frustrating, extremely so. Especially where Janey was concerned.

"I won't ask her any more questions," Alan told Olivia. "But you surely can't mean to not ever permit Janey in the barn again just because I'm here."

At least that remark affected her. Olivia stopped in her tracks, hesitated, then walked on.

Homer and John showed up together a few days later to plant Olivia's garden. Alan wasn't sure how that had come about—if they had come to an understanding on their own or if Olivia had scolded them for fighting over her that afternoon and told them that if they thought they could be civil toward each other they could plant the garden for her.

After they finished the planting, Olivia invited them into the house, and when Alan saw that, he clamped his jaw shut so hard he nearly bit his tongue. John and Homer had *fought* over her, caused a commotion that Ida had assured him only this morning was still being batted around town and laughed about, and yet they had been invited back; they were about to gather around the table with her and Janey right now, where *he* wanted to be. He . . . he had asked Janey a few harmless questions, then expressed concern to Olivia about Janey, and because of his professional concern she had turned a cold shoulder on him and had not spoken to him since. It was absurd. Crazy, mad . . . ridiculous!

He thought repeatedly about cornering her one evening in the barn but quickly decided against that. Bullying her certainly wouldn't make her talk to him. It would only make her withdraw more, he felt certain.

During ensuing mornings he milked the cow and gathered eggs for her before leaving to call on patients. It was an act of good faith to let her know in a subtle way that he only wanted to help her. Yet in the beginning he knew that Olivia might react in one of two ways: she might tell him not to milk the cow and gather the eggs anymore, that she didn't need or want his help, or she might silently accept his help, still refusing to say a word to him. He almost wished she would object. At least then she would be talking to him.

He soon discovered himself trying to finish with patients early enough so that he would be home, in the barn, when Olivia came to clean up after the animals and settle them in for the night. He liked hearing her soft voice, even if she was talking to the animals and not to him. Although of course he would have preferred that she talk to him.

One afternoon he was walking through town, having just finished stitching Charlotte's finger—she had almost sliced the digit clean off—when he spotted Olivia busily arranging her packaged butter, baskets of eggs, and fruits and vegetables in a wagon that was parked at the corner of Front and Ripley Streets. Alan was amazed by the sight. Not only had she not had time to grow fruit trees (oranges, lemons, peaches, and apples), but no vegetable garden could produce that fast. Unless, of course, he had accidentally slept through the growing for a month or two, and he was fairly certain he hadn't. A group of women were already picking over Olivia's goods and bargaining with her about prices. Janey sat on a nearby overturned crate, munching on a peach, juice dripping down her chin.

"Good afternoon, Mrs. Monroe," Alan said, approaching with a grin of amazement on his face. "Where in the world did you come by the fruit and vegetables?"

With customers gathering around her wagon and delighting in the selection, she couldn't possibly think of ignoring one of Davenport's leading citizens.

"Dr. Schuster, isn't this marvelous?" Caroline Brewster asked, approaching him. Lydia Crane and Rebecca Lawrence also fluttered close, their faces alive with color.

"Indeed it is," he responded.

"Good afternoon, Doctor," Olivia said, greeting him with subtle coolness.

"I'll tell you where she came by them," Hank Shears, one of Davenport's leading merchants, growled, barreling up the street to the wagon, his belly flopping around in front of him. "She bought 'em out from under me. Right out from under me! I got word last week that there was a shipment of fruit coming upriver on the *Brazil*. Didn't know what day it was coming, just knew it was coming. Then this morning I saw the ship docked at the landing and when I went down there, all the fruit had been bought, lock, stock, and barrel. It was meant for my store, and she bought it out from under me. Now here she sits on the corner with her wagon, bold as brass!" Hank grabbed an orange, tossed it on the ground, and squashed it under his heavy boot. Then he glared at Olivia.

Her jaw dropped open. "The fruit was for sale to anyone."

"Hank, that's no decent way to act," Alan said, feeling

hair rise on the back of his neck. "You owe Mrs. Monroe the cost of that orange."

Now Hank's jaw dropped open. "Whose side are you on, Doc? Not hers! Why, she comes prancing into town with her high ways . . . Probably spent time with the captain of the ship, charming him the way she's been charming Homer and John. She probably did more to get him to—"

"That's enough, Hank," Alan warned. He had no way of knowing whether or not Olivia had done such a thing, but Hank's behavior and accusations on the street corner, in front of Olivia's customers, were inappropriate. He should at least wait and take up the matter with her in private. Besides, Alan wasn't sure if he really believed that Olivia had "charmed" Homer and John. The two of them were starved for the attention of an unattached woman; both wanted to marry and have families.

"Probably spent the night with him or something," Hank growled.

Caroline, Lydia, and Rebecca gasped. Behind the wagon Olivia's face flushed. She tipped her head and narrowed her eyes, and Alan knew she would not stand idly by while Hank insulted her further. Neither would Alan, for that matter. Hank's lewd accusation not only shocked him, it angered him.

"You now owe Mrs. Monroe an apology, too," he told Hank.

"I don't owe her anything! She stole that shipment right out from under my nose!"

"Hank, apologize!"

"I won't!"

Alan didn't have the belly Hank did, but he was not small when compared to the other men in town. He stood six feet tall, and he was solid from riding every day to call on patients all over the county. Hank had a mean look in his eye, one that suggested that he might like to pull Olivia from behind her wagon and throttle her, woman or no woman, and on top of that threat he had ruined one of her oranges, made ugly insinuations about her and the *Brazil*'s captain, and refused to apologize. The look in his eyes didn't intimidate

Alan in the least; if anything it made him ball his fist all the harder when he raised it and popped Hank square across the jaw, sending him sprawling into the street.

The women gasped again. Behind her wagon Olivia said, "Oh, my God!" Hank rubbed his jaw and stared at Alan in disbelief as shouts rang out, and a crowd began to gather nearby in the street.

"I'll be bringing charges against you for that, Doc!" Hank shouted, having no dignity left.

Alan nodded coolly. "You do that. But you'd better know, Hank, that if I catch you around Mrs. Monroe's wagon insulting her again and destroying her merchandise, the same thing will happen each time. Go home now, and on the way reconsider apologizing and paying her for that orange."

"He defended her virtue!" Lydia said, her head of brown curls bobbing with excitement as she turned to her friends and repeated the announcement several times. They made excited faces and remarked about how heroic the doctor was.

Behind her wagon, Olivia blushed profusely. "You didn't need to do that," she whispered loudly to Alan. "I was prepared to defend myself."

Alan held up a hand, palm out, to stop further objections. "How well I know that you can defend yourself, Mrs. Monroe. But according to my standards, I did need to do that."

She said nothing more. For whatever reason—the thought to do so just struck him—he pulled a handkerchief from his pocket and handed it to Janey, who had stopped eating to stare at the scene that had just been played out in front of her. "Peach juice is sticky when it dries," he said, smiling.

Then he walked off, continuing on his way to the homestead.

The crowd that had gathered to watch Alan defend Olivia's honor lingered even after Hank stumbled off rubbing his jaw and Dr. Schuster walked off down the street whistling, toting the medical bag he had dropped in favor of hitting the insulting man. Olivia stared off after him, feeling shocked that Hank Shears had attempted to defame her in such a way, that anyone would, and that Alan Schuster had, indeed, defended her virtue. He was suddenly a hero in her eyes, too, and that was a startling thought, considering how their acquaintance in Davenport had begun, with his wanting her and Janey out of his house, and with his and Olivia's quarrels over the animals, his autopsies and dissections in the barn room, and Janey's inability to speak.

Olivia forced herself to pay attention to her business when people began approaching again to buy fruit and vegetables, and during the course of the afternoon she sold a good amount of butter and lots of eggs, too. By late afternoon, when she elected to quit for the day and take the wagon home, she was pleasantly exhausted.

Ida came by as Olivia was hitching the wagon to the horse she had bought from Mr. Brewster only yesterday afternoon, and she gave Olivia a proud look and a wink across the wagon. "Did some fine bus'ness t'day, I see. An' Doc helped ya out, from what I hear."

Olivia gave her a tired smile. Then she shook her head in amazement. "I guess I owe him a thank-you."

"Ya guess?" Ida croaked. "I reckon ya do owe 'im that. Wasn't gonna stand for Hank insultin' ya that way, eh? Doc might jes' be gettin' a little soft in the heart for ya."

"Ida," Olivia scolded. Earlier she had set some of her baskets on the ground because she couldn't display all the fruits and vegetables in the wagon. Janey was now lifting a basket of corn to return it to the wagon. The elderly woman stumped over to her and offered her several pieces of hard candy, which Janey eagerly accepted after carefully lowering her basket.

Ida rapped her cane on one corner of Olivia's wagon and narrowed one eye at Olivia. "Don't growl at me fer givin' the girl what she deserves for a hard day's work. She was right here helpin' ya, I heard. Countin' out money an' gettin' yer customers things they needed. I'd say she deserves more'n two pieces of candy fer a day like that!"

"Oh, I wasn't objecting to you giving Janey candy," Olivia assured the woman.

Ida studied her. "That bus'ness 'bout Doc Schuster, then," she said finally. "Might jes' be the truth of things, y'know. An' if Doc's got 'is eyes set on ya, Homer an' John can go to the devil—Doc'll have ya."

Olivia lifted a brow. "Do my feelings enter into this at all?"

More studying. "Well now, we both know we're women with backbone, women who can get on by ourselves in a place where it ain't easy fer a woman to get on by 'erself. But bein' women we get a itch fer males from time to time, too, an' I'd say Doc Schuster might jes' be a good choice fer scratchin' that itch."

Olivia coughed, choking on shock. "I don't"—she coughed again—"recall ever having an itch that needed scratching, Ida," she said in a low voice as she glanced around to see if anyone was within hearing distance. Across the street a man on a ladder was whitewashing a newly constructed building. People passed back and forth in front of the building, but none seemed interested in stopping to have a look at Olivia's remaining fruit and vegetables or to listen to her conversation with Ida.

"I reckon ya have," Ida disputed. "Ya've been raised so proper-like ya wouldn't admit it fer nothin'. If circumstances was right, ya might. High moon, nice music, maybe a few crickets goin' here 'n' there. Ain't nothin' stoppin' a body when the situation's right an' the mood strikes."

Olivia had the horse hitched and all the baskets loaded in the wagon now. Her face was scalding, and she didn't think the warmth of the day had a thing to do with the heat. Ida knew few limits when it came to decency, and she had shocked Olivia almost to the point of mortification.

"I believe we're ready," Olivia said, taking Janey by the hand and leading her to the wagon. She hoisted the girl up onto the seat, bade Ida a good evening, then climbed up herself, took the reins, and clicked the horse into motion. She heard Ida cackle behind them, and Olivia could not keep from shaking her head and smiling a little.

"She likes to shock me," she said aloud to herself. "She really likes to shock me.

"Doc might jes' be gettin' a little soft in the heart fer ya." Olivia pondered that as she guided the horse along the street, stopping once to allow a mother and her small son to pass. She didn't know if Dr. Schuster had gone "soft in the heart" for her, as Ida had said, but Olivia had certainly seen flashes of desire for her in his eyes during the times she had found herself alone in the barn with him. When their fingers and hands had touched, sparks of excitement had shot through her, and she had glanced up during those times to find his eyes becoming smoky and, in her mind, dangerous.

Finding herself alone with him at times, even if it was in a barn filled with animals, was dangerous in itself, not to mention improper. She had been raised to observe certain proprieties—that an unmarried girl never went out unescorted, for instance, and never, ever placed herself in a compromising position. But since coming to Iowa Territory, in her quest for complete independence and survival, she had unconsciously thrown out any and all rules. For one thing, she had allowed John and Homer to call on her without the benefit of a chaperone. Of course, Janey had always been present, but Janey was a child, not an adult female. Olivia had never felt awkward or uncomfortable around Homer or John. She had never felt sparks of excitement when they simply touched her arm or drew near to her. But she felt sparks when Alan Schuster simply touched her arm or drew near.

She had never even considered before she had become so aware of the attraction between herself and Dr. Schuster—before Dr. Schuster had come along—that she had disregarded the rules with which she had been raised regarding unmarried men and herself, an unmarried woman. A woman who had *never* been married. She had never even considered, in her panic over learning that the doctor had returned and that she and Janey might again be looking for a place in which to live, that having him live in the barn while she lived in the house was improper. She had placed herself in a very compromising position, especially given the fact that there undeniably was attraction between her and Dr. Schuster. An "itch," as Ida would call it.

There was no good solution to the dilemma. She and Janey needed to live in the house right now, and he needed to live in the barn room. And this is not Philadelphia, Olivia reminded herself. As Charlotte might have said had she known Olivia's thoughts, *"You're not in Boston anymore,"* and she would have told her how things were different out here in Iowa from back East.

The way of life was different here because everything was new. The people who arrived by way of wagon and steamer were, in many ways, just like her; they were opportunists, desperate newcomers filled with hopes and dreams. People here didn't care about what was proper and what wasn't. And subconsciously, Olivia had already realized that, all the way back in Pittsburgh. While it had shocked her at first, it had also made her realize that possibilities were endless in the West. That was why she and Charlotte had quarreled the day after Olivia had arrived in Davenport, when Charlotte had tried to convince her to return to the East by implying that there were few possibilities for women out here. Charlotte was wrong. There were possibilities, endless ones. In Philadelphia Olivia wouldn't have considered standing on a corner selling fruit and vegetables from behind a wagon. The thought wouldn't even have entered her mind.

He's not getting soft in the heart for me, she thought. *He's not. He simply knows there's something different about me and Janey. He knows we're hiding something, and he's determined to find out what. He's determined to learn why Janey doesn't talk, and he's determined to help her.*

The last part of that, his apparent determination to help Janey, was slowly but surely melting Olivia's resolve, but it also scared her. She sensed that his desire to help was genuine. He milked Eleanor and gathered the eggs almost every morning now, and his handing Janey his handkerchief this afternoon to wipe the peach juice from her chin had been a small but sweet thing. Still, a little voice, the voice of fear, always warned Olivia that no one, absolutely no one, could be trusted with her and Janey's deepest secrets. That Janey had stopped talking the night of her mother's death and that shortly afterward Uncle Edward had begun his drunken rages that became more and more frequent over the next year. That she—Olivia—suspected there was a definite reason why Janey did not talk and that that reason led a straight path back to Uncle Edward, whom Olivia had either murdered or further enraged the night she and Janey fled Philadelphia. If Dr. Schuster helped Janey, somehow made her talk again, would Janey not spill some of their troubled background? She had already mentioned Harry. Why oh why had Edna decided to pack those blocks for Janey anyway? Of course she knew the answer—it was because Edna knew that Janey used them to communicate sometimes, that Janey loved them. And Edna had no idea they could cause trouble.

You'll have to deal with all your ugly secrets one day, Olivia, the voice warned. *Hiding them is impossible.*

But not yet. She would keep Dr. Schuster away from Janey as long as possible. She and Janey had a strong start here in Davenport, and she wasn't going to allow that to be destroyed by Dr. Schuster's curiosity. She wasn't going to allow him to ask Janey any more questions.

CHAPTER
❖ ❖ ❖
TWELVE

INDEPENDENCE DAY WAS celebrated in homes and on the streets of Davenport by a mixture of both wild and decent citizens. But just as Olivia had realized that there were no rules of propriety governing Iowa Territory, she thought her definition of decent might be far different from the next person's. So long as no one made lewd remarks or troubled her and Janey in an offensive way, she meant for them to enjoy the public celebration. With that thought she laughed a little, turned her face up to the sun for a moment, then went off to sit beside Charlotte and Janey on a quilt they had spread on the grass in front of Charlotte's boardinghouse, where they meant to watch the parade that would be along soon.

And soon enough, there was Ida leading the procession from her seat atop a wagon trimmed with red, white, and blue banners. Even she and the harnesses were trimmed with the colors, and when Ida lifted her cane and waved it at the crowd of people that had come from all over Scott County, Olivia saw that it was trimmed with multicolored ribbon, too, and she laughed. Ida tossed little bundles of candy to the children, although adults occasionally reached up and snatched bundles out of the air. Whenever that happened, Ida growled and waved her cane at the adults.

"Hell, Ida, I like candy, too!" one man shouted.

"Watch yer mouth, Zeke Jackson," Ida shouted right back. She waved her cane, motioning all around him. "Young'uns ever'where. Give that boy there a piece or two!"

Zeke did, but not before he scowled at Ida. She just cackled, then turned her attention toward the sack of bundled candy that sat next to her on the wagon seat.

Behind Ida came several painted clowns. One danced over to Janey, waved a handkerchief in front of her, then made a circle with his thumb and forefinger and pushed the handkerchief down into it. When he pulled the handkerchief through the circle and shook it out, a gray bird fluttered out of it. Janey laughed with delight, and Olivia silently marveled, not for the first time, at how wonderful Davenport had been for Janey and herself. The clown tweaked Janey's nose, then plucked a cloth daisy from his sleeve and handed it to Olivia. She glanced into the clown's eyes and realized that it was Homer behind the greasepaint and the silly red, white, and blue clothes. She laughed at him as he pretended to trip over his large shoes. Then he sped off to entertain other children and adults.

A small brass band, complete with trumpets, trombones, and a large drum, came through, playing *Yankee Doodle Dandy*. To Olivia's surprise, Dr. Schuster was playing one of the two trombones, and he playfully marched over to her and Janey and slid the instrument in and out, giving the tune flair and making Olivia and Janey laugh more. Then he rejoined the band as it marched on down the street.

There were more clowns, followed by a division of non-uniformed troops that, according to Charlotte, had been thrown together to protect an area of land along the Missouri–Iowa border that Missourians claimed as their own and Iowans would defend as *their* own.

After the parade, guns blasted and people shouted wildly up and down the street. The pie-baking contest was held in the tent that housed the First Presbyterian Church on Brimstone Corner, and while Charlotte won the contest hands down, Olivia watched with delight as the four judges—Homer among them—tasted her apple pie and made favorable remarks about it.

By now she was pleased with almost every aspect of her own life and Janey's in Iowa. They had made a fine start here; they had been in Davenport for little more than a month, and during that month they had found a decent home in which to live, at least for the immediate future; Janey was happier; Olivia had learned an acceptable amount about cooking; and she had learned, through the sale of their butter, eggs, fruit, and vegetables that there was definitely enough room for another store in Davenport. The day she had purchased the horse from Mr. Brewster he had been in a talkative mood, and he had remarked that a certain saloon owner was interested in selling the lot on which his establishment stood because he wanted to move on, and Olivia had decided right then and there to talk to the proprietor and find out how much he was asking for the property. If she purchased the land, she would have an establishment built for her and Janey, and she would have a second story added in which she and Janey could live. A small barn and barnyard out back would house Edwin, Annie, Eleanor, Martha, and the hog that Olivia had since named Elmor. (It had taken her nearly a week of getting to know him before she had thought of a name for him.)

Slices of the many pies were sold after the judging was complete, and the money went into a fund that would be used for the building of a schoolhouse.

"Which one's yers, Mrs. Monroe?" John Brimmer asked, having put away his rifle. (He had been among the Iowa men who had helped protect and preserve the southern border.)

"Why, Mr. Brimmer, need you ask?" Olivia teased.

He shrank back a little. "I jus' . . . see, I thought . . . Fact is, there's so many pies. Ye're right, I oughtta know but I don't. So if you'll jus' give me a little hint about the general direction, I reckon I'll find it from there."

"There's no more. Not a slice," Homer said, approaching with a scowl on his clown's face.

"Why don't ya go wash that paint off an' change yer clothes, Homer, so ya don't look so silly?" John suggested.

"I'm s'posed to look silly," Homer shot back rather indignantly.

After the argument and fisticuffs over who was going to plow her garden, Olivia had arranged to have Homer and

John meet her at Charlotte's boardinghouse, where she had managed to convince the two men to put their differences aside; she didn't want them fighting over her. In fact, she *hated* the thought of them fighting over her. They were friends before she arrived in Davenport, she had told them, and friends they would remain, despite her presence, or she'd have nothing to do with either of them. She would absolutely have nothing to do with either of them as long as she knew they were fighting over her, she had added. If they wanted to seed her garden, she didn't mind that at all, but they would seed it together, there would be no harsh or sarcastic words between them, and afterward they would share supper with her and Janey. Sharing her was better than not having her at all, apparently, because both men had shown up the next afternoon to seed, and they had both stayed for supper, too.

"Every slice of my pie is gone?" Olivia asked Homer in disbelief.

He nodded, his clown's bow bobbing up and down under his chin. "Every slice. Doc Schuster bought the whole thing. Leastwise, that's what Mrs. Evans just told me."

Olivia blinked in surprise. "Why would he buy the whole thing?"

"Reckon he thought nobody'd buy any," John mused aloud.

"Why would he think that?" Olivia queried. "My pie was wonderful."

"Durn right it was," Homer said. "I knew it was yours, too, minute I tasted it."

Grimacing, John scraped his boot across the planked floor. "Didn't mean it wasn't. Jes' wondered what was goin' on in Doc's head, 'at's all, to make 'im buy every slice."

Homer pouted again. "Didn't leave a piece for anybody. Not a bite."

"Where is he?" John asked.

"Don't rightly know."

"We should go find 'im. Wrestle a piece from 'im."

Homer squinted John a look of agreement. "Now that's a fine idea you have there, John Brimmer."

"Let's do it."

The men started off together, and Olivia stepped forward, not liking the idea of them going to find Dr. Schuster. What did they mean by "wrestling" a piece from him? There might be another argument once they found him, then another fight. All during the Independence Day celebration.

"Mr. Brimmer. Mr. Whitworth," Olivia called in a light, chastising tone.

Both men stopped in their tracks and turned around, shuffling, grimacing, looking for all the world like naughty boys.

"No arguing. No fighting. No fisticuffs."

"Yes, ma'am," Homer said.

"Notion didn't really enter our heads," John said, and Olivia laughed and shook her head when they turned away. She had done well with the pie, it seemed, but she would have felt much better about her cooking skills if John, Homer, and Dr. Schuster had not been the only ones vying for her pie. Right now, she strongly suspected that the three of them might vie for anything she cooked or baked.

"You bought my entire pie," Olivia marveled again later, this time to Dr. Schuster at the corner of Ripley and Main. Janey had joined in a game of skipping rope with a group of girls nearby. Olivia hadn't seen Charlotte in quite some time—not since she had gone off to help Malva Dodge serve ribs at a table up the street. The smell of barbecue drifted this way, making Olivia's stomach growl. But she didn't want to take Janey away from her friends, so she was trying to ignore the rumblings, something that was becoming harder and harder to do.

"I did, and it was delicious," he said proudly.

"Did Homer and John find you?"

He laughed. "I didn't let them."

She wrinkled her brow and gave him a wondering smile. "You mean you saw them coming and—"

"I evaded them, yes."

"How mean."

"How sneaky?"

"How ill-mannered," she teased. "You couldn't have spared them a bite, Doctor?"

"I wish you wouldn't call me that," he said, handing her a mug of lemonade. "You're not my patient, after all. Giving them a bite would have meant two less bites for me."

"A pity, since you had so little pie to begin with."

Laughing, he leaned an elbow against the corner of the stand and regarded her over the rim of his cup. The afternoon sunlight enhanced the green flecks in his eyes, and the breeze ruffled his hair in a boyish way. The grin playing on his mouth made Olivia's heart skip a beat or two—she wasn't entirely sure of how many—and just the way he stood, exuding confidence but not arrogance, sent shivers of excitement through her. She averted her gaze, drank her own lemonade, tried to catch her breath; she had suddenly become short-winded.

He leaned close to one side of her, his breath warm on her hair and ear, and his voice was lower and deeper than usual when he spoke, even a little raspy: "You'll be attending Walt Lincoln's dance this evening?"

She withdrew a little, and without thinking, she dropped her gaze to his mouth. His lips were moist from the lemonade, and a few drops had settled in his beard just below his bottom lip. Again without thinking, Olivia reached up to wipe the lemonade from his whiskers.

He caught her fingers in his hand, brought them to his mouth, and sucked the lemonade off the tips of them. At the same time, he captured her gaze with his. His eyes, darkened and clouded, regarded her with such longing that Olivia felt she might melt into his arms right here and now. She had never been as close to any man as she had been to him numerous times during these past weeks—while he was teaching her to milk Eleanor, and now, with his breath brushing her fingers in a maddening way, with his lips touching them, lingering on them—and the feelings he awakened in her were beginning to drive her a little mad.

She pulled her hand, and her gaze, from him. Then she dropped her hand to the corner of the stand and looked off at Janey.

"Charlotte and I plan to attend Mr. Lincoln's dance," she said in answer to the question he had asked before he had decided to suckle lemonade from the tips of her fingers.

"Good," he said, and Olivia wondered what in heaven's name had made her forget to bring along a fan this afternoon to ward off the July heat. She was blazing suddenly. "You'll save a dance for me?" he asked.

"I'm . . . I'm afraid my dance card is already full," she responded, feeling herself stumble over every word. After first forcing it from her mouth, of course.

He laughed low under his breath. "Walt was raised in the wilds of Wisconsin Territory, Olivia. He doesn't know what a dance card is."

She nearly bit her tongue, she clamped her jaw shut so hard. "Perhaps I could teach him."

"Perhaps you could. In the meantime, consider saving a dance for me," he said, placing his mug on the stand.

He walked off without another word, and Olivia was left staring after him, wondering how she could avoid dancing with him, suspecting that he knew she was wondering.

"I've had far too much to eat this afternoon," she called on a whim. "I had ribs, pie, corn pones . . . My stomach is in knots! I was thinking of telling Charlotte that I can't go."

He turned around and began walking backwards, talking to her at the same time. "A pity. Maybe appendicitis. It certainly couldn't be the ribs and corn pones since you haven't gotten down that way since Louise Gordon and the others began cooking them. You've been standing here watching Janey jump rope."

"You've been spying on me, Dr. Schuster," Olivia accused.

"Yes, I have, Mrs. Monroe."

"Your mother never taught you that spying is rude?"

"I'm afraid not," he said, continuing backwards, grinning now. "But then, in that respect, we're alike. Your mother never taught you either."

That remark made Olivia bristle because she knew she was referring to the way she had spied on him from the loft.

She straightened her sleeves, smoothed her skirt, and fixed a haughty gaze on him.

He laughed. "You're endearing, Olivia Monroe. For all your oddities and primness, you're endearing. You're like a disgruntled hen smoothing her feathers. Never fear, I'll not ruffle them anymore this afternoon. I do expect to see you at Walt's dance this evening, and if you're not there, I'll bring the dance to you. That is a promise," he said, crashing backwards into Homer and John, who parted like the Red Sea and let him stumble and fall.

As irritated with him as she was right now, Olivia couldn't help but laugh. He had sounded so confident, and then he had crashed into Homer and John, and now *he* was gathering *his* dignity, standing and brushing dust from his nice striped waistcoat and trousers.

"Ya bought her whole pie," John accused.

"We'd like a bite," Homer said, and Olivia thought he was trying hard to be civil.

"I'll buy a piece from ya," John offered.

Homer stuck his head between John and Dr. Schuster. "I'll pay you twice what you paid—for the whole thing."

"Now, Homer, ya ain't gonna do no such thing," John responded. "I'm gonna have a piece of Mrs. Monroe's pie."

"I'm afraid neither of you are," Dr. Schuster said. "I ate the entire pie."

Olivia gasped, not because he had eaten the entire pie, but because he was gloating about it, tossing the fact in Homer and John's faces, knowing it would irritate them. He was grinning mischievously, backing away again, and Olivia swore he was teasing them.

"Mr. Brimmer. Mr. Whitworth," she called, hurrying toward them. "You'll both be at Mr. Lincoln's dance this evening. I'll spend the evening dancing with both of you, and I'll bake each of you a pie another day."

"Will you?" Homer asked, perspiration having smeared his makeup.

"That's right gen'rous of ya, Mrs. Monroe," John said.

Dr. Schuster took a step forward. "You didn't offer me a dance."

Olivia almost laughed aloud at the pout on his face. "I know. I have a feeling most women aren't given a chance to offer you a dance because you simply march forth and take one. Come along, Mr. Whitworth, Mr. Brimmer . . . I was about to take Janey and go eat. We would love to have the two of you join us."

That deepened Dr. Schuster's pout. He looked pitiful, dejected, standing with dust all over his clothes and an expression on his face that said no one wanted to play with him so he would just have to take his ball and go home. Olivia almost felt sorry for him. Almost.

Homer and John eagerly offered her an arm each, and taking both arms, Homer on her left, John on her right, she turned away to call to Janey.

CHAPTER THIRTEEN

WALT LINCOLN HAD secured the help of his mother and sisters to decorate his barn. Outside, colorful banners were looped over the doors and from one end of the roof to the other, and inside they swung at intervals from the rafters and from the edge of the loft. They livened up bales of hay and tables on which sat glasses of lemonade and dishes of food. Near the far wall of the barn Frank Coates sang along with the ballad he strummed on his instrument.

'Twas upon a high, high hill,
Two maidens chose their dwellin',
An' one was known both far an' wide,
Was known as Barb'ra Allen.

He strummed more, then sang the second part of the tune:

'Twas in the merry month of May,
All the flow'rs bloomin',
A young man on his deathbed lay
For the love o' Barb'ra Allen.

Olivia became captivated with the tune. She had certainly heard a ballad or two in her life, sung by the baritone voices of sailors near the wharves in Philadelphia, but most of her musical exposure had been to waltzes and quadrilles in ballrooms. Many of the ballads she had heard from sailors had been from her position in the safety of a carriage, and she seized this opportunity to draw close and really listen to the words of Frank Coates's ballad as Janey skipped off after the new friends with whom she had jumped rope this afternoon.

He sent a servant unto her
In the town where she was dwellin'.
"Come, Miss, O Miss to my master dyin'
If yer name be Barb'ra Allen."

As the song had it, Barbara went to the young man, though she shunned his attention because days before, in a local tavern, he had drunk to the health of the ladies present—and yet ignored her. Barbara went home, and on the way she heard the church bell tolling the man's death. She had liked him, loved him from afar, but hadn't wanted him to know for fear that he would turn away. She hadn't really thought he would die, and she realized what a fool she had been now not to see how very ill he had been. A brokenhearted fool.

Sweet William died on a Sat'rd'y night,
An' Barb'ra on a Sund'y.
Her mother died for the love o' them both
She died on Easter mornin'.
William was buried in one graveyard.
Barb'ra in another;
A rose grew on William's grave
An' a brier grew on Barb'ra's.
They grew an' grew to the steeple top,
An' there they grew no higher;
There they tied in a true-lover knot,
The rose clung 'round the brier.

"Oh," Olivia said softly, touching a hand to her breast. It was the sweetest story, and one of the most tragic, she had ever heard. Like *Romeo and Juliet.* It made tears spring to her eyes and slip down her face, and she was so deep in thought, picturing the vines growing together, that she barely heard Charlotte teasing her: "That Frank Coates, he can really sing 'em. Sings a person nearly to tears, he does. I'm going off to find Malva, Ida, and Louise. The four of us together bearing down on Frank oughtta be enough to make him play something a little livelier."

"That was lovely," Olivia said, brushing at her tears. "That was just lovely."

"But we came for a celebration. We didn't come to weep," Charlotte grumbled.

As if on cue, Frank sprang into a lively tune, and he was joined by Elijah Stephenson, Davenport's sole blacksmith, on the banjo. Instead of going off to find Malva, Ida, and Louise, Charlotte began clapping her hands and stomping one foot, bringing her knee up high each time. Now and then she grabbed the sides of her skirts and did a little jig, and Olivia laughed at the sight, never having seen Charlotte act so animated.

Charlotte bolted away to dance with the first man who asked her. Ida appeared in the dance area, kicking up her heels with Curtis Campbell, her "favorite suitor" according to Charlotte, who had pointed him out to Olivia this afternoon during the parade. Louise Gordon and her husband Samuel blazed a path into the dance area, and Malva appeared with Dr. Schuster, flipping her skirts, her long gray braid bouncing around on her shoulder.

John took Olivia by the elbow and coaxed her out into the wild dancing. Frank boomed out the words to the song, and the sizable crowd that had gathered in Walt Lincoln's barn joined in.

We was boomin' down the ole Miss'ip',
One splugeous summer's day,
When the ole man yells, "Now let 'er rip!
I see the Maquoketay!"
But we jus' sez, "We're up to snuff
An' don't keer what ya think.
That crossin' ain't got dep' 'nough"—
Cap'n Jones jes' took a drink!

A gasp went through the crowd, and Olivia quickly realized that it was feigned. "What? Water?" the crowd asked Frank. "Yes, water," he answered, then sang: *Dry up, yer darn ole liar!* "Not water? Yes, water," the crowd shouted, and Frank nodded his head sadly and responded in tune: *Cause his innards was a-fy-ar!"*

The song went on, recounting a youth's gallantry and daring aboard a ship on the "ole Miss'ip'." The youth caught the eye of a girl in one river town only to have her "pap" say "nay." The boy loped away, pretending sadness, then turned back and squinted one eye at the girl, who promptly told her pap good-bye. The boy and girl's story certainly ended better than William and Barbara's had, with the boy and his girl floating off on the ship down the river. Four slapping steps and a shout from the crowd completed the tune, and Olivia thought she'd never had so much fun in her life. Crazy, outrageous fun.

Homer came along, and Olivia shared her dances with him and John, occasionally wondering why Dr. Schuster didn't press the issue of dancing with her. He danced with Ida, Malva, Louise, Charlotte . . . with everyone but her. He laughed with them during reels and pressed them close during waltzes, shocking—and delighting—Louise and Charlotte. He brought them plates of food, glasses of punch . . . He even removed Louise's boots and rubbed her feet when she complained that they were sore. Olivia heard and witnessed that entire exchange as she sat nearby with John on a bale of hay, sipping from the glass of punch he had brought her.

"What nice feet you have, Louise Gordon," Dr. Schuster said, rubbing his thumb over her instep. "Fine and delicate. And such soft skin!"

Louise blushed to her roots. "G'on, Doc. But you shore know how ta rub 'em the right way!" She giggled like a schoolgirl.

"Gonna dance with us agin, Doc?" Malva asked, pressing close, Ida stumping up behind her.

"The rest of the night," he said. "That is, if Curtis doesn't object."

Ida snorted. "Well, he might. Gotta feelin' he might jes' pop a question at me soon, too."

"No!" Dr. Schuster said, feigning surprise. "What the devil gave you that idea, Ida?"

She gave him a light smack on the shoulder with her cane and a playful glare. "Ya wanna hold off with that teasin'."

"I might."

"Enough o' rubbin' Louise's feet there, Doc. They ain't that perty," Malva said, taking him by the elbow.

He laughed. "There's no need to fetch me, Malva. I'll come anytime you call." And he went off with her.

Ridiculous, Olivia thought. *The way he's flirting with women old enough to be his mother.* Not to mention the fact that he had asked her, only this afternoon, to save a dance for him. No, he hadn't asked her to—he had told her to. And as the afternoon hours had passed, as she began unknotting the knot in her belly, she had actually started looking forward to dancing with him. Having him near her was dangerous, because in his presence she felt almost weak at times; if he leaned forward and tried to kiss her, she might not have the strength or the desire to resist him. But the danger made her curious. What would kissing him be like? she wondered suddenly, watching his mouth as he talked to Malva. Exciting. Thrilling. Soft. Moist. Unbelievable.

Unthinkable.

She jerked herself upright, squaring her shoulders. He had caught her staring, it seemed. He was looking straight at her now, a wide grin on his face. "Like he knows exactly what I was thinking," Olivia said aloud.

"What?" John asked.

She inhaled quickly. "Oh. Nothing. Charlotte, she seems to always know exactly what I'm thinking. She coaxed me into coming tonight because she somehow knew I was thinking of staying home."

"Stayin' home?" Homer asked, closing in on the other side of her and trying to press a glass of punch into her free hand. The other hand held the glass of punch John had offered her not five minutes ago.

Olivia had danced the entire evening away with the two

of them, had drunk the numerous glasses of refreshment they had offered her, had politely accepted their sweet attentions, all the while wondering in the back of her mind when Alan Schuster planned to approach and claim a dance with her. But he never had, and now it seemed he had no intention of doing so, and she felt confused and even a little jealous. No, a lot jealous—of three elderly women! Why had he decided not to ask her to dance? What in the world was he thinking? She was surprised by how much she wanted to dance with him.

"I thought you might like more," Homer said, still trying to press the glass into her hand. "What do you mean, you were thinkin' about stayin' home?"

"Nothing," Olivia said sharply. She didn't want to be unpleasant. She really didn't. But she suddenly didn't feel as festive as she had felt earlier today and when the dance began.

She stood and handed John the glass of punch he had given her some time ago. "I'm going outside for a bit," she said, and started off.

Homer and John started to follow.

Olivia turned on them, and although she wanted to be pleasant, doing so was becoming harder and harder. They had followed her everywhere this evening, and she was tired of them, absolutely tired of them. "No. I want to be alone," she said succinctly. "Alone."

They both shrank back, and Olivia was immediately sorry for her harsh words. She thought briefly about apologizing but decided against doing that since she really did want to be alone, and Homer and John had to learn not to follow her. Sometimes their attention was flattering. But other times it was bothersome.

She walked off without another word to them and approached Janey, who was now playing tag with three other girls around bales of hay, to tell her that she was going outside for a walk. Then she went off to do exactly that.

Rustling the leaves and branches of trees, a nice summer breeze carried the earthy smells of freshly turned soil and damp foliage. Dew shimmered on the grass in the moonlight, and lanterns glowed in front of the barn. Light and music drifted from within, becoming more and more distant the farther Olivia walked. Walt lived a mile outside of Davenport, and although Olivia liked the town, she found the quiet here soothing. There were sounds—crickets chirping, a cow lowing faintly in the distance, horses whickering where they stood still hitched to wagons outside the barn—but the sounds were far different from those of the rowdy drunks on Davenport's streets, where a fair share of the drunks roamed from saloon to saloon and gaming house to gaming house at this time of evening.

Olivia wondered, as she had numerous times now, how Edna Ferguson, her uncle's housekeeper in Philadelphia, and Harry, her uncle's driver, had fared after she and Janey fled. Concern for them still crept into her thoughts, as she felt certain it always would, and she also found herself wondering, as she frequently did of late, if there was any way of finding out where they were, what they were doing now, and if they were well. She wondered, too, if there was a way of finding out if Uncle Edward had lived through that blow to the head, and if so, if he was searching high and low for her and Janey. Mrs. Ferguson had a sister in Philadelphia—Anna Thompson—and while Olivia could easily send her a letter, she had never met the woman and was not sure if she could be trusted. Still, she often wondered about sending word to Mrs. Thompson and asking after Mrs. Ferguson. She and Janey had made a good life here, and they would not have been able to do that if Mrs. Ferguson and Harry had not helped them escape. Olivia might not have been able to think of another way out of the nightmarish situation, Janey might have been doomed to a sanitarium, and God only knows what might have happened to Olivia herself. Not knowing what had become of Harry and Mrs. Ferguson was almost unbearable for her at times.

Up ahead was Walt's house, lit by two lanterns on the porch railing on either side of the steps. Olivia turned to the right, where several horses poked their heads over a fence and whickered, seeming to beckon her.

"Good evening," she greeted them softly as she approached, slowly stretching a hand out to stroke one between the eyes. The other horse nuzzled the one Olivia stroked, then stepped back, tossed his head, and whinnied. He dipped his head to the other horse's left hind leg and skittered to the side when she kicked at him.

"Walt must be trying to get a foal or two," someone remarked behind Olivia.

Alan Schuster. Olivia would have known the voice anywhere. Deep but not too deep. Raspy but not too raspy. It had sounded the same the evening of the birthday party aboard the *Star of Ohio,* and then this afternoon near the lemonade stand. It sent a thrill through her, just hearing it, just knowing he was near and that he had followed her out here—that he had decided not to ignore her entirely this evening.

He moved to stand on her left near the fence, and he too reached out to stroke the mare's neck. Olivia glanced over at him, found him watching her, his eyes glistening in the moonlight. She had not left the barn with the intent of drawing him out here; she hadn't even thought about doing that. But she was glad he was here.

Suddenly her heart began skipping, then drumming, in the odd way it did whenever he came close, and she wondered if being out here in the moonlight, all alone with him except for the horses, was a wise thing. She had definitely tossed aside all rules of propriety now.

"She's . . . well he should have no problem with that," Olivia said nervously, turning her eyes back to the mare. "Walt, I mean. Getting a foal. She's in season. The mare, I mean."

Dr. Schuster chuckled, and Olivia's face burned with color.

"The—the mare," she said again, with a little more force this time.

"I know." He laughed again just as the stallion whinnied near the far fence, where he had trotted after the mare's refusal. "I hope you don't mind me following you out here. It's dark, and I worried when I saw you leave alone. Anyone might have followed you."

"Homer and John tried."

Another laugh. "I saw that." He sobered. "If you want to be alone, I'll keep my distance."

"But watch over me in the night?" she teased.

"Yes. If you ever want me to."

His voice was so serious and deep at that moment that Olivia glanced up, startled by his tone—and by the implication. Their relationship was changing—she sensed that, she felt it—having the potential to progress far beyond that of a landlord and tenant. Far beyond where she wanted it to progress. Far beyond what was wise.

His hand crept up, toward where hers rested between the horse's eyes, and although an objection was on the tip of her tongue, it refused to leave her mouth. His fingers brushed hers in another magical touch, and Olivia heard herself gasp. But she didn't pull away.

"You're as skittish as she is," Dr. Schuster teased. "And I'm not trying to get nearly as friendly with you as he is with her."

Olivia squeezed her eyes shut, then popped them open, trying to quiet her pounding heart. "Don't jest at a time like this, Dr. Schuster. Please don't jest," she managed breathlessly.

His fingers slid between hers, traced the bones in her hand, slid down to the inside of her wrist and stroked. So sensitive. So excruciatingly sensitive.

"It's time you stopped addressing me formally, Olivia."

She loved the way the last syllable of her name hung on his tongue, like a dish he was savoring. She watched his hand circle her small wrist.

"Say my name. Say *Alan.*"

His fingers flitted their way up her arm, to the inside of her elbow, where they again lingered, toying with a sensitive place. He leaned forward, and she felt his warm breath in her hair and on her face, as she had that afternoon. Only now they were so alone and the moon bathed them and their surroundings in a soft silver glow. The mare whickered lightly, the crickets chirped, and the branches of nearby trees whispered secrets, perhaps about the many lovers who had gathered, at one time or another, beneath their branches. The stallion returned to the mare, who seemed a little more receptive now, and he nuzzled her, then dipped his head up and down and against her, as if trying to discern her mood.

"Say it, Olivia," the doctor whispered again, and this time Olivia obeyed, saying his first name softly, feeling it touch her lips for the first time.

His fingers went from her elbow to her jaw, where their touch became even more unsettling. Olivia thought she would die with wanting more of his touch, on her face, her neck, her hair . . . She said his name again, with no urging from him this time, and she turned her face toward his, unable to resist the temptation he presented. She wanted him to kiss her. Oh, how she wanted him to kiss her!

And then he *was* kissing her, pressing his lips to hers, softly, sweetly, whispering her name. His arms slipped around her and drew her closer to him, and she dropped her hands to his shoulders, feeling his strength through his waistcoat and shirt. She had so little strength of her own at the moment that she couldn't have pushed him away even if she had wanted to. Which she didn't.

He kissed the tip of her nose, the corner of her mouth, her jaw. Then he kissed her lips again, parting them gently, teasing her tongue with his. His tongue dove deep, and he pressed her closer to him, so close she felt his hardened length through his trousers.

Still, she didn't pull away. She gasped and stiffened with shock, but he kissed her more, lightly now, gently, and she relaxed against him. Seconds later, he lifted his head, and Olivia stared up at him, feeling dazed.

"I've wanted to do that all day," he said, his voice low and thick. He skimmed his fingers along her jaw, then slid them into her hair at the nape of her neck. He urged her head to rest against his chest, and Olivia heard the crazy but reassuring gallop of his heartbeat. "Don't be afraid, Olivia.

I won't hurt you, and I won't ever let anyone else hurt you either."

His last words pierced her heart, because she felt certain that he meant them. They came from his heart. At some point during these past weeks, after his return from St. Louis, he had started caring for her. It showed in his actions—his milking the cow and gathering the eggs every morning to save her the work, his hiring Walt to plow her garden—and his affection touched her deeply.

She cared for him, too, she realized, even as irritating as he could be at times. Because of his compassion and sense of humor, his devotion to his friends and patients (often the same)—and because he had defended her virtue and her food wagon.

What am I doing? Olivia wondered frantically. *I can't possibly think of falling in love right now. I'm in trouble over my head—I stole from my uncle, kidnapped his daughter, and possibly murdered him.*

She would disclose her horrible secrets to no one. And she refused to put anyone in danger alongside her. If her uncle rode into Davenport right now and found her, he could accuse none of the people she had come to know and love these past weeks of hiding her or aiding her in any way. No one in Davenport had any idea of the circumstances that had led her and Janey here, and that was the way she preferred to leave things. She would put no one in jeopardy.

"Don't be afraid," Alan had said. But she was. Extremely afraid.

She had no idea what he was thinking exactly, if he had just wanted to kiss her, or if he intended to try to take the relationship further.

She pushed away from him, shook her head, lifted her skirts, and started to rush off to the barn, thinking to collect Janey and go home.

He stepped in front of her. "Don't go off offended, Olivia."

She glanced up at him. She wasn't. Oh, she wasn't! His kisses had been exquisite, the feel of his arms and the steady sound of his heartbeat comforting. "I'm not," she said simply, and started around him.

He took her by the elbow, stopping her. "Look at me."

She hesitated, then looked up at him.

"Why do I always see fear in your eyes, Olivia? Every time I ask Janey a question, every time I get close to you. Every time you think I might ask you a question. Every time you think I'm getting too close."

Olivia closed her eyes and shook her head. "Don't. I'm not offended. But please don't kiss me like that again. Ever again," she said, opening her eyes. "I—"

"Boston or Philadelphia? Janey spelled Philadelphia with her blocks."

Olivia's eyes widened. "I said don't. That means don't kiss me again and don't ask me questions."

"Do you know what Ida told me this afternoon?" he continued. "That Janey's right arm is bent, as if it was broken at some time and not set to heal properly. And this afternoon when Janey was playing with her new friends, she wrote her name in the dirt, and do you know what surname she wrote?"

God. Olivia's heart stopped, then seemed to leap into her throat and threaten to jump out of her body. She had to think of something, another lie, or at least an explanation for the name she knew Janey had written.

"Do you?" he pressed.

Olivia swallowed. "Janey Morgan. Of course I know what she wrote. She's my unmarried sister and she retains our maiden name."

He narrowed his eyes, as if considering what she had said.

"Her arm?" he queried.

"Was broken once. Having no medical knowledge or training, I have no idea if the physician who tended her was competent in setting her arm."

Well, at least that wasn't a lie.

He considered that, too. Then he asked again: "Philadelphia or Boston?"

"What does it matter?" she shot back, twisting and trying to free her arm. "No more questions!"

He held tight. "I wouldn't ask if I didn't care about you, Olivia. It matters because I care about Janey. You're hiding things about the two of you. Has Janey ever spoken?"

Olivia jerked her arm free finally. "Leave us alone! For God's sake, leave us alone."

"I want to help you and Janey, not hurt you. I wish you would believe that."

"I believe it! But I don't want your help. Yours or anyone else's!" she said, and then she turned and ran away.

She sat on Charlotte's wagon seat for a time, wiping her eyes and fighting more tears, silently cursing him, silently contemplating telling him the entire truth, then deciding against doing that. She wouldn't put him in danger. Him or anyone else in Davenport. She wouldn't have them accused of knowingly helping a criminal.

She returned to the dance some time later, as it was winding down. The crowd had thinned; people had started leaving in their buckboards and on horseback even before she had come back inside. Frank had just started into a waltz, an odd tune coming from his fiddle, considering that he had played ballads and lively, heel-kicking tunes most of the evening. Olivia started over to where she saw Janey sitting with Ida and Charlotte on a bale of hay, and Alan Schuster stepped up and took her by the hand before she could take three steps toward her cousin and friends.

"Dance with me," he said, and his eyes were soft and pleading.

Olivia wouldn't have considered saying no, because people might have wondered why, and gossip began that way. She turned toward him, lifted her arm, placed her hand lightly in his, her other hand on his shoulder, and began twirling with him.

He held her gaze with his.

"Don't be afraid of me, Olivia. I want to help."

"I don't want your help."

"I want to help," he said again, drawing her closer than

what was normally allowed during a waltz. He pressed his chin against her forehead.

"You're not going to leave it alone, are you?" she asked softly, meaning her dilemma and Janey's.

"No, I'm not. Because I care about you and Janey."

She glanced up at him. "I wish you would stop—because I care about you."

She didn't wait to see what his reaction to that would be. She averted her gaze to Frank, who had his eyes closed as he relished the tune he was playing.

CHAPTER FOURTEEN

ALAN KEPT HIS distance from Olivia and Janey for the next few weeks, biding his time. The garden grew and flourished, promising to produce a bounty of summer vegetables to replenish Olivia's wagon—although she might not be working from the wagon much longer. He had recently learned from Ida that Olivia was interested in buying out a saloon owner's interest and planned to do some remodeling of that establishment. Since his journeys all over the county gave him frequent opportunity to view the countryside, he did approach Olivia with several prospects for land on which he and a group of other townsmen could build her a homestead. She thanked him politely, and days later he learned that she had John take her out to look at the land. That infuriated Alan enough that he had to fight down the urge to march into the house, taking her by the shoulders, and shake her. "I only want to help you," he wanted to tell her again. But he *wouldn't* tell her that again. He'd told her enough times.

He wasn't at all surprised when he questioned the captain of the *Brazil*, the ship Olivia had taken from St. Louis to Davenport—a piece of information Charlotte had shared with him—and learned that Olivia had registered on that vessel as Olivia Monroe, but had claimed to be a widow. A quick glance at the ship's log revealed that the *Brazil* had departed St. Louis with her and Janey aboard the same day that the *Star of Ohio,* the ship on which Olivia and Alan initially met, had docked in St. Louis. He and Ida had disembarked, and so had Olivia and Janey—to board the

Brazil. During his next trip to St. Louis, Captain Manning did a little digging for Alan, and upon his next trip to Davenport some four days later, the captain arrived with the news that Olivia had registered only Janey and herself aboard the *Star of Ohio*. Again, no husband. Her story had always been that her husband had died en route, somewhere between St. Louis and Davenport, but that had to be a lie because her husband had never been registered on the *Brazil*.

Which then made Alan wonder if she had run away from her husband, and if Janey was really her daughter, not her sister as she claimed.

"Tarnation!" Ida blurted at him when he presented that theory to her. "She's hidin' somethin', sure. But why would she wanna twist a story that much? She ain't old 'nough to have a child that old."

"Have any of us asked her how old she is?"

"Pshaw! She ain't that old. Nineteen, mebbe. Ya need to simmer down, Doc. I wrote to my friend in Pittsburgh a few weeks ago, when yer suspicions started goin', an' I 'magine he'll do some checkin' over in Philly an' write me back soon. Lessen' he's died or somethin'. Rich is gettin' on in age, like m'self." She shifted in her chair, then glanced up from her stitching and squinted one eye at him. "Listen, I hear Harv Tirado, Hank Shears, an' some other fellers' 'ave got it in fer that gal. I don't mind 'er takin' over my bus'ness, but they mind 'er takin' over theirs, an' it seems the rivermen favor her a bit more than they do Harv, Hank, an' the others when it comes time to sell shipments. Word is, they're doin' their own diggin', jes' to see if they can run 'er outta town. Even plan to drag her sellin' on a street corner to the Council an' see if they can get a ord'nance passed against such doin's. Don't that jes' beat the nation! But I thought ya oughtta know, ya bein' a alderman an' all. If she's really hidin' somethin', we'd better find out what it is b'fore Harv an' the others do, an' see if we can help 'er fix it."

Alan agreed, and with that thought in mind he went off to see if the latest ship had brought Ida any mail, although he knew it was probably too soon for her friend in Pittsburgh to have written back to her.

He was outside standing near the barnyard railing a few evenings later, watching the moon and the stars, and pondering everything, when he heard the house door creak open; the night breeze carried the sound. He twisted around that way, realizing immediately that Olivia didn't see him. She seemed deep in thought. She wore a white shift, and she looked like an angel gliding across the grass on her way to the well, her golden hair spilling down her back in waves, a pitcher in her right hand. He followed her, though he knew she didn't sense him.

She filled the pitcher from the well, then stood, gazed off into the distance, and whispered, "I love this place. I never want to leave. Life is simple here. Unthreatening. Janey is safe here. Please," she whispered in a desperate tone, turning her face up to the heavens, "I don't want to run again."

She seemed so young to him at that moment—vulnerable, innocent, fearful, desperate.

"Olivia, you don't have to leave," he whispered, hearing her shift flap in the breeze. "You don't have to run again."

He watched her hair blow around her face as she spun around, watched the wind blow the night rail against her legs, outlining them. He recalled the softness of her lips pressed against his, the sweet perfume of her hair and skin, the headiness of just holding her, touching her, kissing her.

She sniffed, as if she'd been crying. "I have a friend who works aboard the *Brazil*," she told him.

"Will Clift. I know."

"He says . . ." She sniffed again. "He says you were asking the captain questions."

"Where's your husband, Olivia?" Alan queried, hearing the goats start their bawling in the barn. They didn't cry as much anymore, though they still robbed him of sleep now and then. "He wasn't aboard the *Brazil* or the *Star of Ohio*. Where is he?"

She didn't answer. She turned slightly and watched as her

finger traced the pitcher handle. In the moonlight, he glimpsed the shadow of her breast through her shift, and an ache began in his groin, one he felt all too often of late whenever he looked at her.

Lord help him if her husband were still alive—he'd be coveting another man's wife. While he had certainly had his share and pick of women in his youth, he had never touched a married one—but he had kissed this one the night of Walt's barn dance. Just the thought, the strong suspicion, that Olivia was married to another man made him feel as though someone had put a knife into his chest.

Four strides put him a distance of six feet from her. There he stopped, afraid she might bolt.

"You're going to have to trust someone," he said. "Me, Ida, Charlotte, John, Homer, Malva, Louise, and scores of other people in Davenport want to help you settle here. If you're in trouble, Olivia, we'll help you with that, too. If you ran from your husband because he was cruel to you and Janey, John might know how to go about obtaining a divorce in the state in which you lived. Trust us. We'll try to help you."

No response. She continued studying the pitcher.

His patience ran thin. He had talked to her numerous times now, asked questions and tried to convince her that he meant her no harm, but she was so bullheaded.

"Olivia, I don't like the thought that I kissed a married woman. If you weren't going to tell me the truth about your husband still being alive you might have at least refused to let me kiss you."

"There is no husband," she said so softly he barely heard her.

Alan cocked his head, wanting to know if he had heard right, hoping he had, desperately hoping.

"There is no husband," she said again, just as softly. But he was listening closely this time, and he heard her.

Relief and joy swept through him. He closed the space between them, took her gently by the shoulders, and turned her toward him.

"Before Mr. Lincoln's dance . . . ," she said, still staring down at the pitcher. "Before that night, I had . . . I had never been kissed." She looked up at him, her eyes wide and sparkling. "You kissed me, and it felt so nice. I wanted it to continue forever."

He had been the first to kiss her. *The first.* He wasn't sure how he felt about that. Thrilled. Exhilarated. She was pure and untouched. Except for his kiss, of course. He recalled it, the way she had melted against him, given herself into the kiss, looked full of wonder and surprise afterward. He had thought she was offended. But, no, she had liked the kiss, so much that she had wanted it to continue forever.

She reached out slowly and touched her fingers to his, hesitantly, glancing up at him as if wanting to see how he would react. "More than two weeks since the dance, and I still think about the way you touched me that evening . . . the way you kissed me," she said, her voice little more than a whisper in the night. "I thought that if I had nothing to do with you, if I avoided you, the memory might fade. But it hasn't. I lie awake thinking of it sometimes . . . your kiss." She touched her finger to her lips in wonderment, then laughed a little at herself. "A girl who never went out without a chaperone before coming here."

She twined her fingers through his, and he had to wonder if she knew what she was doing, that she was tempting him to kiss her and show her much more about relations between men and women that would amaze her. She had been awakened with a kiss, and now she longed for more. Well, he would give her more kisses, gladly and without reservation.

He slipped his hand beneath her hair to her nape and drew her to him, feeling the softness of her, reveling in her innocence, her freshness. "Like an untouched flower," he whispered, watching her lips part as they prepared to meet his, watching her eyes close to mere slits.

He stroked her cheek, wound a section of her silky hair around his hand, slid his tongue over her bottom lip, felt her suck in a breath of surprise then release it in a rush. He drank it, just touching his mouth to hers, and felt her slump slightly against him.

Where had she come from, this angel, this woman who had so suddenly become part of his life when he returned from Cincinnati and St. Louis? If she thought for a moment to slip away now, to run again, she should think again. She had captivated him with her stubbornness, oddness, charm, determination, and now innocence, and he intended to keep her in his life.

"Where did you come from?" he whispered aloud against her lips. He expected to feel her stiffen with apprehension. Instead, she laughed.

"From heaven," she jested.

Now he laughed. "That may well be."

He kissed her more deeply, slipping his tongue into her mouth, pressing her close, so close he felt the heaviness of her breasts against his chest. He wanted to touch them, but he didn't want to frighten her. His groin grew heavy with want, and he wondered what she wore beneath her shift, if she wore anything.

The thought was too much.

"Olivia, do you know what the stallion and mare most assuredly did after nuzzling?" he asked, lifting his head, his voice thick and raspy.

Her eyes flared. She stiffened with apprehension.

"The natural progression of relations . . . ," he said, trying to lighten his tone.

"I—I thought only of kisses," she stammered.

"Nuzzles."

He bent to pick up the pitcher she had dropped. A mistake. The shift blew against her legs, outlining their shape, and he was right there, with his nose almost touching her knees. He straightened and handed her the pitcher, asking, "Are you wearing anything under that nightrail?"

She gasped. "Dr. Schuster."

He nodded. "Good. It won't do for us to be on a first-name basis tonight."

She tipped her head and regarded him curiously.

"I'm turning in," he said, then grinned and shook his head at her. "The natural progression of events is not always a good idea."

"Oh, stop that. We're outside, Dr. Schuster. We couldn't possibly . . . progress much further."

He laughed at her naivete. "The grass would make a fine bed, and events could progress quite nicely, believe me. Good night," he said, and turned and began walking away. The most difficult thing he had ever done in his life—walking away from her when he would like to catch her up in his arms, take her into the house, and make love to her on his bed.

The thought suddenly struck him that she had been sleeping on his bed for some time now, on his tick, using his coverlet and pillows. The thought made him smile and then wonder what she looked like sleeping on his bed.

"Do you wonder why I said I was a widow?" she called, as if not wanting him to go.

He turned back, a grin on his face. "I won't be asking you too many more questions about yourself or your life before Davenport."

"Won't be asking me . . . but you'll be asking other people."

He shrugged. "If I must. And apparently I must."

"I wanted to ward you off," she said. "That evening on the ship."

"And you certainly did. But now I know the truth, and now you'll have a devil of a time warding me off, Olivia Monroe. Don't forget the natural progression of events. We already nuzzled. I have incredible powers of self-restraint sometimes."

She grasped her shift above her breasts in a protective manner, and he chuckled. Seconds later, he stepped into the barnyard and then into the barn.

Three days later, on a rainy Tuesday afternoon, Olivia jerked down a notice that had been posted on the front door of the Methodist church and spun around to face Alan, her eyes flashing.

"People will help us? *People will help us?*" she said, shaking the notice in front of his face. Others had been posted around Davenport, near saloon doors and on walkway posts. A town council meeting was to be held this evening in the Methodist Church, and Alan had just finished posting the notice on the front door of that establishment when Olivia arrived and tore the paper down.

"Calm down," Alan said, snatching the notice from her hand. "A meeting of the council doesn't mean there are no people willing to help you."

"All the while you're assuring me that the people of Davenport will help me and Janey, you're planning a meeting of the town council to talk about passing an ordinance that will outlaw our produce wagon," she shot at him without pausing to take a breath. "What comes next—outlawing us?"

"That's ridiculous, Olivia. You're upset, and I understand that. But your best course of action is to show up at the next meeting and argue your case there. Don't lose your temper right here in front of the church and give people something more to talk about."

"Defend my right to sell goods on the streets of an American city? I will not!" Her face was pink with outrage, and she had balled her right fist. Janey stood down near the street holding the ends of two ropes that were tied around Edwin's and Annie's necks, and she pulled a face when she caught Alan glancing at her, as if she knew there was a storm brewing and she would just like to avoid it altogether and go about her business, thank you very much.

"Then you'll probably end up not being able to sell your goods on the streets of this American city," Alan responded, having no patience today for one of Olivia's outbursts. He had been up most of the night nursing Tommy Brewster through another bad bout with tuberculosis, and he had been on his way home to sleep when Harvey Tirado rode up and handed him the stack of notices. Last week Harvey had handed him a petition that he and Hank had circulated and that had been signed by a good number of citizens, and Alan had agreed that a meeting should be held to discuss the matter. He just hadn't expected Harvey and Hank to have the notices printed so soon. And he had never expected them to demand that he, as head of the council, circulate them. If he refused, Harv and Hank were going to get vicious, he just knew it.

Why the hell had he volunteered for civic duty in the first place? he had wondered, grabbing the notices from Harvey. Something about wanting to help Davenport grow and flourish. Something about living in a community he could be proud of. He'd wanted to punch Harvey right in the snout when the man said that he and Hank, as councilmen themselves, were trusting that Alan would not let his new attachment to the Monroe woman cloud his judgment. The notices should be posted, and they should be posted this afternoon since he and Hank had called the meeting for this evening. As president, Alan had asked smartly, shouldn't he himself be the one to call meetings? And Harv had asked right back if he had planned to call one at all. "You're sweet on that woman—Hank saw ya kissin' her at Walt's dance. Your judgment's already clouded," Harv had said, and then he had ridden off, not giving Alan a chance to punch him off his horse.

So the notices had been posted, and the one he was holding now, the one Olivia had torn down right in front of him, was going to be reposted. Because if it didn't get reposted, Harvey and Hank might find out and start spreading ugly rumors about him and Olivia. If they weren't *already* spreading ugly rumors. Rumors about the intimacy of his and Olivia's relationship that probably weren't far from the truth. But gossip had a way of distorting the truth, of making something as sweet as a kiss seem dirty, and for Olivia's sake, Alan meant to do everything in his power to keep that from happening.

He pushed the notice back onto the nail that hung on the door for such postings, making a new hole in the paper. Olivia promptly jerked the notice down again. Alan snatched it out of her hand and put it back up. Olivia grabbed it once more and tore down the steps before he could even think of grabbing it back.

"You're only hurting yourself!" he called, and then he ran down the steps after her.

"You didn't tell me you were a council member," she

said, her face aflame with anger. "Hah! You didn't tell me you were *president* of the town council."

"There was never a need to tell you that."

"Whose idea was it to call this meeting, Mr. President? And why wasn't I told about it? Why did I have to find out by reading a notice? You can't tell me you just found out about it yourself. These things take time," she said, waving the paper. "Printing takes time!"

"I didn't know!"

She wore a white smock over a light green dress today, and she reached into the pockets of the smock and pulled out other papers, all crumpled into balls. She must have gone up and down every street and removed every notice he had spent all morning posting.

"Olivia!" he said in complete disbelief.

She made a face at him, looking triumphant, her eyes bright, as she began tearing one of the papers. "I'm going to shred all of them," she announced.

"No, you're not," he said, and he began grabbing notices from her, snatching them out of the air as she tossed them here and there to blow around. Some tumbled off up the street.

She walked off after them, and as she walked, she picked them up, unballed them, and tore them, a woman gone mad, completely mad. She managed to shred at least half of the papers Harvey and Hank had had printed, and the pieces flew everywhere, on walkways, up and down the street. Alan caught a few, cursing Olivia with every step.

"I'll be here this evening," she said smartly, tipping her head and shredding more. "We shall see if anyone else is."

"The council members will be there, and they're the ones who vote!" he shouted at her. "I don't know what you thought to prove by doing this!"

"It's defiance."

He laughed crazily. "It's a temper tantrum, that is what it is."

"I won't be bullied ever again by anyone, anywhere! I will not be bullied by an individual or by a team of people. I brought a little something nice to Davenport, a little color on a street corner, and I harmed no one by doing it! A meeting even to discuss passing an ordinance to outlaw my wagon is outrageous and insulting. It's several merchants trying to bully another because she's outdoing them and perhaps because she's a woman outdoing them! I'll never be bullied again because I'm weaker and smaller. I'll fight!"

With that, she gave a flip of her skirts, turned, took the ropes from Janey, who regarded her with wide eyes, and started off down the street. As irritated with her as he was, Alan suddenly wanted to applaud her for her speech and even for the way she had so brazenly shredded those notices. He had no idea what circumstances had led to her coming to Davenport, but he suspected that they had a lot to do with her speech and with the fury with which she had shredded the notices.

People had gathered near the church and emerged from nearby buildings to watch the confrontation, and many of them *did* applaud, saluting her and the stand she had just taken. Alan had known that the signatures Harvey and Hank had gathered on that petition represented a minority. Still, seeing the support for her warmed his heart. Most everyone liked Olivia, and that was probably even more true now. Harvey and Hank *were* two merchants crusading to oust her because she threatened their business by doing good business of her own, and if they were to march up the street and begin reposting the remaining intact notices themselves, Alan did not doubt that Olivia would be fearless in snatching the papers down and finishing what she had started.

He joined the crowd in clapping, cheering what she had just done. Olivia turned and gave him an incredulous look. Then she broke into a rather meek smile. Later he might demand an apology from her for thinking that he had anything to do with calling the meeting. For now, her smile would do.

Harvey tore out from between two buildings, and nearly slid right past Alan in the street. "I just heard," he said, out of breath. He waved a hand, indicating the pieces of paper littering the street. "Look at this. Look what she did! Went around town an' pulled them all down. She should be arrested. Yes, she should. Some're still together. Get them an' post them, Councilman. Right now, before they all blow away."

Shaking his head, Alan handed Harvey the pieces of notices he still held. "I'm going home and going to bed, Harv. You chase them," he said and walked away just as a good gust of wind swept up the street, scattering the pieces of paper and intact notices even further afield.

"I'm going to demand your resignation!" Harvey shouted, infuriated.

"You won't have to demand it," Alan said and kept walking.

The meeting was well attended even though Olivia had shredded so many of the notices, and the whispering that started up and the admiring looks that greeted her when she and Janey walked into the meetinghouse made Alan wonder if their confrontation that morning was responsible for the turnout.

People filled every chair, crowded the aisles, and spilled out onto the steps. But the masses parted when Olivia arrived, smartly dressed in a prim dark blue hat and modest dress of the same color. Not that she ever dressed lavishly. But this dress and hat made her look harmless, like a woman who would never dream of snatching public notices from posts and meetinghouses and shredding them in front of the president of the town council. People clapped, whispered, sat up straight, and took notice as she entered the church. They cleared chairs in the front row for her and Janey, and the crowd quieted as soon as Alan brought the meeting to order.

The first thing on the agenda was his resignation. He refused to serve on a council that consisted mostly of members who planned to vote for the passing of an ordinance that would prohibit the selling of goods on any street corner. The ordinance was aimed at Davenport's newest citizen, Olivia Monroe, he said, specifically because she was outselling other leading merchants. "She has harmed no one. She's industrious in buying vegetables from outlying farmers and from incoming steamers, and she's brought color to one of our street corners and added tastefulness to our community."

She sat a little straighter during those moments, and her eyes sparkled with something akin to admiration as she watched him. He had used some of the very words she had used in her speech to him this morning, because she really had brought color to one of Davenport's street corners. She really had added a certain amount of tastefulness to the community.

"Aw, don't resign, Doc!" someone called from the back of the room.

"Leave Missus Monroe an' her wagon be!" someone else called. "We don't need no such ord'nance. Doc Schuster's right. It's just to try to run somebody whose doin' bus'ness off the street. That ain't right."

Other grumblings rose from the gathering, voices of agreement.

"Don't resign, Doc. We need ya," Charlotte said, getting to her feet.

"That's right, we do," Curtis Campbell said, rising next to her.

More calls of "don't resign" and "we need ya" went through the room, and several dozen people got to their feet to show their support.

"With three merchants and myself on the council, I'm outvoted," Alan said. "I've seen enough people gather around Mrs. Monroe's wagon to know how most of you feel. But the fact remains . . . the three merchants who serve on this council don't want Mrs. Monroe doing business on that corner because she detracts from their business."

"Ye're presumin' to know how I'm plannin' on votin'," Jake Coates said, poking his head around Hank Shears at the front table. Jake was Frank's brother and the fourth council member—the third merchant—and Alan had heard rumors that Harv and Hank had been down at Jake's store talking to him all afternoon. He had indeed presumed that the three of them all planned to vote in favor of passing the ordinance.

"I apologize, Councilman, if you haven't allowed Mr. Shears and Mr. Tirado to influence your vote," Alan told Jake.

"Well, I haven't," Jake responded, a bulge of tobacco in his right cheek. He shot a stream of juice at the spittoon on the floor to his left—he always brought his own since Reverend Carpenter refused to keep spittoons in the church for the convenience of the congregation's most disreputable guests from the saloons just up the street. Jake leveled a glare at Hank, then turned it on Harvey. "Thought ya had me, did ya, boys? Thought I might help ya run that gal oughtta Dav'nport? Not a chance. I'd sooner run you two out for what ye're tryin' to do to 'er."

"She's livin' with 'im at his house, her an' her girl!" Hank said, bolting up from his chair behind the long table where the council members sat. "Mrs. Monroe an' Doc Schuster."

"That's enough," Alan warned the man. "She lives in the house, I live in the barn. She rents the house from me—we don't live in it together. You need to remember what I told you the afternoon you visited her wagon, Hank."

"Resignation accepted," Harv said suddenly, trying to snatch the paper on which Alan had prepared his speech.

"Not so fast," Alan said, holding it up high. "A vote of two to two would end the entire matter in a tie. An ordinance passes only if there's a majority vote."

"The American way!" someone shouted.

"Gotcha ya, Harv . . . Hank," another man said.

"There. Now leave Mrs. Monroe alone," a woman commanded. Was that Louise's voice? Alan didn't dare take his eyes off of Hank long enough to find out. Obviously Hank planned to say something more, and Alan meant to send him a silent warning that if he said anything derogatory about Olivia and anything distasteful about their relationship, he would be after him again. Hank needed to be reminded of that more than once, it seemed.

"She's shackin' up with him in that house, that's why he doesn't want to vote for the ord'nance. That's why he's resignin'," Hank said, as if daring Alan to come after him at a public gathering. He was a fool, given the fact that Alan had punched him in a public place before—on a street corner—for insulting Olivia in such a way.

Alan went over Harvey after Hank, upsetting the glasses of water on the table and scattering any papers that the water failed to reach and soak. Women shrieked, and men cheered. Harvey cursed and scrambled to get out of the way. Hank turned tail to run, and Jake cackled as if he'd never seen anything so funny in his life. He grabbed Hank by his shirt and shoved the man over to Alan. Alan raised a fist, preparing to pummel the insulting merchant, but Olivia jumped up on the table suddenly and pushed her way between the two of them, mindless of the fact that water was soaking a portion of her pretty skirt.

"Stop!" she screeched, and fearing that she might pull out her pistol and shoot the church rafters, Alan lowered his fist.

"It doesn't matter what anyone says," she told Alan. "I'll—I'll move back to the boardinghouse. Provided you'll allow me to leave my animals in your barn. And provided I can tend the garden every day and pluck out the weeds."

"There ain't nothin' wrong with you rentin' from Doc," a woman called. "Hell, we've all been waitin' for Doc to get himself a woman anyway!" she said in a lighthearted tone. Laughter sounded around the room. Agreements rose.

Olivia twisted to face the crowd. "I never meant to cause anyone any trouble. Not you," she said, looking back at Alan. She turned back to the crowd. "Not anyone. I've upset the entire town, and I never meant to do that. People have been fighting ever since I came. I won't have the wagon out on the corner anymore. I'll find something to do that's a little more . . . acceptable. I never meant to disrupt anyone's life. I never meant to disrupt the town. I never thought anyone might think . . ."

She shook her head, climbed down off of the table, and took Janey by the hand. Together they started up the aisle, cutting their way between people, and although she held her head high, Alan knew that Olivia was deeply shamed and embarrassed. She felt responsible for all the fighting, and now her reputation had been soiled.

To hell with cutting between people to go after her, he thought, and he climbed up onto the table in front of Harvey, wanting to be seen and heard well. "Mrs. Monroe . . . Mrs. Monroe?" he called, still using the married title to prevent people from asking questions. "I wonder . . . and now seems a good time to ask . . . if you plan to give me an answer to my proposal soon."

She froze. The crowd froze. Olivia turned slightly and slanted him an odd look. "What proposal is that, Dr. Schuster?"

He lifted his brows, feigning surprise. "My proposal of marriage."

Women gasped. Men chuckled. Charlotte said. "Oh, Doc, I knew . . . I just knew it was meant to be!" Louise reached out and patted Olivia's arm and flashed her a brilliant smile. "You can't think of turnin' Doc Schuster down," she said. "No woman in her right mind would."

"You've forgotten already," Alan said, shaking his head.

"No," Olivia said, and she cleared her throat.

"No?" Charlotte pressed. "Olivia Monroe, remember that speech I gave you about being newly arrived from Boston?"

"I mean no, I haven't forgotten."

"Oh." Charlotte fluttered a handkerchief in front of her face. "Well, thank goodness. You haven't completely lost your senses, then."

"No," Olivia said again, looking straight at Alan.

A sigh of disappointment went through the gathering. Charlotte slumped back in her chair. Olivia gave Alan a silent apology with her eyes, pleading with him to forgive her.

"I'm honored that you asked," she said, smiling a little. "Truly honored. But I can't."

As she cut between more people, Louise and Charlotte both grumbled loudly. "I wanna know where Ida is," Charlotte said. "She'd talk sense into her."

Alan bristled at the refusal, but his disappointment was

quickly overshadowed by what Charlotte had just said—*I wanna know where Ida is.*

He looked straight at Charlotte. "Where *is* Ida? She never misses a town meeting."

Charlotte paled. "That's right, she doesn't. She knows about it. We talked about it this afternoon."

Alan jumped down off of the table and began cutting his own path between people, even excusing his way past Olivia and Janey, and tearing right out the front door. And as he ran down the street, he thought over and over, *Ida never misses a town meeting, never, ever . . .*

CHAPTER FIFTEEN

OLIVIA AND JANEY ran after him, but they couldn't catch up, and Alan arrived at Ida's store first. When he called to her and she didn't answer, he charged straight for the back room. She wasn't there either, so he went upstairs, calling her name.

There he found her lying face down on the floor beside the chair that looked out over the top of her store at the street below. A little pool of blood had formed and dried near her forehead, and Alan was just stooping to check the pulse in her neck when he heard Olivia issue a cry from the doorway. She was paler than he had ever seen her. But his immediate concern was for Ida.

"Olivia, if you can't stand the sight of blood, leave," he said, pushing Ida's hair back, trying to locate a wound, if there was one.

"No, it's not that," Olivia said, hurrying forth. "Let me help you."

Together they turned Ida over, and Alan checked her pulse. Strong, but irregular. Her lips were gray. Her skin was mottled beneath the surface. A little cut just above one of her eyebrows had produced the blood. He damn sure never would have guessed that a fall would kill Ida in the end. He had always thought she might dance herself to death or someone might find her "sleeping" in her sewing room one day. Never a fall.

Janey had come over, and she grabbed Olivia's shoulder and shook her hard. "Did you kill him, Livvy? Is he dead?"

she asked, her voice small and soft as she stared at the blood on the floor.

"Janey!" Olivia gaped at her sister, her eyes as large as Alan had ever seen them. *Killed who?* he wondered, but he didn't have time for questions.

Charlotte burst into the room and hurried over to where Ida lay. "Let's get her to the bed," she told Alan. He slipped his arms under Ida's shoulders, Charlotte lifted her feet, and together they carried Ida across the room to her bed.

"She fell," he informed Charlotte. "I think she hit her head on the windowsill."

"Ida's never fallen out of her chair," Charlotte argued.

"Her pulse is erratic. Her heart's been weak for some time now. Maybe she fell after an attack."

"A heart attack?"

He nodded.

"Oh, Ida. You'd be really mad at yourself if you knew you missed the town meeting," Charlotte said.

Olivia had gathered Janey onto her lap on the floor and was now pressing Janey's head to her chest and whispering to the girl. Alan couldn't make out what she was saying, and he didn't want to worry about it right now. He asked Olivia if she would fetch his medical bag from the barn—he had left it there, not planning on needing it during the meeting.

She and Janey went off to get the bag while Charlotte removed Ida's boots and Alan pressed his head to Ida's chest, trying to hear heart sounds.

"I don't know if I killed him, Janey," Olivia said as they hurried toward the homestead. "If I did, I'm sorry. I'm very sorry. I would never intentionally kill another human being. I had to do something. He was trying to stop us from leaving. Do you remember? You do, don't you? I don't think you have all this time . . . since we left. Then you saw Ida lying there. You spoke, Janey. You spoke! Say something else. Please."

"Is Ida dead?"

Olivia stared at her. She hadn't just been hearing things back there in Ida's room. She really hadn't. Janey *had* spoken. In her mind she had suddenly been back in Philadelphia, reliving that horrible night when Olivia had hit Edward with the bookend. Janey hadn't seen Ida lying on the floor moments ago; she had seen her father. And the shock of it after nearly three months of peace had forced words from her mouth.

"No, Ida's not dead, sweetie," Olivia said. "But she's old, and old people tire and pass on one day. Like my father did, remember?"

Janey nodded. "Livvy?"

"Yes, Janey?"

"If Papa's dead and people find out, will they put you in the gaol?"

Olivia inhaled deeply. If only she could have avoided involving Janey in her web of deceit. But there was no way. Janey had been there the night she had hit Edward with the bookend, Janey had accompanied her here, and if Janey told anyone what she had seen that night, Olivia would most assuredly end up in jail.

"They will, Janey. But I don't want you ever to lie to anyone, the way I've lied to people."

"I won't tell anyone anything," Janey said as they reached the homestead. She ran into the barn, and just as Olivia was entering the structure, she emerged from Dr. Schuster's room with his medical bag in hand. She dashed past Olivia, saying, "Hurry, hurry! I found it next to one of those wooden legs he's always playing with."

Olivia didn't bother to ask how Janey knew he was always playing with the wooden legs. That could wait until later.

"Doc, I thought ya had a hankerin' to get fresh with me lately," Ida croaked softly.

Alan lifted his head and grinned down at her. "That's right, I have. And you just had to have an attack so I could, didn't you?"

"G'on with ya. Don't that jes' beat the nation," she said, fighting a grin of her own.

"Ida Bogue," Charlotte whispered excitedly. "You . . . you old woman, you. You gave us quite a scare!"

"I was jes' restin' is all. Hey, Doc."

"Yes, Ida?"

"That box o' papers I keep over 'n the corner. Fetch it fer me, would ya?"

"Ida, I don't think you should be going through a box of papers right now."

Her eyes sparkled angrily, but the sparkles were dull compared to how bright they usually were. "I need my box. Have I gotta get up from here an' fetch the dadburn thing m'self?"

She wanted to get her affairs in order, that's why she wanted that box. It contained her important papers—her deed to the lot on which her store was located, the addresses of the many friends and acquaintances she had made over the years, deeds to other land she and her various husbands had acquired over time . . . She knew she was in a lot of trouble health-wise this time, and she wanted the box close to her. Alan knew Ida well enough to see the fear in her eyes behind her tough front, and he didn't want to fetch the box for her. He didn't want to help her get her affairs in order because he didn't want Ida to go just yet. He wanted to spend at least a few more years with this grumpy old woman. He wanted to dance with her again and call on patients with her, something she hadn't done once with him since returning from Cincinnati. He wouldn't let her get up.

"Well then, get me my box, Doc," she said, settling back on the pillow. "I'm gonna take a nice long nap soon—I ain't never felt s'tired 'n my life. But I gotta look through a few things first. Charlotte, go fetch Frank Coates an' tell 'im I wanna hear a little o' his fiddlin' b'fore I take m'self a nap. Where's that gal . . . Livia?"

"Sure, Ida," Charlotte said, giving the elderly woman an odd look. She glanced at Alan, worry marking her brow, then back at Ida. "I'll do that. I'll fetch Frank and his fiddle. Don't . . . don't go to sleep before I get back now, you hear? I want you to be awake when I come back, Ida Bogue."

"I'll be awake."

"Doc, you keep her awake, you hear?" Charlotte said, and he thought he heard a note of panic in her voice. Charlotte knew, just as he and Ida knew, that Ida's time on earth had just about run out.

"I'll keep her awake, Charlotte. Go get Frank."

Charlotte left, and Alan got the box and brought it to the bed for Ida.

"There's some papers all wrapped up in there," Ida said. "Tied t'gether with a string. Take 'em out. They're yers. Stayed for a spell with the Sauk an' wrote down a lot o' their healin' recipes. Kept 'em all these years. Yer always wonderin' how I mix things, an' I ain't never told ya. Got to thinkin' las' week ya might want those."

Alan started to object, to say he didn't want them because it wasn't time for her to go yet. But that would be denial; he and Ida both knew she was lucky to have lived this long.

He lifted the bundled papers from the box. There were other papers in the bottom of the box, but he ignored them, turning the bundle over in his lap, examining it on the surface.

"They work, Doc," she said, and when he glanced up, she was smiling at him.

He smiled back, despite the heaviness that had settled in his chest. Grief. This was how grief felt. "I know, Ida. I've learned a lot from you, but not nearly enough."

"Listen up," she said, snapping him to attention. She licked her lips and inhaled deeply, as if she needed more air. Her lips were still blue. "Talked to John las' week, too. We drew up a little somethin' 'bout the store an' all the land I own here 'n there."

"Ida, don't. Where's the foxglove I gave you? It's only another arrythmia," Alan said, getting up from the tick and hurrying over to her dresser. He couldn't stand this. He really couldn't. He sat by bedsides many times and watched numerous patients expire, knowing he could do nothing more to help them. But with Ida, there must be something more he could do. Something.

"Sit down, Doc, an' stop fussin' about. My ticker's worn out, is all. Plumb worn out. I'm old. Sit down."

He sat back down on the bed just as Olivia and Janey entered the room with his medical bag.

"There she is," Ida said, straightening, licking her lips again. Her eyelids drooped. She popped them open. "Damn if I ain't tired. Go down'n get some o' that candy, Janey, an' bring up the corn cakes I left sittin' on the counter. G'on. Frank's gonna show up any minute with his fiddle, an' we're gonna have a li'l party."

Janey did as she was told, always prepared to go after candy. Olivia gave Alan a baffled look. He glanced away, blinking back tears. Wasn't it just like Ida to want to have a party at a time like this? Damn her anyway. But wasn't it just like her?

Charlotte came with Frank and his fiddle, and Ida grinned and told him to play her a jig. Janey returned with the candy and cakes, and Ida told everyone to take some. "Smile, ever'one. Doc, take this girl out an' dance with 'er," she said, meaning Olivia. "I wanna see the two o' ya t'gether, an' I mean that. C'mere, Janey. Sit by me fer a minute or two."

Janey climbed up onto the bed while Frank began a lively tune and Alan took Olivia's hand and began dancing with her.

"Reckon I was 'bout yer age when I came out here with my ma an' pa, an' I reckon ya got a good long life ahead o' ya," Ida told Janey.

"What is she doing?" Olivia whispered to Alan. "What is all of this? Has she gone mad?"

Alan shook his head. "She's enjoying herself one last time with some of her friends."

Olivia's eyes flared.

"Keep dancing," he said, and she did.

"Charlotte, ya keep an eye on Louise. Ya know how she likes the bottle."

"I'll do that, Ida," Charlotte said, her eyes glazed.

"Janey, that cat o' mine. The one that's always hidin' when people come around? Take 'er home with ya t'night.

C'mere closer an' I'll tell ya where 'er fav'rite hidin' place is. That's where she's at, I guarantee ya."

Janey moved closer, and Ida whispered in her ear. Then the girl scrambled off of the bed and ran off downstairs again.

"Rest o' the papers in that box, Doc," Ida said. "Take 'em to John, an' he'll make sure they get taken care of. Play another one, Frank. I'm gonna take a rest now. Livia, mind the store good. I know ya will."

Alan had to force Olivia to keep dancing as Ida closed her eyes. Charlotte stood near the window now, and she put both hands over her mouth and breathed deeply, fighting tears. Frank played *When the Farmer Comes to Town*, Ida's favorite tune, and she smiled and nodded moments before drifting off into a deep sleep.

Nearly the entire town turned out for Ida's funeral. Words were spoken in the Methodist Church, first a blessing by the reverend, then an account by John of when he'd first met Ida, the day she was forcing a bull she'd just bought up Main Street to breed with the cow she already had. Alan couldn't help a smile, imagining a younger Ida tugging a bull up Main Street. Homer made a speech, saying how Ida wouldn't want any of them to be sad; she loved a party, she'd gone to sleep in the middle of a party, and she would want everybody to celebrate to remember how she liked to have fun. Therefore, a gathering would be held in his barn this evening, and everyone was invited. Alan choked up in the middle of his own eulogy about how Ida had taught him a lot about medicine that no aspiring doctor could learn in medical school. Ida Bogue had been more than his companion in medicine these past years, he said; she had been his friend.

Frank got the brass band together for Ida's last march up Main Street to the cemetery, and Alan choked back more tears and forced himself to play his trombone. At the graveside he finally spilled his grief into his handkerchief, and then he stayed long after most everyone else left, until the last shovel of dirt was patted down and the stone Elijah

Stephenson had chiseled for Ida was in place. Then he stood to leave.

Olivia watched Alan from the shade of a tall oak, where she had sat on a blanket all afternoon. Janey, Louise, Malva, and Charlotte had sat with her for a while, then Charlotte had suggested that they all go to the boardinghouse for refreshment. Later they should drop in at Homer's barn, she said.

"I might stop by Mr. Whitworth's later," Olivia had responded, "but I think I'll stay here for now."

Charlotte had nodded. "Could I take Janey for you? She could play and help me with things at the boardinghouse. Might be much better for her than having the sun beat down on her out here. Might even be some other children around to play with."

Olivia agreed that Charlotte could take Janey to the boardinghouse with her. But she planned to stay right here with Dr. Schuster. *In the event he wants a shoulder to lay his head on,* Olivia had thought.

While she was waiting for him, John had come by. He offered her a clean handkerchief, and she thanked him as she dabbed at the tears on her cheeks.

"Takin' it pretty hard, ain't he?" John asked, hunching to her level and gazing off at Alan.

Olivia nodded. "She really livened Davenport up, didn't she? It's going to seem quiet with her gone. I'll never forget how much fun she had, leading that parade and then dancing in Mr. Lincoln's barn later."

"Yep. You remind me of 'er a bit."

Olivia smiled at him.

"Speakin' of . . ." He pulled a paper from the inside of his coat. "Reckon now's as good a time as any to give this to ya," he said, handing the paper to her. "That there's a deed to some land a couple o' miles out. Ida lived there with her last husband, an' moved into town to live above the store when he passed. Didn't wanna stay at the place by 'erself. Reckon she's joined 'im now."

Olivia stared at the paper. Ida had given her a piece of land?

"Got plenty o' room fer yer an'mals out there, an' there's a nice cabin that could prob'bly use a good dustin'. There's another deed there, too, to some land here in town." He dug something else out of his pocket. Keys. "The land her store's sittin' on. An' these here keys're to the lock Ida had put on the front door o' the store after some saloon rowdies barrelled in one night. She shot their backside good with buckshot," he said, chuckling. "Anyways, she came callin' on me las' week, sayin' she wanted to change 'er will. She wanted ya to have her store when she passed 'cause she said you'd put yer heart into it, the way she has."

Olivia's jaw seemed to come unhinged. She stared at John as if he'd lost his mind. He grinned at her, then turned her hand over, put the keys in it, and said, "Welcome to Dav'nport, Mrs. Monroe. Yer a bonafide citizen now, fer sure. See ya in Homer's barn later."

Later, in Homer's barn, Alan danced to many of the songs Ida had loved. He danced jigs and reels with Charlotte, Louise, and Malva, and waltzes with Olivia.

"Ida left me her store," Olivia said during one of the last waltzes.

Alan's attention was on Harvey Tirado and Hank Shears as they stood talking near the table where lemonade was being served. "What?" he asked, unsure he had heard Olivia correctly.

"She left me her store. And the homestead where she and her last husband lived."

Alan stared at her. Then he broke into a grin. "I don't imagine that vote went in your favor after I left the Methodist Church yesterday. I realized only this morning that I left behind that note of resignation. Harv probably snatched it right up."

"The vote didn't go well," she said, grinning, too.

"But it doesn't matter."

"No, it doesn't matter."

He chuckled. "Should we go tell them?"

"No," she said. "No fighting at Ida's going-away party."

"I'm going to miss that old hen," he said, reflecting.

"Old hen?" She laughed in disbelief.

"Ida wouldn't mind. She'd turn around and accuse me of being a rooster."

Alan studied Olivia. Her golden hair, so shimmery in the lamplight. Her sparkling blue eyes. Her clear skin. The color that rode high on her cheeks and that deepened when she caught him observing her so intensely. Her fine brows, long lashes, the smooth line of her jaw . . . Her sweet, full lips that he had tasted and wanted to taste again. She was wearing her blue dress again, the one she had worn to the council meeting, only she had replaced the hat with several matching bows. She looked festive though not too festive, but certainly unlike someone in mourning. And that was good because Ida had hated black.

"You sat beneath that tree all afternoon," he said.

Olivia tipped her head, tossing back the curls on one side of her face. "I was worried about you."

"I know."

"I sat up all last night worrying about you, wondering if you were sleeping out in the barn or lying awake thinking of Ida."

"I was lying awake thinking of Ida."

"You should have come to the house. I couldn't sleep, either. We could have shared a cup of cider."

The thought of them doing that made him smile. His gaze drifted to her lips. "You wouldn't have turned me away?"

Coloring more, she slowly shook her head. "No, I wouldn't have turned you away. The offer stands for tonight, too."

He drew a deep breath and teased: "Harv and Hank probably have spies planted."

"It doesn't matter anymore. Maybe John will tell them I no longer have to sell anything on the street corner."

That made him laugh.

"I'd marry you to preserve your good reputation," he said.

She laughed a little, too, rather sadly. "I know you would." But she didn't take him up on the offer.

They twirled, turned, dipped. Alan sighed. "There are things you need to tell me, Olivia Monroe."

"Sh." She shook her head again. "Not tonight. Please not tonight. We've had enough unpleasantness between yesterday and today."

"All right. But I won't be put off much longer."

The dance ended, and Olivia went off with Charlotte and Janey. But not before she gave Alan another long look over her shoulder as she walked toward Homer's barn doors. There had been plenty of those tonight—long looks—but this last one made him seriously consider her offer to share a cup of cider with him later. Tonight, he would much rather be with her in the house she had made into a home than out in the barn, alone with his memories of Ida.

CHAPTER SIXTEEN

Olivia and Janey rode home in Charlotte's wagon. Janey washed at the basin in her room, then Olivia slipped a gown over Janey's head and tucked her in for the night. She was tired herself from the activity of the last few days, especially Ida's funeral today, and then the dance in Mr. Whitworth's barn. But Eleanor needed to be milked, and Olivia thought she should say hello to the other animals, whom she had seen so little of for the last several days. She grabbed a lantern, though she kept several in the barn, and she left the house, hearing Annie and Edwin bleat almost as soon as she stepped off the porch. They wanted milk and a few soothing touches of her hand, no doubt. Olivia wondered if Alan had returned yet, and as soon as she stepped into the barn she saw that he had—he was busy brushing down his horses and settling them in for the night.

Edwin and Annie ran straight to her, affectionately bumping their heads against her thighs. Elmor snorted his way over and pushed between the goats. Atop a pile of hay, Martha stood, fluttered her wings and quacked for good measure. Just to remind Olivia not to forget her.

"Well, it seems everyone is glad to see you," Alan said, chuckling. "I've never seen animals develop such an affinity for one person, nor a person for them."

Olivia smiled. "We have grown fond of each other," she said, stroking Edwin's neck, then Annie's. She rubbed between Elmor's ears. Eleanor mooed from her stall, and Olivia assured her that she would be over in a few moments.

"She just asked me where you were."

"Did she?" Olivia's smile widened.

He folded his arms across a top stall rail. His eyes twinkled in the lamplight. "Oh, certainly. She said, 'Doc, my mistress ain't been in here to see me this evenin'. Don't that jes' beat the nation? Haven't see her, have ya?' "

Olivia inhaled deeply. "Ida always said that—'don't that beat the nation.' "

He withdrew, looked sad for a moment, then returned to the rail. "I know. I'm always going to repeat some of her sayings so I don't forget them, so I always remind myself of how she sounded."

"You won't forget."

He shook his head. "A person forgets, Olivia. The years start passing. Memories fade—though you always remember some things."

"How could anyone forget anything about Ida?" she asked.

He laughed softly. "True. Very true."

Eleanor mooed again, and Olivia said, "All right. I'm coming."

"You visit with those goats. I'll milk," Alan offered, and when Olivia opened her mouth to object, he shook his head. "No harm comes from letting a person help you."

Not with the little things anyway, she thought as they exchanged a meaningful gaze. She wondered how much longer she could avoid telling him why she and Janey had traveled west and come to be in Davenport. He had surely heard Janey yesterday in Ida's room when Janey had asked *"Did you kill him, Livvy?"* and that possibility scared her nearly to death. She had started to contemplate taking Janey and their belongings and running again. But she didn't know where they could go, and she didn't want to start over again. Besides, anywhere she and Janey went, people might start asking questions. She was so frightened . . . so fearful that their lives were about to unravel. And yet, she had decided against running again. She didn't want to have to put their lives together again. She was tired of worrying. She was tired of being afraid. She was tired of keeping secrets. More than a week ago, she had finally forced herself to send Mrs. Ferguson's sister a letter, and she wondered for days now what the response to it would be. Would Mrs. Thompson report her whereabouts to the authorities? Or would she or Mrs. Ferguson simply write back and tell her what had happened with Uncle Edward, Mrs. Ferguson, and Harry after she and Janey fled? Sending the letter had added to her worries.

She had finally gotten used to the hay, thank goodness. She sat on the haystack with Martha while Alan milked. Edwin and Annie sat on either side of her, and Annie rested her head on Olivia's leg. Elmor wasn't usually very friendly, but he did come over and plop down beside the haystack. Martha fluttered her wings at him, and he snorted at her. The two of them never did seem to get along.

Alan began humming something that sounded like a spiritual tune. His voice rose, then dipped, seeming to glide around the barn, and before long, Olivia lay back on the haystack, unable to keep her eyes from closing.

When Alan finished milking Eleanor and noticed that Olivia had fallen asleep on the haystack, he couldn't resist the urge to coax the goats away from her by dividing the milk between them. It was one of the few times they rushed his way; since the first night he had spent in the barn with them, when he had shouted at them several times to be quiet, they had been avoiding him.

He crawled up on the haystack and propped himself up on his elbow beside Olivia. He traced her jaw with his fingertip, and he stared down at her pretty, innocent face, wondering what scared her so much that she couldn't tell him, couldn't trust him. She was so sweet, sitting this afternoon under that tree, waiting for him, worrying about him. Not sleeping last night because she worried about him. Taking care of Janey and these animals.

What had Janey meant when she had asked Olivia *Did you kill him?* The recollection of that had come back to Alan late this afternoon, after his initial grief had started to ebb and after Ida's funeral was behind them. He had also started thinking about how Ida hadn't liked his pressing Olivia for answers about why Janey couldn't speak and why Janey had said they were from Philadelphia when Olivia had said Boston. In fact, Ida had gotten impatient with him because he had pressed Olivia for any answers. "Wait for Rich to write," Ida had said. "Stop naggin' the gal."

Because he wanted to help, he really had been nagging Olivia. Ida was right. And he needed to stop. If Olivia chose to tell him someday why Janey had asked her that question when she'd seen Ida lying there, it would only be after he had won her complete trust. And he would do that by being patient and supportive of her, not by drilling her with questions.

Her lashes fluttered up.

"Hi, sleepyhead," he teased, and he kissed her lightly on the lips.

Olivia stared up at him, looking dazed, from sleep and from the kiss, he thought. She smiled a little nervously, then she lifted her head and kissed him back.

That was a surprise. Wondering what she was thinking and where more kisses might lead, he twirled a finger in a curl that had come loose from the rest of her hair, and he kissed her again, longer this time, slipping his hand to the back of her neck, closing his eyes as she opened her mouth and offered more of herself. Her hands came up to his shoulders, her lips moved against his, sweetly and softly, and he had to wonder if he had suddenly died and gone to heaven.

"Cider might taste good right now," he suggested, lifting his head. At the very least, it might cool him off a little.

"Yes, it would," she agreed.

Something bumped Alan's thigh, and he turned in time to see Edwin dipping his head, preparing to bump him again.

Olivia giggled. Alan scowled at the animal. "Edwin, stop it," she said, trying to push him away with her boot.

"He doesn't like me," Alan remarked. "He gets jealous of me."

"He'll just have to be jealous, then." Olivia moved off the haystack, stood, and brushed strands of hay from her skirt. Her eyes, sparkling as she smiled, met Alan's, and she held out her hand to him, inviting him.

For conversation and a glass of cider, that's all, he told himself. But if more began to happen once they got inside the house, he damn sure wasn't going to stop the natural progression of events tonight. He wanted her, and he wanted her to learn to trust him, and allowing more intimacy to grow between them, both physically and emotionally, might eventually persuade her to do that. Besides, Olivia had turned down his offer of marriage, but in time he hoped to change her mind.

Olivia didn't want him to spend another difficult night alone in the barn with his thoughts and memories of Ida. He seemed all right, but once the quiet settled in he might begin reflecting on the events and happenings of the last few days, and he might begin missing Ida again. Olivia believed that a person needed to grieve—she had certainly grieved when her father died—but she did not believe a person should do it alone. He should have someone to talk to, someone with whom to share his memories of the deceased person, someone who could console him, dry his tears, hold him . . . share a cup of cider with him.

Alan settled his hand around hers and rose. Olivia grabbed the lantern while he grabbed the bucket of milk. Edwin was looking at the haystack where Olivia and Alan had been lying, as if he too might like to lie down on it, and he gave a small bleat just as they slipped out the barn door.

Olivia felt somewhat relieved, slipping out of the barn and stealing across the grass hand in hand with Alan. The feeling was wonderful, especially since she had spent the last weeks and months being so afraid that the circumstances leading to her arrival here might be discovered. She was still afraid; Alan would ask more questions at some point, and she wouldn't lie to him—as she had told Janey to lie to no one. *No more lies, Olivia,* she had told herself this afternoon, hence her relief. She couldn't stand the thought of telling even one more, ever. If Alan began asking questions, she would simply be selective about what she told him, but no more lies. If he asked again if she was from Boston or Philadelphia, she would tell him Philadelphia.

She would not volunteer information, however. She would not ever lie to him about the trouble with her uncle—the fact that she had stolen from the man, then possibly murdered him—she would just not tell him about that ugliness unless she had no alternative. She certainly would not tell him with the intent of enlisting his aid in getting out of the trouble in which she had embroiled herself.

Upon entering the house, Olivia went to the back room for the cider, then returned to the main room and took two cups from a cupboard that was located not far from the stove. She started to put the cups and jug of cider on the table. Then she glanced at the settle and the braided rugs and pretty curtains and opted to take the cups and the jug there. She laughed at the smile of wonderment on Alan's face as she placed the cups and jug on a nearby table and then settled herself on the rug, tucking her legs beneath her.

"If I can nap on a haystack, a braided rug certainly is not too good for me," she said when he joined her. He pulled the cork out of the jug and poured cider into their cups.

"Janey spoke yesterday," he remarked, leaning back against the settle, watching her.

Olivia nodded, feeling a knot of apprehension in her stomach. His questions were about to begin again. She sensed that and she had to make herself stay calm.

She liked him so much. Too much. At times she thought she loved him, particularly these past few days. But she didn't want to be faced with his questions about her and Janey, why Janey hadn't spoken until yesterday, and where they were from. She didn't want to tell him the truth about any of those things because she felt that the less he knew, the better. But she would tell him the truth if she had to. Since she had told him she'd never been married, she had expected him to ask why her last name was different than Janey's—particularly since she had more or less told him that Morgan was their maiden name. He hadn't asked about the names, and that baffled her, made her wonder if he even realized the discrepancy in her explanation.

She felt warm suddenly; there didn't seem to be much air circulating between the two open windows. She took a long drink of cider to cool herself. He refilled her cup, then studied her as she drank more.

"Want to sit on the porch?" he asked. "There's more air."

Normally she might have assumed that he too was unusually warm sitting inside the house. But one look into his eyes revealed that he knew how trapped she felt suddenly.

"Or we could walk," he suggested. "Just around the barn and the house."

That sounded like a nice idea. She didn't want to walk up the street or beyond since Janey was inside the house asleep. But being outside in the open and feeling an occasional evening breeze on her face sounded like a fine idea.

They took a lantern with them, though the moon was high and nearly full, casting a silver glow on the house, the grass, and the barn. Olivia carried out the pail of milk that Alan had carried inside only a short time ago, and she placed it in the well bucket and lowered that into the cool well to keep the milk from spoiling. In the morning she would milk Eleanor again and deliver that milk to Charlotte, as she had been doing for weeks now, since she and Charlotte had made the agreement that Charlotte would teach her to cook in exchange for a pail of milk a day.

"For a city girl, you've learned quite a lot about country living," Alan said, watching her lower the bucket.

"Particularly since I hardly knew a thing about fending for myself when Janey and I first came here," she said, enjoying the compliment.

"I want you to know I really had nothing to do with calling that meeting," he said. "Harv and Hank went over my head to do it."

Sitting on the wooden slats that surrounded the well, Olivia reached up and pressed a finger to his lips. "I know that now. I knew it when you opened the meeting with your resignation speech, and I felt ashamed of myself for even thinking that you might have called the meeting. A number of times these past weeks, I've been guilty of wondering if you teased me so much to try to drive me and Janey from the homestead. I'm ashamed of thinking that too. I think you simply enjoy teasing me."

He caught her finger in his hand. "I do," he said, grinning. "I expected you to pull out your pistol and shoot Harv right between the eyes yesterday morning."

She scowled playfully. "I only have it because the men who frequent the saloons make me nervous."

"As well they should."

"I wouldn't really shoot anyone."

"Livvy, you would have shot me my first night home if you could have seen me clearly! Thank goodness a lamp wasn't burning."

"Indeed. You might have been able to see the furniture. You might not have awakened me until you climbed into bed, and then—"

Her face heated as the image of them in bed together popped into her head.

"That's quite a thought," he said, as if reading her mind.

"No one but Janey has ever called me Livvy," she said, changing the subject.

"If I offend you by calling you that, I won't."

"You don't offend me," she said, rising to walk. "But I must admit, I've wondered how you learned the name. Janey's blocks?"

Alan followed, the lantern in hand, and soon caught up with her. As they walked near the side of the house, he listened to the swish of Olivia's skirts above the whispering trees and the distant shouts, laughter and music that drifted from the saloons. He watched the breeze lift strands of her golden hair, and he inhaled deeply when the direction of the breeze shifted and her scent drifted his way. So sweet, so tempting, so torturous.

She glanced over at him, a question in her glowing eyes.

"The day you burned the food," he explained, sensing that she felt nervous because she thought he meant to question her about Janey and herself again. "Janey woke me that night to thank me for saving you from the smoke. She brought her slate with her to the barn, and she wrote your name as 'Livvy.' That was also when I examined her throat."

"She must trust you a great deal."

He nodded.

Quiet fell between them for a few moments. She seemed tense suddenly, braced for an onslaught of questions.

"I'm not going to ask you any more questions about you and Janey," Alan said, trying to assure her. "I wish you'd let me help you with whatever troubles you, but since you've elected not to . . . that doesn't make me think any less of you, Olivia. Or care about you any less."

Olivia was touched by his desire to help and his acceptance of her even while she was refusing his help. And she knew he was sincere—she saw sincerity glowing in his eyes. She had seen it for days now.

Without giving the matter a second thought, she slipped her hand down into his. When he lifted her hand and kissed the back of it, warmth filled her, the same tingling warmth that had made her light-headed during the times he had kissed her on the mouth. Olivia wondered if he was thinking of kissing her on the lips now, and she nearly laughed aloud, shocked at herself over the thought that *she* just might kiss *him* again.

She turned to watch the stars and the moon, leaning back against the back-porch railing. Being out here with Alan was nice, with the night air caressing her face, with toads croaking and crickets chirping. The noises drifting from the saloons hardly bothered her, the night was so pretty and so serene.

"It's the most terrible thing, knowing you're afraid of me," Alan said, drawing close. "You apparently have other things to be afraid of, Olivia. You needn't be afraid of me."

He placed the lantern on the bottom step, then touched her forearm and skimmed his fingers up to her shoulders. Olivia tipped forward and kissed him boldly, feeling more warmth rush up from her toes. She kissed him again, closing her eyes for a second, pausing on his bottom lip.

"And you, Dr. Schuster," she whispered. "You seem afraid to touch me tonight for fear that I might withdraw."

"Will you?" he queried, his voice thick and low, raspy. "You seem so close sometimes, Livvy, and yet so far away."

"I'm here and I'm not withdrawing."

He stared down at her for a moment, as if trying to measure her mood. Another breeze cooled her face, but her skin still tingled, wanting his touch.,

She threw all caution aside, probably unwisely, or so the apprehensive side of her warned. She placed her open palm against the front of his shirt, then she reached down, took his hand and brought it to her face. She kissed his palm, then his fingers, inhaling his masculine scent, and she drew a sharp breath when his arm brushed the tip of her breast. She had never known she could be so sensitive, that she would even want to be touched so much by a man, be so near to one. That she would ache so. She had ventured out into the world beyond Philadelphia knowing so little, she suddenly realized. Particularly in the area of relations between a man and a woman.

She tipped her head back, moved his hand down to her sensitive neck, and closed her eyes again. He stroked her, whispered her name, drew closer, slipped his other hand up to her neck, then to her jaw.

"You don't realize how tempting you are," he grated, kissing the corner of her mouth. His fingers slid into her hair and through it, bringing a portion of it to his face, where he rubbed it against his cheek. "We're nuzzling again. You need to remember what nuzzling leads to. The—"

"Natural progression of events," she said, opening her eyes.

He studied her, her head still tipped back, her lips parted and ready for his kisses, her body aching more than ever for his touch. He seemed to be holding his breath. She watched him swallow, then lick his lips as if they had suddenly gone dry. Hers certainly had, along with her throat.

"Livvy . . . you look like you're inviting me."

She glanced away, then returned her gaze to his. Her heart was now beating in her ears. "I suppose I am," she said softly.

He went very still. Even his fingers stopped moving in

her hair. "Do you want more to happen? More than innocent kisses?"

"Do you?" she countered.

He gave a small laugh of disbelief. "I'm a man. Of course I do. Remember that—that every man wants a woman to offer herself to him."

"I don't believe that about you, Alan Schuster," Olivia said, touching a finger to his lips. "That you would accept just any woman's offer."

He grinned. "I do have incredible powers of restraint. Sometimes."

She smiled. "I'm glad you added that. When you went over that table after Mr. Shears yesterday, I wondered if you'd gone mad."

"That's not the kind of restraint I'm talking about," he said, kissing her lightly.

She kissed him back, applying a little more pressure this time, touching his shoulders, then his chest again, feeling the strength of him, remembering the rush of feelings she had experienced when he went over the table after Hank, again defending her virtue. Fear, pride, love . . .

"I love you, Livvy," he whispered against her hair. "I think I realized it the day I saw you with your wagon on the street corner. And I love that name . . . Livvy."

Olivia tried to slip away, intending to grab the lamp and go up the back steps. There she meant to invite him back into the house. He planted his hands on the railing on both sides of her, and he dipped his head to her neck and began nipping like a man who had suddenly realized how hungry he was. The abrupt change in him made Olivia gasp.

She listened to his quick breaths, to her own, to the drumming of her heart. Her head tipped back, and her hands went to his head, pressing, encouraging him. She gasped again when he cupped her breast, and when he squeezed slightly, catching her nipple between his thumb and forefinger, she moaned and arched against him.

He lifted his head, withdrew a little, and began unbuttoning her bodice buttons, holding her gaze all the while. "Stop me if you want to," he said, and she wondered if she would have enough willpower to stop him—even if she changed her mind and wanted to.

He unfastened more buttons.

"Oh, my God," Olivia whispered. She swallowed, wondering at her sanity for the first time since she began encouraging him, and though she still ached all over for his touch, his eyes glowed with such intensity that she glanced away, settling her gaze on the porch railing to her right. She didn't want to stop him . . . She didn't.

He pushed her bodice open, revealing the upper swells of her breasts over the top of her corset and chemise. She had always dressed modestly, even when attending parties and balls in Philadelphia; she had not cared for the low necklines favored by so many of the women at evening gatherings. To have so much of herself revealed, even to a man with whom she was contemplating total physical intimacy, embarrassed her greatly. She reached up, grabbed both sides of the open bodice, and brought them together.

"Livvy," Alan said, his voice rich and coaxing. "Don't be ashamed. Don't be embarrassed. You're beautiful. *Beautiful*. Let's go inside." He dipped his head to kiss her again, and he lifted her face to his, forcing her to look at him. Then his hand parted hers, opening the bodice again, and he bent and kissed the tops of her breasts.

The kisses were Olivia's complete undoing. She released a rush of breath and a moan, and she melted against him. He kissed her breasts more, cupped them, savored them. She thought she would die, she now ached so completely and so intensely. She ached in her fingers, in her toes, in her most intimate place . . . She ached everywhere. A sweet, beautiful ache.

"Let's go inside," he said again, and he reached down, took Olivia's hand in his, the lamp in his other hand, then led the way up the steps.

Once inside the house, he led her straight to her bedroom. *His bedroom,* Olivia thought. He placed the lantern on the small secretary to the left of the door, and, still holding her hand, he took his time glancing around the room, taking in her arrangement of it. She had moved the bed, covered it with a quilt that Ida had given her, added a rocking chair—courtesy of Charlotte—and a woven rug that the Presbyterian church ladies had brought to her within days of her renting the house. The ladies had brought her and Janey everything from complete meals to clothing, and considering the fact that they were acting as "the Lord's disciples," she had had a difficult time even thinking of refusing their charity. She had placed another lantern on the chest of drawers, one with a porcelain base on which roses had been painted, and across the top of the chest of drawers lay her silver-handled brush, hand mirror, and several fans painted with a French garden scene. The items had been her mother's, gifts handed down to Olivia by her father when she had reached the age of sixteen.

Alan laughed under his breath.

"I—I know it's different than the way you had it," Olivia said nervously. "It will be changed back, just like the sitting area, when Janey and I leave." She was clutching the front of her unbuttoned bodice again, and she couldn't seem to stop her hands from trembling. She was so frightened suddenly, and yet she had no intention of turning him away.

"And it will stay the same if you don't leave," he said, putting the lamp down and closing the door.

Olivia had time to shoot him a baffled look, and then his lips were on hers again, kissing tenderly while his hands fell on hers and pushed them gently away from her bodice. He unbuttoned more buttons, further loosening the dress that Ida had finished making for her only last week, and he pushed the material over her shoulders and down her arms. The dress soon slid to the floor, but Olivia scarcely noticed, his lips were so hot and delicious on her jaw, her neck, and the upper swells of her breasts.

He stopped only to lift her and carry her to the bed, placing her head gently on the feather pillows. She wore only her undergarments now, and when she turned her head, again feeling self-conscious, he came up to her, hovering over her, and smiled down at her. "Sweet," he whispered, and kissed her again.

He removed her boots, untying and unlacing them quickly, and then he removed his own, shedding them even more quickly. As he began unbuttoning his shirt, Olivia closed her eyes, fighting off more fear and apprehension. She wanted to be with him, though she had heard talk about how a woman's first time with a man hurt. She had also heard that sex was an unpleasant marital task that must be endured by the woman for the sake of conceiving children. But since meeting Alan, she had started to wonder if it was really unpleasant. The feelings leading up to it certainly were not, as she now knew.

"You're trembling," Alan said, removing his shirt.

Olivia stared at the hair on his chest—dark, like his beard—at the small pink nipples peeking from beneath the hair. "Tell me . . ." She swallowed. "Is it unpleasant?"

He lay down beside her, propping himself up on one elbow, his chin in his palm. He began running the tip of his finger along the lace edging the top of her chemise. "What do you think so far? Do you like the way I touch you?"

"Yes," she responded, wondering if she would ever again catch her breath in a normal fashion. "I know only what . . . what I heard my aunt and her friends say over the years . . . what I heard my own friends whisper."

"There's pain the first time, when a man enters a woman. I won't lie to you about that."

She glanced down at his finger, swallowing when it dipped into the hollow between her breasts.

"But not much if it's done right," he said, drawing her gaze back to his face. He kissed the top of her right breast, then the top of her left, looking up at her as he did, a shock of blond hair falling over his brow. "Forget what you heard. Forget what was whispered, Livvy. I'll show you how pleasant it can be."

His finger pushed down the top of her chemise and found a rosy nipple, pushed up by her corset. He twirled his finger around it, and Olivia could not help herself. She moaned and arched, gasping when his mouth closed over it. She'd never imagined that anything could feel so good, never realized that any touch or kiss in the world could be such sweet agony. He suckled, and she pressed his head closer and tossed her own head back on the pillows, baring her throat.

Leaving his fingers to pinch and roll her nipple lightly, he moved his lips up to her throat and he devoured it, biting gently, running his tongue up and down either side of it. Her corset felt so tight, so binding suddenly, robbing her of precious air, that Olivia reached down and released it a clasp at a time, finally pulling it out from under her and dropping it on the floor. Alan pulled the ribbon that formed the neckline of her chemise, and his lips followed his hands as he pushed that garment down off of her shoulders and arms.

She felt his length push up against her thigh, hard and insistent, but instead of jerking away from it as her first instinct urged her to do, Olivia relished the feel of it. He pushed her chemise clear down to her waist, kissing and suckling her nipples one at a time, shocking her when his hand slipped between her thighs and began stroking her most intimate place. Olivia gasped and stiffened, but he kissed her and whispered that she was beautiful and that he loved touching her. "Open, Livvy," he urged twice, and the second time she did, moving her legs apart to allow him better access.

He untied her drawers and began pushing them down, his lips blazing a trail across her breasts and down over her stomach. He touched her freely now, without the drawers between his fingers and her, and as his finger slid back and forth over her sensitive bud, Olivia moaned, and arched . . . became lost in his pleasurable movements. She felt his hot mouth on her stomach, on her hips, on her thighs, on her bud, and she wanted to burst, it felt so wonderful. He suckled, and she arched, hearing her own cries. A storm grew deep in her belly, swelling, finally bursting into a million colors.

"Tell me, Livvy, was that unpleasant?" he whispered in her ear.

"No," she said, lifting her head to kiss his chest. "Oh, no."

He pushed her drawers off completely, then her stockings, grumbling about how many clothes women wore.

Olivia couldn't help a shy smile as she sat up and helped him push the last stocking off. He was sitting up, too, now, and she realized that he was working at undoing the buttons on his trousers. She lay back on the pillows and closed her eyes.

He laughed at her, and Olivia grabbed one of the pillows and tossed it at him. He laughed louder, then he pushed the trousers off and eased between her thighs, lowering himself onto her. Olivia braced herself, clutching the quilt on either side.

"It's not going to be so bad," he said, laughing again, prying her hands free and shaking his hair back from his forehead. "Relax, Livvy. Don't tighten up."

He began kissing her again, caressing her breasts, rubbing her nipples, making her strain and arch. His hand slid between them, down between her thighs, and his fingers eased into her, pushing, gliding in and out. Whatever modesty Olivia had left disappeared as she opened and instinctively began moving her hips up and down with his hand. More pleasure began building deep in her groin, spiraling to a crest, and just before she would have peaked, he moved his hand, slid it around and under her buttocks and brought her up to him. He thrust his hips, and sharp pain shot up through her as he entered her, joining their bodies.

She had gone rigid. He kissed her, whispering assurances, that the hurt would fade and that she would feel nothing but pleasure. He settled in more deeply, and Olivia clung to him, trusting that he was right.

He was. When he began moving in and out of her, the pain began to ease. A deep and exquisite pleasure replaced it, and Olivia moved with him, unable to help herself, pressing her hips to his, moaning and crying his name, arching and writhing, straining with him. A few more thrusts and he gasped, groaned several times, stiffened, and spilled himself in her.

Olivia stroked his hair as he brought his head down to rest on her breast.

CHAPTER SEVENTEEN

When Olivia woke the next morning to birds chirping outside the window, Alan was gone. All that remained of him was the impression his head had left on the pillow next to hers and the dampness between her legs. Both things reminded her that she hadn't dreamed what had happened between them last night. He had been here and they had made love. She wondered if he was in the barn working; he was often gone in the mornings when she and Janey went to the barn, but would he have left this morning without kissing her or at least telling her goodbye?

He wasn't in the barn room, as Olivia discovered when she and Janey went out to tend the animals, and she had to suppress her disappointment while she went about her chores. She milked Eleanor while Janey gathered eggs, and when they completed those tasks they set off up the street to call on Charlotte and deliver the milk to the boardinghouse.

"You're rather quiet this morning," Charlotte said, narrowing one eye at Olivia. "A little more color in your cheeks than normal, but you sure are quiet. You usually come in here chatting."

"Nothing's wrong," Olivia said.

Charlotte raised her brows. "When a person says nothing's wrong, there usually is something wrong. Have you been out to the place Ida left you yet?"

"No. I thought Janey and I might ride out there this afternoon."

"I'll go along with you if you'd like. Sally'll be here to mind the place for a time."

"I'd like that," Olivia said. "We're going to the store right now."

"Well, come by here when you get ready to ride out."

Olivia agreed to do that, then left the boardinghouse with Janey.

John had given Olivia the key to Ida's store, and upon reaching the establishment she pulled the key from a pocket in the smock she had donned earlier. The key slid easily into the lock and turned. Still carrying the basket of eggs, she pushed the door open and let Janey walk in first.

"Are we gonna do the wagon anymore, Livvy?" Janey asked.

Olivia walked in and placed the basket of eggs on the counter. The inside of the store was dim. Someone had pulled the curtains across the two front windows. The door to the back room, where Ida had always done her stitching, was closed.

"You mean, are we going to sell food from the wagon anymore?" Olivia asked Janey.

"Uh-huh."

"No. We don't need to. Ida left an important paper, a will, that said when she died she wanted you and me to have this store. It's sad that Ida died, but, Janey, she gave us her store and everything inside of it," Olivia said excitedly, glancing around, trying to decide if she wanted to throw open the curtains and the front door and begin doing business today.

"She was grumpily," Janey commented, her pronunciation making Olivia smile. She plopped down on the floor in front of a low shelf of canned goods—beans, potatoes, and corn. She liked to rearrange the cans, something she decided to do almost every time they came into Ida's store.

Olivia pulled one of Ida's ledgers from a shelf below the counter. The first order of business was to find out if Ida had been expecting any goods and who her suppliers were. She had ordered from wholesale dealers in Cincinnati from time to time—that much Ida had told Olivia. But when Homer was minding the store, Olivia thought he had mentioned that Ida also ordered from a wholesaler in St. Louis.

"She wasn't grumpy to *you*," Olivia said.

Janey dropped a can. It went rolling down the aisle, and she ran after it. She returned with it seconds later and placed it on the new stack she was making. "She was grumpily to the doctor and to Mr. Whitworth. She was grumpily to Charlotte, too."

"I don't think Ida thought of herself as grumpy. I think she thought of herself as an old woman who had seen a lot of things and people and thought she had wonderful advice to offer," Olivia said. "And she did for the most part."

"She had a lot of candy t'offer, that's for sure! Ever'time we came here. Now we get to come here ever' *day* and there'll be a lot of candy!" Janey said, and she shot up from the floor and headed toward the counter, her eyes fixed on Ida's candy jars.

Olivia laughed. Then she said seriously, "You can have candy every day, provided you eat your meals."

"I know," Janey said, affecting a pout. Then she stuffed her hand into one of the jars and pulled out a handful of gumdrops, using her right arm, the one that had been broken last summer during one of Edward's rages. In the short-sleeved dress she was wearing, the forearm was visible, still bent at a funny angle, though not nearly as badly as it had been bent that night. That night the bone had protruded through the skin, and the sight of it had nauseated and enraged Olivia. She remembered Alan mentioning the arm the night of Mr. Lincoln's dance, and she recalled withdrawing from him and refusing to answer any of his questions or respond to any of his comments. Maybe he had mentioned it because there was something he could do to fix it if it bothered Janey.

"Does your arm ever hurt?" Olivia asked Janey.

The girl shrugged. "Sometimes."

"Very much?"

"Nope."

"What about when you write on your slate?"

"Sometimes," Janey said, stuffing gumdrops into her mouth. She went off to stack the cans again.

Olivia wondered if she should broach the subject of Janey's arm to Alan. If it didn't bother Janey overmuch, she saw no reason to mention it. But if Alan could do something to make it not bother Janey at all, then she *should* mention it. Undecided, Olivia watched Janey use that arm and hand to stack the cans.

Olivia went back to looking at the ledger. A payment here, a payment there, goods received and goods sold . . . The wholesalers and their addresses in Cincinnati were listed in the back of this ledger, as Olivia discovered when she flipped through the pages. Ida had certainly kept good records, at least as good as the ones Olivia's father had kept.

"Livvy?"

"Yes, Janey?"

"Can I tell you something about Mommy?"

Olivia's head snapped up. Since Kathleen Morgan's death, Janey had never mentioned her mother in the few messages she had written on her slate or spelled with her blocks, and she had not mentioned her mother since she had begun talking again. "Yes . . . what is it?"

"Do you think it's all right to talk, Livvy?" Janey asked in a small, trembling voice, glancing up suddenly. Her hand jerked and cans went flying. "Do you think he's dead? Did you kill him?"

Feeling stunned, curious, and worried, Olivia rounded the counter and went to sit beside Janey on the floor. "I don't know if I killed him," she said, stroking her cousin's hair. Janey's eyes had grown wide and were filled with fear. "I don't know. It wasn't right for me to hit your father like that. But I just didn't know what else to do at the time. I hope I didn't kill him. I don't know if I could—"

"I hope you did!" Janey grabbed her and wrapped her arms around Olivia's waist. "I hope you did 'cause he was gonna kill you! That night we ran, Livvy, he was gonna kill you, too, like he kilt Mommy. He told me never to say anything about that, what I saw when Mommy died, or else he would hurt me bad, too. I never said anything, *anything,* and he still hurt me. If he's dead like Mommy is and like the bird we found in the garden that day it's all right to talk. Is it all right to talk, Livvy?"

"Oh, Janey," was all Olivia could say. Her own eyes felt

as wide as Janey's had looked a moment ago, wide and filled with absolute shock. Uncle Edward had told Janey not to say anything . . . *about what?* And she hadn't talked all this time because he had threatened to hurt her if she did?

Olivia took Janey by the shoulders and held her out a little, enough that she could look down into the child's eyes. "It's all right to talk," she assured the girl. "I promise you—no one will ever hurt you again. He told you never to say anything? How do you know he killed your mother? What did you see that night, Janey?"

Janey grabbed Olivia's arms so tight Olivia thought they might drop off. "I know 'cause I saw him! She was standing by the banister when I came out of my room. I had a bad dream and she was there. Then he was there, and he pushed her over, Livvy. Mrs. Ferguson, ever'one . . . they thought she did it, that she kilt herself. I heard talk. But she didn't, Livvy. Papa kilt her. Papa kilt her!"

Olivia could say nothing, she was so shocked. Staring at Janey, she sat blinking now and then, her entire body going cold. She shivered with the force of the jolt. Aunt Kathleen had slipped into a deep depression after the miscarriage of her second child, and she was seen in public so rarely in the six-month period between that event and her death that Olivia had not had a chance to talk to her very much. She was despondent, or so everyone said, but even more, people said the miscarriage had driven her mad, so mad that she threw herself over the banister that night.

But she hadn't thrown herself over. Uncle Edward had pushed her.

"My God," Olivia whispered. "Why would he do that?"

"I don't know, Livvy. But he did. I swear it, he did! And he knew I saw, and he told me not to say anything. And I didn't say anything. I swear it. I hope you kilt him. I do."

"Don't say that, Janey. Don't think such an evil thought. I never wished him dead, even at times when I knew he was hurting you. I only wanted us to escape."

"I know it's bad, and I know maybe I'll burn in hell like the Presbyter'an ladies say about the men who go in those bad places down the street, but I don't care. I don't care, Livvy, 'cause if Papa's dead, he can't hurt you or me anymore!"

"He won't hurt us even if he's alive. We came to a safe place," Olivia said. "He won't hurt us here. He won't even find us here." That probably wasn't a good thing to tell Janey because what if he was alive and he did manage to find them here? "That's what we have to believe," she amended, pressing Janey's head to her breast.

All this time, her little cousin had not spoken because she had been told that if she did, she would be hurt. And Edward had hurt her anyway. What a horrible, evil man.

"I'm glad you're talking," Olivia said, and Janey squeezed her tight around the waist again.

"I thought he would hurt you, too, if I told you."

Olivia wanted to weep, knowing that Janey had kept such a nightmarish secret for so long and that she hadn't told even her, her best friend, because she wanted to protect her. If he was alive and he ever did find them, Olivia was now so angry and outraged that she wondered if she would have any qualms about lifting her pistol and shooting him, fully intending to kill him this time.

She had never contemplated killing anyone. She was, for the most part, gentle, kind, compassionate . . . But she had loved Kathleen, and she loved Janey, and if Uncle Edward was still alive and he ever showed up in Davenport and laid one finger on Janey, Olivia would kill him.

She and Janey stacked and restacked the cans together for a time. Olivia began a list of the merchandise and the wholesaler from whom Ida had ordered each item or group of like items. She planned to write to the wholesalers, inform them of Ida's death, and let them know that Ida had left the store to her and that she planned to keep ordering from them. *Unless a better alternative comes along,* she thought to herself, *a wholesaler who offers a better price.* The years she had spent in her father's Philadelphia shop, tagging along after him and observing most everything he did where the shop was concerned—from ordering items and goods to recording sales and purchases in ledgers—had taught her a lot. She felt at ease in the store, behind the counter, reviewing the books, walking up and down the aisles, straightening items, dusting and sweeping. And Janey reminded her of herself at an earlier age, tagging along, peering over the counter at the ledgers, straightening items, and dusting, too.

Out of respect for Ida, Olivia decided to not open the store for business until the following week.

On the way back to the boardinghouse to pick up Charlotte and go look at the property Ida had left them; a thought dawned on Olivia, one that suddenly made her want to dance with joy: Now that she didn't have to think about buying property on which to build a store and property on which to build a house, and now that she didn't have to have a house built (assuming, of course, that the homestead Ida had left her was in decent living condition), she could think about sending back the money she had taken from Uncle Edward's study, the money she had expected to use for the new start she and Janey had to make. Harry had given her a bag of coins, and she wasn't quite to the bottom of that yet. So far, she hadn't touched a dollar of Uncle Edward's money. Not a dollar. And if she sent it back, she would at least have that off her conscience. She would no longer be a thief.

She put a hand to her face, wanting to shout with joy. Yes! She didn't need his money, money she had justified stealing by telling herself that it was a loan on her trust. She didn't need his money. If he was alive and she returned the money, he couldn't accuse her of stealing it. Returning the money didn't solve the dilemma of her being accused of attempted murder and of kidnapping if he was still alive, but maybe what Janey had told her this afternoon—that he had killed Kathleen and threatened Janey if she told anyone she had seen him push her mother over the banister—could be used to explain Olivia's actions. Janey's life had been in danger. Olivia had had good reason to kidnap her and hit Edward with that bookend when he had tried to stop them from leaving.

More and more she was needing to know what had happened that night after she and Janey had fled Philadelphia: If Uncle Edward had survived the blow, and if so, if

Mrs. Ferguson had managed to find other employment and escape his wrath—and if Uncle Edward had guessed Harry's involvement and sought revenge against Harry, too. Olivia was beginning to realize that she couldn't keep hiding, that she couldn't keep going day by day in Davenport not knowing what had happened in Philadelphia.

John Brimmer was an attorney. He might know if what Janey had told her could be used to lock Uncle Edward away forever. But what would happen to Janey after that? Would she be left with her—Olivia—or would the relatives still think that Olivia's behavior too horrible to be forgiven and try to take Janey away?

She and Janey couldn't be separated, not after all that had happened, not after all they had been through together. Separating them would surely kill Janey and cast Olivia into such a state of depression that people might start accusing her of going mad, as they had accused Kathleen. And she might really go mad; this time the gossip might not be mere rumor.

But how could she possibly think of going to John Brimmer and revealing her ugly secrets to him in hopes that he might offer her hope? She had already decided not to involve anyone in Davenport. No one. She wanted no one to be accused of aiding her in the event she was discovered.

So she would continue worrying alone, but in the meantime she meant to write to Mrs. Ferguson's sister and ask after Mrs. Ferguson and Harry.

"Push, Mrs. Runde," Alan commanded, gently turning the newborn's head. *"Push!"*

The delivering mother grunted and screamed, then bore down with every ounce of strength she had left, which was not a lot. She had been laboring since yesterday afternoon and trying to deliver the child for the past three hours now. It was her first, and first labors and deliveries always took longer than subsequent ones. Her attendants, female relatives, had been wringing their hands and shrieking along with her for the past two hours, it seemed, alternately praying and worrying aloud that the mother and the child might die. Not that they hadn't been of some assistance. They had occasionally mopped his and the mother's perspiring brows, changed the bedsheets, and helped walk the mother from time to time. During every labor and delivery he attended, Alan always found that the force of gravity helped with the progress of the birth. Some mothers cursed him, some clung to him, some shrieked and objected with every step. But all walked the floors, either with him or with their attendants, and he had them lie down only when the child began slipping through the pelvis.

She screamed again and bore down again, freeing one of the infant's shoulders. The other shoulder passed easily, and then one more push shot the child into his hands. A girl, with healthy color despite the long length of time she had spent in the birth canal. She coughed and sputtered blood and mucus, then she began squalling. Life had ended for Ida recently, but here was a life beginning.

Alan couldn't seem to shake that thought, as he tied off the cord and cut it, as he handed the infant to its grandmother, as he stitched the mother where she had torn, and even a bit later, as he washed his hands over a basin, then shared a pipe of celebration with the new father. One life ends . . . another begins.

"The next will be a son," the father boomed, passing him a pint of whiskey.

Alan took a drink, felt it blaze down his throat and into his stomach. He wanted sons and daughters one day, too. One day soon, he thought. He was ready for a family, had been for some time. But now, after spending the night in Olivia's arms in the house she had made into a home, he was more than ready. He wanted to hear the sounds of their children running about, shouting, laughing, crying, calling for their parents. For him and Olivia.

The thought was a nice one, one that warmed him inside.

Holding the infant, now wrapped in a light cotton cloth, he wanted that family even more.

Why had Olivia declined to marry him? he wondered. He hadn't actually proposed, he guessed, and she had to be thinking that the only reason he had mentioned marriage at the town meeting and then later, at Homer's dance, was to preserve her good reputation. In fact, he remembered telling her exactly that, that he would marry her to preserve her good reputation, not that he would marry her because he loved her and wanted to spend the rest of his life with her and Janey and that he wanted them to add to their family. He hadn't proposed marriage in a decent, respectable fashion. He had been trying to rescue her, and Olivia didn't want to be rescued.

With that thought, he handed the infant back to its father, checked on the mother once more to make certain she wasn't hemorrhaging, then he set out for town. He had been called away early this morning by a tap on the front door of the house. It was Mr. Runde, probably prepared to ask if Mrs. Morgan knew where the doctor was. But Alan had answered the door, not wanting the knock to awaken Janey or Olivia. He had sensed that it was one of his patients—who would be calling on Olivia at that hour? He had gone off with Mr. Runde straightaway, and Olivia had probably spent the better part of the day wondering why he had disappeared. Now he intended to ride back to Davenport, tell her why, and propose at the first opportunity.

The property Ida had left Olivia was not in the best of condition. No one had lived here for almost two years, Charlotte said. Several windows needed repair. The front door had blown open at some point and was hanging by the bottom hinge. The barn loft window was hanging, too, and part of the barnyard fence had rotted and crumbled.

"But it's in mighty fine condition considering it's been sitting all this time," Charlotte said, turning from her inspection of the stove that sat to one far side of the main room. "The homestead, that is. A stove is a stove, although this one could use a good cleaning. Ida sure wanted you to be part of Davenport. She liked you the first night she met you. She said you were just the stock we needed to build up our territory. I reckon she was right."

A compliment from Charlotte, however small, was something to be proud of. Olivia smiled at the boardinghouse proprietor who had become her friend, and walked off to open a door near the back of the house.

The house had only one actual bedroom, but there was a loft room where she could arrange Janey's belongings. An old tattered brown curtain hung from the window in the bedroom. Olivia tore it down and looked out the window at the land that sloped for a bit then seemed to drop off for a space.

Wondering if there was a creek just beyond that point, she strode back into the main room. Charlotte had found a small, long-handled metal scoop and a bucket and was scraping ashes from the bottom of the stove. Janey was kneeling beside her, watching, asking if she could help.

"Sure can," Charlotte said, handing the girl the scoop.

"This'll be our home, Charlotte?" Janey asked, scraping more ashes into the bucket.

"I reckon so, if your sister wants it to be. That's why Ida gave it to you."

"The place we live now, it's not really ours," Janey said. "We pay the doctor ever' month so we can live there. Livvy worries about the garden. But all the veg'tables won't be done before we move, and she was wondering if maybe the doctor'll let us live there longer."

"I imagine he'll do that. It won't be for that much longer."

"He doesn't get in such bad tempers anymore. Even when he got in bad tempers, he never did hit Livvy. I was afraid sometimes that he might, but he never did."

Charlotte stared at Janey. "Why would you think Dr. Schuster would do something like that? I've never known him to raise a hand to anyone."

Janey glanced up at the woman, her eyes a little wider than normal, as if she feared she had said something wrong. "He just got in bad tempers, is all."

"Why don't we take a walk outside," Olivia suggested, approaching before Charlotte could ask another question. "I think there might be a creek just down the hill. Janey?" She held out her hand to her cousin. Janey dropped the scoop, brushed her palms together, then took Olivia's hand.

"I swear, she's talked more today than I ever heard her talk," Charlotte remarked, looking at Olivia. "Fact is, I'm trying to remember if I heard her talk before yesterday. All the time you two've been in Davenport now, and I'd never heard her talk before yesterday."

"Janey takes a long time to warm up to people," Olivia responded, and she and Janey headed for the door.

"I'd say. A mighty long time. Never thought about it before."

Olivia hoped Charlotte would accept her explanation of why she hadn't heard Janey talk before yesterday and not question it anymore. After all, some people were so shy they hardly said two words whenever you encountered them.

The creek was littered with twigs and fallen branches, and Olivia decided she would tidy it, though not today. Glancing back at the house and the barn, she felt a rush of pride. This homestead was really hers and Janey's. No one but she could sell it or give it away, as her father had given the Philadelphia store to Uncle Edward in his will. That had been the biggest disappointment of her life. After her father's death she had fully expected to run the store by herself, to go there every day, put the key in the door as she had seen him do many, many times, greet customers, make transactions, and keep up his books. But it seemed he hadn't quite trusted her enough to leave the store to her. He had left it to Uncle Edward. And Edward had sold it and everything in it within a month of his brother's death and told Olivia that she would start acting as a young lady should act, start thinking of running a household and of marrying soon. No more bookkeeping and minding the store. He had sold their house, too, where Olivia had been raised and where she had spent so many wonderful times with her father, and he had told her about the sale with a sneer on his face when she objected. It wasn't her property, it was his, and he would do with it what he wanted; he would put the money from both sales into his accounts, and she would adjust to her new life since her father had named him as her guardian.

But now she had property no one could take from her. And the store in Davenport. Hers. No one could sell either place out from under her and then laugh in her face.

Olivia remembered the feeling of helplessness that had

flooded her the day Edward had sold the store, and she smiled. "Never again," she whispered, feeling empowered. "Never, ever again."

"What's that?" Charlotte asked, walking up from her own inspection of the creek. "Crawfish in there. Good eating. What did you say?"

"Nothing," Olivia said, still smiling. "I was talking to myself."

"That deep in thought?"

"I do that sometimes."

Janey was inspecting a frog that sat sunning himself on a small stone. He croaked, and Janey glanced up at Olivia and laughed. When Janey reached to try to pick him up, the frog hopped away. Janey jerked back, startled by the quick movement, and Olivia laughed this time.

"Give you warts if you're not careful," Charlotte told Janey.

"I thought that applied to toads," Olivia said.

"What's the difference, frogs or toads."

"Toads are bigger," Janey said. "Jeffrey Young in Philadelphia brought one to the garden one time. 'Member that, Livvy?"

Olivia nodded, feeling uncomfortable suddenly. She had always told Charlotte that she and Janey were from Boston.

Janey glanced up at Olivia, paling a little as she realized her blunder. But Olivia couldn't fault her for the slip of tongue. She was an eight-year-old child, and she had lived in Philadelphia until they fled her father's home that night. All her experiences up until a few months ago had taken place in that city.

"When were you ever in Philadelphia, miss?" Charlotte teased, tugging at Janey's dark braid. "That's a ways from Boston."

"I know. I was there," Janey said simply. Then she skipped off down the bank of the creek. She had evaded the question well, but Olivia hated the fact that she had had to evade it at all. It was ridiculous that an eight-year-old child had to be cautious when speaking.

CHAPTER EIGHTEEN

Olivia and Janey were in the barnyard at Alan's homestead, playing with Edwin and Annie, when the doctor arrived home. Olivia spotted him riding up, and she caught and held her breath, watching his blond hair blow about, admiring him sitting so tall and proud in the saddle, his medical bag hanging from the horn. He wore dark trousers and a white shirt with billowing sleeves that were rolled up to just below his elbow. Her gaze went to his hands, which held the reins, and Olivia was flooded with memories of how those hands had touched her last night, how his fingers had stroked her. The image of him hovering over her, moving inside of her, skipped across her mind, and she shook her head, feeling her face grow hot.

He knows what I'm thinking, she thought as he reined his horse to a stop near the barnyard fence and met her gaze. She glanced away, to the ground, to Edwin, who was nudging her leg, to Annie, who had her head turned up to Janey, to Janey, who was laughing at Annie, to the ground . . . to anywhere but him. She couldn't remember the last time, before last night, that anyone had seen her without her clothing. Before coming to Davenport and meeting him, she had never even allowed a man a kiss, much less an intimate touch. She hoped he thought no less of her because she had given herself to him.

The sun was just beginning to lower in the sky, just beginning to deepen its color. He opened the barnyard gate and led his horse inside. Then he stopped in front of her, touched her jaw, and lifted her chin. Olivia dared a glance at him. He smiled. She smiled back.

"Evening," he greeted. "Sorry I had to leave so early this morning. Mrs. Runde's baby decided to make her appearance, only she gave her mother a devil of a time. The labor started yesterday, and little Elizabeth Runde didn't poke her head into the world until this afternoon. I stayed for a few hours afterward to make certain Mrs. Runde didn't hemorrhage."

"You don't need to explain," Olivia said, but she was glad he had. All day she had fought off fears—what he must think of her now, if he thought the intimacy they had shared last night had been a mistake. She also had begun to doubt herself—should she have given herself to him? should she have encouraged him? had she enticed him? That was exactly what she had done. Enticed him. Whenever he came so close, her breath caught in her throat and her heart quickened; she could barely think straight sometimes.

"I do," he insisted. "You probably wondered what happened to me this morning."

"I did," she admitted.

"I didn't leave because I wanted to leave you. I left because of an insistent knock on the door. Mr. Runde—prepared to ask you if you knew where I was."

"You answered the door?" Olivia asked, aghast, her voice dropping to a harsh whisper. "You were dressed, I hope?"

He chuckled softly. "I was dressed," he whispered back.

Olivia turned to pet Edwin, who again nudged her. "After Mr. Shears' declaration at the town meeting, I imagined my reputation couldn't be more muddied. You answering the door to the house, half dressed, however, might top that."

"I was dressed," he assured her again.

All the same, her face blazed with embarrassment.

"The Rundes rarely get into Davenport, Olivia."

"How long do you think it takes to mention that Dr. Schuster came out of Olivia Monroe's residence early one morning in response to a frantic knock, looking like he'd just climbed out of bed?"

"I offered to marry you to preserve your good reputation," he reminded her, smiling.

She tilted her head at him. She couldn't possibly marry him, letting him that much more into her life and heart. She had done some horrible things, and she didn't want to marry a man and keep secrets from him. And what if she did marry him and he later discovered her terrible secrets and regretted their union? She couldn't stand that. Why did he have to be so handsome, so caring and compassionate? Why did he have to have such vivid blue eyes? "And I declined," she said. "I don't need to be rescued, thank you."

Edwin nudged her again, with more force this time. She stroked beneath his neck, where he most enjoyed being touched.

"Have you and Janey eaten supper yet?" he asked.

"No. Charlotte said she would have something for us if we wanted to stop by the boardinghouse for supper."

"I don't imagine she'd mind having a third party join you," he said, as if searching for an invitation.

Edwin decided to nudge Alan's thigh now.

Alan stooped to the goat's level and squinted an eye at him. "We need to talk. You like your mistress. I like your mistress. There's no reason we can't share her."

Edwin stared at him. Then he lowered his head and brought it up quickly, catching Alan in the shoulder with a horn, knocking him off balance.

"Edwin!" Olivia scolded.

"Damn goat," Alan muttered, rubbing his shoulder and getting to his feet.

"Bad, Edwin, bad!" Janey said, rushing over. She looped her arm under and around Edwin's neck and pulled his face toward hers. "That was very bad!"

"Dr. Schuster," Olivia said, giving him a stern look for cursing.

"I have never encountered a jealous goat," he said, rather indignantly.

"He's not jealous. He's—"

"He's jealous," Alan responded. "I'm going to unsaddle

my horse and wash up. Perhaps I'll see you at Charlotte's boardinghouse in a little while."

"Perhaps we'll wait for you," Olivia told him.

"Let's do!" Janey said. "He could go with us."

"I wouldn't want to contribute to muddying your reputation further," he said, eyeing Olivia.

Suddenly she was sorry she had mentioned her reputation at all. He had certainly done nothing to muddy it. She had encouraged him to kiss her, and she had encouraged him to make love to her. He had answered a frantic knock on the front door of his own house, probably half asleep and not giving a thought to who might be on the other side or what that person might think. He might even have stumbled out of bed and answered the door out of habit.

He started to walk away, to lead his horse into the barn. Olivia placed her hand on his arm. He stopped and looked at her over his shoulder.

"You won't be," she said, smiling a little, hoping to allay his fear. Fear prompted by her cutting remark about Hank Shears and *his* remarks at the town meeting. "Muddying my reputation, that is."

He studied her for a long moment. "I don't ever want you to have to be ashamed to be with me, Olivia."

She shook her head. "I'm not. Go ahead now. We'll wait for you."

A short time later he emerged from the barn looking fresh, his hair combed, a different shirt on, this one a blue linen that made the blue of his eyes seem more prominent. He was without his medical bag, and he was just tying on a neckcloth when he walked out and gazed up at the sunset.

"Pretty, isn't it?" he said to Olivia. She and Janey were seated on the top rail of the barnyard fence, kicking their legs back and forth while Elmor munched on some corncobs they had tossed on the ground to him. Edwin and Annie were close by, of course, lying near the fence. Edwin got slowly to his feet upon seeing Alan, and Alan scowled at him.

Olivia couldn't help a laugh. "It is pretty."

"These animals and I don't live well together," he told her.

She scooted off of the rail, holding her skirt to prevent it from snagging. "Well, they won't be here much longer. Charlotte went with me and Janey out to the place Ida left us this afternoon. It's in fairly good condition. A few minor repairs are needed. Charlotte gave me the name of a man I could hire to do them for me. They shouldn't take long, and then Janey and I and the animals will move. Provided you let us come tend the garden now and then and harvest the remaining vegetables."

"We're leaving pretty soon, Livvy?" Janey asked from the rail. "To live at Ida's place?"

Alan frowned. His hands stopped working at the neckcloth. He was tying it wrong anyway, not paying attention to what he was doing. "You're leaving so soon? You have until the end of August. It's only the middle of July."

"As soon as the repairs are made on the house, there's no reason why we shouldn't move," Olivia told them both, walking over to Alan. "Here . . ." She moved his hands and began straightening the neckcloth. "I tied my father's almost every day after my mother died."

"There's no reason why you shouldn't move . . . ," he mumbled. "What if I want you to stay here, Olivia? What if I want the two of you to stay in the house you've made into a home?"

"And you'd keep living in the barn?"

"Of course not. I'd live in the house with you. We'd get married."

She stopped straightening the neckcloth to fix an impatient look on him. "I told you I can't marry you."

"No . . . you turned down my proposal because you think I gave it only to save your reputation. But that's not true, Olivia. I love you. I don't want you to leave."

"Livvy, he wants to marry you," Janey said excitedly, bouncing a little. "He wants to marry you!"

Olivia caught her breath. "Alan . . . stop. We should talk about this at another time, in private. Janey, be quiet now."

"But, Livvy, your papa always said you'd get lots of proposals some day. Now here's your first. But I don't think you should wait for more. I think you should take the doctor's. I think— "

"Janey," Olivia scolded. "Stop bouncing before you—"

Too late. Janey fell off the rail backwards, turning a somersault on the grass on the other side of the fence. Both Olivia and Alan heard her head thump on the bottom rail, and both tore out of the barnyard to see if she was all right. Alan reached her first, and he scooped her up into his arms. She stared up at him, not a tear in her eye. But her face was red, as if she was fighting hard not to cry.

"Ouch. That hurts," she said.

He asked her where it hurt, and when she pointed to the right side of her forehead, he squinted an eye at it, studying it, and a few seconds later he told her he knew exactly what to do to take away the lump that was starting.

"What?" she asked.

"Take it away," he said simply, and he pretended to take the lump away from her head.

She scowled at him. "You can't just take it away."

"I surely can." He jerked his hand back and pretended to throw the lump out into the grass.

She felt her head. "It still hurts a little."

"Well, what do you expect? I took the lump off. It'll hurt for a bit longer, just a little, and then the hurt will be gone. Why, I imagine by the time we reach Charlotte's boarding-house, you'll have forgotten all about it."

"Livvy, the doctor took my lump away," Janey said, still scowling at him. "Is that all right?"

Olivia wasn't sure what to say for a few seconds. Then she said the first thing that came to mind. "Do you want the lump?"

"No."

"Then it's all right."

"Why do you call me 'the doctor?' " Alan asked Janey.

She wriggled to get down. " 'Cause that's what you are."

"No . . . I'm Alan. Besides, I'm not the only doctor around here."

"Yes, you are."

"Nope. Dr. Lane lives over two streets. Dr. Sandburg lives over near the river."

"Well, you're the only doctor I can see, that I see all the time," she said, sounding a little impatient with him.

"Good, 'cause if you were seeing two doctors, I'd worry that I didn't take that lump away good enough."

She huffed and gave him a stern look, having quite enough of his teasing. Then she skipped off, announcing, "I'm going to see Charlotte now. I'm going to play with Mary Beth and Sue Owens. They live across from her."

Olivia was smiling, looking after Janey and silently thanking God that she seemed like a normal child once again, having happy, carefree times once again.

"Shame on you, Dr. Schuster, for teasing a child like that," Olivia scolded playfully.

He chuckled. "She's already forgotten about possibly having a lump."

"There was no lump to begin with."

"Wasn't there?" he asked slyly. He offered her his arm. "Shall we go see what Charlotte has cooked up this evening?"

Olivia placed her hand on his arm, but she still slanted him a reprimanding look. They closed the barnyard gate, then walked off up the street toward the boardinghouse. She was surprised he didn't broach the subject of marriage again. She was glad. She thought he was serious—that he really wasn't offering anymore for the sake of preserving her reputation, and that realization made her uneasy.

Alan Schuster was responsible for a lot of practical jokes, it seemed, and some were revealed over supper that evening. Charlotte had invited Homer and John to join them because both men had spent a great deal of time with Ida at her store when she was alive; now that she was gone they were feeling her loss at least as much as Doc Schuster might be if he weren't staying so busy all the time, as the boardinghouse proprietor told Olivia shortly after she arrived with Janey and Alan. Supper consisted of cornbread and fried squirrel, potatoes and corn, and as usual Charlotte's meal was delicious. She had two boarders in at the moment, a Jonathan Galt and a Bill Collins, and both men seemed to enjoy devouring the meal and meeting other Davenport citizens.

While serving himself a second round, Homer, who was known for his storytelling, launched into a tale about a talking mule. The mule's owner sent his boy down to get the mule—they had some hides they needed to pack up and take to the trading post. Except that when the boy tried slipping the bridle over the mule's neck, the mule twisted his head and told him he could toss that bridle away; he'd gotten hardly any sleep the night before and he didn't feel like hauling those hides. The shocked boy of course went back to his pa and told him the mule was talking and refusing to work. The ole man went down himself, not believing his boy, and, sure enough, when *he* tried to slip the bridle over the mule's neck, the mule twisted around and said the same to him. The ole man got scared and ran off through the woods with his dog, and when he came back, he and his boy hauled the hides themselves. "Far as I know," Homer said, "that mule's still enjoyin' himself, eatin' all day an' sleepin' all night. Hasn't said a word since, but he's enjoyin' himself."

The men laughed. Charlotte snorted. "Homer Whitworth, you've gotta new one every week. You sit out at that farm of yours and make them up, don't you?"

"They just kinda occur to me, Charlotte," he said, grinning.

He and John seemed to be getting along fine again. They had arrived together and had had no harsh words for each other since the meal began. In fact, as far as Olivia knew, they had had no harsh words for each other in days. She liked seeing peace between them.

"An' some of 'em ain't always made up either," Homer went on. "Especially the ones involvin' Doc here. He's a bit tame these days, but when he first settled in Davenport and he was gettin' to know people a few years back, he was always up to some prank. Remember, Charlotte, when he told ole Ryan Callison to tie that cow's tail to his bootstrap to keep her from switching in his face and in the milk?"

Charlotte's eyes flared. She laughed behind her hand. "I'd forgotten about that."

Alan leaned back in his chair and chuckled.

"Told Callison it was a Dutch way of keepin' that cow from gettin' her tail in the milk an' in his face. Some cows have longer tails than others," Homer told Olivia," an' this one's was longer than most. So Doc tells Callison to tie it to his bootstrap while he's milkin'."

"I was only trying to help Mr. Callison," Alan said, feigning innocence.

"Doc, ya were playin' a prank an' ya know it," John said, laughing.

Alan shrugged. "Just wanted to see if he'd really do it."

"And did he?" Olivia asked.

Charlotte, Homer, and John all laughed. Alan finally laughed along with them. "He did," he said, but didn't go on.

"We didn't find out about it till the next day, o' course," John said. "Callison rode into town cursin' 'cause he was bruised up from that cow draggin' him around ever'where. Seems somethin' spooked 'er, still don't know what. She jerked him plumb off his milkin' stool b'fore he could do a thing about her tail bein' tied to his bootstrap, an' she dragged him all around the barnyard, through the mud an' almost out into the brush."

"She stopped once," Homer said. "Long enough that Callison got on his feet, then off she went again."

Charlotte was laughing so hard she was crying. Mr. Galt and Mr. Collins were chuckling. John slapped his knee and said, "Hah!" Homer grinned.

"He wasn't on the ground no more," John said. "Part of the time he had his hands on her hips, and part of the time he had her by the tail."

"An' *all* the time he was runnin'," Homer finished.

"The bootstrap did finally give way," Alan told Olivia.

"Thank goodness," she said. It was comical, thinking of the man trusting Alan enough that he would tie the cow's tail to his bootstrap, and she supposed his being dragged around by the cow was comical, too, but she also wondered how the poor man had managed to walk around for days. He must have been so bruised and beaten.

"All the time . . ." Charlotte wiped her eyes. "Oh, Lord. All the time Ryan Callison and that cow of his were playing leapfrog, the rest of the family was laughing to beat the band."

"Callison sure swelled up afterward," John said. "Next week he told Homer here he didn't care to try anymore o' Doc's Dutch tricks."

Everyone laughed now, the boarders, Charlotte, Homer, John, Alan, and Olivia. Janey and Mary Beth were playing with rag dolls in another area of the common room. Charlotte rose to pour everyone more cider.

"For the longest time he had Jack Audrey thinkin' Ida was castin' spells over those rag dolls she makes," Homer said, still laughing some. "For a good two months, ever' time Jack saw Ida comin' up the street, he'd get the most gawd-awful look on his face. Then he'd tear off, lest she look at him and decide to do one of her spells on him."

John hooted. "Then, while he had Jack thinkin' that, he put one o' them dolls in Jack's bed an' Jack found it that night. He tore outta his house like his britches were on fire."

Alan held his stomach and laughed.

"It was a good month before Jack would even go back in his house," Charlotte said. "He stayed here. Ida finally took issue with Doc and made him come and tell Jack he'd been storying to him all that time. She was hot that Jack wouldn't even go back in his house."

"Ain't never seen a grown man so scared," John said.

Olivia laughed, too, but then she shook her head at Alan. "Why do you do such things?"

"So we can sit together and laugh about them later, like we're doing now. I get bored. Day in and day out living in Davenport can get a little boring if someone doesn't do something to liven things up."

"Then he had those newcomers, Tom Strines and his

boys, hunting snippers out in the woods," Charlotte said, and this time *she* shook her head at him.

"Now wait a minute," Alan objected. "John was in on that one."

"What are snippers?" Olivia asked.

"Good question," Charlotte said.

Homer cackled. "They're nothin', that's just it. He had 'em huntin' nothin'. They hunted all night, too, an' into the next day, an' they were dog tired when they got back to Davenport."

Laughter sounded around the table.

"We even had 'em set traps an' check 'em," John said, grinning.

Alan took a drink of cider and said, "Tom was pretty good-natured about it."

"All in all," Homer added. "I remember he had a few hot words for you."

"Those boys o' his sure split a side when they learned they'd had a joke played on 'em," John said.

Charlotte went off to the kitchen to bring out dessert, and Olivia went to help her. Charlotte sliced the cheesecake she had made that morning and put the slices onto plates, and Olivia took the plates out to the common room. Homer ate his cheesecake, then said he had promised to meet Walt Lincoln for cards in a bit. Charlotte scowled at him, not approving, and John coughed and said he thought he was supposed to take part in that game, too.

"Both of you are surely going to the devil," Alan said, a grin playing on his mouth.

Homer grunted at him. John shot him a scowl. Then they both rose and prepared to leave for their card game, complimenting Charlotte on a delicious meal. Mr. Galt also thanked her for the meal and said he was turning in early, and after a round of handshakes, he went off to do just that. Janey was yawning, so to speed things up Olivia helped Charlotte clear the table and take the dishes to the kitchen.

Almost as soon as they stepped into the kitchen Charlotte leaned Olivia's way and whispered, "What do you think of Mr. Collins?"

Olivia lifted a brow. Charlotte was blushing, positively blushing. "You mean do I think he's handsome?"

Charlotte nodded, her eyes bright.

Olivia laughed. "Why, Mrs. Lind, I think you may be sweet on that man."

Charlotte giggled like a schoolgirl.

"I think he's handsome," Olivia said truthfully. "A few days of your cooking will surely put more weight on him."

Charlotte waved a hand. "I don't care about that. He asked me to go for a buggy ride and a picnic with him tomorrow afternoon. Louise said I'd better go, that she'd mind the place while I'm gone."

"If you want to go, you should go."

"Ain't that just like you," Charlotte complained, putting her dishes down on the block table. "Common sense. Don't you ever get flustered when you're around Doc Schuster?" She put a hand to her breast. "My goodness, I haven't felt this way in ages."

"Then go," Olivia said, laughing, "and you'll have a marvelous outing, I'm sure."

Charlotte glanced down at herself, at her blue-and-white gingham and the white apron she had tied around her waist. "What'll I wear? And I'm so pale these last few days since Ida died. What in the world does he see in me anyway? I ain't had a man interested in me in so long, I don't know what to think. I don't know how to act, for heaven's sake."

"Calm down," Olivia advised. "What time tomorrow afternoon?"

"Wha—? Oh. One, he said."

"Then I'll come at noon and help you dress, and I'll fix your hair."

Charlotte looked relieved by that. "Will you?"

Olivia nodded. "But remember that he must like you for the way you are right now. So don't criticize yourself."

"You're right. He must. Oh, when you and Doc Schuster leave, he'll be here and he'll want to visit more."

"Then leave the dishes for one night and visit with him. Make coffee or tea."

Charlotte took a deep breath. "All right . . . I can do

that . . . coffee . . . I'll make coffee. Stop laughing at me, now. I've never been so nervous in my life. Did you notice the looks he was giving me over supper?"

"I didn't." The truth was, Olivia had been so caught up in listening to Charlotte, Homer, and John relate some of the many pranks Alan had pulled over the years that she hadn't paid much notice to Mr. Collins. Rude of her, now that she considered it, especially since he was Charlotte's guest. Fortunately, Charlotte was apparently too excited to note—or care.

"He has an insurance business in St. Louis, and he's making stops in different river towns to see if there's a need for his business. Oh, I know you have to go. Janey's looking tired, poor girl."

"Yes, she is. I should take her home soon."

"You and Doc . . . you seem like peas in a pod the last few days," Charlotte said, looking as if she wondered how Olivia would respond to that.

"Yes, well . . . he took Ida's passing hard, you know. He really loved her."

"He sure did. We all did. You know what she told me about the two of you—'it's a match made'n heav'n, Charlotte.' 'Heav'n made,' that's what she called the two of you."

Olivia gave her a patient smile. "I have to go."

"All right. I know. I'll see you tomorrow, then. And I'll let these dishes sit," Charlotte said, approaching a cupboard and looking up at it, searching with her eyes. She glanced down at herself for a moment. "I should get rid of this apron, that's for sure. Now, where did Sally put the pot this morning after she cleaned up? She came to help because I was baking bread for the week and—"

"Good night, Charlotte."

Charlotte turned around. "Oh . . . night now." She laughed at herself. "Reckon I'm talking up a storm, ain't I?"

Nodding, Olivia smiled. "Calm down," she advised just before slipping out of the kitchen.

In the common room, Janey had lain down on one of Charlotte's braided rugs and fallen asleep. Mary Beth was nowhere to be found, and Alan told Olivia that the girl's mother had come for her. Alan scooped Janey up from the rug as if she weighed only a few pounds—as he had in front of the barnyard earlier—and they left the boardinghouse.

"You have quite a mischievous streak, Dr. Schuster," Olivia said as they passed several rowdy saloons. She spotted a woman inside, dressed scantily in red and black, her breasts swelling above the neckline of her clothing. Olivia glanced away, more than a little shocked. Since being in Davenport she had never even dared a quick look into one of the saloons.

"Yes, I do, when I become bored," Alan said, smiling slightly at her reaction to what she had seen. "They have to make a living, the saloon girls—like everyone else. Not many arrive with the intent of working the saloons. Some are young women who traveled west with their families or relatives and found themselves alone for one reason or another."

"The day after I arrived, Charlotte tried to convince me to go back east."

"With good reason. She saw a beautiful woman with a young girl to care for and no resources."

"I had money when I arrived," Olivia objected. "I still do."

"I'm only telling you what Charlotte's experienced mind probably thought when she saw you. She had no idea how resourceful you would be at the time. She had no way of knowing if you had only a few dollars or a hundred."

I have a lot more than that, Olivia thought, *and most of it was stolen from my uncle Edward. And you wouldn't look at me with such respect and admiration if you knew that. You wouldn't. You would look at me in shock and disbelief and then disappointment, and I couldn't stand that.*

She never wanted him to know. Never.

They took Janey into the house, where Olivia lit a lamp and then turned down the coverlet on her bed. Alan laid Janey down, and Olivia removed her boots and her stockings. Alan pulled the coverlet up over Janey, then followed Olivia out of the room.

He turned her around and had her in his arms before Olivia could even think of objecting. She caught her breath and tipped her head to stare up at him in the short hall. The lantern Olivia still held flickered light on his face.

"Alan, I shouldn't have—"

"I love you, Olivia," he whispered. "With my heart and soul. I've needed to tell you that all evening."

She didn't want to hear him say he loved her. She didn't. "Alan, I—"

"Sh. Don't tell me that you think what happened last night was a mistake, because I'd know you were lying. You don't think that, Olivia, not really. Calm down and listen to what I have to say. Not much, and then I'll leave. Don't worry—I don't plan to try to make love to you tonight. Something is wrong. Today you've acted as if I'm reading more into what happened last night than I should be, and I believe that's because something has you scared. I love you, and I believe you love me. I see it in your eyes, Olivia. I felt it in your touch last night, in the way you gave yourself to me. You're not the kind of woman who would give herself to just any man, and yet today you acted as though I'd gone mad when I told you I loved you and when I proposed to you. A proposal is what a lady would normally expect at this point, and yet . . ." He shook his head. "You want me in your bed tonight, but you're scared to have me in your bed tonight. I'm not blind or insensitive. You're scared to let me get close to you, and I'm not happy with that. I won't be content with that. The thing with Janey was strange, how she suddenly started talking when she saw Ida lying on the floor, how she asked you if you'd killed someone. Did you kill someone, Olivia? Or are you afraid you might have? No, don't turn away, not yet," he said, when she held her breath and started to twist away.

"You promised . . . no more questions," she said, suddenly feeling light-headed. Too much had already been said, and he was too close to the truth.

"I know I promised. But I want to help you. Why won't you let me help you?"

"Why don't you simply hold me and not ask questions?" she asked hoarsely.

"Because I think you're in trouble, or could be, and I want to help you."

"No."

He stared at her, studying her, finally shaking his head in frustration. He ran an open hand across his mouth and rubbed his jaw. "Why shouldn't I ask questions? The most incredible time I've ever had with a woman, I had with you last night because I've fallen in love with you. I delivered Mrs. Runde's baby today, and afterward I held the infant and thought, I want to marry Olivia and have a family with her. If you get past being scared of whatever you're so scared of, you might start thinking along those lines, too."

He paused again, as if expecting her to start talking. Did he actually expect her to tell him her ugly secrets? She wouldn't. She couldn't.

"I know you," he said, stroking her jaw. "I've seen your gentleness and kindness for weeks now. I don't believe you would intentionally kill anyone. Don't be scared of me. Don't be afraid to be truthful with me. I love you, Olivia, and I'll love you no matter what."

He kissed her, a lingering kiss. Then he finished by saying, "You know where to find me if you want to talk."

She wanted him to hold her. Simply hold her. Instead he walked away from her, and Olivia felt her heart crumble a little in her chest.

She *did* love him—something she had realized days ago, only the feeling was growing more intense. Dear God. Falling in love was not something she had planned on doing, with anyone, when she came to Davenport. She had wanted to find a quiet place to settle, and she had wanted a relatively quiet life for herself and Janey, a quaint life. Well, she had found those things, only she had found even more in the process.

She heard the front door brush open, then shut, and she put her back to the wall. She didn't know what to do. She did love him, and she didn't know what to do.

CHAPTER NINETEEN

I love you, Olivia, and I'll love you no matter what.

Throughout the following days his words resounded over and over in her head—as she and Janey helped Charlotte prepare for her afternoon outing; as they cleaned at the homestead and located the man Homer had suggested for the repairs she needed; throughout tasks such as milking Eleanor and feeding the animals, when Olivia often heard Alan moving about in the next room; while she was making butter and cooking. He was frequently there, talking to her and Janey while they churned, helping them weed the garden, playing with Janey in the grass, sometimes helping Olivia clean up after the animals. He was always polite and friendly, and she was polite and friendly back. But he was very careful about not touching her, even when handing her a pail of milk.

At times Olivia wanted to slip her hand over his, touch him, kiss him again, but she restrained herself, not wanting to be turned away. She knew what his conditions where—that she keep no more secrets from him, that if she were in some sort of trouble she tell him about it so that together they could search for a solution. But she didn't want him involved in her problems, and so she said nothing to him about her troubles.

At night Olivia sometimes sat in front of one of the windows in the main room of the house and stared out at the barn, watching the faint glimmer of light that crept between the boards that formed the room where he stayed. She wondered what he was doing, if he was working or simply lying awake, as she often did of late. She wondered if he was working on more artificial legs, carving them with painstaking precision, taking apart another real leg and studying the workings of the knee.

One night, nearly a week after the supper at Charlotte's boardinghouse, she spotted him walking along the barnyard fence. She was stitching together blocks of material that would eventually form a quilt, and her hands stopped working when she saw him. She sat watching him for the longest time, and he finally turned and saw her. He stared at her, for how long she couldn't be sure, though it seemed like a long time. Time probably spent silently questioning her—*what keeps this distance between us, Olivia? What troubles you? Why won't you let me help you?*

In the end he turned and walked away, in much the same fashion he had walked away from her in the hall that night, with his hands stuffed into his trouser pockets, with a steady gait. Olivia's hands trembled so when she tried to stitch again that she finally dropped the quilt blocks into the basket that sat on the floor beside her chair.

She didn't know how much longer she could go on like this. She wanted to touch him and be with him again. But he was uncompromising when it came to her keeping secrets from him. As long as she insisted on doing so, he meant to keep his distance. It was all or nothing with him, Olivia realized as she stared at the window again.

Raindrops splattered the panes. Thunder rumbled. Lightning flashed in the distance, Olivia leaned her head back against the slats of the chair and closed her eyes. Her heart felt heavy. She was scared. She had to find solutions . . . she had to send her uncle's money back, as she had decided more than a week ago. But she didn't want to send it from Davenport, which would allow Edward, if alive, to trace the parcel. She had written to the wholesale dealers in St. Louis, and a business trip up that way was not out of the question. Even a trip to Cincinnati wouldn't be out of the question. But a journey to St. Louis would take far less time. She could mail the money from there. So Edward could trace it to St. Louis. She didn't live in St. Louis. The city still seemed too close for Olivia's peace of mind, but in reality, it wasn't close. It was several hundred miles away. She had to send the money back and get the theft off her conscience.

So she began planning a trip to St. Louis, albeit a brief one. Charlotte saw no reason why she should even think about making such a journey—meeting the wholesalers wasn't necessary.

"I disagree," Olivia said. And Charlotte just gave her an impatient look, knowing better than to argue with her; when Olivia's mind was made up, it was made up.

"Well, at least leave Janey here," Charlotte said. "She can keep me company and help around the boardinghouse. She'll like that."

Olivia said she would think about that. Then she eyed her friend, having been curious about Charlotte's beau for a week now. "You never have said if you enjoyed your afternoon with Mr. Collins." It was true. Charlotte hadn't said a word, and Olivia hadn't asked before now because she thought that Charlotte would offer something. She knew that Mr. Collins had left the day before yesterday, bound for Dubuque this time, and she had heard from Homer that Charlotte had become very friendly with the man in the meantime.

Charlotte smiled—and blushed. She patted her cheek. "I'm trying to keep some sense about me, the way you do. He's gonna stop here again on the way back down river. I reckon that afternoon went fairly well, and other afternoons after that. I'm being courted, but I've got to keep some sense about me. I've been here for years. I can't just start thinking one day of running off to St. Louis and getting married."

That remark caught Olivia by surprise. "Has he asked?"

"Well, no. But he talks about how he wants to get married again one day. You know his first wife died of cholera some five years ago. I think he gets lonely. Now that I think of it, that's a good reason why you shouldn't think of going up there, leastwise not right now. Cholera runs rampant in big cities like St. Louis in the summertime. Olivia, meeting those wholesalers can wait."

"Cholera runs rampant in Philadelphia, too, in the summertime, and I never caught it once in all the years I grew up—" Olivia caught herself. She was letting her guard down, becoming far too much at ease with Charlotte. She had said Philadelphia without even thinking that she should say Boston, and now Charlotte was looking at her in a strange way.

"You grew up in Philadelphia?" Charlotte asked. "You never mentioned that. Janey spent some time there, too, apparently."

"We both did," Olivia said, reaching for the pail in which she had put Charlotte's milk yesterday morning.

"You'll leave her here when you go to St. Louis? I know your mind's made up to go."

"I'll think about it."

John offered to go with her because he didn't like the idea of a woman traveling alone. Bad enough she'd had to do that when coming to Davenport. Olivia politely declined, saying that she wouldn't dream of taking him away from his business here. John started to insist, but Olivia squeezed his hand and said, "Thank you, but I'll be fine."

She arranged to have Homer mind the store, tend her garden, and feed the animals while she was gone. He commented, "In the I don't know how many years Ida ran that store, she didn't go but once a year or so to meet with those people in St. Louis and Cincinnati, and she met with 'em once this year already. Don't understand why you have to meet 'em again."

"I want to introduce myself," Olivia said, and Homer seemed satisfied with that. She couldn't resist teasing him: "Mr. Whitworth, I don't want to come home to find that any of my belongings have been rented out, especially my animals."

John whooped at that and slapped his leg. Homer winced, then laughed a little. They were all three standing on the walkway in front of the store when Alan approached and asked what John and Olivia found so funny. John told him about her comment to Homer. Alan chuckled a little—apparently he was finally able to look back on Homer's rental of his home with some humor—then sobered as he glanced at Olivia.

"Wait a minute," he said. "Why will Homer be minding your animals and store for a time?"

"I'm going to St. Louis to meet my wholesale dealers," Olivia explained.

His bristle was predictable. "Alone?"

"I might take Janey along."

"You shouldn't have made the trip here alone," he said, giving her a scrutinizing look.

Now she bristled. "I had no choice."

"That's right," Homer said in her defense. "Her husband died along the way. Was she supposed to turn back?"

Olivia wondered if Alan would reveal that she had never had a husband, that she had set out and made the journey from the east by herself, with Janey in tow. Instead his scrutinizing look continued, as if he wondered what she was up to now.

"I'm going with you," he told her later, while she was cleaning up after Edwin and Annie.

"Alan, you have patients here who need you," she said, knowing that convincing him that she didn't need his protection would be a fight. But she couldn't have him going to St. Louis with her. She needed to go to the post office there alone, not with him beside her every step of the way, possibly asking what she was mailing to Philadelphia.

"You shouldn't go to St. Louis alone, Olivia. You know no one there."

"I'll manage, I'm sure."

"I'm sure you will. But I'd feel better about your safety if I went with you." He grabbed a spade from one corner of the barn, took up a position alongside her, and piled dung in the wheelbarrow that sat nearby. Olivia always took the wheelbarrow out afterward and dumped its contents in the garden, as she had been advised to do by Homer soon after he and John had planted her garden. Alan still milked Eleanor and gathered eggs most every morning, and occasionally Olivia found her garden weeded and hoed, and she knew he was responsible.

"I haven't asked for your protection," she said irritably, not wanting to argue with him about this.

He inhaled deeply. "No, you haven't. Just like you never ask for my help. You *won't*. That's what this is about. You not wanting me to help you with anything. We could go to St. Louis, the three of us—you, me, and Janey. I have friends there, one with a daughter just a year or so older than Janey. We could stay with them, and Janey could play with Maggie, and I wouldn't worry about the two of you."

Olivia stopped working to stare at him. She didn't want him going with her, wondering what was in her parcel. She didn't want him to know that she was mailing something to Philadelphia. She had to put a stop to his insistence that he travel with her.

"We're not a family," she said, knowing it was a cold thing to say, that it would hurt him deeply, so much that he might turn away from her forever. "And I don't want us presented as one. I don't want us traveling as one."

He stopped working, too, and slammed his spade down on the barn floor. "You're not going to St. Louis alone, Livvy."

"Yes, I am. I'm a grown woman with good business sense and good judgment. I don't need anyone watching over me, observing every move I make and presuming to tell me what I can and cannot do."

"I only want to go with you to make sure you and Janey are safe."

"I can do it alone," she insisted, grabbing his spade from the floor.

He gritted his teeth. "You're so damn stubborn, just like Ida. I'm going along, Livvy, whether or not you want me to."

And he did. A week later, when Olivia climbed down off the wagon seat in front of the wharf where the *Brazil* was docked, he was waiting beside the steamer.

She had decided to take Janey with her—they hadn't been separated for months now, and she didn't like the idea of spending any time away from her cousin—and she wrestled now with getting their two trunks out of the wagon bed. Mr. Clift came out to help her, telling her how glad he was to see her, and Alan took one of the trunks from him and loaded it onto the ship. He was going, it seemed, and since there was nothing she could do to stop him she might as well start thinking right now about how she could mail the parcel without his knowledge.

After he loaded the trunk onto the ship, he looked down into Janey's bright face as she told him that Charlotte had told her only yesterday that he had a friend in St. Louis with a little girl who was only a bit older than she and that she bet that little girl would play with her until she was exhausted. "Every day," Janey told him. "Every *day* until I'm exhausted!"

"I do indeed," he said, pulling her up into his arms, "and she will indeed." Then he walked off a ways with her, telling her all about Maggie Murphy, what a delightful child she was, how she had set out to meet a certain actress last year—though her father forbade her from going anywhere near the St. Louis theater where the actress was performing—how she had hidden in a trunk in the actress's dressing room, befriended her, took her home with her, then deceived her father by pretending that the actress was someone else. "Delightful, yes," he said about Maggie, "but she has a mischievous streak that never fails to entertain, and sometimes frustrate, a person. Her father and the actress were married only last year, and Miss Murphy right now is expecting a new brother or sister near the end of September, and she was bubbling with joy over it when I saw her in June. Yes, indeed, Margaret Anne Murphy will exhaust you—but she'll entertain you, too."

He lifted Janey to his shoulders, and perching there she called to Olivia: "Look at me, Livvy. Look how high up I am! I can see clear to the other side." And she hooded her eyes with one hand and pretended to gaze that way. "I could be the captain's look out."

"Ahoy, you surely could!" Alan said, entering into her game. "Let's go see what the captain's plan is, then." And before Olivia could object and spirit Janey off for a rest in their cabin, he was gone with her.

"He's a wonder with the girl," Mr. Clift said behind Olivia, chuckling.

"Yes, he is, isn't he?" she murmured.

"He'll make a fine father to 'is own children someday," the man remarked.

Olivia already knew that to be true. "I'm going to my cabin, Mr. Clift, if they decide to look for me."

"Ye're all right, ma'am?"

She nodded, and walked off. No, she wasn't all right. She didn't want to be reminded of what a good father Alan would be to his own children someday. She didn't want to see him interact so sweetly with Janey. She didn't want to see his blond hair blowing in the breeze. She didn't want to see his smile and his vivid blue gaze every time she closed her eyes. She was going to her cabin to rest, and she hoped she slept the afternoon away.

She did, pretty much. Janey woke her, her little hands rubbing Olivia's cheeks, her lips kissing Olivia's nose. She talked faster than Olivia had ever heard her talk.

"Mr. Clift caught fish from the river and the cook fried them. There's vegetables and bread, too, Livvy. You've just gotta come eat. Are you sick? I hope you're not sick. We had the most wonderful time in the pilot house. The captain let me steer the ship for a while. But it was hard work so I stopped. We played dice on the deck and Alan told me more about Maggie in St. Louis. I can't wait till we get there, Livvy. I can't wait!"

"That's nice, Janey," Olivia said unenthusiastically. Not only was she still sleepy, but she really didn't look forward to reaching St. Louis, Once there, she would have to figure out a way to escape Alan and his friends for an afternoon. Once Uncle Edward's money was on its way back to Philadelphia, though, she would feel a little better. Even if he was dead and had no use for it anymore, she didn't want it in her possession.

"You're missing all the fun, Livvy. Wake up," Janey insisted. "You never sleep in the afternoons."

Olivia rolled onto her side. The heaviness, the worry

about everything—that was what made her feel so tired. She felt the weight on her shoulders, on her chest, pressing with such force that she had trouble catching her breath at times. It was hot in the cabin, she thought, pushing the blanket aside.

"Are you coming, Livvy? Are you coming?" Janey asked, kissing her again.

Olivia forced a smile. "I'll be along. I have to wash and dress."

"I'll help. You're always taking care of me. I'll take care of you."

With that, Janey bounded off of the bed, flew to the trunks on the opposite side of the small cabin, and threw one open. "What should my cousin Livvy wear t'day?" she mused aloud, tapping a finger against her temple.

Olivia laughed at her antics. She herself might not be enjoying the trip and the thought of arriving in St. Louis, but Janey was having a grand time, from the sound and sight of things. Her cheeks were rosy, her eyes glowed, her smile was brighter than Olivia had ever seen it as she pulled a gown of blue silk from the trunk. The gown had a square, low corsage, short, puffy sleeves, and ruching for trim. The one silk dress she had managed to bring from Philadelphia. Just as well, she had thought many times, since she had no use for elaborate gowns in Iowa Territory. She had packed the dress for this trip, though, not wanting to seem too simple while in St. Louis, and she had packed the black lace sacque that went along with the gown.

Olivia frowned at the dress. "No, it's far too much for an evening aboard a ship."

Janey put the gown back and pulled out a walking dress of imitation pongee in deep green and white stripes. Olivia had made the dress herself from material in Ida's store. She had stitched white flounces onto the dress and trimmed it with green ruching and ribbons. She had longed for something a little more elegant than the ginghams and calicos she had worn for weeks and weeks now, and so she had created a dress in between the silk gown and the plain everyday dresses.

"Please?" Janey asked. "It looks so pretty on you."

But it still might be a bit much for a supper aboard a steamer. Olivia twisted her lips and lifted her brows, expressing for Janey's benefit her indecision.

"Oh, all right," she finally said. "But I made you a new dress, too, and you haven't worn it yet. I'll wear my new dress if you'll wear yours."

Right now Janey was wearing a dark blue linen dress with a ribbon tied around her waist. "I will," she said excitedly, and she nearly tripped on Olivia's dress while carrying it to the bunk. She scrambled back to the trunks and threw open the other one, singing, "You're gonna look pretty, yes you are!"

"So are you," Olivia sang back at her. She sat up on the bunk, awake suddenly, though she still felt that sense of heaviness. Surely nothing woke an adult faster than an energetic child.

Olivia washed her face, neck, and arms over a basin that sat on a stand near the bunk. She wrapped her corset around her chemise and began lacing it. Janey tied the laces in back for her, then Olivia bent down and let Janey slip the dress over her head. Olivia took it from there, pulling it down over her shoulders, slipping her arms into the armholes, smoothing the skirt around her hips. Janey fastened the clasps in the back, closing the placket, and then Olivia tied the ribbon around her waist.

Janey brushed Olivia's hair, doting over her, helping Olivia twist and pin. They left several spiraling curls to rest on Olivia's left shoulder. The hair tickled her collarbone and ended just above her left breast.

"Your turn," Olivia told Janey, and they went to work on her, washing, dressing, clasping, brushing, and pinning.

"We look lovely!" Janey announced when they had finished. "I hope they didn't eat without us. I want some of Mr. Clift's fish. He promised I could have some."

"Then I'm certain he saved you some. Come along now," Olivia said, taking her cousin's hand and opening the door.

"And Alan said I could sit by him."

"Then I'm certain your chair is waiting, Princess Janey."

Janey giggled. "I'm not a princess."

"Oh, but you look like one tonight. So you've decided to stop calling him 'the doctor'?"

Janey shrugged. "He's really *not* the only doctor. It just seems like it sometimes. You're not gonna marry him, huh, Livvy?"

"I'm . . ." The question caught Olivia off guard. She started to say that if she decided to she would have to tell him about everything first, about the money and about Janey's father. But Janey didn't know about the money, and she seemed so happy this evening that Olivia didn't want to mention Edward. Doing so might make Janey frown. Thoughts of him and the cruelty she had suffered at his hands might cast a cloud over an evening she looked forward to. "I don't think so," Olivia said.

Janey sighed. "Well, I like John and Homer, too, so it doesn't much matter who you choose," she said, then she skipped off ahead of Olivia before Olivia could tell her that she wasn't considering marrying John or Homer either.

A short distance up the hall Janey turned to the right and went up some steps. Clearly she didn't intend to wait for her cousin, so Olivia lifted her skirts and hurried after her, slowing when she reached the deck. Sunset was beginning, a pool of pastels across the sky with a center of glowing reddish orange. A breeze skipped across the river, rippling the waters as the ship glided along. She heard the engines, felt their vibrations, watched smoke billow from the stacks. The land looked wild and uninhabited on either side of the water. Tree roots hung out over the banks, twisting and tangling, and the undergrowth was heavy. Olivia walked along the deck, turning her face up to the sky, feeling the cool breeze on her neck. She was still somewhat tired; she would be able to sleep through the evening and the night. Sleep blotted out her troubles, made them disappear for a time, and a big part of her would have liked to sleep through the entire trip and the visit to St. Louis.

At the steps that led down to the dining saloon, a riverman tipped his hat to her, saying, "Evenin', Mrs. Monroe." She didn't know him, but she flashed him a smile, then lifted her skirts and started down the steps. The door to the saloon was open and the sounds of conversation and laughter, mostly male, drifted out.

They died down when she walked into the saloon, then they stopped altogether.

She was being stared at by Alan, by Captain Manning, by Mr. Clift . . . by another man she didn't know. A plumpish, matronly woman sat to his right. The table was nicely, though not elegantly, set. Olivia paused just inside the doorway, wondering if something were wrong with her appearance.

The man she didn't know was the first to stand, a show of respect for the lady who had just entered the room. Alan stood next, nearly knocking over a glass of water in the process. Grinning, Captain Manning and Mr. Clift got to their feet.

The captain, a tall, distinguished-looking man with a snow-white beard and hair, approached Olivia as Janey tugged on Alan's arm. "I told you she looked pretty. I told you!"

"Yes, you did," Alan murmured, and Olivia felt her face grow warm. No wonder Janey had run off ahead of her—to announce her.

"Evening," the captain said, offering Olivia his arm. She placed her hand on it and allowed him to lead her to the table. There, he introduced her to the man and woman she didn't know—Mr. and Mrs. Coleman, who were traveling to St. Louis from Dubuque to visit with their daughter and her family. Mrs. Coleman offered a broad smile. The smile, her grandmotherly demeanor, and her conservative traveling dress all reminded Olivia of the Presbyterian ladies in Davenport. Mr. Coleman was more reserved, seeming to inspect her with his hard gray eyes, and Olivia had the distinct impression that no two people could ever be more opposite than this husband and wife.

Olivia was seated to Captain Manning's right, between him and William Clift, who immediately, his eyes bright with pleasure, commented about her hard work in Davenport and the good fortune she had found there. He had been talking to Alan, she realized as the men took their seats. Janey sat to Alan's left and asked him if he knew when the fish would arrive.

"I'm famined," Janey said, and everyone laughed except for Mr. Coleman, who sat stoically, as if wondering if he could endure an entire meal with a child.

"You mean famished," Alan said. "Famine means there's no food or hardly any food."

"And we have plenty of food tonight, thanks to Mr. Clift," Captain Manning said.

"A *lot* of hard work and a *lot* of good fortune," Olivia was telling William. "I was prepared to open my own mercantile soon, but Mrs. Bogue recently passed away and left me her store and everything in it."

"Because she knew it would survive under your management," Alan commented.

She made the mistake of looking at him, and the love and pride shining in his eyes as he held her gaze made her heart quicken. The cook arrived with platters of fish, rice, and vegetables, and Olivia was thankful for the distraction. Being on this small steamer with Alan for days and sharing every meal with him while they traveled to St. Louis would not be easy.

CHAPTER ✣✣✣ TWENTY

THE ST. LOUIS levee bustled with people and activity. Three other steamers besides the *Brazil* had just docked. Cabs and horses lined the entire opposite side of the street that ran alongside the levee; warehouses and buildings stood behind the cabs and horses. Men and boys hustled here and there, carrying luggage and instructing passengers. Crates were being unloaded from one ship, trunks from another. As people came off the vessels, they either greeted waiting friends and relatives or had their luggage loaded into the trunk of one of the cabs and away they went. The levee smelled of fish, of perspiration, of dirt, of horses.

Alan lost no time in approaching one of the cab drivers. Soon his companions' trunks were loaded into the back of the cab. Then he handed Olivia and Janey up into the conveyance and off the three of them went, Olivia and Janey on one seat (with Janey peering excitedly out the window), and Alan opposite them. On her lap Olivia held a small gray bag that she had insisted on handling herself. She clutched it with both hands, exactly as she had while boarding the ship back in Davenport.

She had been cool and distant for weeks now, ever since he had told her he wasn't content with her being afraid of him, that he thought she was in some sort of trouble and that he wanted to help her. He believed in openness, in trust. He had no friends or acquaintances who felt they couldn't trust him, and the thought that Olivia refused to unnerved and frustrated him. He was her friend first, above all else, and he felt he had shown her that in a number of ways. He didn't know what was wrong; he only knew that when he had asked her outright about Janey's questions on the day of Ida's collapse, Olivia hadn't denied either killing someone or suspecting that she had.

He meant what he had told her—that he didn't believe her capable of murdering someone. He had witnessed her gentleness and compassion and knew she wasn't capable of cruelty; not one time after Ida's death had she flaunted before Harvey and Hank the fact that Ida had left her her store and that, no matter how their council vote had gone, she didn't have to operate her business from the street corner anymore. She had taken over the store with quiet dignity, with a professionalism that Alan respected and admired. Despite her coolness toward him these past weeks, he had fallen even more in love with her. But not so deeply in love that he wasn't bothered by her distrust of him.

"Almost there?" Janey asked Alan, bouncing a little.

He laughed. "Almost there."

"The noise and the stench . . . the crowds," Olivia remarked, clicking open a fan and slowly waving it beneath her chin. "I'd forgotten how unpleasant big cities could be."

"That's why I'm a country doctor," Alan said. "But, don't judge all of St. Louis by the levee and surrounding streets. I'd be happy to show you the fine points of the city. There's—"

"I don't know how long Janey and I will be staying," she said, glancing away—to her bag, out the window. "I don't know how long my business with the wholesalers will take. Perhaps only a day or two."

She and Janey . . . it was always "Janey and I." She always excluded him. She and Janey were a family, that was that, and he shouldn't try to insinuate himself into their lives. Sometimes she made that painfully clear.

"Relax a little and you might find some enjoyment here. You might even decide to stay longer than two days."

"I have a store to run," she reminded him, snapping her head around. Her eyes flashed.

"I'm aware of that. I'm also aware that you left the store in Homer's capable care."

"It's my store."

"Olivia, I'm your friend."

She quieted at that, but it was a stubborn, sullen quiet. Something was wrong. Something had been wrong since they left Davenport. Since before. Why the sudden urge to go to St. Louis? And why had she not wanted anyone to accompany her? John had volunteered, too, as Alan had learned soon after telling Olivia that he didn't want her to go alone, and she had politely refused John's offer. Ida had received a shipment of goods from her wholesalers in St. Louis not long before her death, and the store appeared fully stocked. She kept good books, too, so Alan couldn't imagine that questions about the shipment were what drove Olivia to the city. And . . . the store hadn't been under her management for long. This seemed a critical time, a time when she should be settling in and making certain everything was running smoothly. Add to all that the fact that she had been tense, quiet, and preoccupied for weeks now, and Alan couldn't help but feel that something was wrong. He wondered if the reason was the fact that he had insisted on accompanying her, but gut instinct told him that was wrong. He kept going back to the fact that Ida had just received a shipment of goods from her St. Louis wholesalers, and that Ida kept thorough books. There was no good reason for Olivia to be in St. Louis right now. No solid reason. From the time he had met her, he had always felt that she was hiding something, and he had that feeling even more strongly right now.

The cab rattled and bumped its way up Main Street, past Walnut, Market, Chestnut, Pine, and Olive. It passed Locust and Saint Charles streets, then turned up Washington Avenue. The scenery began changing, from the warehouses of the wharf and dry docks to residential areas with small clusters of businesses—coffee houses, bookshops, shops for shoes and hats. The houses became bigger and nicer, even elegant. Olivia was looking out the window now, appearing interested at least. Before, she had looked detached, and her remark about the unpleasantness of big cities had made Alan suspect that she didn't really want to be here, that she probably hadn't planned this trip because she was excited by the idea of meeting her wholesalers.

So why had she planned the trip? Alan couldn't get the question out of his mind—*why was she here?* Her decision to make the journey seemed to have been such a quick one, and it was an odd one, too.

The cab finally stopped in front of a residence he knew well, a two-story brick house with a neatly kept lawn and a walkway that led straight to the front door.

"We're here, really? At last?" Janey said, her voice high-pitched with excitement.

"Now, the ride from the levee didn't take so long," Alan teased.

She jiggled the door handle. "But altogether everything did. The ship and the ride here."

The cab door opened just as Olivia smiled and said, "Patience, Janey." It wasn't her usual open smile; it was stiff, and she stared at the house as if inspecting it, as if wondering what the residents were like. "These are your friends, Alan. Perhaps Janey and I should stay in a hotel."

"No." He leaned forward. "Livvy, I won't have you and Janey staying in a hotel in a city that's foreign to you. If you're worried about appearances, *I'll* stay in a hotel."

"They're *your* friends. I wouldn't dream of having you stay somewhere else while Janey and I stay here."

"They're your friends, too," Alan said. "Because you're my friend."

The cab door opened and the driver stood aside while Alan climbed down out of the conveyance. Janey fairly hopped into his arms, then he handed Olivia down while the driver removed their trunks from the cab. Olivia looked prim and lovely, clutching her bag, wearing the blue dress and hat she had worn the evening of the council meeting, and Alan held her hand longer than necessary after she stepped down.

He leaned close to her. "One more time . . . if you're in trouble, Livvy—and I believe you are—I'm your friend and I'll be glad to help. I won't judge you or condemn you."

She stared at him, her brow wrinkled, uncertainty and

fear flashing in her eyes. He could have urged her head to his chest right then and she wouldn't have resisted. As it was, excited voices clamored behind him on the walkway. He heard Maggie Murphy squeal his name and knew that only seconds, literally seconds, remained for this meaningful exchange with Olivia.

"I love you," he told her, "and I'll love you no matter what."

She had time to whisper "Thank you"—an improvement over the last time he had told her that—and then Maggie was at his heels, jerking on his arm, words flying out of her mouth.

"Alan, Alan! You didn't write and tell us you were coming. You should see Josephine. The baby's growing! It'll be here in just a few months, Papa says. You brought friends. Did you get married? You brought a lady—and a girl, too! Hello, I'm Margaret Anne Murphy," Maggie said, prancing around Alan and poking her hand out to Janey before Alan could say a word to her. "Most friends call me Maggie."

Janey looked a little surprised at Maggie's forwardness. Alan laughed. Olivia smiled. Mrs. O'Brien, Maggie's nursemaid, and Josie, her middle swollen with child, reached the gathering just as Janey took Maggie's hand and gave it a vigorous shake. "Not Dr. Schuster," Janey informed the girl. "He calls you 'the Maggie hurricane' most times."

Alan knew what sort of reaction that would draw from Maggie. She plopped her hands on her hips and twirled to scowl playfully at him. "I am not a hurricane," she said succinctly.

"Oh yes, you are," he shot right back. He tugged on one of her golden curls, then turned to Josie and Mrs. O'Brien, kissing them both on the lips, causing the portly Mrs. O'Brien to turn bright red and clap her hand over her mouth.

"Oh! Dr. Schuster! My goodness, I'm glad to see you, too, but—"

"Nothing like a kiss to put a little color in the cheeks, eh, Mrs. O'Brien?"

"Dr. Schuster!" she said, and giggled.

"Mrs. Murphy, you're glowing," he told Josie, and she glowed more. "Or is that growing?"

Laughing, she pushed the length of her wavy dark hair over her shoulder. She looked healthy and carefree, better than he had ever seen her look onstage. She looked happy.

"I'd say both," she said, and kissed him back. "What a surprise this is! You were just here in June. And you brought friends, as Margaret said. Good friends, Doctor?"

Alan caught the glint in her eyes, the hope, the curiosity. "Ah, you've got the devil in your eyes, Josie, as Thomas might say. Behave yourself. Good friends, yes. Let me introduce you." He drew Olivia forth with a hand, gently placed, on her elbow, and he caught Janey by the hand just as Maggie suggested that the two of them should go investigate the garden paths. "Wait, wait," he told Janey. He made introductions all the way around, then the girls skipped off to play.

"Well, they've taken an instant liking to each other," Olivia remarked.

"Maggie has a way of making people feel welcome," Josie said.

Alan paid the driver, speaking to the women as he did. "They both have spirit—and special women in their lives."

Josie gave him a wide smile, a brilliant smile, which she turned on Olivia a few seconds later. She took Olivia's hand and looped it through her arm. "Welcome to our home," she said, tipping her head in her charming way. Then she urged Olivia up the walkway, leading the way to the home Alan always found warm and inviting. Pride rushed through him, and excitement that he was introducing Olivia to his best friends.

After taking refreshment with Josie and Olivia in the parlor, Alan elected to call on Thomas at his office. Olivia was glad—while he was gone, she could find a post and send Uncle Edward's money back to Philadelphia. She had bundled it, wrapped it in plain brown paper from the store, secured the paper with twine, then placed it in the bag she had hardly let out of her sight since leaving Davenport. Now that she was in St. Louis, she felt nearly frantic with the need to get the money off her hands. Weeks had passed since she had sent the letter to Anna Thompson, Mrs. Ferguson's sister in Philadelphia, and so far, she still had heard nothing back. It was too soon, of course. A letter might take a month or more to reach Philadelphia from here, and then if Mrs. Thompson responded, her letter might take another month or more. But the waiting was becoming excruciating, especially since Olivia had made the decision to act. She had to know what had become of Mrs. Ferguson and Harry. She had to.

Alan left for Dr. Murphy's office, and Olivia asked Josephine Murphy where she might find a post. She had an important package to be mailed, she said, rubbing her thumb along one handle of her bag.

"Please . . . call me Josie," Mrs. Murphy requested, glancing curiously at the bag. "Everyone does. I'll have someone take the package for you. Why, you just arrived. You must be exhausted. Surely you don't want to run right back out and—"

"I'd prefer to take the package myself."

Josie's brows went up a little at Olivia's abruptness. "Of course. I'll have someone take you then—the groom, since we don't keep a regular driver. We don't use one often enough. Thomas takes his own horse and buggy out to see his patients and to his office. I was about to ask if you wanted to go sit in the garden where the girls are playing."

"Perhaps when I return. I'll be taking Janey with me. We won't be gone long." She liked Josie Murphy. She really did. And she was certain she would feel more at ease around her, in this house, in St. Louis, and more at ease in general, once she concluded the business that had brought her here. Josie was obviously wondering why she had to run out again so soon. Olivia could tell she thought it odd, but was too polite to ask why Olivia had to mail the package herself. Olivia wanted to sleep again. She was tired, weary of lying, hiding, and evading.

"All right," Josie said. "I'll—I'll go fetch the groom." And she went off to do that.

Finding Janey and trying to pull her away from Maggie for a short time was a task. She whined that they'd just arrived and that she didn't want to go yet, that she'd just started playing with Maggie.

"She'll be fine here if you want to leave her," Josie offered, and Olivia struggled with indecision. She probably would, but they had just met the Murphys, and she and Janey had been separated so rarely.

"I wanna stay," Janey said, stomping her foot once.

"Janey," Olivia admonished.

Janey scowled. "I've been wanting to meet Maggie Hurricane for a long time. We just got here, and now we have to go somewhere else."

"Maggie Hurricane?" Margaret objected, giggling. "I'm not as bad as that. Hurricanes blow through real hard, Jonathan Drury says. They knock down buildings and everything. I don't do that! I wish everyone would stop calling me that!"

"Things do have a way of scattering when you blow in," Josie teased, tugging Maggie against her side. She hugged the girl, and Maggie beamed up at her, then rubbed a hand on Josie's belly.

"She's going to let me help take care of the baby," Maggie told Janey.

But Janey's mind was still on whether or not she could stay and play with Margaret right now. "I don't wanna go anywhere right now, Livvy. I'll be fine here," she said, repeating what Josie had said. "Please? Oh, please?"

There had been a day when Janey wouldn't have let Olivia out of her sight. Olivia watching her now, with the birds chirping overhead in the trees, with the sun shining between leaves and branches and making patterns on the stone walkways. Nearby a frog croaked from where he sat sunning himself on a rock in a small, brick-lined pond. The Murphys were Alan's good friends, therefore they could be trusted with Janey, Olivia finally decided as she watched a small fish leap in the water. And Janey . . . well, she didn't want Janey to always cling to her. She wanted her to heal inside. Still, Janey's weaning herself was a little painful for Olivia. She now knew how a mother must feel when a child found independence, no longer needing as much maternal care. She was proud of Janey—as recently as three months ago, Janey had been a silent, haunted child—but she also felt a pang of sadness that Janey no longer needed her as much.

"All right," Olivia conceded finally. "But play with Maggie. Mrs. Murphy is in no condition to run after the two of you."

"Mrs. O'Brien does that," Maggie said, pulling a face.

Josie laughed. "Yes, she does make certain you attend every lesson and that you eat meals at regular times."

Janey jumped up and down, pulling on Maggie's arm. "Let's go, let's go, let's go!"

"All right, all right, all right!" Maggie said, and they dashed off, racing by the frog, who leaped into the water to avoid them. Seconds later they had disappeared from sight, and their shouts and laughter filtered through the trees.

"She really will be fine here," Josie assured Olivia.

"I know," Olivia said, and she did. She truly did.

Riding in the carriage, Olivia soon lost track of the many streets they passed. The trip to the post office seemed much farther than it probably was because she was so anxious to be rid of the money. Dust swirled up from some streets, choking Olivia at times; others were paved with brick, and the conveyance bounced and grated over those so, she wondered if she might be vibrated right out of her skin. St. Louis seemed as noisy and as crowded as Philadelphia—people spilled from shops, hustled up and down walkways, strolled or rushed across streets; they shouted, laughed, talked, hailed others.

In places, where people had pitched tents or thrown up buildings so fast that they leaned and groaned with every gust of wind, the city also seemed as crude and harsh as Pittsburgh. Every city had its saloons and gaming houses, it seemed, and St. Louis was no different, though Olivia spotted many such disreputable establishments that were clearly no longer thriving—they were boarded up and littered with temperance-movement and religious postings.

Shouts and frantic cries rose from somewhere close. The carriage started through yet another intersection, and Olivia gasped when she spotted another conveyance flying toward them. The horses' eyes were wild, and their hooves pounded the street so, their legs were barely discernible through the dust. She screamed at the groom—Mr. Leavensworth, she'd heard Josie call him—but too late. The other carriage clipped the back of theirs and tipped it.

Olivia screamed again when the conveyance toppled over and sent her and her bag flying to the other side of the carriage. Horses, an entire herd of them, it seemed, screamed shrilly as Olivia rammed into the opposite door and pain exploded in her right shoulder and arm and the ribs on that side. The other door slammed open. Despite being in pain and unable to breathe at the moment, she wondered where her bag was. Not in her hand anymore.

She drew a ragged, painful breath, and began searching around for it. More shouts rose outside the carriage. Mr. Leavensworth peeked down in at her, asking if she was all right. No, she wasn't. She could barely breathe, and her bag was gone—she didn't see it anywhere inside the carriage.

"My bag," she managed hoarsely. "I need my bag."

"We've gotta get her out of there!" someone said.

"Enough of us together can pull this thing upright again!" someone else said.

"My bag . . . where's my bag, Mr. Leavens . . . Mr. Leavensworth, where's my bag?"

She didn't see him anymore; he had withdrawn. She didn't see her bag either. She felt pressure on the right side of her chest and more pain—in her ribs, arm, and shoulder on that side. But despite that, she had to find her bag.

She reached up, gasping, and caught hold of both sides of the carriage door opening, meaning to pull herself up and out somehow. The conveyance began tipping again, rocking, and when it tipped upright, Olivia rolled over and planted her back against the floor, not wanting to get another jolt. It slammed upright onto all four wheels.

Mr. Leavensworth and two other men helped her from the carriage. Olivia straightened, pain burning her entire right side. But the bag was still her main concern. Where was it? She searched all around the carriage, and Mr. Leavensworth followed, asking over and over if she was all right.

She finally spotted the bag lying a good fifty yards away, near a walkway in front of an apothecary, turned upside down. A group of dirty, bedraggled boys began kicking it around, batting it between them. Olivia opened her mouth to shout at them and started to run across the street. More pain blasted in her side, and she snapped her mouth shut. But pain or no pain, she tore off between people, determined to retrieve the bag that contained the money. She meant to send every dollar back to Philadelphia, and she meant to do it today.

The bag snapped open. The package, no larger than the two-inch stack of bundled bills it contained, tumbled out. One boy picked it up and began ripping open the brown paper.

"Don't," Olivia managed, but the word came out weak because she still could barely catch her breath.

Mr. Leavensworth closed in behind her, grabbing at her arm. "Mrs. Morgan, where are you going? What are you doing? The carriage is back on its wheels. I'll check the horses, then we'll be on our way. We'll go to the post office just like you want."

"My bag . . . the money!" She had to get the package. Once the ragged group of boys found—

The boy's mouth dropped open as he stared down at the package. He shouted something at his friends—*money!*—then he tore off, stuffing the half-opened parcel into a jacket pocket. His friends tore off after him, and he continued shouting at them, words Olivia couldn't discern.

Her heart seemed to have stopped beating. Her side burned now with heat and pain that seemed to start on her skin and singe inward. Her shoulder and arm were on fire, and once her heart started up again, it hammered in her chest. The dizziness she'd felt inside the carriage had returned. But she ran anyway, trying to ignore the burning pain. She meant to catch those boys, the thieves. She had to.

"Mrs. Morgan . . . ?" Mr. Leavensworth again, from behind her.

The boys kicked up dust as they ran, getting farther and farther away. Olivia fought for air, fought against the dizziness. Mr. Leavensworth caught up with her finally.

"Catch them," she gasped. "My . . . bag. Money. Catch them!" She tripped, then righted herself, lifting her skirts. She swayed against the groom, smelling horses and leather, feeling nauseous as everything began spinning—people, buildings, horses, Mr. Leavensworth.

Uncle Edward's money, she thought as the groom caught her. Then everything snapped out, all sunlight, all images, all worry.

CHAPTER TWENTY-ONE

When Olivia regained consciousness, she didn't know how much time had passed. She was lying in a bed with something binding her middle. A wrap. Alan was bent over her, and he held her left shoulder down while someone yanked her right arm so hard that Olivia expected to see the person stumble backwards with her arm in his or her hand, having pulled it off. She had been in pain before, but the yank produced something worse than pain—agony.

She screamed, and then Alan was soothing her, talking softly to her, and the agony died down to a dull throb. Whatever the person had done, her shoulder and arm now felt better.

"Dislocated shoulder and a few broken ribs," said someone who spoke with a distinct Irish brogue. "Yer lucky you didn't end up in worse shape, lassie. You could've."

"It's all right now," Alan said, trying to soothe her as he seated himself on the edge of the bed. He smoothed back the hair from her face and stared down at her. "I didn't know you needed to go anywhere this afternoon or I would have taken you myself."

"The money . . . those boys stole the money. My bag," Olivia said, remembering everything, how she had tried to run after the thieves, how they had been too fast for her, how Mr. Leavensworth had chased her down.

He exchanged a worried look with a man who stood on the right side of the bed, doubtless the man who had yanked her arm and who spoke with the brogue.

"Olivia, this is my good friend and colleague, Dr. Thomas Murphy," Alan said, his brow still wrinkled.

But Olivia didn't care to meet anyone right now. Her shoulder felt better and so did her side unless she moved—when she moved, pain shot through her side again—and she had to know if Mr. Leavensworth had recovered her package from those boys. She desperately needed to know.

"The package . . . I had a package with me, Alan. In my bag. When the carriage tipped, the bag flew out. I was going to retrieve it. A boy picked it up, took the package, and ran off with it. I need that package."

"You need to rest, Olivia."

"No!" She tried to sit up. But her side hurt so badly, she plopped back on the pillows.

"A package isn't worth risking your life over, Olivia. You could have been run down in the street. Mr. Leavensworth said you were oblivious to everything but that package and those boys."

Closing her eyes, she fought down the pain, swallowed, then looked up at him again. She couldn't go anywhere, it seemed. She would have to share at least one of her secrets with him, involve him in a way she didn't want to involve him. But who else could she turn to? She barely knew Josephine Murphy, and she knew no one else at all in St. Louis. She would have to tell him that she had stolen money from her uncle, and then she would have to lie here and watch the love for her in his eyes change to disbelief. His respect for her would plummet, a thought she couldn't stand. But she had done something wrong—she had stolen—and ironically, in turn, what she had stolen had been stolen from her. And now, even more was about to be taken. Alan had proposed to her, but without knowing that she was no better than those boys, that she had taken the bundle of money and run, too. Only she had done it months ago.

She swallowed again. "You don't understand . . . the package . . . money . . . a lot of money . . . It's not mine. I have to return it. I have to get it back. We have to find those boys."

"You're right, Livvy," he said, his voice tight. "There are

a few things I don't understand, and it's past time you told me about them." He looked as though he had run clean out of patience, as if this accident—followed by her nearly getting run down in the street trying to chase the little thieves—was the last straw.

Thomas Murphy coughed. "I'll uh . . . I'm thinkin' I should go visit a bit with Maggie and Josie, and make my introduction to Janey. No quick movements there, Miss Monroe, or those ribs won't heal properly."

She nodded at him, feeling as nauseous as she had just before she'd lost consciousness, and she felt certain the feeling rose, not from the pain but from the knowledge that the money had been stolen and from the fear that the boys would never be found. They might be halfway to New Orleans by now, feeling as though a fortune lined their pockets. To boys as tattered as those four had looked, it was indeed a fortune.

Alan pulled a fiddleback chair from the hearth to the side of the bed, and there he sat.

"How did I get here?" Olivia asked, not sure, right away, where she was. But she realized that the room looked familiar—it was where she and Janey had been brought when they arrived; Alan had carried their trunks up to the room.

"Mr. Leavensworth hailed a cab and brought you here. Then he went back for the carriage," he said.

He sat, waiting.

Olivia glanced away, not wanting to do this. But it was time she forced herself to tell him a few things. With her barely being able to move at the moment, he might be her only chance for recovering the money. "I haven't wanted to tell . . . to tell anyone anything. I haven't wanted to involve anyone." She looked back at him, found him still sitting, waiting, a stoic look on his face.

"Janey's not my sister. She's my cousin," she said quietly.

When he didn't respond, she went on.

"Things happened . . . Her mother miscarried a child. It's been several years now. Kathleen and Edward—Janey's mother and father—seemed happy, but only on the surface . . . I don't think they really were. Kathleen at times seemed removed, unusually reserved. At other times she was a festive, social woman. Edward . . . Edward was given to drink, but no matter how much he drank he was always able to keep his affairs in order."

She paused again, not especially wanting to launch into the ugliness of Edward's abuse of Janey and the fact that she had recently learned that Janey had witnessed her mother's death at her father's hands. But she went on anyway, knowing she had to, knowing there was no other way now.

"After the miscarriage, Kathleen went into seclusion. There were whispers, rumblings, that she had gone mad. I—I didn't know. Janey and I were friends as well as cousins; I adored her from the day she was born. If Kathleen had gone mad, I thought asking Janey about her would be painful for Janey. So I never did. I know she rarely saw her mother during those long months anyway. Then Kathleen died, and Janey stopped talking. Edward claimed Kathleen had a fit and threw herself over the banister. Janey tells a different story. But I didn't hear it until after we had been in Davenport for some time . . . I have to tell you about Edward first."

I have to make him understand that I had no choice . . . no good choice . . . that I had to take the money or Janey and I might not have survived.

Alan sat considering her, his hand now rubbing his dark, close, neatly trimmed beard.

"My father died not long after Kathleen's death. He owned a shop in Philadelphia, and he had a number of other business interests . . . stocks, things like that. I had always helped him in the shop, and I thought he would surely will it to me. He didn't. He gave it to Uncle Edward, who refused to let me keep it open. He sold it within weeks. My father also left me a large inheritance that will mature when I turn twenty-one. Unfortunately, he also made my uncle my legal guardian.

"From the time I moved into his house I knew something was wrong, terribly wrong. Janey never laughed or smiled or spoke anymore, but she cried. A lot. She cried and screamed in the middle of the night, having nightmares that

Uncle Edward had no patience for. He had no patience for me going to her and comforting her either. Janey stopped crying even, stopped making sounds at all. She used to hide when she heard his carriage in the drive. He frequently came home drunk and tore through the house until he found her, then he called her names, told her things like she was as stupid as her mother."

Olivia put the back of her hand to her mouth and blinked back tears, remember the terror, the bleakness of their situation, the wild fear she had always seen in Janey's eyes whenever they heard Edward's carriage pull into the drive.

"He frightened me, but he frightened me more whenever he dragged Janey into her room and locked the door. I always noticed bruises later. Then there was her arm. It was hanging limp, and the bone . . . the bone had broken through the skin. I told Uncle Edward to send for a doctor. He refused. He said she had broken her arm by running into the side of an armoire while fleeing him, and he said she could live with it. I argued. He dragged me to my room and locked me inside.

"The next morning I found the door unlocked. I tended Janey myself the best way I knew how, and I swore to her, while I was wrapping her arm and securing it to her chest, that I'd find a way to escape. Edward had broken her arm. I knew that, and I also knew that he might kill Janey during one of his rages. I'm not a doctor," Olivia said, glancing down at the bed. "I did the best with her arm that I could. I've never set a bone, and I never want to attempt it again."

Alan moved to sit on the side of the tick. He leaned over her and wiped a tear from her cheek, his expression tight with concern and alarm.

"I knew he might kill Janey," she went on, "and that's what I feared most. But I thought about my inheritance, too, and about how outraged Uncle Edward was at the reading of the will. I didn't know why he had turned so much anger on Janey. What prevented him from killing me and Janey, too? As my guardian, he might find a way of getting his hands on the money my father had left to me. Crazy thoughts went through my head . . . so many of them. I went to my aunt, his sister, and I didn't know what to think of her reaction when I told her that Edward was responsible for all the bruises Janey had acquired, and for her broken arm. Shock . . . fear . . . disbelief . . . I didn't know what to think of her reaction. She ordered me to leave, then she went directly to Uncle Edward with what I had told her. Needless to say, he was furious. Janey and I both spent two days and nights locked in our rooms without food or water. Everyone—all the servants were frightened of him, and of where they might find positions elsewhere if he dismissed them."

Alan ran the back of his hand along her cheek in a soothing gesture. Sympathy and understanding shone in his eyes. But would they still be there when she told him what she had done? That she had hidden in the study for three nights in a row, waiting for Edward to unlock his safe so she might know where the lock and safe were? In a compartment hidden by a sliding bookcase . . .

"We . . . we had to leave, Alan. We had to get out of that house and out of Philadelphia. I asked no one for help. I thought the servants were too frightened of Uncle Edward. Then one day, Harry, the driver, was brushing down a horse in the stable when I came in, looking to go out shopping for a few hours for Janey. He told me that if I ever took the notion to take Janey somewhere else, somewhere far away, he would help. Such a risk! I had already decided to do exactly that, but I wasn't sure how I would accomplish it. But Harry would help, and that was a great relief.

"So then I—I stole money from Uncle Edward's study. I had so little of my own. I was so frightened, I simply grabbed a bundle, slammed the safe shut, and ran. I've never stolen anything in my life. Never, Alan."

"I believe you," he whispered, and she felt a rush of sweet relief. "How did you get away?"

"We planned it, Harry and I. I would pack bags for me and Janey, and Harry would be waiting downstairs with a carriage. I didn't count on Mrs. Ferguson, the housekeeper, helping. But there she was, packing Janey's bag for me and seeing us downstairs."

She couldn't tell him the part about her hitting Uncle

Edward and possibly killing him. She just couldn't. A murderess on top of being a thief. She couldn't tell him. She could barely stomach the thought herself. She could still hear the crack of the bookend against Edward's head, still hear the sound of him slumping to the floor . . . still see the blood pooling around his head.

"We took a stagecoach to Pittsburgh," she said softly. "From there on, we boarded steamer after steamer. Oh . . ." She realized she'd left out an important part. "Harry gave us money, a bag of coins. I didn't refuse his offer because he would have been insulted. My plan was to find employment somewhere out west and to pay Uncle Edward back every dollar when I turned twenty-one and could get access to my inheritance. I took the money from his study only because I didn't want us to starve. I wanted us to be able to start over, to survive on our own. I used the bag of coins, and I still had some coins left when Ida died and left me her store. Then I realized I didn't need the stolen money anymore. But I didn't want to send it back from Davenport."

Alan opened his mouth as though he had just realized something. He had: "So you came to St. Louis to mail it to Philadelphia."

She nodded.

"Livvy, do you know the thoughts that have run through my mind?" he asked, bending to kiss her, closing his eyes and heaving a breath of release against her lips. "I've wondered if you killed someone and ran. I didn't know how I could help you out of that sort of situation."

Olivia's breath lodged in her throat. He didn't realize that she'd gone rigid; he was too wrapped up in relief, in thinking that he'd been wrong to wonder if she had killed someone and ran. He didn't realize that he had discovered the truth without even knowing, that she *might* have killed someone—Uncle Edward.

"How much?" he asked.

She breathed again, but not easily. Not easily at all. "How much what?"

"Money."

"Why?"

He raised his head. "Because we'll try to recover it, Olivia. And if we can't, we'll raise the amount and send it to the scoundrel."

He wasn't reacting the way she'd thought he would react, with disbelief, then condemnation. He wasn't judging her. He didn't regard her as a common thief.

"I would have done the same," he said, and the love glowing in his eyes made her want to throw herself into his arms.

"I didn't want you involved in this, Alan. I still don't."

"*I'm* involving myself."

"I don't want your money."

"Olivia." His eyes flashed.

"I need to find those boys, that's all," she said.

"And what if we can't?"

"Then I suppose I'll pay the money back as I can and have the theft on my conscience until I do. I don't know . . . I need to find them. If you don't want to help me do that, then as soon as I'm able, I'll get out of this bed and search St. Louis myself. I don't want to send other people's money to Uncle Edward."

He moved from the bed and began pacing the floor slowly in front of the fireplace. He raked a hand through his hair. Seconds later he stopped pacing and faced her. "You're stubborn, Olivia. Pay back whoever raises the money then. Sending the money back is a good idea because your uncle can't charge you with robbery if you do. Janey's another issue altogether," he said, and began pacing again.

Olivia tensed again. "I can't let him find her, ever, Alan. Ever. Something I didn't tell you . . . Kathleen didn't throw herself over that banister. Edward pushed her."

He had stopped pacing again. He stared at her in alarm. "How do you know that?"

"Janey saw him. She saw the entire thing. He told her not to say anything, *anything,* so she hasn't. All this time, she hasn't spoken because she saw Edward push Kathleen over that banister, and she's been afraid he might do something similar to her."

"Son of a . . . Something similar might have been merciful compared to the hell he put her through," Alan grated. "If he ever touches Janey again, I'll kill him."

"Alan."

"I swear it, Olivia. Her arm . . ."

"I won't let him find her, ever," Olivia vowed. "I promised Janey a new life, and I've given her that. I won't allow him to take it from her. I won't allow him to take her from me."

"He could charge you with kidnapping."

"Not if he never finds Janey."

"You plan to hide her away for the rest of her life?" Alan asked, shaking his head. "No, have your uncle charged with Kathleen's murder. Janey's a witness."

She couldn't do that, charge Uncle Edward with murder, not when she was uncertain whether or not he was alive. And she couldn't tell Alan she thought Edward was dead, that she feared she'd killed him.

"You don't want Janey to have to face him in court, do you?" Alan asked quietly.

"No," Olivia said, truthfully.

"I understand that. But if he threatens to charge you with kidnapping, you might have to. Janey might have to testify."

"Right now I have to find that money. I stole it, and then someone stole it from me." Olivia shook her head, not believing the nightmarish situation she was in, wishing she would wake and realize it was only a bad dream.

"How much?" he asked for the second time.

Olivia squirmed, glanced away, then glanced back. "A thousand."

He nodded slowly. She wanted to pull the coverlet up over her face.

"I'm sorry," she said.

"I told you—I would have done the same. No, I think I might have killed the man with my bare hands. What kind of man terrorizes a child? Breaks a child's arm?" He asked the questions of no one in particular; he simply had trouble believing such a man existed.

"I'm going to walk in the garden and think," he said. "You stay in that bed."

She nodded.

"She shot at you three different times?" Josie asked Alan over the supper table that evening. She put her hand to her face and laughed, then exchanged disbelieving glances with Thomas and laughed more. Mrs. O'Brien had taken Maggie and Janey to play with one of Maggie's friends, leaving Josie, Thomas, and Alan to have supper together in the Murphy's dining room. Alan had been relating how he and Olivia had met, first on the ship traveling along the Ohio River, then in his house.

"Goats and a duck?" Thomas asked, leaning forward, looking as if he wasn't sure he had heard right.

"You heard right, my friend," Alan assured him. "I assumed Homer was responsible for the animals and the rearranged furnishings. Then this woman started shooting at me."

"What a sight you must've been covered with molasses and feathers!" Thomas remarked.

Josie giggled. "Tarred and feathered. I suppose Olivia was only protecting Janey and herself at the time."

Alan nodded. "She thought I was an intruder, no doubt a drunk from a saloon. She told me much later that she had the gun because she was afraid of the drunks."

"With good reason," Josie said.

"So she shot at you three times," Thomas marveled, sipping from a glass of burgundy.

"That she did," Alan said. "Two times before I wrestled her to the floor. Once afterward."

Josie gasped. "Alan! You wrestled her to the floor?"

He pulled a face. "Well, what was I supposed to do? At the time I knew only that my furniture had been rearranged, that animals had taken up residence in my house, that I'd had a bucket of molasses slammed down over my head, been beaten with a pillow, and that a strange woman was in my house shooting at me. Yes, I wrestled her to the floor."

Now Thomas laughed, a deep chuckle, as he relaxed back in his chair. "Chaos."

"Exactly. Next thing, John Brimmer is booming at me from the doorway to get off Mrs. Monroe. Ida's telling me I ought to be shot, or something like that, and Homer's hiding outside, scared I'm going to twist his neck—and I might have if John hadn't been standing there. All the while, the goats are bleating and the duck is running races around the room, quacking as if someone wants to wring *her* neck."

Josie was laughing uncontrollably now. She put her fork down and tried to stifle the laughter behind her hands.

"Careful, Mrs. Murphy, lest you laugh that infant into an early birth," Alan teased.

"Unbelievable," Thomas said.

"Goats and a duck . . . Molasses and feathers . . . ," Josie managed. "And you and Olivia on the floor . . . on the floor when John, Ida, and Homer came." She stopped laughing long enough to take a deep breath and run her hands down her swollen middle, then she laughed again. "Do you realize how funny that is? I can see it, and it's funny!"

Alan chuckled. "It is now. Then, it wasn't."

"It's funny, all right," Thomas agreed. "But what happened? Olivia ended up stayin' in the house, but how'd that come about?"

Alan sipped from his own glass of wine, then chuckled again. "Funny thing. Seems Homer and John worked everything out with Olivia while Ida and I were here. Seems both men had their eyes on her, and—"

"Oh, that must have been interesting," Josie said. "And once you got home all three of you clamoring for her attention."

"Well, *I* never clamored," Alan said, grinning.

"Oh, of course not, Dr. Schuster."

"Anyway, Homer had decided to find her and Janey a nice place to live—my home—and, of course, John was right there offering to do the legal work. As my agent, Homer signed a rental agreement with Olivia."

Josie's jaw dropped open.

"Interestin'," Thomas observed.

"I'd say."

"Where have you been living all this time?" Josie asked.

Alan scowled playfully. "In the barn with the noisy animals."

He told them how he and Olivia had worked out their own agreement when she visited him at Charlotte's boardinghouse—that she and Janey remain in the house and he live in the barn room. "That was satisfactory," he said, then related the madness that had gone on during his first few nights in the barn, how the goats had upset the duck, the hog, and the cow—

"The hog?" Thomas asked, looking baffled.

"I didn't know you owned a cow," Josie said.

"I don't. Olivia had bought them both that afternoon," Alan explained. "Homer took her to look at a cow, and she bought the cow, all right. But she rescued the hog from Charlotte's butcher knife, too. Mr. Brewster meant to sell him to Charlotte, who's one of the local boardinghouse owners, and she meant to make smoked ham and bacon of him. Olivia couldn't stand the thought, so she bought the hog, just like she'd bought the duck from Charlotte herself when Charlotte had her ax in hand. Olivia paid Mr. Brewster twice what Charlotte meant to pay him, then she marched off into the hog pen and waded through the slop to save him."

Josie giggled. "My goodness, Dr. Schuster, you've had quite an eventful summer."

Thomas laughed.

"That's not the half of it," Alan told them. "Let's see . . ." He scratched his head. "I was knocked over by the charging hog. A few days later, Olivia decided to learn to cook, and I came home and found smoke pouring from the house. She decided to garden, too, and Homer and John went to fisticuffs over who was going to till the area for her. Of course . . ." He rubbed his jaw, a little embarrassed by the next thing he related: "Somehow I ended up in the middle of that. Then Homer told Olivia that I did autopsies in the barn room—the truth. She decided to spy on me one evening while I was in the room working on artificial legs. She saw the legs and assumed I'd been robbing graves. She fell out of the loft into the room. I guessed what she was thinking, and I . . . well I couldn't resist . . ."

"You let her *believe* you'd been robbing graves?" Josie asked, her eyes widening. She giggled again. "Alan!"

"Quite an eventful summer indeed," Thomas said, agreeing with Josie's earlier comment.

"Yes, it has been," Alan said. "Thinking about it makes me rather tired."

"*Hearin'* about it makes me tired," Thomas remarked, shaking his head.

"But while Olivia and Janey lived in the house and you lived in the barn, you and Olivia came to know each other," Josie said, tipping her head and smiling in a knowing way.

Alan grinned at her. "Mrs. Murphy, I believe you are nearly bursting with curiosity."

Her smile widened.

"Her resourcefulness and her energy and spunk impressed me. Everything. She seemed tireless. She learned to cook and make butter. She bought vegetables from the farmers and fruit from the steamers. She loaded it all into her wagon, and she parked the wagon on a street corner and opened for business. Other merchants complained about her selling on the street corner, but Olivia persisted. They complained because she outsold them."

Josie's eyes sparkled with admiration. "All that so soon after her husband's death. Such courage and strength!"

Alan stiffened a little at that. He himself had related to Josie and Thomas, while telling how he'd met Olivia, that Olivia had told him her husband had died between St. Louis and Davenport. But there was no point in letting them believe that. Hours ago, Olivia had told him the truth about herself and Janey and how they had ended up in Davenport, and since Thomas and Josie were his closest friends and could be trusted explicitly, Alan elected to confide in them. He glanced at the open door, however, not wanting anyone else—not even trusted servants—to hear what he was about to tell the Murphys.

"Is something wrong?" Josie queried.

Alan went to close the door. Then he returned to the table, with Josie and Thomas gazing curiously at him.

"Olivia was never married," Alan said, serious now.

"What?" Josie said. "I thought you said she told you—"

"Exactly. I said that when I first met her she told me she was married. Later she claimed that her husband had died between St. Louis and Davenport. I always felt she was hiding something, and she finally confided that there had never been a husband."

"Why would she lie about such a thing?" Thomas asked, steepling his fingers and resting his chin on them.

"Because he and Janey are in trouble, and she didn't want anyone asking why they were traveling alone."

That silenced them both for a few seconds.

"What kind of trouble?" Josie finally asked.

Alan took a deep breath, wondering where he should begin relating what Olivia had told him this afternoon. He was still digesting it all himself, sorting through it, imagining how terrified Janey and Olivia must have been, how frightened Olivia still was, how determined she was that her uncle should never find them.

He elected to start with Olivia's father's death and how she had been forced to live in her uncle's house. He backtracked at times, to relate Janey's mother's miscarriage, supposed madness, and death, and Janey's silence afterward. Then he told Thomas and Josie what Olivia had told him about her uncle's abuse of Janey—and of herself, too, for that matter, though Olivia's primary concern had been Janey. He told them about Janey's broken arm and how Olivia had set it herself, or attempted to, after pleading with her uncle to get a doctor.

"He refused?" Thomas asked, clearly outraged. Being a physician himself, and a damn good one, Alan knew how that struck him. A bone that was not set right could lead to a number of problems, the least being an inability to use the limb, the worse being infection, which could lead to gangrene and death.

"He refused," Alan said.

"The monster," Josie whispered, horrified. Her eyes were wide, her face was pale. "I noticed Janey's arm. The shape . . . it's awkward."

Alan nodded. "Olivia tried. She made up her mind to take Janey and leave. She wasn't concerned about where. They just had to leave. The housekeeper and the driver helped them. And . . ." He sighed, because he wasn't sure what to do about this last part, how to locate the boys who had stolen the money and how to avoid having Olivia charged with kidnapping. At the very least, he meant to send the money off to Philadelphia himself and clear up that part of the situation. "Olivia took money from her uncle's study to ensure that she and Janey had a healthy start wherever they ended up. Her father left her a large inheritance, but Olivia won't get it until she turns twenty-one. At that time she means to pay back the money she took."

Josie had put her hands to her mouth. "They must have been frightened nearly out of their minds, she and Janey."

"Olivia still is," Alan said. "She finally told me everything this afternoon, after the money was stolen by a group of boys when the carriage tipped over."

"That's what she meant when she woke," Thomas said.

Josie glanced at him.

"She was talking about money when she woke," Alan explained. "After Ida willed Olivia her store, Olivia saw no need to keep the money anymore. But she didn't want to mail it to Philadelphia from Davenport and have her uncle learn where she was from the address."

"I offered to have someone, a servant, mail the package for her," Josie said. "She wanted to do it herself. I thought she was acting odd. She was nervous, grasping the handles of her bag so tightly her knuckles were white."

Alan nodded. "I knew something was wrong, too. I've known for some time. But I knew for certain when I realized that Olivia had no good reason to be taking a trip to St. Louis, at least not for the store. Ida had just received a shipment from her wholesalers here, and she met with them in June, only three months ago, to talk about further shipments. Olivia wasn't changing anything about the store, the goods or anything, that I knew about. There was just no good reason for the trip," he repeated. "And it was so sudden."

"She *could* be charged with kidnapping if her uncle finds her," Thomas said, looking thoughtful; he stared off across the room, his eyes squinting slightly.

"Or the uncle could be charged with murder," Alan said, chilling when he thought of the man pushing his wife over a banister railing.

Josie had been looking at Thomas, but at Alan's last words, her gaze snapped back to him. "What are you talking about? Janey's still alive."

"She saw him kill her mother."

"What?" Thomas asked, straightening in his chair.

"Oh my God," Josie gasped.

"Janey saw her father kill her mother," Alan repeated. "She saw him push her mother over that banister railing. Her mother didn't jump to her death—she was pushed."

"Damn right he could be charged with murder," Thomas muttered.

Alan shook his head. "Olivia won't have it. She doesn't want Janey to have to face her father again, ever."

"But if that's the only way . . . ," Josie said, glancing at Thomas.

Thomas nodded. "If that's the only way to put the man out o' their lives for good, I'm thinkin' like Josie—Janey may have to."

"I agree," Alan said. "Now, I have to convince Olivia."

Josie reached for her water glass. "No. *We*. If she's your friend—and she is, perhaps more—she's our friend, too. We'll help."

Thomas's brows shot up. He slanted a smile at his wife. "I believe I've just been volunteered."

"I believe you have," she said, smiling back.

"She is more," Alan told them. "I think the only reason she refused my proposal a few weeks ago was because she was frightened of what I might think of her taking her uncle's money."

"What else could she have done?" Thomas asked.

"Precisely my thinking," Alan agreed.

"She must be terribly frightened," Josie said, shaking her head. "I can't imagine. No wonder she went after her bag and those boys. Mr. Leavensworth said she looked frantic. She was."

Squeals and the tapping of small boots in the hallway outside the dining room drew their attention that way. Mrs. O'Brien could be heard through the door, scolding the girls for running in the house.

Thomas laughed. Josie shrugged and stood, saying, "Well, at least Margaret doesn't run off to the theater by herself anymore." She smoothed her skirt over her stomach and started for the door.

Thomas reached out and grabbed her hand, tugging her toward him. "Of course she doesn't," he teased, standing. "She has someone to take her now, Mrs. Murphy. Someone who encourages her to be a little actress." He kissed her and dropped a hand to the child that grew within her.

Josie blushed. "Now, Dr. Murphy, I encourage no such thing."

"Mrs. Murphy," he said, kissing her again, "you do. And under your influence, Maggie's sure to grow into a poised and well-mannered young lady."

"Maggie, mannered?" Alan scoffed. "She wouldn't be Maggie."

"True, very true," Thomas said, rubbing Josie's belly. A second later, he jerked his hand back, muttering, "Strong little devil. If that's any indication, we're in for a time of it."

Josie laughed. "Perhaps he doesn't appreciate you embarrassing his mother."

Alan opened his mouth to say "He?" just as the door flew open and Maggie and Janey burst into the room giggling. Their hair was braided in a wild fashion, in a least eight plaits all over their heads with ribbons of various colors tied onto the ends of the braids. Both Thomas and Alan reared back and gave them odd looks. Josie asked what in the world they had done to their hair. Giggling, Maggie jumped up into her father's arms, saying, "Look at us, Papa, aren't we lovely?"

A smiling Janey stared at father and daughter together for a few seconds, then she headed for Alan and climbed up onto his lap.

"One of my ribbons fell out in the carriage," she said, her face bright. She handed it to him, a small pink strip. "I tried to tie it back on and couldn't. Maggie was too busy giggling and poking her head out the carriage window, and Mrs. O'Brien was too busy trying to pull her back in."

"Here," Alan said, taking the ribbon from her. "I'll fix it."

And he did, with Josie looking on and smiling.

CHAPTER TWENTY-TWO

In a gentle way, Josie tried to convince Olivia to let Janey testify. Thomas did, too, with Alan standing by. Olivia wanted to hide her face, her entire body, knowing that Alan had told Josie and Thomas what she had confided to him. But she had the other secret, which she wasn't about to reveal because it was more terrible than the thievery—Uncle Edward might not even be alive for Janey to testify against.

Still, they were sweet, Josie and Thomas. Josie brought her tea, sat on the edge of the bed and assured that they were her friends and that they wanted to help. Thomas asked for descriptions of the boys and told her he would alert the constables and even send out people of his own to look for them. He asked for her uncle's Philadelphia address in case the money was found. Olivia gave it, but she later wondered if that had been a wise thing to do. If the money wasn't found, Alan might get the address from Thomas and send the amount himself. She didn't want him doing that. She had already involved him, Josie, and Thomas more than she wanted to.

Three days later the boys and the money still had not been found. Olivia's ribs were healing, and she decided that rather than spend her days lying in bed or sitting in the garden, she should be back in her store, working hard so she might earn and save enough money to pay Uncle Edward back. That was certainly a better alternative than waiting until she was twenty-one when her trust would become available—better than living until then with the guilt of having stolen the money. If she wasn't charged with murder before then . . . Somehow she had to put *that* thought from her mind and stop allowing it to consume her days.

"Janey and I are going back to Davenport tomorrow," she told Alan that evening, as they walked together along the garden paths. Summer roses bloomed nearby, their scent sweet and unmistakable. Birds chirped in the trees. The garden stones were still slightly damp from an afternoon thunderstorm.

"And you expect me to stay here?" he asked. "Is that why you said Janey and I?" Olivia did not miss the sarcasm in his voice.

She glanced over at him, wondering at his thoughts. "I didn't know if you would be ready to leave yet."

He turned suddenly on the path, took her by the shoulders, and stared down at her. "I came because I didn't want you and Janey making the journey alone," he said tightly. "Why is it always you and Janey, not you, me, and Janey, Olivia? Even now that you no longer have to be afraid that I might condemn you for taking that money, you're still distant. Good God, you slept in my arms. You let me make love to you! Why did you, if you had no intention of allowing more to happen? I love you, and I love Janey, and I want us to be a family."

She didn't know what to say. She stood staring at him. In many ways, she was glad that he had accompanied them to St. Louis and that he had introduced her to Josie and Thomas, and Janey to Maggie. Janey was having the time of her life. The girls seemed to adore each other, and Josie and Thomas had welcomed her and Janey into their home as if they had known them forever and loved them. The trouble was that this visit, being around Josie, Thomas, and Maggie—a family similar to the one she, Alan, and Janey might make if her troubles were ever resolved—seemed to have increased Alan's longing for a family of his own. For her and Janey to be that family.

"I want to make love to you and sleep with you again," he said, dipping his head to kiss her.

"Alan." She withdrew, startled. She would react differently if Mrs. Ferguson's sister wrote with good news—that Mrs. Ferguson was fine and that the blow hadn't killed Uncle Edward. She wouldn't be so afraid then . . . she wouldn't worry that Alan, if he married her, could become a widower if she had killed Uncle Edward and if she were found. She would surely be tried for his murder and possibly hung. A nightmarish thought.

"Is that all you have to say, Livvy?" Alan demanded.

She still didn't know what to say. That she had another secret, this one more horrible than the last?

"Let me know what time you want to leave tomorrow," he said, his voice heavy. "I believe the *Brazil* leaves St. Louis at noon."

The following morning Thomas, Josie, and Maggie went with them to the levee, and when the *Brazil* set out at noon, Olivia, Alan, and Janey waved to the Murphys from the deck of the steamer. Janey didn't especially want to leave Maggie, but she had told Maggie, before boarding the ship, that she would be back when the baby was born. Olivia was surprised by their plans, but she couldn't help but feel some excited anticipation over that event herself. Josie and Thomas Murphy were by far the sweetest and the mostly happily married couple she had ever seen, and the family's excitement over the infant's upcoming birth was infectious. She too would be happy to make the journey again in a few months to greet the newest member of the Murphy family. In fact, she'd make it as soon as word reached them that the baby had been born.

Edwin and Annie, the goats, were delighted to see Olivia and Janey. Not as delighted to see Alan, however; Edwin started after Alan with his horns almost as soon as Alan walked into the barn. Alan grumbled at him, and Edwin bleated and jumped back. Elmor came over to rub against Olivia's leg, and Martha flapped her wings and stood atop the haystack as if *expecting* notice—she certainly didn't intend to go out of her way to get it. Olivia could come to her. Eleanor chomped hay as she stared at her mistress, no doubt wondering where she had been for so long.

After spending a good hour visiting with the animals, Olivia and Janey went off to the house, exhausted and glad to be home, and Alan walked off up the street to call on Charlotte, since Homer had told them at the wharf that she had a cold.

"Steam," Alan told Charlotte after listening to her heart and lungs. "Your chest is clear. Lungs sound good. The congestion is all upper. We'll use steam to help clear your head. Boil some water, drape a cloth over your head, and put your head over the water."

"Won't it burn me?" Charlotte asked, looking startled.

"Well, let the water cool a little. Don't put your head over it while it's still boiling. How have things been in town these past few weeks?"

"About the same. People going in and out, stopping for a spell, wondering if they want to settle in Iowa Territory. There's always the regulars—Harv and Hank, who I don't particularly like anymore since that town council business. Homer, John, Walt . . . speaking of John, he was here just this afternoon, wondering if I knew when you might be back. Seemed a little edgy around the gills, shifting around, saying he needed to talk to you real bad. I told him I knew you'd intended to stay at your friend Dr. Murphy's home while you were in St. Louis, like you almost always do, and he said he thought he might send a letter to you since no one knew when you and Olivia might be back. How'd she do with her wholesalers anyway?" Charlotte asked. "I still think that business could have waited. Made no sense to me. Dragging Janey off all the way to St. Louis and—"

"Now what could be so urgent that John would go to the trouble of sending me a letter?" Alan asked, thinking aloud. "You're right—Olivia didn't have that much business to attend. She never meant to stay in St. Louis for weeks and weeks."

Charlotte shrugged, making a sound in the back of her throat. "None of it's made sense to me since it started. Why she had to go in the first place, and why she didn't just leave Janey here."

"She's never left Janey," he said, understanding at least that part. And knowing more, much more, than Charlotte about Olivia and Janey's lives prior to Davenport, he understood perfectly Olivia not wanting to leave Janey in one town and territory while she went to another. He understood her protectiveness.

"Well," he said, rising from Charlotte's kitchen table. "I'm off to find John and see what that business is about. The *Brazil* certainly got in later than we expected. We hit a few snags in the river. It's running low."

"Hasn't been much rain," she remarked.

"Do the steam, then go to bed and let Sally take over tomorrow," the doctor ordered. "You don't seem to know when to stop and rest, Charlotte."

"Oh, don't grumble at me. I'll be going to see Olivia and Janey tomorrow, that's what I'll be doing," she said. "I've missed those two. Need to hear that girl's boots clacking up and down my hall, and I'd rather see Olivia's sweet face first thing in the mornings, delivering me milk and butter, than Homer's. Did you know he could make butter?"

Alan chuckled. "No, I didn't."

"He surely can. Olivia's is better, but he can make butter. I made sure he didn't rent out anything at you and Olivia's place either. The house . . . animals . . ."

"I thank you for keeping an eye on him," Alan said, grinning. He bent and plopped a kiss on her cheek, glad to be home and happy to see her.

Charlotte reared back and gaped at him as if he'd smacked her or something. "That's enough of you for one evening, Doc. Outta here. Go on. Get, now!" Her face turned red.

"I'm going, I'm going. I wouldn't want to give you an apoplectic fit on top of that cold."

"Shoo. Don't you flatter yourself!"

"Good night, Charlotte," he said, heading for the door.

"Night, Doc. Watch who you go around kissing."

"Oh, I will," he promised. "I'll have my eyes wide open."

She cackled.

As Ida had done for years with her store and home, John

had his legal office on the first floor of a two-story house on Main Street, and his living quarters on the second floor. Light glowed from an upstairs window, and assuming that John was still awake, Alan rapped hard on the front door, then waited. Two more raps and the door finally opened. John stood there in a nightshirt and cap, holding a candle up near his face.

"Doc?" he said, looking uncertain at first. Then he looked relieved. "Doc! Come in here. I've been wonderin' what I should do. Didn't wanna talk to anyone else but you 'bout the matter. Come on in," he said again, stepping out of the way and opening the door wide.

Alan couldn't imagine what might have John so unnerved that he felt he couldn't discuss it with anyone but him. Alan stepped into the front room of John's house—his office—where the desk was completely cluttered with papers. How in the world John managed to find anything in the mess was beyond Alan. Alan took a seat near the fireplace and asked John what had him so troubled.

"I'm takin' care of Ida's unfinished business, ya know? Tryin' to locate her sister, who was out'n Ohio somewhere, last Ida heard. Things like that." He had rounded his desk and now stood studying the piles of papers.

"I didn't realize Ida had a sister," Alan said.

"Reckon she didn't get on with her too well, so she didn't mention her to too many folks. She left her a little money, though, if she ever turns up. Reckon I consider it my respons'bility to try an' locate her."

"I can understand that."

"So I take care of just 'bout anything that comes along fer Ida, even if it's personal bus'ness, since she ain't got no family but the sister she lost track of," John said, finally deciding to tackle a certain pile.

"Should I light that lantern?" Alan asked, meaning the lantern that sat on a small table across the room.

"Reckon that might be helpful," John mumbled. "Ain't much to see by in here."

Alan laughed to himself, wondering, as he sometimes did, how the man managed to get along.

"Matches in the tin box on the mantle," John said.

Alan crossed to the fireplace, found the tin box, and soon had the lantern lit. He carried it over and held it near John's desk.

"Well now, that's consider'ble help. Thanks, Doc!" John said, glancing up for a second. He dug into a pile of papers. "Let's see now . . . If I cleaned up the place, I couldn't find anything." He chuckled at himself as he shuffled through the pile. Alan felt tired and a little impatient at the moment, wanting nothing more than to go home and sleep.

"Letter came for Ida, an' somethin' else along with it. From Richard somethin' or other over in Pittsburgh."

Alan ears pricked up at that. Could this be from the friend Ida had written to some time ago to see if he knew anything about Monroes in Philadelphia? "Slim chance," Ida had told him at the time. "But askin' ain't gonna hurt a thing, Doc, not a thing. If that girl's in trouble, runnin' from a husband or somethin', an' if the husband's lookin' fer her, Rich might've heard somethin'."

"What did the letter say, John?" Alan asked, wide awake now, feeling certain it must have said something important or John wouldn't have felt such a need to locate him. "Do you remember? Is it about Olivia?"

John's gaze snapped up to him. "How'd you know that?"

Alan didn't want to reveal too much about Olivia's predicament to too many people. But if the look on John's face was any indication, he already knew, from reading that letter, that she was in trouble. "Because I felt she was in trouble, and Ida told me she would write to her friend in Pittsburgh and ask if he'd heard anything in Pennsylvania. Olivia told everyone here that she and Janey were from Boston, but Janey mentioned Philadelphia once, and so did Olivia on another occasion."

"It's really her then, ain't it, Doc?" John asked, shuffling again. "That ain't her name . . . Monroe. She doesn't seem capable . . . she seems harmless. That girl ain't her sister, she's her cousin. She ain't a Missus, either, an' her husband didn't die between here an' St. Louis. She snatched that girl outta her uncle's home, stole money from 'im, an' tried to kill him. I wouldn't've believed it, Doc. Not 'bout Mrs. Monroe . . . or whatever 'er name is. No way in hell I would've believed it."

"Tried to kill him . . . ?" Alan blurted. *What?*

"That's what the piece of newspaper says."

"Find it," Alan ordered, digging now, too, although he believed already. He didn't need to see the letter or the piece of newspaper. The first words he'd ever heard Janey say hit him like a brick in the chest suddenly: *Did you kill him, Livvy? Did you?* He suddenly *knew.* Olivia had tried to kill her uncle, and if Janey was uncertain whether or not she had, perhaps Olivia still was, too. Perhaps it had all happened the day they had run away, and she still seemed distant and cold because she hadn't told him everything. She'd told him about her uncle's cruelty toward herself and Janey, how she'd known that she had to take Janey away or he would kill her, and how she'd taken the money from her uncle's study. But she hadn't told him that she'd tried to kill her uncle.

"I've got it, Doc," John said, pulling out some papers. "I was tryin' to organize a bit earlier. Made a bigger mess an' buried it."

Alan snatched the papers out of his hand and leveled a glare on John, wanting to make something clear. "Listen to me. Maybe Olivia's not who she claims to be. Maybe Janey is her cousin and not her sister. Maybe she did 'kidnap' her, or so it would seem to a lot of people. Maybe she did steal from her uncle, and maybe, just maybe she did try to kill him. But you, and others, don't know the entire story, John. You don't know Olivia and Janey's side of the story, the hell that man put them through. Desperate people do desperate things. Olivia's not proud of anything she had to do, but she did it all to save Janey's life. I believe that because I know Olivia. You're having a hard time believing it because you know Olivia, too. No matter what, it's best not to say anything to anyone else right now, John, at least not until I decide what to do."

John stared at him. "Doc . . . I know you love 'er. But maybe yer not seein' real clear 'cause of that. Reckon—"

"Listen," Alan said, in a harder tone this time. He told John everything Olivia had told him in St. Louis about the events that had led to her coming to Davenport with Janey. He told him about Janey's father killing her mother, and about Janey's arm, and how Olivia had not had a good choice—she could either steal from her uncle's study and take Janey away, or sit and wait for him to kill Janey, too.

"I reckon I'm beginnin' to understand, Doc," John said slowly.

"Good," Alan said, and then he turned his attention to reading the letter and the piece of newspaper.

Ida's friend's name was Richard George, and he said he thought Ida's descriptions of Olivia and Janey Monroe matched those given in an advertisement that had been running in a Pittsburgh newspaper for months now, though their last names were different. The advertisement had appeared in several Philadelphia newspapers, too, as well as in others in big cities in neighboring states. Edward Morgan even had associates looking for the girls in Pittsburgh, so determined was he to find his niece and daughter and make certain the niece was properly charged for her crimes. Alan chilled when he read that. And what was Edward Morgan to be charged with? Nothing?

The piece of newspaper contained good descriptions of Janey and Olivia, and sketches of both. The crimes involved were kidnapping, robbery, and assault—and there was an award offered to anyone who could provide information on the girls' whereabouts. Ironically, the amount offered was one thousand dollars. Alan cursed under his breath when he read that.

"What do we do, Doc?" John asked. "After what ya told me, I wouldn't let the man get his hands on those two. What other cities did he put that in, ya think? It's been runnin' for months, so he's mighty determined. Sooner or later, he jus' might find 'em here in our little town."

"I don't know what to do, exactly," Alan said. "We certainly have enough homes to hide them in should he turn up."

"Yer right 'bout that. Lots of people here took a likin' to Missus Monroe, er, Miss Morgan, right away."

"Then again, some didn't. Right now, I plan to go see Olivia and let her know that she didn't kill her uncle. I have a feeling she's still wondering if she did."

"That'll put her mind at ease, but only a little, Doc," John said. "She's still got some mighty big troubles."

Alan agreed. But he wondered again if having Edward Morgan charged with murder was the solution. He felt quite certain that it was. Still, convincing Olivia to let Janey testify was another matter altogether. Without Janey's testimony, her father couldn't even be charged.

The hour wasn't that late, perhaps ten o'clock, but Olivia and Janey had gone to bed already. Pounding on the front door woke Olivia, and she pulled a wrap around her shift, took her pistol from a drawer in the table beside the bed (in case her visitor was an unwelcome one), picked up the lantern from the table top, and went to the door.

"Who is it?" she asked at the front door.

"Alan."

He hadn't come to the house to see her since the evening he had left her in the hallway. She hastened to unbolt and open the door. He stood, his medical bag in hand, his shirtsleeves rolled up past his elbows, looking as he had earlier this evening when he had left them.

"You didn't tell me everything, Livvy," he said softly. "You didn't tell me you tried to kill your uncle."

Her first reaction was to gasp. Her second was to try and close the door. She didn't want him knowing that, and she didn't want to talk about it either.

"No," he said, putting his hand on the door to stop her from closing it all the way. "We're going to talk more. We're going to clear the air."

She stared at him, suddenly wondering if she would ever breathe again. God . . . oh, God, how did he know? "H-how did you find out?" she asked. Something else occurred to her, too: "He's not dead? Why did you say *tried?*"

"Open the door and let me in."

She left the door, giving it up to him, and walked over to the settles in front of the fireplace. She sank down onto one and stared across at the other one. She again remembered the thump of the bookend on Uncle Edward's head, the sound of him slumping to the floor, the dark blood that oozed from his head.

"He's not dead, is he?" she asked again, and for a second she felt deeply ashamed because she wished that Uncle Edward *was* dead—and she had never in her life wished anyone dead. All these months she had been so afraid of being accused of murder, and now that she felt certain he was still alive, she would have preferred to be accused of murder. She didn't want to live with knowing he was alive, with fearing that he might find her and Janey any day, with jumping at every knock on her door.

"No, he's not," Alan said, sitting beside her.

"You must think—"

"I think you should have told me. And don't tell me you didn't want to involve me because I've been deeply involved with you for months now. I am part of your life."

He reached for her, pulled her into his arms, and urged her head to his chest. "Tell me now, Olivia. Tell me what happened."

"How did you find out?" she asked again, and he held up a letter and what looked like part of a newspaper. Olivia took both, sat up straight and read them, feeling the blood drain from her face and her stomach twist into knots.

"He's been running the advertisement in Pennsylvania newspapers and in newspapers in surrounding states," Alan said. "The letter is from a friend of Ida's in Pittsburgh."

"He's offered a reward," Olivia mumbled.

He nodded. "Notice the amount."

"I did."

"Sooner or later, he may find you, Olivia. You're going to have to decide what to do. Tell me what happened."

"He came home as I was getting Janey out of bed to leave," she said slowly. "He—he was drunk, stumbling. He knew about the money I'd taken. He'd guessed that I was planning something. He was so drunk I wondered which of us was stronger. He hit Mrs. Ferguson, the housekeeper, and that was all I could stand. When he fell and was struggling to his feet, I remembered the brass bookends, and I grabbed one."

She glanced over at Alan, then down at her trembling hands that held the piece of newspaper and the letter. Her entire body felt like a quivering mess of nerves. Even her voice trembled. "It's . . . I wasn't trying to kill him, Alan. I swear it. He would rather have killed us both than let us leave that house. There hasn't been a day since that I haven't worried about Mrs. Ferguson. I feared that if he was still alive, he'd make certain she never found employment in any other household. I worried about Harry, too. If Uncle Edward guessed his involvement, he surely made life hell for Harry, too.

"I—I didn't have an alternative," she said, turning her face into his linen shirt. Fear swelled in her throat. Her eyes burned with tears. "If I hadn't hit him with something, Janey and I wouldn't have escaped. I didn't know what else to do."

"I know," Alan said. He exhaled heavily, tiredly, and ran his hand down over his face. "I know what you've told me about him and the things he did to you and Janey, and I believe you did the right thing, in everything—in taking Janey and the money, in leaving Philadelphia and Pennsylvania. I believe you did the right thing, but will others if you never allow Janey to tell a court about the things her father did to her? If you return the money, that charge is gone, and with your testimony and Janey's about the things he did, how could any court condemn you for taking her away? Kidnapping, yes, but with just cause. How could any court not convict him of murder?"

Olivia stood, walked over to the western window and stared out blankly. Janey . . . testify? Such pain that would cause Janey, reliving all the terror, all the suffering. She had put it all behind her, and now Olivia had to consider drudging it all up.

"I can't do that to Janey," she said, turning around to face Alan. "There must be another way . . . I'll testify on her behalf. I'll face him, but I won't allow anyone to force Janey into doing it."

"That might not work, Olivia. You must know that."

"Why wouldn't it?"

"Because Janey is the witness, you know."

"I could try."

"Yes, you could," he said, shaking his head, looking exasperated. "But I'm telling you, your testimony on her behalf may not be acceptable in court. If Janey testifies, the man is done. He'll hang for murder."

Olivia spun back around to face the window. She couldn't . . . she couldn't make Janey face Edward again, ever. "No," she said, setting her jaw.

"Olivia."

He came up behind her, placed his hands on her shoulders, and tugged her back against him. "All right, we won't talk about this anymore right now." He planted a kiss on the top of her head and spoke softly: "Even before this evening, before I knew what had happened with your uncle, I imagined how frightened you and Janey must have been in Philadelphia, how frightened you still are. Then I read that letter and newspaper, and I can't imagine anymore. I've never had to run for my life. I've never had to leave everything and everyone familiar to me. Stagecoaches, ships . . . no home."

"Leaving was the easy part," she whispered, "though if I had stopped to think for long, I would have found it terrifying. Janey and I slept for more than a day after we boarded the steamer in Cincinnati. We didn't have a cabin from Pittsburgh to Ohio, and trying to sleep somewhere on the deck of that ship was exhausting. But, dead or alive, Uncle Edward was hundreds of miles away, and that was a comfort."

"I love you," he murmured. "Never forget that, Olivia."

She twisted in his arms, buried her face in his chest again, inhaling his masculine scent, wanting to stay like this, in his arms, forever. "I didn't know what you would think of me. If we were found, I didn't want anyone to have reason to accuse you of aiding us. I wanted you to be able to say truthfully that we rented from you, and that was all. Now you know everything, and you're hiding a criminal."

"Livvy." He slid his hand under her jaw and tipped her head up. "You're not a criminal."

"I've felt like one for months."

"Yes, you took his money. Yes, you hit him with that bookend. But what else could you have done?" He shook his head. "Nothing."

He kissed her on the lips, gently, lightly, then smoothed the hair back from her face. "You're not a criminal, and I could never think of you that way. The way you saved Janey . . . You're kind and compassionate to people and animals. Animals! You nearly drove me mad with all those animals in the barn, but when I made myself sit down and stop being grumpy, I realized how sweet you were and how large your heart was. Those animals still nearly drive me mad at times, especially Edwin, but they're part of you, and at least Martha and Elmor are in the barn because sweet, gentle Olivia couldn't stand the thought of them in a kettle or a smokehouse. But"—he pointed a finger at her, half grinning—"if you even think about adding more to your collection of barnyard children, we must talk."

"About building a bigger barn?" she queried, smiling genuinely for the first time in weeks. She had been troubled during the entire journey to and from St. Louis and during the days they had stayed with the Murphys, and not having to force a smile now was a good feeling.

He laughed. "I'll build a bigger house, but not a bigger barn."

"And why would you do that? More room for animals?"

"No, no." He lowered his head closer to hers. "More room for children."

He still wanted her to marry him, even after knowing her ugly secrets. The knowledge shouldn't surprise her—over and over, he had told her he loved her—but it did. She slid her arms up around his neck, asking, "How many children, Dr. Schuster?"

"I haven't thought that far ahead yet," he said, his voice deeper now, throatier. "Not too far past wanting to make them."

Not too far past wanting to make them? Olivia's face

warmed immediately. She glanced away, embarrassed by the implication of the statement, her heart jumping in her chest. He laughed under his breath, and a few seconds later she tilted a shy smile up at him.

He placed his hands on the window frame at either side of her head, nuzzling one side of his face against hers, breathing deeply, inhaling her scent the way she had inhaled his. "I've wanted to be this close to you for weeks now, for so long I've wondered if I would burst. And you, in your night rail again. Tsk, Livvy. Do you know how tempting that is? Do you know what I want to do?"

She imagined, and the images were enough to make her face burn red now. But the embarrassment was not enough to make her want to escape him. She turned her face to his and brushed a kiss on his lips. He sobered and stared down at her, deeply into her eyes as if searching her soul.

"Nothing short of marriage, Livvy," he said, reaching for the drawstring just above her breasts. "Nothing less."

She swallowed. "I wouldn't have dreamed of accepting less before if I hadn't had such ugly secrets to keep—and people to protect."

"My Olivia," he whispered, pulling the string. "Devoted . . . committed to those she loves."

She pushed her fingers into the hair at his nape, and brought his head down to hers. She wanted to feel his lips on hers again, his hot mouth on her breasts. She wanted to taste him, hold him, merge with him. "To you," she murmured.

His hands cupped her breasts, then loosened her night rail as he dipped his head and nipped at her neck, working his way down. Olivia tossed her hair back, savoring, and seconds later he lifted her in one sweeping motion and carried her off into the bedroom, where he laid her tenderly on his bed.

He discarded his clothes, then her night rail, and when he came down to her moments later, Olivia opened to him like the petals of a spring flower to the sun, welcoming, wanting. . . .

CHAPTER ❖❖❖ TWENTY-THREE

THEY MADE LOVE again in the morning, at dawn, while the pinks and purples of sunrise flowed together above the eastern horizon. They played this time, laughing and nipping, curling their bodies together. Afterward, Alan pulled on his trousers, fetched a basin of water from the well, and they washed and dressed each other, then raced off outside hand in hand to gather eggs from the barn. When they returned to the house a short time later, they cooked breakfast together, Olivia making biscuits and Alan frying eggs and slices of smoked ham.

"Do you know what this once was?" he asked, forking a piece of ham, holding it up and eyeing Olivia. "What it was once part of?"

"Stop that," she scolded playfully.

He laughed. "Elmor."

"I beg your pardon. Elmor's in the barn. I just saw him."

"Oh. Well, perhaps it was Elmor's brother, then. He was sold weeks before Elmor was, you know."

"No, I didn't know," she said, plopping her hands on her hips. "Stop teasing me."

"People are afraid to tell you when they plan to have a butchering," Alan said, chuckling. "I think Charlotte's done hers by the light of the moon for the last several months."

Olivia rolled her eyes and cut another biscuit. "How does anyone stand the *thought* of killing an animal?"

He held up the ham again. "You have no qualms about eating one."

She shot him a playful look of warning just as Janey

walked into the main room rubbing sleep from her eyes. She blinked, spotted Alan, blinked again, then stumbled sleepily toward him.

"Careful, Janey," Olivia warned. "He's cooking eggs and ham. The grease could burn you." It was amazing how Janey always went right to him, how she had taken to Alan shortly after meeting him. Aside from Olivia, there wasn't another person in her life she had taken to as quickly, or whom she trusted as much.

"You're never here in the morning," Janey told Alan, her voice slightly slurred.

"Aren't you a sleepyhead," he teased. "A little frowsy there, Miss Morgan?"

Janey's eyes widened at that. She whipped her head around to Olivia, looking shocked that he had used her real last name. Olivia exchanged concerned glances with Alan, then she put aside the tin cup she had been using to cut biscuits, approached Janey, and knelt in front of her.

"Alan knows everything about us, and it's all right for him to know," she told her cousin. "He'll help in any way he can. He and Mr. Brimmer know, and I'm sure they'll both help us. I didn't want to involve anyone else because I didn't trust anyone—and I was afraid that anyone who helped us could get in trouble, too. But it's all right. Everything will be all right."

"You're sure, Livvy?" Janey asked in a small voice.

Alan hunched beside Olivia and took Janey by the shoulders. "*I'm* sure. I love you and Livvy, and I'm sure. You both have me and some other very good friends in Davenport, friends who won't let anything bad happen to either of you, ever."

"Promise? Like when you didn't let the smoke take her away?"

He nodded. "Like when I didn't let the smoke take her away." He stood then, lightening the situation somewhat by commenting that the eggs and ham would burn if he didn't keep an eye on them. They could go out and milk Eleanor together after breakfast, if she wanted to, he told Janey.

"We'll take milk and eggs to Charlotte soon and make

butter later today," Olivia told Janey as she returned to cutting biscuits. "I wonder how Homer's done at the store."

"Careful of your ribs while churning," Alan warned. "They might not be healed completely."

Olivia laughed. The warning was rather absurd, considering that if her ribs were going to come apart again if she exerted herself too much, they surely would have during last night's and then this morning's activities. She caught Alan's gaze and thought he read her laughter and look; for the first time she saw him blush.

He made a noise in the back of his throat, a sound of embarrassment. "You're right. If *that* didn't hurt them, churning won't."

"Surely not," Olivia agreed.

He flipped the ham and eggs.

When Olivia and Janey delivered the milk and eggs, Janey wanted to stay with Charlotte, eat some more, of Charlotte's cooking this time, and help around the boardinghouse. Word had gotten around town that Olivia, Janey, and Alan were back, and when the cousins arrived Charlotte was ready with hotcakes, Janey's favorite food. No matter that Janey had already eaten a good amount of breakfast earlier—she went right after the hotcakes.

"My feller might be coming back down this way soon," Charlotte whispered to Olivia. "Got a letter from him this morning."

"Did you?" Olivia asked, smiling, thinking Charlotte's excitement and anticipation cute.

"Sure did. My heart hasn't bopped around so much in my chest for years."

"Well, when he arrives, if you want to go for another outing, Janey and I will be glad to dress your hair again."

"Is there more?" Janey asked.

"Surely is," Charlotte said, getting up to fetch more hotcakes from the stove.

"I'm going," Olivia announced. "I want to see how Homer's done with the store. I'll walk back down in a few hours to get you," she told Janey, and Janey nodded just as Charlotte plopped more hotcakes on her plate.

Homer wasn't as neat as Ida had been about entering purchases in the ledger—in places, Olivia could hardly even read his scrawl. But at least he'd taken the time to write down the date, the item, and the cost. He also had entered the customers' names.

She had been in the store all of ten minutes when Homer appeared, telling her he was glad to see her and Doc Schuster back and that business had been fine while she'd been gone. The church ladies hadn't particularly cared for Ida's brash manner and so they'd chosen to go to other stores in town while she was alive. But now that Olivia owned and operated the store, they did a good amount of their business here, Homer said. "'Nough that you oughtta be proud."

Another quick look at the ledger, and Olivia saw that he was right.

"That one goat of yours is a tough one," he remarked. "That male."

"I don't think he likes too many people besides me and Janey," Olivia said, smiling.

"I reckon not. Don't know how many times he butted me in the leg when I was tryin' to collect eggs in the mornin's. Didn't want me in that barn."

She apologized for Edwin. "I'm afraid he decides right away whether he likes a person or wants that person in his home."

"Well, I'm goin' over to see John for a piece," Homer said, turning away from the counter. For the last month, he and John had seemed like complete friends again, no doubt since realizing she wasn't romantically interested in either of them. They would still scurry to do just about anything for her, she felt certain, but in a friendly, neighborly way now.

Olivia left the front door open as a way of letting people know that the store was open for business. She straightened the candy jars, and realizing she had room for more bolts of material on the shelves behind the counter, she went off to the back room, thinking to bring more out.

She heard someone enter the store, heard boots clomp on the wooden floor and the front door click shut. Her first customer of the day. But why had the person shut the door?

Olivia picked up two bolts of material and carried them with her out into the store area, thinking she would place them on the counter, wait on her customer, then arrange the bolts on the shelves. She was humming when she left the back room, a tune Janey had always enjoyed when she was younger. A man stepped out into the aisle, and a scream froze in Olivia's throat.

Uncle Edward—wearing a top hat and immaculate black suit and white shirt, a cravat neatly tied at his neck, a walking stick in his right hand. He appeared sober and well-kempt, which was more than she could say for the last time she had been unfortunate enough to lay eyes on him—when he had been drunk, unshaven, slovenly, and mad.

The entire time Olivia stood assessing him—seconds that seemed like hours—she didn't breathe. His glowing green eyes told all: he had found her, and now she would pay for her crimes.

Her heart hammered against the walls of her chest. Her gaze skittered to the closed door, to the drawn curtains—she had opened them not a half hour before. He stood in the middle of the aisle. Even if she dropped the bolts and managed to get past him, she didn't think she could reach the door without his catching her. The distance was too short.

He slammed the tip of his walking stick down onto the floor and warned, "Do not try it."

Her knees felt like liquid. She wondered how long she could keep from screaming.

"So," he said. "Here you are, residing in this *barbaric* place, just like that riffraff in St. Louis said. People will talk for money. People in Pittsburgh, people in Cincinnati . . . the captains of ships, even if they've seen only a glimpse of you. No one is above bribery. And so, here you are, living on my stolen money, no doubt, determined to be a storekeeper even after I sold your father's shop."

"You murdered Kathleen," Olivia said, shocking herself. She had opened her mouth to tell him that the Philadelphia store should have been hers upon her father's death, that she was a fine storekeeper—despite being a woman. Instead she told him matter-of-factly what she knew.

Nerves leaped around his eyes, only a little, but enough to tell her that she had alarmed him. She felt a twinge of confidence. She could use that—the knowledge that he had killed Kathleen. She could use it to make him reconsider whatever he was contemplating.

"You murdered her," she said, taking a step forward. "I'll see you hang, I swear to you. I'll watch you. You murdered her, and you would have murdered your own daughter, too."

"She's not my daughter," he growled. "Delivered six weeks earlier than she should have been, but full-size. Kathleen didn't want to marry me—her father forced her to. She got her revenge, by bedding the man she loved before our wedding. She had his child, and when she lost ours she was happy." He spat the last word, ramming the end of his walking stick on the floor again.

He didn't frighten her as much as he had back in Philadelphia and as he had when he'd stepped into the aisle. *He* was frightened of *her*, of what she knew, and that gave her confidence a surge.

Olivia shook her head slowly. "Kathleen wasn't happy when she lost that child, no matter that it was yours. She grieved. You pushed her over that banister. She didn't jump. You *pushed* her."

More nerves leaped around his eyes. "Where is Janey?" he demanded.

"Why? She's not your daughter, after all. You've made that clear."

"According to the law, she is."

"You tried to kill her, too."

"I never . . . !" He banged the walking stick down twice more. His face had grown red.

"You did," she said, taking two more steps forward. She

kept a pistol under the counter. She meant to reach it. "You killed her mother, and you tried numerous times to kill her. Get out of here. Get off of my property. Leave Davenport and never trouble us again. If you do, I swear I'll make certain you hang for murdering Kathleen."

She walked forward, her head held high, silently daring him to stop her. Once she had the pistol in her hands, she meant to drive him out of the store.

She caught a glimpse of him jerk his walking stick up like a sword, but she had no time to react; the end of it, a brass ornament of some sort, hit her hard. Pain exploded in her head, and Olivia crashed against the counter and slid to the floor. The shelves, the floor, the ceiling . . . everything spun. The door rattled open—or was she hearing things? She tried to open her mouth and scream, but nothing happened.

"Edward?" A female voice, a familiar one. "There you are. I thought I saw you come in— Oh my God. It's her. It *is* her. What have you done to her?" The voice became shrill with the last sentence.

"She grabbed my walking stick and tried to hit me with it," he lied. "I grabbed it back and defended myself."

"I'll get a constable," the woman said. "There must be a constable—"

"Fool woman! Shut the door! I want my money and my daughter. Olivia can rot in hell, after she bleeds to death."

"Edward!"

Olivia knew the voice now. Aunt Elaine, who had not believed her when she had told her about Uncle Edward beating Janey whenever he drank. Apparently Elaine had come to help him collect Janey. And what would they do with her once they had her? Edward would kill her, because he knew Janey had seen him murder Kathleen.

Thank God Janey had stayed at the boardinghouse this morning. Thank God.

They aren't going to get her.

Neither one of them. She wasn't going to let them get Janey.

Hearing the door click shut, as Aunt Elaine presumably

stepped all the way into the store, she twisted her body, began crawling on the floor, meaning to get around the counter and get the pistol.

Olivia's hair was braided in one plait down her back. Edward grabbed her by the braid and jerked her head back. "Where is she?" he growled near her ear. "Tell me where she is."

"A constable, Edward," Aunt Elaine mumbled. "We need a constable. You cannot take matters into—"

"Shut up, woman!"

Silence.

"Where is Janey?" he asked Olivia, pulling her head back more.

"You murdered Kathleen!" she screamed, wanting Aunt Elaine to hear every word. "Janey saw you! You pushed Kathleen over the banister. You murdered her. Janey saw you, that's why she didn't—"

He hit her in the head with his fist. More pain exploded inside her skull. He might kill her, too, but before he did, she meant to make certain Elaine knew about Kathleen. She might not believe her, as she'd refused to believe her when Olivia had told her about the beating. But Olivia had to take that chance.

She screamed again; "Janey saw you push Kathleen over the banister! You told her not to say anything, so she didn't. She said nothing! You murdered Kathleen!"

"Shut up!" he shouted, forgetting himself.

"What is she talking about?" Elaine asked hoarsely, stepping forward. "Edward, what is she saying about Kathleen? Janey saw you push her . . . ?"

"Shut up, you fool woman!" He pushed Olivia's face into the floor, then moved away from her. "She's lying, as she always has. When she came to you last year, you didn't believe a word she said. Why would you believe her now? Why would you believe the rantings of a crazed woman? Of a woman who stole from me, kidnapped my daughter, and tried to kill me? Tell me why you would believe I killed Kathleen!"

He continued, completely mad, shouting in Elaine's face.

Olivia had turned her head and was watching them, though blood dripped into her left eye from somewhere on her head. Elaine cringed backward, he ranted more, and Olivia realized that this was her chance.

In ordinary circumstances, if she had been so injured, she wouldn't have had the strength to finish crawling around the counter, reach up, and wrap her hand around the handle of the pistol; these, however, were not ordinary circumstances. If she didn't stop him and he found Janey, he would kill her because of what she had seen. And Aunt Elaine didn't realize it yet, but she was in danger now, too. She now knew the truth about Kathleen's death, too, and Edward would try to make certain that none of them repeated the truth.

"Did you?" she heard Aunt Elaine ask him in a small voice.

He drew a swift breath. "You believe her!"

"You did," Elaine whispered, clearly horrified. "She's telling the truth, isn't she? I knew she was when she came to see me about you beating Jane. I knew it, and I was afraid of you myself. I knew . . . All these months, you haven't been looking for Jane because you love her and want her back, as you claim. You've been afraid that she might talk and tell people what she saw. You did kill Kathleen. I wouldn't have imagined that. I wouldn't have, I wouldn't have. Oh, Edward! what have you done? What have you—"

The sound of him striking her was unmistakable—and it made Olivia find even more strength. She wrapped both hands around the handle of her pistol, struggled to her feet behind the counter, pointed the barrel at him just as he raised his hand over Aunt Elaine again, and fired.

Elaine screamed.

Uncle Edward clutched his shoulder where the bullet had caught him *"Put that gun down and tell me where to find the money and Janey, right now!"* he roared. He flew toward the counter, and Olivia swore he would have flown right over it at her if she hadn't fired again, this time hitting him in the chest.

His eyes widened. A gurgle rose from his throat as he

stared at her. He was as good as dead. She knew it. He knew it.

When he finally fell over a second later, Olivia slumped down behind the counter. Everything was spinning again, spinning darker and darker . . . She might be dying, but at least she'd made certain he would never again hurt Janey. She might go to hell for the thought, for taking a life. But that seemed a small price to pay in exchange for Janey's life.

Janey woke her with a song and by rubbing her cheek with her soft fingers. She was in a bed, in Alan's bed, Olivia realized when she managed to orient herself to her surroundings. She also realized that she was still alive.

"You're awake!" Janey whispered loudly, disbelieving. She pressed a kiss to Olivia's cheek, and when Olivia felt wetness, she realized that Janey was crying.

"Oh, Livvy, I thought you might die. I did! Your head looked so bad. The other side of your face is blue and puffy. Alan said you'd be fine, but I didn't believe him."

Olivia stroked her hair and cried with her. She was glad to be alive, glad to be there with Janey, glad they would never have to worry again. Unless Aunt Elaine wanted to take Janey back to Philadelphia.

As if reading her thoughts, Elaine approached the bed from where she had been sitting in a chair near the window. Olivia saw her from the corner of her eye.

"I didn't listen to you," Elaine said, pressing a handkerchief to her nose. "I didn't listen to you, and I should have. I am sorry, Olivia, for all of us. For Janey, for you, for Kathleen . . . I am truly sorry."

Olivia reached out and squeezed her hand. "There was nothing anyone could have done for Kathleen."

"I know, but if I had listened—"

"Don't," Olivia said. "It's over."

Elaine's face was bruised and swollen, too. She dabbed tears from her cheeks.

"I'm gonna go tell Alan you're awake!" Janey said excitedly. "He's out in the barn. He'll wanna know. I know he will! I just know it."

With that, she scrambled out of the room.

"I cannot tell you what a relief it is to hear her talking, to see her looking so happy," Elaine remarked, staring at the doorway after Janey had disappeared through it.

"She's content here," Olivia said. "The people of Davenport have become our family."

"I've noticed that. They love you and Janey. The church women bring food by for every meal. Charlotte Lind bangs on the door to look in on you every few hours. Mr. Brimmer and Mr. Whitworth have tended your animals. Dr. Schuster said he would do that, but they insisted. They said he needed to keep his attention on your recovery."

"How long have I been here?" Olivia asked.

"The entire day."

"What happened after . . . after . . . ? He would have killed you, too. Once you knew the truth about Kathleen's death, he would have found a way to kill you, too, Aunt Elaine. I wasn't going to let him find Janey, and I wasn't going to let him hurt us anymore. Anyone."

Olivia was crying now, too. She wondered if every time she closed her eyes she would see the image of Uncle Edward clutching his chest and staring at her in disbelief. Not forever, surely. Time had a way of healing wounds, of distancing a person from unpleasant memories. She had to believe that.

Aunt Elaine touched her hand. "You did what you had to do," she said, repeating what Alan had told her. "I know that."

Olivia nodded, wincing at the dull pain in her head. Her face felt as though it was on fire. "Janey . . . she loves it here. I know she's only my cousin and that I don't have a legal right to her, but she loves it here."

"I have no plans to try and take her from you," Elaine assured her, "and I doubt that anyone else in the family will, either, when I tell them the truth about everything."

"Thank you," Olivia said, closing her eyes. "I couldn't imagine her . . . us not being here—and I would go wherever Janey had to go."

Aunt Elaine dabbed at Olivia's tears with her handkerchief. "Here now. No more tears from either of us."

Olivia nodded. "How long have I been lying here? Who brought me here? I was in the store, behind the counter. That's the last thing I remember."

"Some men heard the shots and rushed in," Elaine explained. "Mr. Brimmer carried you here, then went to find Dr. Schuster."

"And the doctor opened his medical bag and pulled out a lot of prayer," Alan said from the doorway.

He and Janey walked into the room. She climbed up on the tick while Alan stood staring at Olivia from the foot of the bed. "You'll be fine," he promised. "Once the bruises and other wounds heal, you'll be fine." He spoke in a tone of great relief, and Olivia had to wonder if he was reassuring himself as well as her.

She held out her hand to him, and he came to her, sat on the edge of the bed, took her hand in his and smiled down at her.

"Thank you for waking," he said. "I promised Janey I would make certain nothing happened to the two of you, and then this happened. She might not have spoken to me ever again."

"She would have. She loves you. I love you."

Grinning, he exchanged glances with Aunt Elaine. "My, my, Olivia Morgan. You take a chance saying that right now. I have a witness. Two. Should I ask their blessing?"

Elaine's mouth formed an *O*. "The two of you?"

Alan nodded. "I'm asking for your niece's hand."

Elaine put a hand to her throat. "Why I . . . I suppose if she loves you, and you love her and promise to take care of her—"

"I can take care of myself," Olivia reminded them.

"No one would dispute that," Alan said, shaking his head.

"Cherish her then," Aunt Elaine amended.

"I already do."

Elaine clasped her hands in front of her breasts and beamed, looking delighted. "Then you have my blessing."

Alan bent and kissed Olivia, lightly, as if he was afraid of hurting her.

"I must look horrible," she said, laughing a little.

"You're gonna get married?" Janey asked excitedly, bouncing slightly on the bed.

"Sit still now," Aunt Elaine told her. "That is exactly what they plan to do."

"I knew! I knew! I knew they would one day."

"One day soon," Alan said.

Olivia smiled. "Of course. We'll have to get you out of the barn very soon after Edwin learns of our plans."

"I hope you have room for me here for a time," Elaine said. "I shall be staying for my niece's wedding."

Olivia told her they would make room—Janey could sleep with her, and she could have the room Janey had been using.

Aunt Elaine fetched a chair from near the fireplace and placed it as close to the bed as possible. Then she sat, and she and Olivia began discussing wedding plans, where the ceremony should be held, who should perform it, the food and cake . . .

"*You* must leave now," she told Alan, when Olivia asked her aunt if she would help make her dress. "You'll see her in the dress we're planning when she's presented to you on your wedding day."

He tossed her a playful pout, then he kissed Olivia again and dutifully left the room.

EPILOGUE

THEY WERE MARRIED in the Presbyterian church just four weeks later since Aunt Elaine couldn't stay in Davenport for months and months awaiting the ceremony. Every pew was filled; people even stood in the outer aisles. A gathering complete with food was held in Homer's barn afterward, and it was held in true Davenport style, with food and games for the young and old. Homer had somehow convinced Elaine to let him oversee a greased-pig contest, of all things, and John had set up a candy stand where the children took turns guessing how many gumdrops were in different jars. Frank played his fiddle, and at times, Olivia caught sight of Aunt Elaine, portly though she was, laughing and trying to learn to jig. Like Olivia and Janey, she had come to Davenport and been captivated by the warmth of most of the town's citizens.

Mrs. Ferguson had been living with her sister since the night she had helped Olivia and Janey flee Philadelphia, Aunt Elaine had told Olivia. As Olivia had feared, Mrs. Ferguson had been unable to find another reputable household position in the city after Uncle Edward recovered from his head wound and began circulating the fact that the woman had aided Olivia that night. Harry had already lined up another position in Philadelphia, though, and the employers he'd had before Uncle Edward had become his employer had given him the highest recommendations. Though Edward had strongly suspected Harry of aiding Olivia and Janey in their flight that fateful night, Harry had adamantly denied doing so—protecting them, Olivia was sure.

"I'll make certain the air is cleared for Mrs. Ferguson when I return home," Aunt Elaine promised Olivia, and then Olivia also made her promise to ask Mrs. Ferguson to write to her.

Olivia and Alan had agreed that the homestead Ida had left to Olivia should be repaired and then rented out to a family. They had talked a great deal about the property, with Alan at first saying that they should sell it. But Ida had left it to her, and Olivia couldn't part with it right now. Someday perhaps she would, but for right now, she preferred to keep it. So she and Alan compromised—repair it and rent it. "Besides," she had teased him, "I might need the barn once ours starts overflowing with animals. My collection, you know." He had laughed, as she'd known he would.

"I love you," he told Olivia now, as they waltzed. "You look beautiful, but I think we should leave soon so I can take this gown off of you."

Aunt Elaine had spent days doing nothing but stitching the gown, making a beautiful creation of white silk and lace. Olivia had been touched. She still was.

"Patience, Dr. Schuster," Olivia teased.

"I've been patient. Listen carefully, because I think there's a plan in the making. Homer and John keep putting their heads together, and Walt has a wagon waiting out back. I saw it when I took care of private business earlier. These folks like practical jokes—not to say that I don't—"

"Of course not. You've pulled a few yourself, from what I hear," she said, recalling the evening at Charlotte's boardinghouse when she had sat and listened to Homer, John, and Charlotte tell about some of the pranks Alan had pulled.

"Well, at least I've never stolen a bride from her husband on their wedding night," he grumbled. "We're leaving soon."

"Feeling a little nervous?"

"A lot nervous."

His nervousness right then was all for naught. No

one—Homer, John, Walt—tried to whisk her away during the remaining half hour they stayed at the gathering. Alan had their own wagon waiting, and they spirited out quietly, without trouble, wanting to be alone. They had had hardly a moment to themselves with Aunt Elaine staying at the homestead these past weeks (she and Janey would be staying with Charlotte for the next few days), and once inside the house, it didn't take them long to discard each other's clothing.

They had just tumbled onto the bed when the noise began outside—rattling, banging, shouting, guns firing . . . Alan began laughing, Olivia tried to sit up in bed. "What in the world . . . ?"

"Just music," he said, tugging her back down. "*That's* what they had planned. A shivaree."

"A what?" Olivia demanded. "They're all out there? While we're in here together, doing . . ."

"Doing what?"

She tossed a pillow at him. He caught it and tossed it back.

"We should go out and tell them to leave," she said, embarrassed.

"No," he said, kissing her, pressing her head back onto the pillows and his body against hers, "we'll continue."

She started to object, but he kissed her again, more deeply this time. Desire flared low in her belly, and suddenly Olivia didn't care how much noise was going on outside the house. She and Alan were inside, together, beneath the coverlet.

"Do you know what Ida told Charlotte shortly after we met?" Olivia murmured against his lips.

"No, what?"

"That the match was heaven made."

"Blessed by Ida," Alan remarked, and laughed.

Then he dipped his head to her breasts, and Olivia became lost in the touch of his lips and mouth.